continued . . .

"Well-written . . . Makes you want to keep turning the pages to see what happens next." —*The (Columbia, SC) State*

"Martin's inventive take on opposites attracting is funny and poignant." —*Booklist*

"A heartwarming story of passion, acceptance, and, most importantly, love, this book is definitely a *Total Rush*." —*Romance Reviews Today*

"Fast-paced, sexy, fun yet tender, the pages of *Total Rush* practically turn themselves. This is Deirdre Martin's third novel and is as sensational as the first two . . . A definite winner." —*Romance Junkies*

Fair Play

"Martin depicts the worlds of both professional hockey and ethnic Brooklyn with deftness and smart detail. She has an unerring eye for humorous family dynamics [and] sweet buoyancy." —*Publishers Weekly*

"Fast-paced, wisecracking, and an enjoyable story . . . Makes you feel like you're flying." —*Rendezvous*

"A fun and witty story . . . The depth of characterizations and the unexpectedly moving passages make this an exceptional romance and a must-read for all fans of the genre." —*Booklist*

"A fine sports romance that will score big-time . . . Martin has provided a winner." —*Midwest Book Review*

"Sure to delight both fans of professional ice hockey and those who enjoy a good romance." —*Affaire de Coeur*

Body Check

"Heartwarming."

—Booklist

"Combines sports and romance in a way that reminded me of Susan Elizabeth Phillips's *It Had to Be You*, but Deirdre Martin has her own style and voice. *Body Check* is one of the best first novels I have read in a long time."

—All About Romance (Desert Isle Keeper)

"Deirdre Martin aims for the net and scores with *Body Check*."

—The Romance Reader (Four Hearts)

"You don't have to be a hockey fan to cheer for *Body Check*. Deirdre Martin brings readers a story that scores."

—The Word on Romance

"Fun, fast-paced, and sexy, *Body Check* is a dazzling debut."

—USA Today bestselling author Millie Criswell

"Fun, delightful, emotional, and sexy, *Body Check* is an utterly enthralling, fast-paced novel. This is one author I eagerly look forward to reading more from."

—Romance Reviews Today

"An engaging romance that scores a hat trick [with] a fine supporting cast."

—The Best Reviews

Deirdre Martin

BERKLEY SENSATION, NEW YORK

THE BERKLEY PUBLISHING GROUP
Published by the Penguin Group
Penguin Group (USA) Inc.
375 Hudson Street, New York, New York 10014, USA
Penguin Group (Canada), 90 Eglinton Avenue East, Suite 700, Toronto, Ontario M4P 2Y3, Canada
(a division of Pearson Penguin Canada Inc.)
Penguin Books Ltd., 80 Strand, London WC2R 0RL, England
Penguin Group Ireland, 25 St. Stephen's Green, Dublin 2, Ireland (a division of Penguin Books Ltd.)
Penguin Group (Australia), 250 Camberwell Road, Camberwell, Victoria 3124, Australia
(a division of Pearson Australia Group Pty. Ltd.)
Penguin Books India Pvt. Ltd., 11 Community Centre, Panchsheel Park, New Delhi—110 017, India
Penguin Group (NZ), 67 Apollo Drive, Mairangi Bay, Auckland 1310, New Zealand
(a division of Pearson New Zealand Ltd.)
Penguin Books (South Africa) (Pty.) Ltd., 24 Sturdee Avenue, Rosebank, Joahnnesburg 2196,
South Africa

Penguin Books Ltd., Registered Offices: 80 Strand, London WC2R 0RL, England

This is a work of fiction. Names, characters, places, and incidents either are the product of the author's imagination or are used fictitiously, and any resemblance to actual persons, living or dead, business establishments, events, or locales is entirely coincidental. The publisher does not have any control over and does not assume any responsibility for author or third-party websites or their content.

CHASING STANLEY

A Berkley Sensation Book / published by arrangement with the author

PRINTING HISTORY
Berkley Sensation mass-market edition / February 2007

Copyright © 2007 by Deirdre Martin.
Cover art by Monica Lind.
Cover design by Lesley Worrell.
Interior text design by Kristin del Rosario.

ISBN: 978-0-425-21447-3

BERKLEY SENSATION®
Berkley Sensation Books are published by The Berkley Publishing Group,
a division of Penguin Group (USA) Inc.,
375 Hudson Street, New York, New York 10014.
BERKLEY SENSATION is a registered trademark of Penguin Group (USA) Inc.
The "B" design is a trademark belonging to Penguin Group (USA) Inc.

PRINTED IN THE UNITED STATES OF AMERICA

10 9 8 7 6 5 4 3 2 1

For my baby sister, Beth.
Love you, kiddo.

Acknowledgments

Special thanks to:

Jojo Plachta, who graciously allowed me to follow her around Manhattan so I could see what the life of a NYC dog walker/trainer/boarder is really like.

Dog trainer/lover/search-and-rescue expert Tom Connors, who answered all my canine questions both large and small.

Thanks also to:

My husband, Mark.

Miriam Kriss and Kate Seaver.

Elaine English and Allison McCabe.

Binnie Braunstein and Nancy Gonce.

The "posse": Jody Novins, Alisa Kwitney, Liz Maverick, Karen Kendall, Mary Giery Smith, and Nancy Harkness.

Mom, Dad, Bill, Allison, Beth, Jane, Dave, and Tom.

Rocky, Winston, and Molly.

CHASING STANLEY

CHAPTER 01

He was big and handsome, with wavy black hair that gleamed in the sun and warm brown eyes that could tease out a girl's deepest secrets. Delilah Gould's heart flapped madly in her chest just looking at him. Her fingers itched; what she wouldn't give to run them through that thick, lustrous hair! Unable to stop herself, she edged closer. Their eyes met. Delilah's heart melted into a puddle, especially when he started wagging his tail. He was the most stunning Newfoundland she'd ever seen.

Delilah had taken her three dogs for a quick midday walk around her Upper West Side neighborhood. According to local weathercasters, the temperature was hovering around ninety-five degrees, with the mercury expected to hit one hundred by late afternoon. Delilah was anxious for Sherman, her golden retriever, Shiloh, a cairn terrier, and Belle, a white mutt, to do their business quickly so she could hustle them right back inside into air-conditioning. After only a few minutes, sweat was pasting her clothes to her body, while the stifling humidity had shocked the hair around her head into a brunette halo.

Despite the heat, the streets were still crowded, though most people were moving like sleepwalkers and looked about as happy to be outside as Delilah was. Rounding the corner of West Eighty-first and Madison, she paused to take a sip from her water bottle. That's when she saw him.

"C'mon, Stanley. Don't do this to me." A well-built man with hair dark as his dog's and brown eyes just as tender, sounded desperate, cajoling the dog. "Stanley!" The man's voice turned harsh. *"Get up."* He moved behind the dog and tried pushing him. Stanley didn't budge. "C'mon, you big slug. I don't have time for this." Hooking his fingers under the dog's collar, he pulled. That's when Delilah sprang into action.

"Don't do that!"

Delilah commanded her own dogs to lie down and stay. They did so dutifully as she approached the Newf and his owner, who was eying her suspiciously.

"Do what?"

"Pull on his collar like that." She clucked her tongue, noting how heavily the poor dog was panting. "How long have you had him outside like this? Don't you know big dogs suffer more in the heat? Especially black dogs. Black absorbs the rays of the sun. Look how heavily he's panting! How would you like to be out in this weather wearing a big fur coat?"

The man stared at her. "Do I *know* you?"

Delilah ignored him. She took her water bottle and squeezed some water into the grateful dog's mouth before pulling a bandanna from her pocket and wiping his dripping jowls. The dog owner watched, dumbstruck. Sizing him up as discreetly as she could, Delilah noticed he seemed unaffected by the heat, his tennis shirt dry as a bone, not a trace of moisture on his rugged, tanned face, almost as if he was *above* sweating. Delilah felt like a total *zhlub* standing there with her sticky T-shirt and shorts covered in dog hair. As casually as she could, she touched the top of her head, pretending to push some hair into place. It was just as she suspected: she was close to sporting an afro. Frazzled, she shoved her bandanna back in her pocket.

The dog owner looked bemused. "Do you always rush up to strangers' dogs and give them water?"

"No. Just the ones who are dying in the heat."

The man's teeth gritted. "In case you haven't noticed, I'm trying to get him to move."

"Not very effectively. You're totally clueless," Delilah blurted. Oh, God. It was happening. Whenever she got nervous, her mouth went into overdrive. She either blurted the first thing that came to her head or babbled incoherently. Sometimes both. Today appeared to be a blurt day.

The man folded his arms across his chest. "You know, I'd heard New Yorkers could be jerks, but until now, I didn't believe it."

"I'm not a jerk," Delilah insisted weakly. "I just know a lot about dogs."

"Think you can get him to move?"

"Yes."

"Oh yeah? Then be my guest. *Please.*"

Delilah pulled a piece of hot dog from her fanny pack and held it out to Stanley, slowly walking backward away from him. Stanley immediately scrambled to his feet, lumbering after her. Delilah stopped moving. Stanley stood in front of her, eyes glued to the treat in her hand.

Delilah casually picked up his leash. Stanley's eyes remained riveted on her hand, his jowls dripping. "Stanley, sit," Delilah said firmly, raising the treat high over Stanley's head. Stanley sat. "Good boy," Delilah cooed, feeding him the hot dog slice. She turned back to Stanley's owner. "See? That wasn't too hard."

The owner frowned. "Except now he's sitting again." He gestured at Delilah's fanny pack. "Got any more hot dog chunks in there?"

"Why?"

"To bribe him into moving."

"*No*, the secret is using food as a *reward* for *listening* to a *command.*"

"Right. Listen, um—what's your name?"

"Delilah."

"I'm Jason. Delilah, if you could give me another piece of hot dog so I can just get him home, I'd really appreciate it."

"Where do you live?"

"Three blocks up on Eighty-fourth. Why?"

"You can't make him walk three blocks dangling a treat in front of his face! It's inhumane!"

At the sound of the word *treat*, Stanley jerked his head in Delilah's direction, sending a thick string of drool sailing toward her. It landed on the left sleeve of her T-shirt.

Jason looked mortified. "I'm sorry."

"No biggie." Delilah pulled out her bandanna again and wiped off her arm before wiping Stanley's mouth again. "You don't see many Newfs in the city," she noted.

Jason seemed pleased by this observation. "You don't see many Newfs, period. That's why I wanted one."

Delilah frowned with dismay. "Is this some kind of status thing for you?"

"No." Jason seemed offended. "This is some kind of *breed* thing for me. A friend of mine growing up had a Newf, and the dog was great. When I had a chance to get one myself, I grabbed it."

"Newfs are kind of special," Delilah agreed. There had once been a Newfie named Cyrus who lived in the neighborhood for three years, until his owners moved to the burbs. Delilah had adored Cyrus; he was intelligent, affectionate, and extremely protective—not just of Delilah, but of everyone he bonded with. Some people were repulsed by his drool, but not Delilah. When necessary, she lovingly wiped the long strings of spittle from his mouth, oblivious to the stains smeared on her clothing.

Delilah stuffed her bandanna back into her pocket. "You really need to train him."

"I don't have time."

Delilah shrugged. "Then don't complain about how long it takes to get him to move." She picked up her own dogs' leashes, commanded them to "Go," and resumed walking down the block.

"Wait!" Jason yelled after her. "You're just going to leave me here?"

"Yes!" Delilah called back over her shoulder. Poor Stanley.

She was halfway up the block when Jason's voice again rang out. "Goddamn . . . Delilah, help!"

Delilah turned. Stanley had wound his leash around Jason's legs.

Delilah walked back to them, shaking her head in admonishment. "Stanley's a delinquent. You do realize that, don't you?"

Jason scowled. "Think you could help me out first and lecture me later?"

Delilah pulled another piece of hot dog from her pack and led Stanley counterclockwise around his master the maypole. When she was done, she again commanded him to sit. This time he obeyed without hesitation.

"Good boy!" Delilah praised him, feeding him his treat and giving his ears a rub for good measure. Her tone was considerably cooler as she addressed Jason. "He's not leash trained, is he?"

Jason looked sheepish as he shook his head.

"You're not doing him any favors."

"He's not a city dog. At least he wasn't until last week." Jason crouched down so he was eye level with Stanley. "Isn't that right, boy?" Stanley began licking his face. "Some people thought I should have left you behind, but we're a team, aren't we, big guy?"

Clueless though he was, Delilah found herself softening toward Jason. "I can see you really love him," she said, "but a dog of Stanley's size needs to be trained—especially living in the city." Delilah couldn't shake the image of Stanley barreling down the sidewalk, mindlessly mowing down innocent pedestrians in his wake. Or worse, trotting out into traffic and getting hit by a car.

Delilah had a waiting list of owners dying for her to train

their dogs, but she'd always been a sucker for the neediest cases. "I'm a dog trainer," she confessed.

"I had a feeling you were some kind of animal nut."

"I am *not* a nut!"

Jason looked apologetic as he rose to his feet. "Let me rephrase that. I had a feeling you were a trainer or walker or something."

"Both, actually. I board dogs, too." She reached into the zippered compartment of her fanny pack and pulled out her business card, handing it to Jason.

"'The Bed and Biscuit, Delilah Gould, Owner,'" Jason read aloud. "You're a godsend."

"Why's that?" Delilah's attention was divided between Stanley, who had sauntered over to sniff her dogs, and Jason, who was giving her the once-over. Delilah felt her stomach contract. Sweaty face plus frizzy hair plus fur-coated walking shorts equaled major bowwow. She was sure of it.

Jason was smiling proudly. "I'm a hockey player for the New York Blades."

"Are those your real teeth?" Delilah blurted.

Jason did a small double take. *"What?"*

Delilah took a deep breath, fighting the impulse for flight. Her foot was so deep in her mouth she could feel the toe of her sneaker kicking against her rib cage. "I'm sorry. I didn't mean to say that. It just—came out."

Jason's expression was guarded. "Apology accepted."

"Thank you," Delilah said gratefully. "Now tell me why I'm a godsend."

"I'll be traveling a lot during the season, and I'll need a place to board Stanley. How much do you charge?"

"Fifty dollars a day."

"In Minnesota it was only twenty-five!"

"You're not in Kansas anymore, Toto."

He looked over her card before slipping it into his pocket. "I guess if that's the going rate, I'll pay it."

"Not so fast. I only board dogs who are trained."

Jason frowned. "And how much do you charge for that?"

"It depends."

"Ballpark estimate." Jason tugged on the leash in an attempt to pull Stanley back from approaching an elderly woman who clearly thought a bear cub had escaped from the zoo. "Excuse me a minute," he said to Delilah as he grabbed Stanley's collar, restraining him. "He's harmless!" he assured the woman, who looked terrified as she hurried to cross the street. He turned back to Delilah. "I know, I know: he needs to be trained. When can you start?"

"When can *you* start?"

Jason looked confused. "Can't I just drop him at your place and pick him up when the lesson's over?"

"No. His success depends on your cooperation and dedication. You need to observe what I'm doing and practice with him between lessons."

"You're pulling my leg, right?"

Delilah was silent.

"Guess not." Jason rubbed his chin thoughtfully. "Okay, look. How about I look at my schedule and give you a call, and we can figure out a time and place for our first lesson?"

"I need to interview you first."

Jason blinked. "Huh?"

"I don't take on just anybody. I like to get a sense of the dogs and their owners first, see how they interact."

"You've seen how we interact! I beg Stanley to do something, Stanley ignores me, and if I'm lucky, he gets bored and eventually obeys!"

Delilah found herself smiling. "I need to see how the two of you interact in your home environment," she continued, nervously running her sweaty palms down the front of her shorts. Dumb move. Now her hands were coated with dog hair. She laced them behind her back. "I know it sounds like a bit much. But it's worth it, believe me. I'm very good at what I do."

"I can see that."

"Stanley has a wonderful temperament," Delilah gushed. "And he obviously learns quickly. Training the two of you should be a snap."

Jason smiled. "Does that mean you think I have a wonderful temperament, too?"

Delilah didn't know what to say. This was one of the reasons she preferred dogs to people: they didn't flirt or make you flustered. "I need to get going," she mumbled.

"Oh. Okay." Jason seemed reluctant to end contact. "So, I'll call you, and we'll set something up?"

"Sure," said Delilah.

"Do I need to wear a tie for my interview?"

Delilah blushed, glancing down at Stanley, whose tail began wagging the second their eyes made contact. No doubt about it: he was a charmer. She bent down and kissed Stanley on the top of the head.

"How am I supposed to get him home?" Jason lamented.

"How have you been getting him home before today?"

"Well, I kinda wait till he's ready to move."

"And how long does that take?"

"Sometimes minutes. Sometimes—longer."

"You stand here in the middle of a city block and make people go around you?" Before Jason could answer, Delilah pulled out another piece of hot dog from her fanny pack, slipping it discreetly into Jason's palm. "Lead him home with this—but just this once! Otherwise he'll expect it every time, and it will make training a nightmare."

Jason looked grateful. "Thank you." Stanley was sniffing the air. A second later he was back on his feet, nudging Jason's hand with his nose.

Delilah pursed her lips disapprovingly. "That's one bad boy you've got there."

"But you're gonna whip him into shape, right?"

"I'm going to whip both of you into shape. Figuratively. Not literally. I mean, I'm not a doggie dominatrix or anything. If such a thing even exists. Which would be pretty weird if you think about it. I mean—"

Jason held out his hand. "Nice to meet you."

Delilah hesitated. No way was she shaking his hand when hers was sweaty. Not knowing what else to do, she bowed. Jason looked confused, then bowed back.

"Well, that was a first," he murmured.

"So, uh, call me," Delilah mumbled.

Jason winked. "Looking forward to it, Miss Gould."

"Check it out."

Jason passed that day's *Daily News* to his brother, Eric. It was open to a full-page article about him. Eric gave the article a cursory glance and handed it back.

"So you're flavor of the week. Big deal. Tomorrow it will be someone else."

"Did the *News* do a full-page article on *you* when you came to play for Jersey?" Jason needled.

Eric snorted. "Yeah. And they did an article on me in *Sports Illustrated*, too. One of us in this room has won the Cup, and it ain't you."

"Yet."

Eric snorted again. "Don't hold your breath, little brother." He returned to watching a rerun of *Lost* on Jason's brand new plasma TV. Stanley lay at Eric's feet, snoring louder than their father ever had. It was easy to forget sometimes he was a dog.

Jason picked up the paper again, staring at the image of himself flanked by the Blades' head coach, Ty Gallagher, and the team's new captain, Michael Dante, who had taken over after Kevin Gill's retirement. After three years of playing for the Minnesota Mosquitoes, Jason had been traded to the big time: one of the original six and the team of his dreams. Most players dreamed of playing with or under Gallagher—even Eric, though he'd never admit it now that he played for Jersey.

Little brother . . . yeah, by three whole minutes. The family joked the only reason Eric emerged first was because he'd elbowed Jason out of the way. He'd been doing it ever since. For as far back as Jason could remember, the two had competed against each other in everything: grades, girls, their parents' affection, and especially hockey.

There wasn't much to do in Flasher, North Dakota, but

play hockey, and the twins had excelled at it. The pond on the family farm froze early and thawed late, and it wasn't unusual for the two of them to play one-on-one for hours. In school, they played on the same team, Jason on the wing and Eric on defense. Sometimes Jason resented the way the town spoke of them as "the Mitchell Boys," as if they were one entity rather than two individuals.

At least they weren't identical. Eric took after their blonde, blue-eyed mother, while Jason, with his unruly dark hair and deep-set brown eyes, was the spitting image of their father. Their only physical similarity was stature: both were big and broad. Their mom said they were built like her grandfather, who'd worked the farm until he dropped dead among the corn at ninety-one. Both boys figured out early on that with their less-than-stellar grades, the only ways out of Flasher were hockey or the military. Both had made the NHL. But of course, Eric did it first.

Jason looked at his brother, slack-jawed as he watched the action on TV. Eric's penchant for watching TV amazed him. "Let's take a walk," he suggested.

"Screw that. It's ninety-eight degrees out there. I prefer air-conditioned splendor, thank you very much."

Jason frowned, restless. All his life he'd dreamed of coming to New York. He wanted to be outside so the city could soak into his skin—its sounds, its smells, even the taste of the air. Instead he was cooped up in his new apartment with his brother, his dog, and his TV.

Stanley woke up, and after a big yawn that sounded like a creaky door opening, began licking Eric's feet. Eric jerked them away. "Jesus! Why does he do that?"

"He's just telling you he loves you. Don't be such a wuss."

"I still can't believe you brought him here. You should have left him with Mom and Dad."

Jason looked down at Stanley, who'd taken Eric's rejection in stride. That Eric could even suggest leaving Stanley behind was proof Eric had no clue about the sacred bond between a man and his dog. Jason had bought Stanley as a pup in Minnesota. They'd grown up together. Stanley was his rock. When Jason had a bad night on the ice, he had the comfort of knowing that when he'd get home, Stanley would be thrilled to see him, and it would lift his spirits. There was nothing that relaxed Jason more than hanging out with Stanley in the backyard playing fetch or taking Stanley swimming in his parents' pond. Of course, now he didn't have a yard. Or a pond.

"Do you know if there's a dog run or anything around here?"

Eric scratched his arm. "No idea."

"How long have you been living here?"

Eric looked at him. "Three years. But you may have noticed I don't have a dog. I'm not needy like you."

Jason gave Eric the finger and bent down to pet Stanley. Delilah would know if there was a dog run. He pulled her business card from his back pocket and looked at it. Delilah Gould. You didn't hear names like that in North Dakota, or in Minnesota, for that matter.

"Whatcha got there?" Eric plucked the card from Jason's fingers. " You thinkin' of boarding Stan the Man?"

"I'm going to have to during road trips, aren't I?" Jason took Delilah's business card from his brother and slipped it back into his pocket.

"What did you do with him in Minnesota?"

"David Kavli's little sister would stay with him at the house for twenty-five bucks a day." Kavli was one of Jason's teammates on the Mosquitoes.

"Kavs couldn't put one in the net if his life depended on it," Eric declared.

"Yeah, no shit." For once he and Eric were in agreement.

"Was the sister cute?" Eric asked.

Jason shrugged. "I never really noticed."

Which was true. Delilah Gould, however, was another story. Jason noticed right away that she was pretty. She had big, brown doe eyes and light brown hair that fell in soft waves around her shoulders. Her baggy shorts and loose T-shirt made it hard to tell if she had a good body, but her

calves were shapely. He'd been a little annoyed with her attitude at first, but his irritation evaporated as soon as he saw
how quickly she was able to get Stan's ass in gear. She was
right: Stan *was* a delinquent, and it was all his fault. Still, he
had no idea how he was going to fit obedience lessons into
his schedule.

Eric suddenly turned to him, sniffing the air with a ques-
tioning look on his face. "Are you cooking *hot dogs*?"

"Yeah, for Stanley."

"Since when does Stanley eat hot dogs?"

"Since I discovered it's the only way to get him to do
what I ask." Delilah would kill him if she knew he intended
to keep using the hot dog trick with Stanley, but he'd worry
about that later.

"Do you have any idea what's *in* those?" Eric was asking.

"No, but I'm sure you'll tell me."

"Nitrates and trites and God knows what else. You're
killing him slowly."

"Thanks for your input, Eric."

"Any time." Eric glanced around Jason's apartment. "I
did pretty well for you, didn't I?"

"I have to admit, you did." Jason was genuinely grateful
to his brother, who managed to find and secure this apartment for him before Jason even got to town. Some people
might find it weird that they lived on the same block, but
considering they'd spent the first sixteen years of their lives
sharing the same room, this was a vast improvement.

He took the TV remote from his brother and turned off
the TV. "I was wondering something."

"What? Why I'm a great player and you're mediocre?"

Jason ignored him. "Why do you live in Manhattan if
you play for Jersey?"

"Because there's fuck all to do in Jersey if you're single,
that's why." Eric snatched the remote back from Jason's
hand and turned the TV back on. "Why not live in the city?
My commute is short, and this is where all the fun stuff happens. I'm not the only Jersey player taking bites from the

Big Apple, bro. A bunch of other single guys on the team live here, too."

Jason nodded. It made perfect sense. What better playground for young, single guys making a ton of money than Manhattan? Being professional athletes didn't hurt, either. Jason had already noticed the adoration that sprang into people's eyes when he mentioned he played for the Blades. He liked that.

Jason rose to go check on the hot dogs. Stanley followed him. "Yeah, you know what's cooking in the pot, don't you, buddy?" He reached down to scratch the top of Stanley's nose. Stanley basked in the attention, then stretched out right in front of the stove. Jason laughed. When he sat at the kitchen table, Stanley sat right beside him. When he stretched out on the couch, Stanley did the same on the floor. It wasn't unusual for Jason to emerge from the bathroom to find Stanley sitting right outside the door.

Eric appeared in the kitchen doorway. "I'm kinda hungry."

"Hold on." Jason swung the door of the refrigerator open. "I've got some eggs."

"Screw that. Gimme a hot dog."

Jason closed the fridge, staring at him. "You're a piece of work, you know that?"

"And you're a friggin' pantywaist whose ass I'm gonna kick up and down the ice this season. Now shut up and give me a dog before I call Mom and tell her you're dating a tranny named Lola."

Jason shook his head. " You know what, Eric?"

"What?"

"I can't believe I'm related to an asshole like you."

"You are ten minutes late, Miss Thang."

Delilah hunched her shoulders apologetically as she joined her assistant, Marcus, on "their" bench at the local dog run. She and Marcus had a standing Saturday afternoon date, more to catch up on gossip than anything else. Delilah considered canceling, given the heat, but she knew Marcus. "If we were working you wouldn't be able to cancel," he'd chide her, and he'd be right. Being a dog walker was like being a mail carrier: come rain or shine, you had no choice but to do your job. Sunny days were known as "the dog walker's revenge": you got to work outside in the gorgeous weather, while most people were stuck inside toiling behind desks. But when it rained, snowed, or was blazing hot, no one wanted Delilah's job, Delilah included.

"Where are the kids?" Marcus asked.

"I left them at home in the AC. Which is where *we* should be." Delilah looked around the small, wooded park. Usually it was packed, especially on the weekends. The combination of the heat and summer vacation accounted for the thinning of the ranks. "Have you seen Gin?"

Marcus's eyes got moist. "Cha-Cha died this morning."

"Oh, no." Delilah held back tears. Cha-Cha was their friend Ginny's beloved Chihuahua, who'd been battling cancer for over a year. "I'll pick up a sympathy card on Monday and bring it over here so we can all sign it."

"I knew it was Cha-Cha's time," said Marcus. "When Ginny carried him over here on Thursday, he looked straight at me and said, 'Amigo, I'm ready to go home to the casa of the Lord.' "

Delilah held her tongue. She believed animals and humans *were* connected. If you knew a dog well enough, you knew when he was in pain, or sad, or agitated. But Delilah did *not* believe people who put their ear to a dog's mouth and announced things like, "She says she wants you to take her to Mexico because she's always dreamed of seeing the Mayan ruins," or "He hates those drapes in the living room; they clash with the parrot." Delilah had been attuned to her pets for years, and not once had any of them "told" her anything of significance beyond *Love me, Feed me, Take me out, Pet me, Play with me, I'm bored,* or *Leave me the hell alone.* Occasionally one of her animals might convey that he felt threatened, afraid, or confused, but rarely. That was because she kept her dogs to a strict routine, which they needed and thrived on. Dogs didn't do well with mixed signals. Neither did Delilah.

"I saw a Newf today," she told Marcus.

"Really? Where?"

"On Eighty-first and Madison. He was sitting in the middle of the sidewalk and wouldn't budge. His owner was beside himself."

"People shouldn't have dogs they can't handle," Marcus sniffed.

"I agree."

"What was the owner like? Big and dumb like the dog, right?"

"Newfs aren't dumb!"

"They're no Border collies, honey." Marcus took out a pack of gum, unwrapping a stick for himself before passing the rest to Delilah. "The owner?"

Delilah hesitated. "He's a hockey player. For the Blades."

"Oooh, a jock." Marcus popped the gum into his mouth. "Hot?"

Delilah absently fingered the gum. "I don't know. I guess."

"You *guess*? Tell me you didn't notice what he looked like."

"Okay, maybe I did. A little."

Marcus tapped his foot. "I'm waiting."

"Big, broad shoulders, darkish hair, brown eyes. Tennis shirt. Hiking shorts. Black Tevas."

"You remember the color of his *footwear*?"

"So?" Delilah began chewing her gum.

"Well, to me that says, 'Smitten kitten.'"

"I am not smitten," Delilah insisted, watching Marcus as he walked to the nearest garbage pail to throw out their gum wrappers. She loved the way Marcus moved; he was muscular yet sinewy, a natural-born dancer. Striking, too, with a gleaming shaved head and caramel-colored skin. Delilah hoped he got his big break soon, even though it would make her life hellish until she found another assistant.

"You're smitten," Marcus insisted, returning to the bench. "I'm glad." He gestured indelicately toward her crotch. "I was beginning to think the amusement park was closed down for the season."

"Marcus!"

"Seriously: when's the last time you got laid?"

"I don't know!"

"If you don't know, then it's been too long."

"No, wait! It was with Dennis."

Dennis MacFadyen had been her boyfriend for six months. Things were fine until he brought her home to meet his parents. Delilah walked through their front door, and the first thing her nervous eyes latched onto was a painting of a handsome, bearded man. "Is that your brother?" she blurted to Dennis in front of his mother. It wasn't. It was Jesus. Things went downhill from there.

Marcus's gaze was filled with pity. "That was over a year ago, Lilah."

"You're the one who's counting, not me." She moved to wipe some sweat off her forehead. There was no air moving at all. It felt as if someone had taken a steaming, wet towel and was pressing it against her face. She thought back to her encounter with Jason and how awful she must have looked. He, on the other hand, had appeared cool as a cucumber. He must have had his sweat glands removed.

Marcus began fanning himself with a rolled-up copy of the *Times*. "I assume you gave Wayne Gretzky your card?"

"Of course. I might be taking them on as clients."

"For what? Obedience, boarding, or walking?"

"All three, probably." Delilah thought of Stanley's noble but lovable face and smiled.

"Honey, we've got a waiting list a mile long," Marcus reminded her.

"I know. But this dog really needs training."

Marcus stopped fanning himself. "Oh, you've got it bad for Hockey Boy. B-A-D bad."

"No, I don't," Delilah insisted again, though she could feel her face burning. She kept remembering the way

Jason's face looked when he'd asked if she thought he had a wonderful temperament like Stanley. The look was kind of flirtatious, or so she thought. Not that it mattered. The last thing on earth she wanted was a relationship. Dogs were better, hands down. They didn't make fun of you for being shy. The only way they could hurt you was by dying.

Marcus wagged a finger in her face. "She who blushes is the one with the crushes."

"Says who?"

"Me. I just made that up. Am I clever or what?" Marcus looked pleased with himself.

"You're very clever," Delilah acknowledged, taking the newspaper from him to fan herself for a moment, "but in this case, you're wrong. Just because I notice a guy is good-looking doesn't mean I want to date him."

"Well, maybe you should think about it. I don't want you winding up one of those crazy dog ladies with a hundred pets and no man in your bed."

Delilah laughed. "I *am* one of those crazy dog ladies, Marcus! Or hadn't you noticed?"

Marcus's gaze turned serious as he plucked the paper from her fingers. "I *have* noticed, believe me. But we're going to fix that."

CHAPTER

02

"Get off of her!"

The minute Jason opened his apartment door, Stanley jumped up on Delilah. His massive paws landed on her shoulders, sending Delilah stumbling back before steadying herself. For a moment, it looked as though they were dancing. Had Delilah not been quite as agile, Stanley would have knocked her flat.

"Stanley, down!" Delilah commanded. Stanley ignored her, licking her face instead. Sighing with momentary resignation, Delilah held still while Stanley gleefully lapped at her cheeks.

"He doesn't know 'Down,' does he?"

"No," Jason admitted guiltily.

Shaking her head, Delilah grabbed Stanley's front paws and gently lowered him to the ground. Stanley looked at her, then indelicately thrust his head between her legs. Jason wished he had a gun so he could shoot himself.

"Stanley!"

"It's okay," Delilah said, scratching Stanley's back. "He knows we're mad at him, so he's looking for reassurance."

Jason couldn't believe it. Stanley had nearly knocked her down, he'd slobbered all over her face, and now he had bull-dozed her—somewhat vulgarly—into affection. Yet Delilah was unfazed.

She continued scratching Stanley's back for awhile be-fore lightly tapping his rump. "Okay, that's it. Rubbies are over for now." Stanley played deaf. Delilah backed up so she was no longer straddling him. Stanley charged her play-fully, hoping for a repeat performance. This time Delilah stopped him in his tracks.

"Stan!" She moved out of reach, eyeing Jason above the unruly beast's head. "This isn't good. If he butts someone in the crotch, it could seriously hurt them."

"Tell me about it." Jason left to go to the kitchen, return-ing with a slice of hot dog. "Watch this." He walked over to Stanley, who had Delilah cornered. His giant tail was wag-ging so hard it created a breeze. "Stanley!"

The dog turned and lumbered over to Jason, who held the hot dog chunk high above Stanley's head. "Sit!" Stanley sat. Jason gave him his reward, smiling proudly at Delilah. "Impressive, eh?"

Delilah didn't look impressed. "You've been using hot dogs to bribe him all week, haven't you? Getting him to come in, getting him to go out . . . Am I right?"

"Well, yeah. But I was using it as a reward, like you said!"

"You're supposed to reward him for obeying a specific *command*."

" 'Sit' is a command," Jason pointed out.

"True. So are 'Up,' 'Out,' 'Down' and 'In.' Are you telling me he knows those?"

"No. I just kind of hold the hot dog out to him and—"

Delilah winced. "Don't tell me. I don't want to know how much he'll have to unlearn."

"Sorry." Jason sulked his way over to his couch. "Want to sit down?"

"Sure." Delilah sat, once again unfazed when Stanley followed her, sitting down right on her feet. "Typical Newf," she murmured, affectionately stroking Stanley's back. "Wants to be right where you are."

"Always," said Jason, stifling a huge yawn. He'd been out partying with his brother and some of his new teammates. He could already tell he was going to love living in Manhattan; there was so much to do and see, so many different places to hang. Eric had told him to get used to being the center of attention because he was a Blade, but it wasn't until last night, with women throwing themselves at him and bartenders giving him free drinks, that Jason believed him.

"Can I get you something to drink?" he asked.

"Some water would be great."

"Coming right up."

Jason returned to the kitchen. He'd been nervous about Delilah coming over to interview him and Stan. He knew she'd bust him on his flagrant hot dog abuse, but there was more to it than that. He wanted to make a good impression. He had the feeling she thought he was a big dumb jock who knew squat about the best way to care for his dog. She was partly right. It was one thing when he owned a house in Minnesota and could just open the back door to let Stan out to play or do his business. But now that they lived in the city, things had to change. Stan's behavior was a hazard, both to himself and others. Jason knew he had no choice but to acclimate him as quickly as possible.

Grabbing two bottles of mineral water from the fridge, he headed back out into the living room. Stanley was now stretched out on the floor with his head in Delilah's lap, gazing up at her adoringly. Delilah looked amused as she took her bottle of water from Jason.

"This is one affectionate little boy you've got here."

"Total love whore. I won't deny it." Jason sat beside her, wondering if he should turn on some music to relax them. Delilah seemed nervous.

"So, is that your official dog walker uniform?" he asked in a lame attempt to break the ice.

Delilah looked down at her shorts, T-shirt, sneakers, and

fanny pack. "I suppose. You can't take care of fifteen dogs a day and care about fashion." She sounded almost apologetic.

"No, of course not," Jason agreed, worried she might have taken his question as a criticism. He wondered: What did she wear when she wasn't taking care of dogs? Tight jeans? Tight T-shirts? She didn't seem the type to flaunt her assets. Then again, how did he know what type she was? All he knew was that she loved dogs.

Delilah was looking around the living room, her right hand absently stroking Stanley's head. "This place is huge." Her eyes fastened on his new mountain bike, propped up in the corner. "Nice bike."

"Thanks." Jason gestured around the nearly empty living room. "I probably should have waited and gotten some furniture first, but what the hell? I wanted it." He took a slug of water, pointing to Stanley with his bottle. "Look at him," he murmured. "He's totally blissed out." It was true: Stanley's eyes had glazed over with pleasure. Delilah could stroke his head for hours, and it still wouldn't be enough for him.

"He really is a charmer," Delilah noted. "That's why it's going to be doubly hard to break him of all those bad habits you let him develop. So tell me: What's Stanley's background?"

"Well, he used to be a puppy. Then he grew."

"Very funny." Actually, she did look amused, which pleased Jason.

"Let's get back to business," she said crisply. For the next twenty minutes she proceeded to ply him with questions. What did Stan eat? Did he have all his shots? Were his parents OFA-certified? (Whatever the hell *that* meant.) When was the last time he saw a vet? Her "interview" was beginning to feel like an interrogation. All that was missing was a hard wooden chair and a blinding light in his eyes. Finally, Jason couldn't take it anymore.

"Look, I love him, and I try to take care of him the best I can. If he's undisciplined, it's not because I'm lazy; it's because when we were in Minnesota, he didn't have to be disciplined. You probably think it was wrong of me to take him to New York with me, but there was no way I was going to stash him with my folks or some friends. He's *my dog.* Know what I mean?"

"Of course I do," Delilah replied quietly. Her eyes glistened. "And I don't think it was wrong of you to bring him to New York. I couldn't imagine life without my three dogs."

Jason nodded. "It's obvious you love dogs and know all about them. Stan is my best friend. I'd feel very comfortable leaving him in your care—if you'll have us."

"Here's the deal," said Delilah. "I'd like to meet with you and Stanley once a week. I charge fifty dollars for an hour-long lesson, and expect owners"—her gaze was unnervingly direct—"to practice with their dogs for a minimum of fifteen minutes every day. Like I said last week: I'm not just training Stanley, I'm training you, too." She started scratching Stanley behind the ears. "Dogs live to please the leader of their pack. If you assume that role and stick to it, Stan will do the rest."

Jason nodded. "Okay." He was pretty sure he could carve out fifteen minutes a day to work with Stan.

"Once he's trained," Delilah continued, "we can set up a schedule for me to walk him. I charge twenty-five dollars for an hour-long walk, fifteen dollars for a half an hour, and twelve dollars for your basic pee and poo."

"And boarding him?"

"That'll cost you fifty dollars a night if I have room. But like I said before, I won't take him in as a boarder until he's trained."

This wasn't what Jason wanted to hear. Suppose Stanley was a bad pupil and wasn't anywhere near trained by the time of the Blades' first road trip of the season? What then? It wasn't like he could always get Eric to do it; he might also be on the road. Jason would just have to make sure he and Stan were whipped into shape by the time the season formally began.

"I think that's it." Delilah's fingers began fiddling with

the zipper of her fanny pack. "Is there anything you want to ask me?"

"What got you into this?"

"I've loved dogs from the time I was a little girl. I got my first dog when I was five, a miniature poodle named Harry. He was gray and white with the cutest little nose and I got him this little pink collar and—" She stopped, checking her watch. "I hate to be rude, but I have to go." She stood. "I have another client I have to meet with."

Jason wondered if she was telling the truth. She couldn't be *that* shy; her business put her in contact with lots of people. Maybe she just felt shy around him?

Meanwhile, Stanley had stood, too, and was once again trying to nudge his way through Delilah's legs.

"He doesn't want you to go," said Jason.

"It's okay, big guy," Delilah cooed. "We'll see each other soon." As if he understood, Stanley backed off and headed for the kitchen; there came the sound of loud slurping. Jason sighed.

"Half the water he drinks winds up on the floor," he told Delilah.

"It's that way with every Newf."

Delilah seemed to relax again now that they were back to discussing dogs. She intrigued him. She was cute, smart, and kinda shy. Best of all, she wasn't repulsed by big, ol', hairy, drooly Stanley. If anything, it was the opposite.

"When can we meet for our first lesson?" Jason asked, trying not to sound too eager.

Delilah pulled a PalmPilot out of one of the compartments of her fanny pack. "How does Thursday afternoon sound, around four?"

"Hang on." Jason's eyes scoured the room. What the hell had he done with his Blades schedule? Most of his life was still in boxes, though he was trying to unpack as fast as he could so he'd start to feel at home. He spotted the schedule peeking out from under a pile of newspapers and grabbed it, giving it a quick glance. "Thursday at four looks good. Where?"

"I'll meet you guys here. It's important we start out in a

familiar setting. I think the first thing Stanley needs to learn is the proper way to behave on a leash."

"You mean twining himself around me is unacceptable?"

"Stanley has so many unacceptable behaviors I don't know where to begin."

Jason laughed uncertainly. Was that a reprimand or a good-natured tease? He shot a sidelong glance at Delilah. She was ribbing him.

"Anything special you need me to have here before our first lesson?" Jason offered.

"A copy of your schedule would be great, too. Just for future reference."

For a split second Jason entertained the fantasy of asking her to the Blades home opener, but then he realized: she'd be watching Stanley.

"I'd also like you to go to the pet store and get him a Halti. It's a type of training collar that looks just the same as a horse's bridle, and more or less works on the same principle: if he starts to pull, his head will turn toward you. Just remember to tell the clerk how much Stanley weighs so they give you the right size."

"Maybe you could come with me?" Jason suggested.

"You'll be fine," Delilah said, edging toward the door. She seemed anxious to leave, so much so that she was having trouble unlocking the door.

"Allow me," said Jason. He opened the door for her. "Thanks for stopping by."

"You, too." Delilah's shoulder bumped the doorframe as she shot out into the hall. "I mean, thanks for having me stop by. Yes. Right."

Jason watched her walking down the hall toward the elevator but then stopped, worried she might sense he was watching. He closed the door and turned; Stanley was right behind him.

"Me and my shadow." Jason chuckled, sidestepping Stan. "Delilah Gould," he murmured to himself. "What's your story?"

•   •   •

Stopping off at Marcus's, Delilah was greeted by the sight of her dear friend and assistant limbering up in his living room with an oxygen mask on.

"Marcus?"

"Yes?"

"Are you all right?"

"Yes."

"Then—?"

"It's for an audition. It's a musical version of *Blue Velvet*, and I'm trying out for the part of Frank. I think the mask will help, don't you?"

"Could you take it off, please? I feel like I'm talking to Darth Vader."

Marcus peeled off the mask with a huff. "Better?"

"Much."

Delilah handed him his pay for the week—all in cash, since Marcus worked off the books.

"You need to talk to Mrs. Schemering about the collar she's got on Muffin," said Marcus. "Muffin says it's affecting her singing voice."

"Muffin sings?"

"Yes. I'm sure it just sounds like barking to you."

"How come Muffin never talks to me?"

"'Cause I've got the shine, and you don't."

"I think the hockey player likes me," Delilah blurted.

Marcus swiped at fake tears. "Frank, our little girl is turning into a woman!"

"Shut up." Delilah was in no mood to be teased.

Marcus patted her shoulder. "Tell Uncle Marcus all about it while he puts up the kettle."

Delilah followed him into the tiny kitchen, whose cupboards were almost always bare. She suspected part of the reason Marcus was so lithe was because he barely ate.

"I take it he passed his interview," said Marcus.

"Yes. I'm going to begin training them on Thursday."

Marcus's face fell. "I was hoping you could cover for me Thursday morning. That's when my audition is."

"It won't be a problem. The lesson's not until the afternoon."

"Thank God." Marcus held up two boxes of tea, shaking them. "I've got some plain old Lipton that's probably five years old, and some echinacea that's supposed to help with colds but does diddly."

"I'll take the echinacea." Delilah worried perhaps Marcus might not be the best person to talk to about Jason. Maybe she should run it by one of her girlfriends at the dog park. The problem was that, like her, they preferred the company of canines to people, so their track records when it came to romance weren't exactly stellar. Marcus was a man; he'd be able to analyze guy behavior for her. Plus he was always going to dance concerts and gallery openings and parties. He knew how people in the non–dog world operated. Delilah's idea of a good time was cozying up on her couch with her dogs and a bowl of mint chocolate chip ice cream, watching *Animal Planet*.

"Why do you think he likes you?"

"Well, he wanted to know all about my dogs and how I got into the dog walking business. Then, when I told him he should get a Halti at the pet shop, he said, 'Maybe you could come with me.' "

"So, you're thinking he might want to put the moves on you while perusing pooper scoopers."

Delilah scowled. "I know you think you're being hilarious, but you're not."

"I'm sorry, kitten." He patted the top of her head. "Continue."

"That's it, really. Any thoughts?"

"How were you with him?"

"What do you mean?"

"You know what I mean. Which of your two anxious personalities came out: Betsy Blurt or Babbling Brook?"

"I think I may have babbled a little. I'm not sure."

"Well, if you babbled and you still think he likes you, then that says something."

"Like what?"

Marcus sighed. "Hard to say, since I haven't actually met him."

"Great." Delilah slumped against the wall. "You know when a dog thinks she's Gwen Stefani, but you can't give me any insights on male behavior."

Marcus pursed his lips. "This is what I think."

Delilah waited.

"Asking you how you came to be a dog walker *could* just be basic human curiosity—or he might like you. Similarly, asking you to go to the pet shop with him *could* be because he's nervous about buying the right collar—or he might have been flirting with you. My question to you is: Does it matter?"

"What do you mean?"

"Let's say for the sake of argument he does like you. Are you going to do anything about it? If he asked you out, would you accept?"

Delilah hesitated. "I don't know."

Marcus put the kettle on the stove. "Then why are we even having this conversation?"

"You're right." Delilah pulled up a kitchen chair. "I did take a closer look at him this time," she admitted. "He *is* attractive. And nice. And he *really* loves his dog."

"But."

"But I can't—I don't—he—"

"You'd feel more comfortable if he had four legs rather than two."

"Yes."

Marcus sat down beside her. "Lilah, you've got to get over your shyness—*and* your fear. Just because your parents' marriage went up in flames like the *Hindenburg*, doesn't mean they all wind up that way."

Marcus was right. All those years of doors slamming, plates crashing, and name-calling had left its mark. So had the always confusing aftermath, when her parents would make up and vow undying love—until the next time they fought. It had taken her years to allow herself to have a serious relationship, and when she did, her anxiety had blown it.

"I'm not sure I'm willing to take the risk," Delilah admitted.

Marcus pushed back from the table. "Then continue living a half life."

His words stung. "I'm frightened, Marcus. Please don't be cross with me."

"I'm sorry, babycakes." He placed the teabags in their cups. "It just gets so frustrating sometimes! You're this sweet, wonderful woman, yet you choose to hide your light beneath a bushel of dog hair. Haven't you ever heard the expression 'Better to have loved and lost than never to have loved at all'?"

"Of course."

"Well, take heed. If it turns out Halti Boy likes you and you like him, too, what have you got to lose?"

Delilah swallowed. "My heart."

"You've already lost it to animals. Don't you think it's time to broaden your horizons?"

"Don't worry about the traffic. We'll be in Brooklyn soon."

Michael Dante turned around to explain to Jason why it was taking them longer than expected to get to Dante's, the restaurant Michael co-owned with his brother, Anthony. Earlier in the day, Jason had to suppress a grin when Michael and Ty invited him to join them for dinner. It was a ritual for the captain and head coach to take new guys out individually for a meal and pep talk.

Sometimes Jason still couldn't believe he was in New York playing for the Blades. Back in North Dakota, he and Eric used to lie awake in their room at night, fantasizing about who they longed to play for. Eric had a hard-on for playing for Boston. But Jason always dreamed about playing for New York, in "the world's greatest arena." Under

Gallagher's stewardship, the team had won two Stanley Cups. Jason wanted to be there when they won the third.

Michael grumbled something under his breath that made Ty chuckle. "I hope you don't talk like that in front of your kids," he said.

"I do, but usually it's in Italian, so it doesn't matter."

Jason leaned forward. "How many kids do you have, Cap?" He wanted to show them that he wasn't nervous, even though he was. It was the right question to ask; if it were possible to bottle and sell the look of pride transforming Michael's face, Jason would be set for life.

"Two, with one on the way."

"How old are they?"

"Dominica's six, little Anthony is four, and the baby is due in January."

"Michael's trying to start his own hockey team," Ty ribbed.

Jason glanced between the two men. "Your wives work together, right?"

"Right," said Ty. "They run their own company, FM PR."

"Though Theresa's dropped down to part-time, what with the kids and all," said Michael. He glanced back at Jason. "You looking for a publicist?"

Ty shot Michael a warning look. "That's the last thing he needs."

"I was making a joke. Relax, will ya?"

Ty grunted and looked out the window.

"How 'bout you, Coach?" Jason's voice sounded a little too chipper to his own ears, so he toned it down a bit. "You've got one kid, right?"

Ty nodded. "Patrick. He's five."

"Shoulda named him after me," Michael put in.

Ty just rolled his eyes.

Jason sat back. The rapport between the two men was comforting. He knew from watching them at practice that they had immense respect for each other, but it was nice to see they were friends as well. In Minnesota, the new coach and longtime captain could barely stand each other. The effect on team morale was devastating. Jason was convinced it was the reason the Mosquitoes hadn't made the playoffs in two years. Loyalties were divided when everyone's attention should have been focused on winning.

"So, has your big brother been showing you the sights?" Ty asked.

Jason frowned. He knew the conversation would get around to Eric eventually. It always did.

"Bigger than me by three whole minutes," Jason muttered.

His gaze caught Ty's in the rearview mirror. Ty looked surprised. "I didn't know you two were twins."

"You been living under a rock or what?" said Michael, weaving in and out of traffic like a lunatic. Ty shot him a withering glance before resuming eye contact with Jason.

"Eric's a great hockey player," Ty continued.

"I'm better."

"Yeah?" Ty sounded amused. "We'll see."

Jason had never been to a place like Dante's. Photos of priests and paintings of gondoliers lined the red walls, while the tables were draped in red and white checkered tablecloths. The decibel level was loud but relaxed; people were genuinely enjoying themselves as they ate. Floating above the din was the sound of Italian love songs piped through the sound system. Jason immediately felt comfortable; it had a real family atmosphere.

He, the coach, and the captain were no sooner seated than a large, swarthy man bounded out of the kitchen, heading straight for the table. There was a big smile on his face as he playfully grabbed Michael in a headlock.

"You here to bust my balls or what, Mikey?"

Michael pushed his brother away with a choke. "Jesus, what are you cooking back there? You stink!"

"I'm cooking fish, *cafone*. Anchovy sauce and other delights." He gave Ty a hearty pat on the back before looking at Jason with unmistakable sympathy. "Is this the latest sacrificial lamb?"

Michael's expression was reassuring as he turned to Jason. "Pay no attention to that man behind the apron." His attention shifted back to his brother. "What do you recommend tonight?"

"To start? Crostini bianchi—that's ricotta and anchovy canapes."

Michael glanced around the table. "That okay with you guys?"

"Fine," said Ty.

Jason just nodded. The only time he'd ever had anchovies was on pizza.

"Next?" Michael prompted.

"Tagliatelle with Bolognese sauce. As a side I'd recommend breaded, fried finocchio."

Jason felt lost. "What's finocchio?" he asked Michael.

"Geppetto's other son," Anthony replied.

"Enough with the wisecracks," Michael said to Anthony. "It's fennel. It's good; trust me."

Anthony folded his arms across his chest. "We all set, then?"

"I am," said Michael. He looked at Ty. "You?"

"You know me: I need a fix of Anthony's scungilli before I can even think of anything else."

"You got it," said Anthony.

"You?" Michael said to Jason. Jason wondered if the anxiety starting to mount inside him showed. Michael's voice seemed unusually kind.

"Whatever you recommend is fine with me."

Anthony gave a curt nod. "If that will be all, gentlemen, I will repair to my humble kitchen to slave over a hot stove for your pleasure."

"Who the hell are you kidding?" said Michael. "It's for *your* pleasure."

Anthony shook his head. "See the thanks I get?" He disappeared behind the swinging doors of the kitchen.

"Don't let Anthony unnerve you," Michael said as soon

as his brother disappeared. "He may come off as a wise-cracking SOB, but inside he's a pussycat."

"Yeah, like Torkelson," Ty added wryly, taking a piece of bread.

Every player in the NHL had a story about Ulf Torkelson, who had recently been acquired by the Blades in a trade with Ottawa. Jason himself had tangled with him on the ice a few times, and the notorious Swede had put an end to Paul van Dorn's career. Jason was glad he'd now be playing with Ulfie and not against him.

"How are you adjusting?" Ty asked.

Jason shrugged. "Great."

"You all moved in?" asked Michael. Jason nodded, reaching for a piece of bread. He was starving, but he hadn't wanted to dip into the bread basket until Michael or Ty had done so first. "Where you living?" Michael continued.

"Upper West Side."

"Nice."

"Don't take the subway," Ty warned. "Use the car service." He jerked his thumb at Michael. "Mikey D over here used to take the subway so he could mingle with his peeps. He was always late—till I started fining him. Do *not* make the same mistake."

"I won't," Jason promised.

The banter was easy through dinner, with Ty and Michael asking him questions about growing up in North Dakota and, of course, about playing for the Mosquitoes. It wasn't until dessert came (some kind of cheese fritter drenched in honey) that they got down to the crux of the matter.

"You've got a reputation as a hard worker out on the ice," said Ty. "Which is good, because we're a team that prides itself on excellence." He took a sip of sambuca. "Want to know why I won three Cups in St. Louis and two here in New York?"

Jason hated being put on the spot this way, but he had no choice but to respond. "Skill. Hard work. Dedication. A burning desire to win."

Ty nodded approvingly. "What else?"

Jason drew a blank. He felt like a dolt.

Ty nudged Michael in the ribs. "Tell him what else."

"Discipline. In all areas of your life, hockey has to come first. Always. Before partying, before hanging out with your friends, before everything. *Capisce?*"

"I hear you," said Jason, squirming with irritation. He'd spent the first sixteen years of his life dreaming of making it to the Big Apple, and now they were telling him to live like a monk?

"I don't like guys who are distracted," Ty continued. "You need to live hockey. You need to eat and breathe it. It has to be the only thing you think about. The only thing you *dream* about."

Ty flashed Jason his trademark glare, and Jason shrank in his seat. That look made grown men want to dive for cover. It was fierce and unforgiving.

Michael smiled. "All we're saying is: Don't forget your priorities. Because if you slack on this team, both of us are going to ride your ass so hard, you're going to wish you'd never been born."

"You got a girlfriend?" Ty asked.

"Not right now," said Jason.

"Good," Ty said emphatically. "Less distractions."

Michael rolled his eyes. "Girlfriends are fine. Just make sure—"

"The team comes first," Jason finished for him, trying not to chafe. These guys had wives and kids and managed to juggle it all. Why couldn't he?

CHAPTER

03

"Do you always lay your head in a girl's lap right after she walks in the door?"

Delilah clucked her tongue. She had no sooner entered Jason's apartment and sat down than Stanley hopped up on the couch beside her and laid his massive head in her lap. He looked so comfortable she hated to move him, but she had to. Stanley had to learn getting up on the furniture was unacceptable. Delilah delicately pushed him off her, rumbling the word *"down"* in her most commanding voice. Stanley gave her a dirty look and grumbled, but he did as she said.

"Let me guess," she said to Jason, who watched in amusement as the scene unfolded. "You let him up on the couch to watch TV with you."

Jason rocked on his heels. "Well . . ."

He looked like a little kid caught in a fib, Delilah thought. She wasn't sure what she'd do if he ever asked her on a date. All that "Don't look too eager/Wait till he calls/Let him chase you" stuff her mother was always preaching confused her. Delilah had never been good at this; in fact, she found it excruciating.

Besides, who was she kidding? Why would a hot pro athlete want to go out with *her*? She wasn't gorgeous. She wasn't rich. She was a bumbling blurter. To top it all off, she knew *bubkes* about sports.

"I got that *thing* you told me to get." Jason disappeared into what Delilah assumed to be his bedroom, returning with the Halti, holding it out before him as if were a noose.

"Stanley, come," Delilah coaxed. Stanley came. "Good boy." She gave him a slice of hot dog then pulled out another. "Stanley, sit." Stanley sat. "Good boy," Delilah repeated enthusiastically, feeding him another treat. Delilah slowly extended her free hand to Jason.

"Halti," she whispered.

Jason passed her the Halti.

"Rub Stanley's belly and tell him what a wonderful boy he is," she told him.

Jason knelt before Stanley, doing as Delilah said. Stanley lapped up his master's praise, barely making a fuss as Delilah put the Halti on him. "Good boy!" she boomed, giving him another treat.

Jason rose to his feet. "Well, that was easy."

Delilah took off the Halti and handed it to Jason. "Your turn."

Delilah sensed Jason's anxiety as he took the Halti from her. He seemed to be stalling, staring down at it as if it were some puzzle to be solved.

"You okay?" Delilah asked.

"I'm afraid I'm going to choke him."

"You're not. That's the whole point. This is a better way to train him than a choke collar."

"Maybe you could help me?"

Delilah was caught off guard. "Help you how?"

"Help me guide it onto his muzzle. Just until I get the hang of it."

Delilah swallowed. "I could do that."

Delilah gently placed her hands over Jason's. Together

they guided the Halti onto Stanley's muzzle. "See?" Jason's hands beneath hers felt strong and warm. "It's easy." Delilah withdrew her hands, discreetly trying to wipe them off on her jeans; she was afraid they'd been sweaty. "You try."

Jason's gaze lingered on her a long time before he began slipping the Halti on and off Stanley on his own.

"How am I doing?" Jason asked.

"Great. Let's take a five-minute break, and then we'll start putting it on him and attaching his leash."

Delilah stared at Stanley. Jason stared at Stanley. Stanley looked from one to the other. Seconds passed. Delilah nearly jumped when Jason abruptly turned to her.

"How did you get into this again?"

Same question as last time they'd seen each other, when Delilah had cut him short. Determined to prove she could hold a conversation without running on at the mouth like a ninny, she smiled.

"I've always loved dogs. Like I told you, I got my first dog when I was five, and I trained him. The rest is history. By the time I was in high school I had my own business, walking and training dogs. I guess you could say it was my destiny."

Jason laughed appreciatively. "I hear you. There's only one thing I've ever wanted to do in my life, and that's play hockey. I guess that gives us something in common."

"Yes," Delilah managed. Thoughts were breaking up into fragments, making it hard to know what to say next. Ask about work—play—girlfriend—family—home—dog? See Spot run. See Delilah speak. See Delilah try not to sound like a moron.

Delilah cleared her throat. "How do you like New York?"

"I like it," Jason said after a careful pause. "Now that the culture shock has worn off, I'm starting to feel at home here." His expression turned curious. "You a native New Yorker?"

"Me? No. I mean, I grew up in New York. New York State, I mean, Long Island, well, that's part of New York, so I guess, hmm, technically yes but not the city, no." Mortified by her incoherence, she shut up and petted Stanley's head, glad for the hairy prop. *This is why dogs are better,* she thought. *You never have to worry about making a fool out of yourself.* "Where are you from?" she asked, eager to deflect attention from herself.

"Flasher, North Dakota." His expression turned playful. "If you tell me you've heard of it, I'll know you're lying."

Delilah blushed. "No, I've never heard of it."

"It's small, rural, and boring as hell. I got out of there as soon as I could."

"And now you play hockey."

"Now I play hockey. First in Minnesota, and now here." Delilah had stopped petting Stanley, so Jason took over. "I bet it's not half as interesting as walking and training dogs, though."

"Please," Delilah scoffed.

"Seriously: you must see some interesting stuff."

Delilah swallowed nervously. It couldn't hurt to open up just a little. She could always retreat if her tongue began tripping over itself.

"There's this one little pug I walk named Quigley. I have to go through this little ritual before I can even get him out the door: I pet him five times, coo, 'Quigley Wiggly you da man,' and then give him a biscuit."

Jason looked perturbed. "Really?"

"I didn't come up with the ritual! His owners did." Delilah was horrified he'd think her capable of such silliness, though if he ever heard the little songs she made up and sang to her dogs, he'd probably have her committed.

"That can't be as bad as it gets," Jason prompted.

"Oh, it's not," Delilah assured him, warming to the topic. "I walk one dog whose owner has covered every inch of wall space with pictures of Andy Griffith."

"Male or female?"

"Male."

Jason looked queasy. "Sweet Lord deliver us, as my grandfather used to say."

"Then there's this black Lab named Betty over on West

Seventy-ninth whose owners are"—Delilah lowered her voice—"Satanists."

"How do you know?"

"They leave their mail on table by the front door, and they've got a subscription to some magazine called *Black Mass Monthly*. Plus there's a huge painting of Satan hanging over the fireplace."

Jason whistled through his teeth. "Man, I'd love to spend a day with you. I bet I'd learn a lot."

Delilah blushed, wondering he was referring to her clients or to her. "We'd better get back to Stanley." She spent the remainder of the lesson getting Stanley used to wearing the Halti.

"You need to keep practicing with him," Delilah told Jason. "Keep the Halti and the leash on for a little bit longer each day. After about three days, start walking him around your apartment with it on. If he pulls in a direction you don't want him to go, stop a minute and tell him, 'This way,' or, 'Let's go.' If he does what you say, give him a t-r-e-a-t. Never punish him if he does something wrong. Reward him if he does something right." Delilah pulled out her PalmPilot. "So, next Thursday?"

Jason grimaced. "Look, is there some kind of accelerated program we can put Stanley on?"

"Why?"

"Because my first road trip is in about three weeks, and I'm worried he won't be properly trained and you won't board him."

Delilah crouched down so she was face-to-face with Stan. "You'll be ready by then, won't you, big guy?" Stanley's response was to lick her face with a big slurp. "See?" she said to Jason. "He'll be ready. No extra lessons necessary."

"If you say so," said Jason. Delilah thought he looked disappointed.

"I guess that's it, then. See you next week."

"Next week," Jason echoed.

"Don't forget to practice."

"I won't." He paused. "Thanks for your help." Before Delilah knew what was happening, Jason leaned in to give her a quick peck on the cheek. Dazed, she floated in the direction of his front door.

"Bye, Stanley," she called over her shoulder on her way out. She hated to admit it, but next Thursday suddenly felt like a long time away.

"Heads up, here comes the mayor."

Jason turned from where he sat with Eric at an outdoor café, expecting to see Rudy Giuliani or Michael Bloomberg strolling down the street. Instead, a wizened old man in a shabby suit was slowly ambling their way, pausing every few feet to stop and chat with everyone who crossed his path. Jason and Eric were no exceptions.

"Hello, boys, hello."

"Hello, Mr. Mayor," said Eric. "Beautiful day, isn't it?"

"A rare September gem," the mayor said before continuing on his way. He was barely out of earshot before Eric turned to Jason. "Total lunatic. Makes the rounds every day. He's harmless, though."

Jason nodded, watching the mayor until he'd toddled completely out of view. Eric waved to a willowy woman clad like a Bedouin across the street, piquing Jason's curiosity. "Who's that?"

"Sheena. She lives in my building. She's some kind of puppet master or something."

"How the hell can anyone make a living as a puppet master?"

"You'd be amazed at some of the ways people make a living in this city."

"You seem to know everyone," Jason observed, making sure he sounded impressed.

"Well, I have been living here awhile," Eric replied with the boastfulness Jason had deliberately sought to stoke.

"Do you know that dog walker?" Jason asked casually.

"Who, that cute little chick who walks around covered in dog hair and drool?"

Jason nodded, mildly annoyed by Eric's use of the word *cute*. His physical description of Delilah wasn't very flattering, either. Jason hadn't noticed either dog hair *or* drool.

"I've seen her around," said Eric, breaking off a piece of crumb cake from Jason's plate and popping it in his mouth, a habit from childhood that still drove Jason up the wall. "But I can't say I *know* her." He looked at Jason. "Why? You know her?"

"She's training Stanley."

"No kidding. How's it coming? Has Oscar Mayer called to thank you for keeping his empire afloat?"

"Har-har." Jason stretched out his legs. "I was just wondering what the word around the neighborhood is about her, that kind of stuff."

Eric grinned at him. "You're hot for her."

"*No.* I just like to know as much as I can about the person who's going to be taking care of my dog."

"Mmm." Eric seemed distracted as he watched a leggy blonde in a short skirt saunter by. "Man, they sure don't make 'em like that in North Dakota, eh, bro?"

"The dog walker?" Jason prompted.

"Oh. Right." Eric turned back to him. "All I know is that she loves her dogs and everyone else's, but keeps them in line. You know, the whole tough love thing that Mom and Dad tried with us but didn't work."

Jason laughed appreciatively.

"Sometimes I see her at the Starbucks around the corner with some tall, skinny, black guy."

"Her boyfriend?" Jason asked, hoping he wasn't too obvious.

"Nah. He's a queen. I think he's a coworker or something. I've seen him out walking dogs, too." Eric narrowed his eyes suspiciously. "You gonna ask this chick out or what?"

"Will you quit calling her a chick? This isn't an episode of *The Mod Squad*."

"Nice attempted deflection," Eric drawled. "What's the deal?"

"I already told you," Jason replied, playing up his exasperation. "She's probably going to wind up spending more time with Stanley than I am. I need to get as much info on her as I can."

Eric looked skeptical. "Didn't you interview her?"

"Of course I did. I'm looking for off-the-record stuff; dirt you might have heard about her on the street."

Eric snorted. "Look who's talking like Linc's sidekick now."

"Don't bust my balls, Eric."

"I haven't heard anything bad about her, and that's the truth. What's her name?"

"Delilah."

"Delilah," Eric repeated slowly. "She good with Stanley?"

"She's great with Stanley. Lets him lick her face and everything."

"That is totally gross."

"You'll understand when you become a father," Jason teased.

Eric looked thoughtful. "Well, she's cute, I'll give her that much," he repeated.

Jason suppressed a scowl. That was the second time his brother had used the word *cute* in connection with Delilah. It set his teeth on edge.

"I'd do her," Eric continued.

"Who wouldn't you do?" Jason retorted.

"Hmm. Good question. I'll get back to you on that."

While his brother ran down a mental checklist searching for any woman he wouldn't bed, Jason found himself wondering what Delilah was doing. Probably walking dogs. Or feeding dogs. Or something else dog-related. She'd be proud to know he'd been practicing the Halti/leash trick with Stanley, and it was working like a charm; Stan paraded around the house with it on, no problem.

He was looking forward to their next dog training lesson.

He considered it a coup that he'd gotten her to talk about herself. It was clear she was painfully shy.

"You ready to get your ass kicked tomorrow night?" he asked Eric. Tomorrow was the Blades home opener against New Jersey. Jason couldn't wait to get on the ice and play his first game as a Blade. That he'd be facing off against his brother made it that much sweeter.

Eric's mouth curled into a sneer. "Fuck you. You're the one who's gonna be crying for Mama tomorrow night, not me."

"Right."

"Haven't you been reading the sports pages?"

"I try to avoid it," said Jason with a yawn. "It gets kind of boring reading about how great I am."

Eric rolled his eyes. "Gee, I musta missed that article. The ones I keep seeing are those talking about what a powerhouse Jersey is." He reached across the table to swipe Jason's final morsel of cake. "Be afraid, little brother. Be very, very afraid. 'Cause I'm gonna show no mercy."

Jason laughed dismissively. "I'm shaking in my skates."

Jason was well-acquainted with the adrenaline rush that came with preparing to play, but dressing for his first game as a Blade, he was close to giddy. Lacing up his skates on the bench in front of him sat the Blades' new goalie, David Hewson, while across the room, the team's new defenseman, Ulf Torkelson, was slipping on his Blades jersey for the first time. The locker room hummed with an odd mixture of solemnity and excitement. Barry Fontaine, a gritty veteran, grinned at Jason as he worked on affixing his shoulder pads.

"Nervous?"

"Nah," Jason lied.

"As long as you play your balls off, you'll be fine," Fontaine advised, moving to turn down the volume on the pregame music.

"Hey!" Denny O'Malley, the Blades backup goalie, protested. "I was gettin' pumped!"

"Maybe you can get your mojo workin' without turning me into frickin' Helen Keller in the process," Fontaine growled. O'Malley backed off.

Jason turned to his locker, slipping the small gold crucifix his mother had given him when he was seven around his neck. It was his good luck charm out on the ice. Down the hall in the visiting team's locker room, he imagined Eric doing the same thing. He, too, wore a cross from their mother as his good luck charm. Sometimes Jason worried the two of them wearing the same talisman might somehow divide whatever luck there was to be had between them. But so far, they'd both seemed to do okay.

He had just pulled his sweater over his head when Michael Dante entered the locker room, already dressed. Michael wasn't the scowling type, but his hot temper could be a force to reckon with.

"Okay, listen up." Michael's voice matched his gaze: calm. "I want us to set the tone for the season from the moment we step out on the ice. We need to let those Jersey assholes and every other team know that no one fucks with us."

As if on cue, Ty Gallagher entered. There was total silence as he looked at each and every player in turn. When his gaze fell on Jason, it took every ounce of Jason's concentration not to look away.

"Talent means shit. Will beats skill every time. We play to win the game—every game. That means I don't care if it's the first game of the season or the fiftieth. If you don't give your all out there, you sit. The Blades have one goal every year: winning the Cup." Players started banging their sticks on the floor. "All right; let's get out there and hit 'em in the mouth."

"Get off me, you pussy."

Jason laughed at his brother's taunt. He'd just crushed Eric with a body check so satisfying, he wished he could

smoke a cigarette afterward. There was something gratifying about jamming Eric up against the boards; always had
been. Sniggering, Jason returned to the Blades' bench with
the rest of the second line, watching avidly as the first line
returned to the ice. Jersey was trying to open things up, but
the Blades were having none of it. Instead of getting into a
pond hockey game, the Blades were playing dump and
chase in order to establish physical dominance.

Jason couldn't believe the energy rippling through Met
Gar. The fans in Minnesota were enthusiastic, but these
New Yorkers were nuts, their fanaticism infectious. Jason
said a silent prayer thanking the hockey gods for granting
his wish to play for the Blades, and waited for Ty to send his
line back out onto the ice. They were doing pretty well. His
forechecking had led to a couple of scoring chances, and
he'd gotten the second assist on Thad Meyers's goal, the
only score of the first period.

Back on the ice, he was skating the left wing, looking for
a breakout pass from defenseman Nick Roberts. They failed
to connect, thanks to Eric, who interrupted the attempt and
chipped it deep into the Blades' zone.

"You wearin' concrete skates or what, asshole?" Eric
jeered.

"Fuck you," Jason snapped.

And so it went for the rest of the game. Every time Jason
met up with his brother, insults were traded along with
checks. While Eric didn't play as chippy as Torkelson, he
had his moments. With less than three minutes left in a 2–2
tie, Jason carried the puck into Jersey's zone when Eric met
him with a high hit that included a two-glove face wash.

"You are one fuckin' wuss, baby bro," Eric taunted.

"Yeah?" Jason panted. They were battling for the puck in
the corner. Eric dug it free and cleared it. They were both on
the bench when Michael Dante scored on a seeing eye wrist
shot from the top of the circle.

When the horn sounded, Jason and the rest of the Blades
rushed off the bench to congratulate David Hewson. As the

two teams slowly cleared the ice, Jason couldn't resist getting in one more dig.

"What happened? I thought you were gonna kick my ass!" Jason called to Eric, who was heading off ice for the locker room. "Decide you'd rather kiss it instead?"

"It's a long season, asshole, and payback is a bitch," Eric called over his shoulder.

"We'll see!" yelled Jason.

Exhilarated, he headed back in to the Blades locker room.

"Good game!" Michael Dante commended as Jason headed toward the shower. He patted Jason on the back.

"Thanks, Cap."

"You and Eric always go at it like that?"

Jason shrugged. "Yeah. It's been that way since we were kids."

"Hey, I know. My brother and I still lock horns. Something about sibs, I guess."

"I guess."

"Well, keep up the good work," said Michael.

"Will do."

Jason watched his captain walk away. Michael Dante had never had speed or great skills, but he was relentless and never backed down. If Jason showed half the grit and determination Michael did, he'd make his mark on New York.

"Yo, country boy."

Jason turned at the sound of Denny O'Malley's voice. Malls, as he was known, wasn't the sharpest tack in the box, but he was a nice guy, and he knew how to have a good time. Jason had already been out on the town with Malls, Eric, and a couple of other guys before the season started.

"A bunch of us are going over to the Chapter House for a few brews. You in?"

"Definitely," said Jason.

"Meet me in the Green Room, and we'll split a cab."

"Cool."

Jason continued on to the showers, grinning like a fool. He'd heard about the Chapter House; it was the Blades' un-official bar, a place where they could shoot pool and sink a few drinks without being hassled. Jason had yet to set foot inside. That was about to change.

CHAPTER

04

"What a dump!"

Jason was delighted with the Chapter House. The juke-box was older than dirt, the windows hadn't been washed since Prohibition, and none of the rickety tables had matching chairs. But that was its charm; besides, not one head turned when he and a few of his teammates strolled in. Jason wouldn't have minded being recognized, but he knew the other guys relished the bar as one of the few places they could drink without hassle. His ego could deal with anonymity for one night.

"Total shit hole," Denny O'Malley agreed in a voice laced with affection. "But to me, it's a second home."

"That doesn't bode well for your first home, dude," quipped Barry Fontaine, who'd tapped Jason to pay, since he was "one of the new guys." Jason didn't mind. Ulf Torkelson would pay next, and besides, it all evened out in the end. What mattered was hanging out with these guys *here.* If it wasn't so dorky, he'd pull out his cell and call Guillaume Steves, his buddy back in Minnesota who was still playing for the Mosquitoes. "Guess where I am?" he'd

say. "At the Chapter House!" Guillaume, who worshipped
Ty Gallagher like a god, would understand.

Ulf slapped him on the back. "So, how are you liking
New York?"

"How are *you* liking it?" Ulf played for Ottawa before
being traded to New York just before Jason.

"Amazing." Ulf shook his head in wonder. "The food, the
people . . ."

"The women," added Thad Meyers.

"That, too," said Ulf with a grin. "So many babes, so little time."

"Hear, hear!" said Malls as they all raised their glasses
high.

"You got a girlfriend?" Ulf asked Jason.

An image of Delilah flashed in his mind. "Not right now.
You?"

"Divorced. Finally. Thank God."

Jason didn't know what to say. He didn't know Ulf's
wife, but judging from the approving nods of his teammates, Jason gathered Ulf was better off sans Mrs. T.

An hour and a half passed in the blink of an eye. Talk became decidedly more raucous as booze and increasing fa-
miliarity loosened their tongues. Malls, Thad, and Barry
were cracking Jason and Ulf up telling them about their ad-
ventures on the Blades. Malls looked pissed when Barry reminded him of the time he'd told a magazine he liked
women with "Big kazungas" and Ty's wife, working PR for
the Blades at the time, had had to do damage control. All
agreed it sucked that Paul van Dorn had to hang up his
skates.

Ulf slapped a hand against the edge of the table. "We will
win the Cup this year! I know it!" He clinked his beer glass
against Jason's. "I might have to cripple your brother to do
it, though."

"Who's his brother?" Barry Fontaine asked.

Denny stared at him. "You're shittin' me, right?"

Barry looked haplessly around the table. "What am I
missing here?"

"Your fuckin' brain," Denny O'Malley snorted. "This is Jason Mitchell, right?" Barry nodded. "His brother is *Eric* Mitchell."

"No shit. I didn't make the connection." He chugged the remains of his beer, wiping the foam off the top of his lip with the back of his hand. "He's one tough fucker, your brother."

Jason frowned. "Whatever." The last thing he felt like talking about tonight was Eric—unless, of course, they cared to point out how he'd nailed his brother's ass out on the ice tonight. That would be okay.

"He's older than you, right?" queried Thad.

Jason clenched his jaw. "By three minutes."

"You guys are twins?" Barry looked confused. "You don't look alike."

"Not all twins are identical."

"I always thought they were."

"You also think Don Cherry's a sharp dresser," Thad pointed out. Barry replied with a one-fingered salute.

Drinking with his teammates, time seemed to come unbound. Jason was completely in the moment—until Barry Fontaine stood up and announced he was leaving.

"I'm afraid I have to call it a night, guys. The wife is waiting at home, and she'll kill me if I get too late."

That's when Jason realized: He'd forgotten about Stanley.

Delilah associated Starbucks with three things: cinnamon scones, café mocha, and Marcus. She was unprepared, therefore, when Jason hustled through the door and made a beeline straight for their table.

"Delilah." He was panting lightly. "I'm so glad I found you."

Delilah put down her fork. "What's wrong with Stanley?"

"Nothing. I mean, not really. But I need your help. Hi," he said to Marcus, extending his hand. "I'm Jason."

"Oh, I know who you are," Marcus replied, returning the handshake. "I've heard all about you." He sipped demurely at his coffee. "About your dog, I mean." His clarification was the only thing stopping Delilah from sliding beneath the table and slithering away in mortification.

"I'm Marcus," he continued. "C'mon, park your carc. I'd scooch over to make room for you next to me, but I've got some personal space issues. It's a dancer thing."

Marcus winked at Delilah, who kicked him as discreetly as she could before making room for Jason, who looked desperate.

"I know you don't want to set up a formal schedule to walk Stan until he's fully trained," he said to Delilah. "But I need your help *now*. Last night was the Blades' home opener, and by the time I got home, Stanley had had an accident—totally my fault, not his. I don't want that to happen again. I need someone to take him out on the nights I'm playing."

"Someone?" Marcus sniffed.

Jason rolled his eyes. "Okay, Delilah. I need Delilah."

Delilah pushed pieces of scone around her plate. Now that Jason was here, she was no longer hungry. It was hard to eat when your heart was going crazy in your chest. "I don't understand. Don't hockey games last just a few hours?"

"Yeah, but there's more than time spent out on the ice. We usually get to Met Gar early to work on our skates and sticks, and then we warm up and skate. Then after the game we have to shower, and—"

"I get the picture."

"Not me. I need to hear more about the shower," said Marcus. Delilah gave him another small kick under the table.

Delilah turned to Jason. She was determined to keep focused, making sure her sentences were straightforward and simple so she didn't turn into Babbling Brook or Betsy Blurt and embarrass herself. "When you have a game, what time do you leave Stanley, and what time do you come home?"

"Well, in Minneapolis, I would usually leave my place any time between three and four, and I'd get home whenever." His gaze darted away.

"Whenever," Marcus repeated with a purr. "Now there's a nice vague phrase." A look passed between the two men. Delilah was unsure whether Jason was amused or annoyed.

"You walk him before you go to Met Gar?" she continued, trying to piece together a timeline in her mind. Jason nodded.

"So, you'd want me to come by and walk him at what— eight? Nine?"

"Between nine and ten would probably be good."

"Mmm." Delilah snuck a sideways glance at him. He looked tired; his face was slightly drawn, and there was the faint beginnings of bags beneath his eyes. Still, he exuded a certain masculine vitality even at this early hour. Delilah wondered if that was true of all athletes, or if it was something unique to Jason. She'd ask Marcus after Jason left. If anyone would have an opinion on the matter, it would be Marcus.

A thought struck Delilah. "How did you manage to come home 'whenever' when you had home games in Minnesota?"

"I had a doggie door in my house. He could go in and out as he pleased."

"I would *kill* to see a doggie door big enough for a Newf," Marcus chortled.

Jason chuckled in response, but there was no mistaking the continuing appeal in his eyes as he looked at Delilah.

"Can you help me out? Please?"

Delilah sighed. "Here's the thing." *You're sitting so close to me that our legs are touching and I'm having a hard time concentrating.* "The only dogs I walk at night are those boarding with me, as well as my own, obviously."

"But couldn't you make an exception? I'd pay you double. Triple. Whatever you want."

"Let me think." Delilah suppressed a yelp as the toe of Marcus's sneaker connected firmly with her shin.

"Oh, c'mon, Lilah, you can do it," Marcus urged. "You're always at home at night anyway." Delilah glared at him. "What I mean is, Delilah can be a bit of homebody," Marcus quickly amended, flashing Jason a very charming smile. "I didn't mean to make it sound like she doesn't have a life." *Even though you don't*, Marcus's expression said as he sucked in his cheeks disparagingly.

"Delilah, I'm begging." Jason's gaze remained riveted to her face. Delilah felt her pulse stutter. His eyes were gorgeous, especially right now as they pleaded with her. Delilah wondered how many other women had fallen prey to their charm.

Delilah broke eye contact. "Okay, here's the deal," she said, taking a sip of coffee. "I'll do it as long as it's not every night."

"It's not! Only on game nights."

"Only on game nights during the week," Delilah amended for him. "Weekends are out unless he's boarding with me. I do have a life, you know." She shot Marcus a pointed look. Marcus pressed his lips together. Delilah could tell he was suppressing a snort.

Jason frowned. "Maybe we could negotiate something if it happens to be a weekend and you're free."

"Maybe," said Delilah, wondering if this was what her mother meant when she would say, "Make him chase you." If she had a bag of kibble for every time she'd heard that, she'd never have to buy dog food again.

"So, it's a go?" Jason pressed.

"Sure. Obviously I'll need a key to your apartment, your game schedule, and a number where I can reach you in case of emergency."

"No problem. Thanks so much." Jason gave her leg an affectionate squeeze, and Delilah nearly rocketed to the ceiling. "I can't thank you enough. Seriously."

Delilah just nodded. Her mind was still back at his touch.

Jason cocked his head quizzically. "How much money—?"

"We'll work that out."

Jason checked his watch. "Shoot, I have to run to practice." He smiled at Delilah. "I'll call you later, and we can iron out the details, okay?"

"Sounds good."

"Catch you later." He headed toward the door.

"Have you been practicing with Stanley?" Delilah called after him.

Jason flashed a grin over his shoulder. "Of course. What do you think I am?"

He pushed open the door and was gone.

"What a good boy you are!"

Delilah was praising Stanley, but it was Jason who was feeling the pride. They'd just finished their latest training session, and Stanley had exceeded expectations. Not only had he behaved like a perfect gentleman on his leash all the way over to Central Park, but with the help of Delilah's ever-present hot dog chunks, he'd also mastered a variety of new commands. Jason had always known Stanley was bright; it was gratifying to see Delilah thought so, too.

"Want to sit down?" Jason asked. Delilah nodded, following him and Stanley to a nearby bench. Jason couldn't believe how busy the park was, even on a weekday. There were couples strolling, bladers, cyclists, and joggers galore. People were stretched out on the grass reading; others practiced tai chi. Jason loved it; he could sit on the bench all day just people-watching and never get bored.

"Hi, Captain Wiggles."

Delilah's voice rang out as she waved to an elderly woman in a blue cape walking a decrepit Dalmation. The woman squinted a moment before waving back at Delilah. Jason turned to Delilah.

"She named her dog *Captain Wiggles*?"

"Oh, and Stanley's a more dignified name?"

Jason drew himself up indignantly. "Hey, don't make fun of the name Stanley. It's sacred!"

Delilah looked amused as she pushed a stray lock of hair off her face. "Why's that?"

"He's named after the Stanley Cup, the greatest trophy in sports."

Delilah scratched behind Stanley's ear. "No offense, but it's a total *schlemiel* name." She leaned over to kiss the dog's head. "It's okay, boy," she said to him. "It's not your fault."

"What the hell is a *schlemiel*?"

"A loser," Delilah explained.

Before Jason could counter, a dumpy middle-aged couple in matching maroon track suits strolled by, walking what looked to him like two bug-eyed rodents.

"Hi, Mercutio!" trilled Delilah. "Hi, Macbeth!"

The couple stopped in front of the bench. "Hello," they greeted Delilah warmly. "Where's the three babies today?" the man asked.

"Home. I'm actually winding up a private lesson right now." Delilah patted Stanley's head. "This is Stanley."

The woman recoiled. "He's awfully big. And drooly," she added, staring in disgust at Stan's moist, sagging jowls.

Jason scowled. Who the hell was she to be repulsed by Stanley when she had a belly the size of a Butterball turkey and was parading around in public with a rat on a leash? He opened his mouth to protest but then thought better of it, not wanting to embarrass Delilah in front of her "friends." He settled for a quick glare as he pulled a hankie from his pocket and restored Stan's dignity.

"We've got to run," said the man, pushing his slipping sunglasses back up on his bulbous nose. "The kids here are invited to a birthday party, and we don't want to be late."

"Have fun," Delilah called after them as they continued on their way. Jason couldn't wait for them to be out of earshot.

"A *birthday* party? For *dogs*?"

Delilah shuddered. "I know."

"What do they do? Play pin the tail on the boxer?"

"You got me. I haven't been to a birthday party since my Bat Mitzvah."

"What kind of dogs were those?"

"Italian greyhounds."

"Stanley shits bigger than that!"

Delilah laughed. What a light and pleasant sound it was. Jason had once had a girlfriend whose laugh sounded like a horse. Eric's nickname for her was Mr. Ed.

"Nice of you to introduce Stanley to your friends and not me," Jason ribbed.

"Oh." Pink rushed to Delilah's cheeks. "I'm so sorry. I didn't think they'd stop and then when they did and asked about my dogs I had to be polite and besides I don't really know their names plus—"

"It's okay. You don't need to apologize. It's obvious you like Stanley more than you like me."

Delilah smile was shy. "That's not true."

Jason saw an in and smiled back at her, ready to ask her out. That's when Stanley burped. So much for seizing the moment.

"You seem to know a lot of people," Jason observed in an attempt to restart conversation.

"I know their dogs. Not them. I don't know many humans. Who aren't clients, I mean."

Stanley started pawing at Jason's knee insistently in a none too subtle bid for affection. "You're very demanding today, Stan," Jason noted as he leaned forward to scratch the dog's back.

"Well, he worked very hard," said Delilah. "He deserves extra TLC."

"Anything new with Mr. and Mrs. Beelzebub?" Ever since Delilah told him she had clients who were Satanists, Jason found himself checking out every couple strolling the neighborhood, wondering: *Is it them?*

"Not really."

"And the Andy Griffith fan?"

Delilah considered the question. "Well, I did notice he

has the whole first season of *Matlock* on DVD. The case was lying on his coffee table."

"I bet you could write a book. Or do some heavy duty blackmailing if you wanted to."

"I suppose. Marcus suggested it once when the Devil couple were behind on their account, but I just couldn't do it. I mean, suppose they were just going through a rough patch?"

Jason chuckled to himself. Delilah seemed completely without guile, the type of person who actually believed politicians, or found herself shocked to hear bad things happened in the world. It was refreshing.

He stopped scratching Stanley, stretching his arms out along the back of the bench. Tilting his head back, he closed his eyes, the better to enjoy the breeze playing over his face. "Have you had a chance to look at my schedule?"

"Yes. I can walk Stanley tomorrow night and next Monday night. But not next Tuesday."

"Okay." Jason wondered what he would do with Stanley Tuesday night. He also wondered what Delilah was doing that night that made her unavailable. "Date?" he asked casually, keeping his eyes resolutely shut.

"What?" Delilah sounded confused. That was good. Confused was better than sharp. Or offended. Sharp or offended would be bad.

"Next Tuesday night," Jason continued, face still tilted in the air. He opened his eyes, readjusting to the light as a convoy of clouds slowly crossed the sky. "Going on a date or something?"

"Oh, no, I'm having my tarot cards read. I thought it might be fun."

"Gonna ask about me?" Jason teased.

"Probably," Delilah blurted, then looked away. "Damn," he heard her whisper to herself.

Jason didn't press it. "Well, let me know how it goes. I'd be curious to hear about it."

Delilah gave a half smile, kind of like the *Mona Lisa*. She looked nice today, Jason noticed. The weather was beginning to cool off, and she had on a long-sleeved T-shirt that seemed a bit more form-fitting than usual. Also, her lips looked very shiny. Lip gloss? Whatever it was, it had him noticing how pink her lips were, how plump. Angelina Jolie had nothing on Delilah Gould.

It was too much to resist. Slowly, and with great care, he leaned over and kissed Delilah. Her eyes registered shock, but then he felt her give herself over to it, but only for a moment. Not wanting to push, he gently broke contact. Delilah blushed, studying her hands in her lap.

"That was nice," she murmured.

"Yes, it was. Would you like to go for coffee?"

Delilah blinked. "With you?"

Jason laughed. "No," he teased, "with the other guy who just kissed you. Of course, with me. Me and Stan," he amended, hoping that might make her less nervous.

Delilah squirmed. "I don't know. I mean"—she licked her delectable lips—"I'm not sure."

"Hey, I know you like coffee. I've seen you drink it."

"I know, it's just . . ." Her voice drifted off as she stared down at her feet.

"Afraid kissing coupled with caffeine might drive us to do something crazy?" Jason joked.

Delilah appeared not to have heard him. She'd stopped staring at her feet and had instead turned her attention to a man in a pin-striped suit walking a German shepherd. The guy was the size of a meat locker; he reminded Jason of one of those omnipresent bodyguards hip-hoppers seemed to surround themselves with. Jason watched as the shepherd squatted and did his business before master and dog began sauntering away.

"Excuse me!" shouted Delilah. She sped toward the man and dog as if shot from a cannon. "Hey!" she yelled. The man stopped. So did Jason's heart.

"You're supposed to clean up after your dog," Delilah scolded him. "It's a law."

The man stared down at her contemptuously. "Yeah?"

"Yeah." Delilah put her hands on her hips. "How would you like it if you stepped in dog shit and ruined those lovely

shoes you're wearing, because some *schmuck* like you didn't clean up after his dog?"

The man thrust his boulder-sized head forward. "Yo, what did you call me?" he asked as his dog began to growl.

"Quiet!" Delilah barked at the dog. Shockingly, at least to Jason, the dog shut up. Delilah's expression was angry as she continued looking up into the man's face. "Please clean up after your dog." Like a magician pulling a rabbit out of a hat, she made a poop bag appear from out of her fanny pack and held it out to him.

The man sniggered. "I'm not cleanin' up any *shit*." His expression turned menacing as he took a step toward Delilah, towering over her.

"C'mon, Stan." Jason picked up Stanley's leash and hustled over to Delilah and the Man Who Refused to Scoop Poop. Stanley let out a couple of barks and a low, long growl, something he rarely did. He knew this guy was a threat to Delilah. The sharp-dressed man took one look at Stanley and took a big step back.

"What's going on?" Jason demanded. He couldn't believe Delilah had picked this guy for a civics lesson; he was three times her size and looked like the type who drop-kicked toddlers for fun.

"What the hell kind of dog is that?" the man asked nervously.

Jason yawned. "Newfoundland. Canadian attack dog."

"Keep that dog away from me, bro," said the man.

Jason glowered at him. "Then do as the lady asks."

Muttering curses, the man snatched the poop bag from Delilah's hand and scooped up his dog's mess.

"Happy?" he jeered, though he continued to peer fearfully at Stanley.

Delilah pointed to a nearby garbage can. "If you could throw it in there, that would be great." The man begrudgingly obliged. "Thanks!" Delilah said brightly.

"C'mon, Tyson." The man snapped his shepherd's leash. "Newfoundland," Jason heard him murmur to himself as he hurriedly walked away. "Damn, I gotta get me one of those."

CHAPTER

05

"Can I ask you a question?"

Jason could barely keep up with Delilah as she bounded out of the park. She seemed to be annoyed with him, which was completely mystifying since he'd just saved her from being a headline in tomorrow's *Post*.

"What?" Delilah's voice was clipped.

"Are you out of your goddamn mind?"

She increased her pace. "I don't know what you're talking about."

"I'm talking about that stupid display of bravado back there. In case you didn't notice, that guy looked like he ate women your size for breakfast. What were you thinking?!"

Delilah stopped short, forcing Jason and Stanley to do the same.

"Don't take this the wrong way, okay?" Delilah's big brown eyes smoldered with anger. "But I'm perfectly capable of taking care of myself. I didn't need you to come over there and act all macho."

"I was just trying to help!"

"I didn't need your help. I wasn't afraid of him."

"Well, I was!" Jason retorted.

Delilah frowned dismissively. "I deal with jerks like him all the time."

"Yeah? So how come you're fearless when it comes to canine crusading, but when I ask you out for a simple cup of coffee, you get all twittery?"

"I do not!"

"Well, well, well. Speak of the Devil. I was just about to call your cell, baby bro."

Jason's shoulders sank at the sound of Eric's voice. It was just like his evil twin to show up at exactly the wrong moment.

Jason tried to ignore the puckish look in his brother's eye as he made introductions. "Delilah, I want you to meet my brother, Eric."

Delilah peered questioningly at Eric as she shook his hand. "You look really familiar to me."

"You've probably seen me around the neighborhood," he explained. "I live right down the block from Mr. Cosmopolitan here." He tilted his head toward Jason.

Delilah no longer looked angry; she looked puzzled. "You never mentioned you had a brother," she said to Jason.

"You never mentioned you turned into Wonder Woman when total strangers don't pick up after their dogs."

Eric looked amused. "Am I interrupting something here?"

"Not at all," Delilah assured him.

"Yes," said Jason, glaring at Eric. "We're training Stanley," he added lamely, hoping to appease Delilah.

"Stan the Man." Eric crouched down in front of Stanley, rubbing him vigorously behind his big, floppy ears. "Isn't he the greatest?" he said, beaming up at Delilah.

"He is," Delilah agreed, clearly moved by Eric's love of the dog.

You SOB, thought Jason. Usually Eric treated Stanley as if he were the canine equivalent of the Elephant Man. But now that impressing a woman was involved, he suddenly acted like a charter member of the AKC. Jason wanted to throttle him.

"Aren't you late for your cross-dresser's support meeting?" Jason asked his brother. "Or maybe you were calling me to come over because you forgot what a real hockey player looks like."

"Anytime I want to see a real hockey player, I just look in the mirror, asshole." His gaze cut quickly to Delilah. "Sorry. Sometimes my brother's immature behavior drives me to speak without thinking."

Delilah looked back and forth between the two men. "You both play hockey?"

Jason nodded. "He plays for Jersey. You were looking for me because—?" He wanted to wrap this up. The longer they lingered, chitchatting with Eric, the greater the odds his brother would try to show him up in front of Delilah.

"A bunch of us are going out tonight for some pizza and beer," said Eric. "Thought you might want to come."

"Who's going?" Jason asked. Eric rattled off a bunch of Jersey players, all of whom Jason had hung out with before. It was a no-brainer. "Sure. Okay."

"Wives and girlfriends are coming along, too." Eric's expression was gallant as he once again regarded Delilah. "Would you like to join us?"

"No."

Eric seemed shocked at the rapidity of her response. "My treat, of course," he continued.

"Can't." Delilah's eyes darted wildly as if looking for the nearest escape route. The canine crusader was gone, replaced by the twittery woman Jason was determined to coax out of her shell. He smiled to himself. Delilah's blunt rejection of Eric *rocked*. That would teach the pathetic egomaniac not to stick his nose where it didn't belong.

Delilah pushed her hair off her face as her anxious gaze finally settled on Jason. "So, um, I have the spare key to your place and I'll walk Stan tomorrow night between nine and ten." She kissed Stanley on the top of the head. "Bye, boy. Don't forget to practice with him this week," she added for Jason's benefit.

"I won't," Jason assured her as she started away.

"Nice meeting you," Eric called after her.

"Oh." Delilah jerked to a halt. "You, too." For a split second she looked unsure of what to do. Then she hustled on.

Jason stared down at the sidewalk with a heavy sigh. He knew Eric; the minute Delilah turned the corner, his brother would be on him like a puma on his prey, toying with him mercilessly until zeroing in for the kill.

"Cute," Eric murmured as she disappeared from view. "*Very* cute."

Jason snapped his head up, glaring. "What the hell was that about?"

"What?"

"Pretending you give a rat's ass about Stanley! Asking her out!"

Eric smirked. "What, that bothered you? I thought you didn't have the hots for her."

"I don't!"

"My ass."

Jason began petting Stanley's head, hoping the soothing, repetitive motion might help calm him down. "Just keep away from her, okay? She's a nice girl, nothing like the trolls you usually hang out with."

"I wasn't really interested in her," Eric admitted with a yawn. "I was just trying to break your balls."

"What a guy."

"She smells a bit doggy, don't you think? Has a touch of Eau de Damp Pooch about her."

"No, she doesn't," Jason replied, offended. Eric was nuts. Delilah smelled great. Then he realized: puma time. The tormenting had begun.

"What were you two lovebirds quarreling about when I so rudely interrupted?"

"Nothing," Jason muttered.

"Tell big brother," Eric cajoled. "Maybe I can help. We

both know I have lots more experience when it comes to the opposite sex."

Jason ignored the barb. "We were in the park, right? And this guy the size of a Hummer lets his dog take a crap and doesn't clean it up. So what does Delilah do? She runs over there and reads him the riot act. This guy was totally menacing, okay? It looked like he was seconds away from just reaching out and crushing her windpipe, I'm not kidding. So Stan and I came to her rescue. But rather than being grateful, she was pissed! Care to explain that to me?"

"Yo, Mr. I Have No Impulse Control, this is not Flasher, okay?" said Eric as he watched two giggly coeds in NYU sweatshirts bounce along the street. "New York women can take care of themselves. Delilah might be small, but she's obviously got spunk."

"What am I supposed to do now?" Jason asked. "Apologize to her for being a nice guy?"

"Absolute-a-mento. Chicks dig it when guys admit they're wrong." Eric put his arm around Jason's shoulder. "Look, I know you like her. If she's stupid enough to like you back, it can't hurt to act all chastened and shit, like you really didn't mean to offend her or overstep your bounds or whatever. She'll be eating out of your hand."

Jason removed his brother's arm. "You really need to cancel your subscription to *Maxim*, you know that? It's starting to rot your brain."

"You asked me what you should do. I told you."

Jason grunted. He had no problem apologizing. He was willing to do whatever it took to restore himself to her good graces. He hated that she might think he was some kind of macho jerk.

"I gotta get going," he told Eric, prompted by Stanley's newly persistent pawing, which meant only one thing: hunger. "What's the drill tonight?"

"I'll swing by at around eight, and we'll head down to McDougal's to meet the rest of the guys."

"Sounds good."

"If I run into Delilah, do you want me to say anything on your behalf?"

Jason scowled. "*No.* I can handle things on my own."

Eric snorted as he walked away. "Keep tellin' yourself that."

"Your mother's here."

The doorman's voice was cheerful as it crackled over the intercom, a stark contrast to Delilah's own mood. For weeks, Mitzi Gould had been hounding her daughter to get together, completely ignoring Delilah's busy schedule. Finally, unable to take the endless dramatic messages left on her answering machine ("You have time to train dogs to sit, but you can't make time for your own mother?" "You haven't called in three days. I could be dead for all you know."), Delilah broke down and invited her mother into the city for lunch. The closer the date drew near, the more tense Delilah grew. She hadn't slept at all the night before, which meant only one thing: within five minutes of letting her mother in the door, she'd tell Delilah how awful she looked.

"Send her up."

Maddening as Mitzi could be, Delilah was hopeful lunch would her take her mind off Jason. Did she really act "twittery" when he asked her out for coffee? She knew she'd hesitated a bit, but overall, she thought she was doing well. If they hadn't been interrupted by that jerk who didn't pick up after his dog, she probably would have gone for coffee with him. And Stan. No, not probably. She would have. Especially after that kiss.

Running into his brother had thrown her a bit, too. Not only because Jason had never mentioned having a brother, but because Eric was so flirty with her, so fast. Delilah might be more attuned to animals than people, but even she could tell Eric was trying to get Jason's goat by asking her to join them for pizza. She didn't appreciate being a toy in the competition between the two.

"Helloooo." The voice on the other side of Delilah's door

was quiet yet imperious, the knock accompanying it coming later than Delilah expected. Her mother must have taken the stairs rather than the elevator in her never-ending quest to "burn extra calories"—as if she were even in need of such thing. Mitzi Gould weighed ninety pounds soaking wet, if that.

Delilah took a good look around her apartment before opening the door. She'd dusted and vacuumed, transforming disarray into order as best she could, no easy task when you owned three dogs and boarded others. She'd gone out of her way to get all her mother's favorite foods for lunch: bagels, lox, smoked whitefish, even herring in cream sauce, which Delilah found revolting. If her mother saw she'd made an effort to please, she might think twice about criticizing. The odds were slim, but it was worth a shot.

Squaring her shoulders, Delilah finally opened the door. There stood her platinum-blonde mother in a full-length raincoat.

"Hi, Mom." Delilah leaned over to kiss the powdered cheek, having learned as a little girl never to kiss her on the mouth, since it might mess up her lipstick.

"Hello." Her mother stepped over the threshold. "You've put on weight."

"Thanks, Mom. Nice to see you, too." Delilah glanced quickly at the window. "Why do you have that raincoat on? It's not raining."

Her mother's disdainful glance zeroed in on Delilah's three dogs, all of whom were sleeping peacefully on the living room rug. They were so well-trained they didn't even stir when someone entered the apartment. "I don't want to go home covered in dog hair and drool."

"None of them drool," Delilah felt compelled to point out.

"Well, they shed," her mother replied tersely. "I'm keeping the coat on."

"Suit yourself."

Delilah had sworn she wouldn't let her mother rattle her. But less than two minutes into their lunch, Delilah was los-

ing the battle. "How was the train?" Delilah asked in an effort to shift the topic from the dogs to her mother's favorite
subject: herself.

Her mother clucked her tongue. "Eck, disgusting. I
should have driven. I remember when the LIRR used to
clean their carriages. Now they're just petri dishes on
wheels." She peered into Delilah's face. "You look terrible.
Aren't you sleeping?"

"I had some trouble falling asleep last night."

"Poor baby. You should get a prescription for Ambien.
Works like a charm." Her mother seemed genuinely sympathetic as she reached out to cradle Delilah's cheek. "You
know, a little makeup would help cover up those dark circles
under your eyes."

"It's fine, Mom. Really." Delilah signaled for her mother
to follow her into the kitchen. "Come on. I've made lunch."
Her mother made a face as she sidestepped one of
Sherman's squeaky toys.

Delilah could feel her mother's deliberate gaze scouring
every surface as she put up the coffee and pulled the lunch
items out of the fridge. If there was a flaw in the room, no
matter how small, her mother would find it. Stomach in
knots, Delilah awaited the inevitable critique, shocked when
it was semi-positive.

"You've done a nice job in here. I wouldn't have painted
the cabinets that light a shade of blue—in fact I think dusty
rose might have worked better—but it's your apartment.
You have to do what works for you."

"Thank you." Thrilled to have gotten off so lightly,
Delilah gestured toward the kitchen table, where the food
was now spread out. "See? I got all your favorites."

Her mother looked horrified. "Do you have any idea how
fattening all that is?"

"I thought you loved this stuff!"

"That doesn't mean I allow myself to eat it."

"Fine." Annoyed, Delilah began loading food back into
the refrigerator. "We'll go out."

"No, no, don't be silly," her mother insisted. "Half a bagel won't kill me. I guess."

Delilah rested her forehead against the refrigerator door. "Are you *sure*? Because if you're going to sit here making comments, I'd rather go out."

"This is fine," her mother assured her. "Wonderful."

"You're sure."

"Put out the food, Delilah."

"If you say so." Delilah began unloading the food.

"So," her mother began coyly, "have you talked to your father lately?"

"Not lately."

"I heard he's got some new little tootsie. I was wondering if you knew anything."

"No, but why should you care?"

After twenty-eight years of acrimonious wedlock, her parents had finally divorced. The final straw had been her father's supposed affair with his longtime secretary, Junie. Delilah believed him when he denied it, but not her mother.

Her mother appeared insulted. "I *don't* care," she insisted. "I'm just curious." She took the plates Delilah handed her. "Is he still *schtupping* Junie?"

Delilah put the silverware in her hand down with a clatter. "I don't know, Mom. Why don't you call him yourself and ask him?"

"The day I call that prick is the day hell freezes over." Her mother's lips puckered sourly as she folded a paper napkin in half and put it under one of the forks. "He can screw whoever he wants now. I've got my own love life to keep me busy."

"Really?" Delilah was surprised. What man could deal with her mother's unique blend of criticism and bitterness?

"Uh-huh." Her mother's perfectly made-up face glowed. "His name is Bruce Holstein. I met him at the temple's mixer for singles. He's smart, rich—a widower."

"How long has he been widowed?"

"About six months. Cancer. You know men: the wife

dies, and before you know it, they're on the prowl. They can't stand being alone."

"Can't stand doing their own laundry is more like it."

"Sweetheart, Bruce has no interest in my doing his laundry. He much prefers I do *him*."

"Mom!"

"What, that shocks you? I'm just in it for the sex, Leelee. And let me tell you, it's been fantastic. He's a great lover. Much better than your father ever was, and that's saying something, because your father was an absolute tiger in the sack. Bruce does this thing with his toes—"

"Ma!" Delilah's hands flew to her ears. "I don't need to hear this, okay?!"

Her mother looked wounded. "Fine. We can talk all about you, if you'd like. Forget about me."

"We can talk about you without talking about your sex life, can't we?"

Her mother shrugged. "I guess. Though where you get this prudishness from is beyond me. I certainly didn't raise you to be that way." She looked at the stove with longing. "Is that coffee almost done?"

"Just sit down and relax, Mom. It'll be done in a minute." Delilah put two cups down on the table and went to fetch the coffee. "I wish you'd take off that raincoat. You look ridiculous."

"Some women don't mind being covered in dog hair. Others do." She held her coffee cup up for Delilah to fill. "Is this decaf?"

"No."

"I thought I told you I only drink decaf now."

"No, Mom, you didn't."

"It must have been your cousin Dory. She calls me all the time just to talk."

Delilah chose to ignore the implicit barb. "Do you want the coffee or not?"

Her mother sighed. "Half a cup won't kill me. I guess."

No, but I might, Delilah thought.

"That's enough!" her mother commanded when Delilah

had filled the cup halfway. "You have skim milk, right?" She sounded nervous.

"No, only cream. I'm going to tie you to the chair and make you drink it while watching your hips expand. Of course I have skim milk. That's what I drink."

"Thank God."

Delilah fetched the milk from the fridge as she and her mother finally sat at the table. Only ten minutes had passed, and already Delilah felt exhausted. She'd have no problem falling asleep tonight.

"How's work?" Delilah asked.

"Busy. I could use an assistant, if you ever decide you want a real job."

Delilah's mother was an interior designer in Roslyn on Long Island. She catered to clients much like herself: wealthy North Shore residents who turned their homes into showpieces. Their willingness to spare no expense had made Delilah's mother a rich woman.

Delilah's voice was even as she buttered her bagel. "I have a real job, Mom. I run my own business, just like you."

"You call cleaning up dog poop a business?" Her mother shook her head sadly. "I worry about you, Leelee. Truly."

Here it comes, Delilah thought. "Why's that?" she made herself ask.

"You're not getting any younger."

"I'm not even thirty, Mom."

"You do nothing to capitalize on your assets." Her mother reached across the table. Delilah swore she could see herself reflected in the high gloss of her mother's red nails. "A little makeup wouldn't kill you, you know. You have such beautiful eyes."

"I don't like makeup. You know that. Besides, I don't want anything chemical on my face in case one of the dogs licks me."

Delilah's mother shuddered. "Don't tell me any more, or I won't be able to eat." She ran her thumb back and forth over the top of Delilah's hand. "If you wanted, I could pay to send you to a professional, someone who could show you the right makeup to buy and how to apply it."

"How many times do I have to tell you?" Delilah was incredulous. "I don't like makeup."

Her mother sighed. "How about you let me take you shopping, then? We could get some nice clothes for you."

"I have nice clothes, thank you."

"How come I never see them?"

"Because no matter what I wear or say or do, it's never good enough for you."

"That's not true. I just want the best for you."

"Then leave me alone about this stuff, okay?"

Her mother withdrew her hand. "Fine. I will."

"Good."

Desperate to salvage what little chance of decent conversation was left, Delilah turned the subject back to her mother's life. She got to hear all about her mother's mahjongg group (the longest-running group in Roslyn!), her mother's best friend Edie, her mother's new white carpet, and her mother's bid for the presidency of the temple board. But midway through her mother's recitation, it dawned on Delilah that their conversation, if you could call it that, was strictly one-way. Not once did her mother ask about her business, her dogs, her friends, or even if Delilah was seeing anyone. Did she think Delilah was such a loser there was no point in asking?

"You know, things are going really well for me," Delilah interrupted in the middle of her mother's story about how Sandi Mintz's son-in-law had made partner. (Delilah had no idea who Sandi Mintz was).

"Mmm?" Her mother sounded unconvinced as she spread a thin layer of whitefish salad on a hollowed-out bagel half.

"My business is thriving."

"That's nice, sweetheart."

"And I'm seeing someone."

Delilah knew she was digging a hole for herself, but she couldn't help it. She wanted her mother's attention. And judging by the expression of wide-eyed delight on her mother's face, she had it.

"Oh, Leelee! Why did you wait so long to tell me?"

"I was waiting for the right time," Delilah mumbled. It was the worst possible thing she could have said.

"Oh my God." Her mother clutched the lip of the table. "Is it serious?"

Delilah could feel her feet beginning to sweat in her sneakers. "No. Not yet. I mean, it could be. In time. But not yet. I mean, we've only just started seeing each other."

"When?"

"Two weeks ago," Delilah fibbed.

Her mother bounced eagerly in her chair. "Name, I want a name."

"Jason Mitchell."

"Is he—?"

"No, Mom, he's not."

"Not a problem," her mother trilled. "He can always convert." The news of Delilah's relationship seemed to have a profound effect on her mother's appetite. Delilah watched in fascination as her mother piled more whitefish salad atop her bagel and bit into it lustily.

"What does he do?" her mother warbled through the food in her mouth.

"He's a hockey player."

Her mother looked at her blankly. "A what?"

"A hockey player," Delilah repeated with annoyance. "For the New York Blades."

"Never heard of them." Her mother looked uneasy. "Does he have his own teeth?"

"Yes, Mother," Delilah huffed, though she was embarrassed she'd asked the same thing.

"And he makes a decent living hockey-ing?"

"He's a professional athlete. What do you think?"

"As long as he can support my little girl, that's all that matters."

"Mom!" Delilah was mortified.

"I know, I know, it's early yet. But the news that you

have a boyfriend—" She took a deep breath as her eyes misted over. "Excuse me a minute." She reached into the pocket of her raincoat and pulled out a tissue, dabbing her eyes. "That's better." She put the tissue back in her pocket. "When do I get to meet him?"

Delilah panicked. "Not for a while. I mean, he plays hockey a lot. A lot. And he has lots of away games. I mean I barely see him myself."

"I'm sure he can make time for brunch with his future mother-in-law." Her mother winked.

Delilah's hands linked tightly beneath the table. "I wish you wouldn't say things like that."

"Afraid I'll jinx it?"

Delilah nodded, not knowing what else to do.

"Mum's the word, then. For now." Beaming, Delilah's mother rose and came to stand behind her daughter. "I'm so, so happy," she said as she wrapped her arms around Delilah's neck and kissed the side of her face. "I have to be honest, I was getting a little worried. That last one you brought home was such a loser. And then you were spending so much time with that *feygele* dancer, I thought, *She'll never meet a nice boy.* But you have, and I'm thrilled. *Thrilled.*" Her mother hugged her tighter. "Let me just say one more thing."

"If you must."

Her mother showered the top of her head with kisses. "I have a feeling about this, Leelee."

So do I, Delilah thought. *I have a feeling I've just painted myself into the tightest corner in the world.*

CHAPTER

06

"*You're skating like* shit. Get your ass over here."

The disgust in Ty Gallagher's voice made Jason slink off the ice like a puppy with his tail between his legs. Moronically, Jason had hoped his coach might not notice he was moving at half speed this morning, the result of one of the worst hangovers of his life. Five minutes of practice confirmed everything he'd heard about Ty: the guy didn't miss a trick.

Skull pounding, Jason stopped at the bench where Ty sat with a stopwatch and a clipboard, and waited. And waited. His humiliation grew the longer Ty ignored him. By the time Ty deigned to look up at him, Jason longed to sink through the floorboards.

"What's the problem?" Ty demanded.

Jason swallowed. "I'm not feeling too hot, Coach. I think I'm getting a cold."

"I had the flu and was running a fever of one hundred and one when I won my second Cup. Don't give me this 'My nose is stuffed up' bullshit."

Jason winced and glanced away, unsure of how to re-

spond. Should he just come clean and tell him he was out
drinking with Eric and other assorted hockey players until
three a.m.?

He hadn't meant to get trashed. But he and Eric were
having such a great time that one drink led to another, and
before he knew it, late night had somehow turned to early
morning. Yet the evening was great only in hindsight; right
now, with a head filled with lead and his coach looking at
him like he was the lowest form of scum, the previous
evening seemed far from worth it.

Jason forced his gaze back to Ty, who was still staring at
him with contempt. "You're hungover, aren't you?"

"Yeah." There was no point in lying. "I'm sorry," Jason
added, heartfelt.

"Me, too. Because we're playing Chicago tonight, and I
really could have used you. Instead you're not dressing
tonight—*and* you owe me five hundred bucks."

The thought of not being allowed to play was torture. "It
won't happen again, Coach! I swear!"

"You're fucking right it won't happen again," Ty snarled.
"'Cause if it does, you're gonna spend the rest of the season
as the stick boy."

"Coach." Jason was seconds away from tossing all dignity aside and pleading. "I really didn't mean for it to happen. I was out with someone and—"

"Who?"

"My brother, Eric." Jason removed his helmet and ran a
hand through his sweaty hair. "He can get a little wild sometimes and—"

"Jason?"

"Coach?"

"Let me point something out to you." Ty still sounded
disgusted. "We have a game tonight. New Jersey doesn't."

Jason was confused. "So?"

"Did it ever cross your beer-sozzled mind that your
brother, who just happens to play for a rival team, got you
drunk on purpose so you wouldn't be one hundred percent?
Or so you couldn't play at all?"

"Uh, no, that never crossed my mind." The thought made Jason vaguely ill.

"Well, maybe the next time your brother invites you out for a brew, you'll check to see if *Jersey* has a game the next day before accepting."

"I will," Jason replied lamely.

"Good. Now get back out there and skate until you puke. You can give me my check for five hundred dollars before the game."

"*I'm not sure* I'm up for this."

Delilah's mouth felt dry as Marcus ushered her across the threshold of the Golden Bough, a New Age store down in Greenwich Village. Though she'd initially been excited by the prospect of a tarot card reading, now that she was actually here, she wasn't so sure. What if this woman could read her mind and her long-running, secret crush on Wolf Blitzer was revealed? What if the cards said she hadn't a hope in hell with Jason?

Marcus inhaled deeply as he closed the door behind them. "Mmm, lavender. I love coming in here. It always smells so peaceful."

Delilah nodded in agreement. Marcus was right; the store smelled lovely, and the atmosphere created by the antique rugs and plump armchairs was welcoming. Delilah cocked her head, listening. Celtic music was playing softly.

At the back of the store, a woman sat on a high stool behind a small wooden counter. She was small and curvy, with a wild tangle of red hair and the friendliest green eyes Delilah had ever seen. Spotting Marcus and Delilah coming toward her, she smiled. "Hello. I'm Gemma."

"Hi, hon." Marcus rounded the counter and kissed her cheek. "I want you to meet my friend Delilah."

Gemma held out her hand. "Nice to meet you."

"You, too," said Delilah, who couldn't help but notice the antique sapphire ring on Gemma's left ring finger as it dazzled in the light. "That ring is beautiful."

"Thank you." Gemma blushed with pleasure. "It was my grandmother's."

"How do you two know each other?" Delilah asked.

"Gemma is good friends with my friend Theo," Marcus explained.

"Theo." Delilah was drawing a blank.

"The performance artist? The one who made a bra out of two CDs and licorice and crashed the Victoria's Secret runway show?"

"Oh. Now I remember."

Marcus leaned close to Gemma, flicking a thumb at Delilah. "This one doesn't remember anything unless it has to do with dogs," he drawled.

"That's not true!" Delilah protested.

Gemma smiled and patted the empty stool next to her. "Here, sit down," she urged Delilah. Delilah sat. "I can do a bunch of different spreads for you. The simplest is a one-card spread, which might not be a bad way to start off if you've never had a reading before."

"I haven't," said Delilah.

Gemma smiled kindly. "Well, there's nothing to be afraid of, I promise." She reached beneath the counter and pulled out a small purple velvet bag, from which she removed a well-worn deck of tarot cards. "Now. What you need to do is think of one question, any question you want, and then shuffle the deck as many times as you want. When you're done, just put the deck down on the counter and turn over the top card."

"Okay." Delilah took the cards from Gemma. They were battered, almost flaccid; how many other people had sat right where she was sitting now, hoping for answers and insights? She kept waiting for some feeling of electricity or energy to shoot from the cards to her fingertips, but nothing happened. She decided to concentrate on her first question.

She waited to see what her mind tossed up. An image of Belle swam before her. Delilah quietly asked, "Will Belle's other eye need surgery?"

"You're asking about one of your dogs?!" Marcus yelped.

Delilah's eyes flew open. "This is *my* reading and I'm doing it *my* way! If you don't like, just leave!"

Gemma raised her hands in a gesture of calm. "We need to get centered here, people. This negative energy is not good."

Marcus made a zipping motion across his lips. "Not another word from me. I swear on Bob Fosse's grave."

"Go ahead and shuffle," Gemma urged Delilah.

Delilah once again closed her eyes. She waited until she felt calm again before shuffling the cards. She shuffled twenty times, because it just felt right. Then she put the deck down, opened her eyes, and turned over the top card. The image on the top card looked like ten tree branches sawed perfectly straight at the top and bottom.

Delilah held her breath as Gemma nodded slowly, looking pleased. "It's the Ten of Wands. A very good card in terms of your dog's health. It means problems are solved."

Delilah let out a sigh of relief. "Oh, good. Can I ask another?"

Gemma looked amused. "That's what you're paying me for."

Delilah nodded gratefully and took the cards. She liked Gemma. She seemed to know just who she was. Delilah wondered: What did it take to achieve that kind of equanimity? To feel so at home in your own skin?

She asked a bunch of questions about her business, her parents, even Marcus. Finally, she picked up the cards and thought of Jason. *Is there any chance my friendship with him could grow into romance?*

It felt like she was shuffling endlessly. Worried that the universe—and Gemma—might be losing patience, she put down the cards and turned over the top card. Staring back at her was a scythe-wielding skeleton stalking a barren landscape.

"Oh, God." Delilah's eyes began filling with tears. Someone was going to die.

"Relax." Gemma patted Delilah's arm reassuringly. "This is a very, very good card."

Delilah looked at her through watery eyes. "Really?"

"Absolutely. The Death card means an overturning of the old life, of rebirth. It means regeneration. Change. Transformation. Shuffle one more time and think of Jason."

Delilah gasped. "How did you know—?"

Gemma smiled enigmatically. Shaken, Delilah did as she was told. The card she turned up showed three chalices. Gemma grinned.

"Three of Cups. It symbolizes emotional growth, love, fulfillment in marriage or a relationship. That sounds good!"

"It does," Delilah agreed uneasily.

Gemma gathered up her cards and returned them to their velvet pouch. "These things aren't carved in stone, nor will the universe just hand them to you. *You* have to play an active role in your own destiny."

"How do I do that?"

Gemma's gaze was unnervingly direct. "Stop being so afraid."

"Please don't let her kick my ass, please don't let her kick my ass, please don't let her kick my ass . . ."

Jason knew his chant was in vain as he and Stanley hustled toward Central Park for their next obedience lesson with Delilah. They were supposed to have practiced the "down stay" command, the next logical step after the "sit stay." But Jason had been so depressed by not dressing for Chicago, everything else had flown out the window. He spent every spare minute he had preparing mentally and physically for the next game so he would be at his peak. It wasn't until he checked his schedule this morning that he realized he had another lesson with Delilah and had done nothing to prepare for it.

His trepidation abated somewhat as he caught sight of her waiting at their usual bench. She was oblivious to his approach, oblivious to how sweet she looked sitting there all on her own, watching a ponytailed dog owner play Frisbee with his dappled mutt.

"Hey." Jason couldn't resist breaking into a big smile as he finally came to where Delilah was sitting and told Stanley to sit and stay. He wondered if he should bring up the last time they met, when he'd asked her for coffee and she'd squirmed, despite obviously enjoying their brief kiss. Maybe it was better to let it go for now.

"Hi."

Jason loved the way Delilah's face lit up when she saw Stanley. She always leaned over to give him a big kiss. How sad was it that he envied his own dog?

"So, how's it been going?" Jason asked. He wanted to keep her talking. The less time they spent on an actual lesson, the better for him.

"Pretty good," Delilah answered. "You?"

"Okay." He sat down on the bench next to her. "How was your tarot card reading?"

"Oh." She seemed surprised to be asked. "It was all right."

"Learn anything interesting?"

"A few things," Delilah answered evasively.

"Like?"

Delilah squinted into the middle distance. "I have to stop being afraid of things."

"Mmm." Jason took this as a good sign. Maybe she'd simply smile and say "Yes" the next time he asked her out.

Delilah stood up, seemingly eager to get things rolling. "Time to show me how you boys have been faring with the 'down stay.' "

"Of course." Jason rose. He could will Stanley to do this, even though they hadn't practiced. He knew he could. He looked deeply into Stanley's eyes. "Stan, down." Stanley stretched out on all fours. "Stan, stay." Stanley didn't move as Jason detached his leash from his collar.

"There you go," Jason said to Delilah. Damn, he and Stan were good.

"Now walk away with me," Delilah said.

Jason's face fell. "What?"

"The whole point of the command is that he stays down

until you command him otherwise." Delilah put a hand on
her hip. "You did practice this with him, right?"

"Yeah, of course," Jason scoffed. Once again he stared
deeply into Stanley's eyes in his new role as canine hypno-
tist. *Don't move a muscle, pal, please.*

Together with Delilah, he slowly started walking away.
Though his back was to him, he could hear Stanley scrambling to his feet. Next thing he knew Stanley was trotting
beside him.

Delilah stopped. "Stan, sit." Stan sat. "Good boy." She
fed him a treat while regarding Jason with suspicion. "You
said you practiced this with him."

"I did. He must just be excited to see you or something."

"Then let's try it again."

Shit, thought Jason.

"Stan, down." Delilah's voice was firm but loving. Stan
obeyed. "Stan, stay." Taking Jason's elbow, Delilah began
steering him away. They'd only managed a few steps before
Stanley joined them, thrusting his head between Jason's legs.

"I guess he's not in the mood to be alone," Jason said
lamely, scratching Stan's back.

"And I'm not in the mood to have my time wasted."

"I'm sorry." Jason scanned Delilah's face. She looked
more annoyed than flat-out angry. He decided to come
clean. "I meant to practice with him this week, but time got
away from me. It won't happen again."

"We can work on the 'down stay' today," Delilah said
briskly. "I was hoping we could really challenge him by
walking completely out of his line of sight, but he's not—"

Stanley was off. A scurrying squirrel had made the tacti-
cal error of directly crossing Stanley's path, and now he was
running faster than Jason had ever seen him move in his life.

"Stanley!" Jason yelled after him. "Halt!" Stanley kept
running. "Oh, shit. Excuse me a minute."

Leash in hand, Jason chased after Stanley, Delilah speed-
ing right after him. He gained on Stanley easily, grabbing
him by the collar. The squirrel disappeared up a tree and out
of sight. That didn't stop Stan from straining so hard he was

close to breaking Jason's fingers as he held tight to Stan's harness. While restraining him, Jason was reminded of what a powerful dog Stanley could be. Out of the corner of his eye, he saw Delilah standing by anxiously. No way could she have restrained Stan when he had this kind of adrenaline pumping through him.

Jason fastened the leash to the collar and jerked it. "Stan, *sit*." Stanley continued trying to pull toward the base of the tree. Jason jerked harder. *"Sit."* Reluctantly, Stanley listened. Jason heaved a sigh of relief and waited for Delilah to tell him how he was the worst dog owner on the face of the earth.

Instead he got, "Are you okay?"

"I'm fine. A little shaken up."

Delilah crouched before Stanley. "You're the Devil in disguise, mister." Her expression was serious as she looked up at Jason. "Now do you understand why absolute mastery of the 'down stay' is so important?"

Jason was dubious. "C'mon. Tell me that even the best-trained dog won't go nuts if a squirrel teases him."

"Squirrels don't tease."

"Sure they do. That guy who ran in front of Stan? Total tease."

Jason could see that Delilah wanted to smile. She didn't give in, though. "The better trained the dog is, the less likely it is to happen."

"Stan's doing pretty well in general, though, right? I mean, he's not retarded in dog terms or anything."

"Retarded in dog terms?"

"Slow learner," Jason clarified. "That's what I meant."

"No, he's not slow. You, on the other hand . . ." Delilah shook her head good-naturedly.

Jason smiled. "That's why I need you to teach me, Miss Gould."

Delilah's face turned beet red, and she looked away. Shit. Had he pushed it? How could he have? She was the one who started it. Hadn't she just flirted with him?

He put his hand on her shoulder. "Did I just embarrass you? Because if I did, I'm sorry."

Delilah looked up at him. "Life embarrasses me," she confessed.

Jason smiled. "You're making progress."

"Progress to what? From where?"

"From insanely shy to totally shy. By my reckoning, you should reach 'not shy at all' right around the time you're ready to collect Social Security."

"That's pretty far away."

"I was thinking in dog years."

Delilah laughed. Jason was thrilled he'd been able to salvage the moment. "About Stan the Man here," he continued, stroking Stan's back. "You can still board him tomorrow, right? Even though he's a total failure at the 'down stay'?" Tomorrow the Blades left for their first road trip of the season. Jason would be away three nights.

"No problem," Delilah assured him. "He's basically trained. You just need to tell me what time you plan to bring him by."

Jason grimaced. "See, here's the thing. We're leaving really early in the morning. Is there any chance you could swing by and get him? You've already got the keys to my place. I'd pay extra."

"As long as you leave me a list of instructions about feeding him as well as enough food for him, that should be fine. And yes, it *will* cost you extra."

Jason leaned in close. "I'm willing to do whatever it takes. You know that."

"Yes, I do," Delilah murmured. She was blushing, but she hadn't turned away. Jason leaned in closer and gently skimmed his lips over Delilah's before taking a chance and kissing her more fully. He could feel her trembling as he took her into his arms, anchoring her to him. *See? Nothing to be afraid of.* Slowly but surely, she was learning to trust. He need only be patient.

Breaking their embrace, Jason smiled. Perhaps Operation Coffee would commence sooner than expected.

CHAPTER 07

"He's quite the Casanova."

Delilah could tell Marcus was genuinely impressed as they entered Jason's apartment, and her favorite big black furry friend rose to cover her with kisses. Normally she would have swung by on her own to pick up Stan, but considering Stanley's size and the fact she had no idea how much food she might also be lugging, she decided to bring Marcus along. He was coming back to her place anyway, so they could watch *The Turning Point* together.

Delilah skimmed the note Jason had left her. Stanley's food regimen was straightforward: two cups of water-soaked kibble twice a day, followed by five small biscuits after each meal. Ten biscuits a day! Delilah made a mental note to talk to Jason about that.

"Why can't I get any of the men I want to do this?" Marcus sighed.

Delilah glanced up from Jason's instructions to see Stanley's head stuck between Marcus's legs.

Marcus abruptly held up a hand. "Hold on: message coming through from Stanley."

Delilah tried to hide her skepticism as Marcus disentangled himself from Stanley and knelt in front of him. "Okay. He says his dogdruff isn't being caused by the change in the weather. He's allergic to the new dog food Jason switched him to."

The hair stood up on the back of Delilah's neck. She hadn't voiced her thoughts about Stan's dogdruff aloud. Maybe there was something to this animal telepathy thing after all.

"What's that, Stan?" Marcus closed his eyes and put his ear to Stanley's muzzle. "Uh-huh. Uh-huh. Knew it." His expression was smug as he opened his eyes and looked Delilah. "He says Jason likes you. *A lot.*"

"You're making that up."

"I most certainly am not. And Stanley is offended you would even think that." Marcus sprang to his feet, rubbing his hands together excitedly. "Let's go check out his bedroom!"

"Marcus!"

"Don't you want to see how big it is? His bed, I mean."

"No!" Marcus looked crestfallen. "It's an invasion of privacy." Delilah peered at her friend worriedly. "Please don't tell me you go poking around people's apartments when you're working for me."

"Of course not!" Marcus bit his lip. "Well, maybe a few."

Delilah's mouth fell open. "Marcus!"

"You know that button-down guy on Seventy-eighth with the springer spaniel named Kingsley?" Delilah nodded fearfully. "Well, one time I brought Kingsley back to the apartment, and while I was there someone left a message on the machine saying, 'Hello, Leather Daddy, this is Dungeon Monkey. I'm looking forward to playing Twister at six.' So naturally I had to poke around."

"No, you didn't, but continue." Now that Marcus had started his story, Delilah felt she had an obligation to hear it through. It was only polite.

"I sniffed around the living room—not the bedroom"—

he added pointedly—"and you will not believe what I found in the broom closet."

"A broom?"

"A black leather mask, a cat-o'-nine tails, *and* a Twister board bearing no resemblance to any *I'd* ever seen."

"That's nice." Delilah pushed back the hair from her forehead. "Marcus? Please don't ever do that again! I could lose my business if someone ever found out!"

Marcus looked disappointed. "I guess that means I can't go into Halti Boy's bedroom and report any unusual findings back to you."

"You better not," Delilah warned.

"You're no fun anymore. Can I at least go into his kitchen for a drink of water?"

"Of course. Can you grab the dog food while you're in there?"

"No problem." Marcus disappeared into the kitchen. "Oh, Lilah," he sang out. "I think you better get in here. *Now.*"

Bracing herself for the sight of poop-christened Pergo, she joined Marcus. Sitting on Jason's kitchen table was a small coffee press, a bag of hazelnut coffee, and two New York Blades mugs. Propped up against one of the mugs was an envelope addressed to her. But before Delilah even had a chance to reach for it, Marcus snatched it up.

"Let's see what he has to say."

"Excuse me!" Delilah snatched the envelope back. "That's addressed to *me*."

Marcus's nostrils flared. "Yes, but *I* came upon the booty first, so you're obligated to share with me whatever the note says."

"Since when?"

"Since I'm the one helping you *schlep* all this dog food back to your place."

"Fine," Delilah muttered. She steadied herself as she opened the envelope. Inside was a note written on a piece of loose-leaf paper that said, "Sorry about yesterday's lesson, but I did enjoy the kissing part. Just try getting out of coffee

with me now! Thanks for taking such good care of Stan.
Jason." Delilah folded the letter back into the envelope and
held it to her chest, smiling.

"Well?" Marcus asked impatiently.

"He wants to have coffee with me when he gets back,"
Delilah whispered. She was amazed he'd gone through the
effort to buy the mugs, the coffee, the press. Obviously he'd
meant it when he'd said he was willing to do "whatever it
takes."

"If you tell me you need to think about this, I'm going to
slap you senseless," Marcus threatened.

"No, I'll have coffee with him. I guess. I mean how could
I not? I want to. Plus, I'd look like a total bitch if I turned
him down because he went through all this effort to buy this
stuff. It's just coffee, right? I mean—"

Marcus's hand flew to cover her mouth. "He likes you.
You like him. You're having coffee with him. The end." He
removed his hand. "Dogs don't lie, girl."

For once, Delilah couldn't argue.

*All right, big boy. Time to show the old man you've got
the goods.* The minute Jason hit the ice for his first shift
against San Diego, the angry voice in his head took over.
But rather than let his rage fester, he decided to use it out on
the ice. Did Eric really think he could fuck him up? Did Ty
really think the Blades could win without him? *Then watch
this.*

The buzzer sounded, and Thad Meyers won the face-off,
dumping the puck deep into San Diego's zone. Jason flew in
after it. *Dig, you stupid bastard, dig!* he exhorted himself as
he scrambled to free the puck from the corner. Out of the
corner of his eye he spotted Marty Cuff, one of San Diego's
chippiest defensemen, barreling toward him. *Crush the
fucker, but keep your elbows down!* Teeth gritted, Jason
smashed into Marty. The hometown crowd booed, prompting Jason to grin. *How 'bout that, Gallagher? That a good
enough hit for you, you hard-assed bastard?*

Pumped, Jason threw the loosened puck behind the net, then skated out into the crease. "Fuck you," San Diego's goalie Wingo Charleston jeered through his mask as he whacked Jason on the legs.

"I know you'd love to," Jason shot back as he subtly slapped Wingo's glove with his stick. The puck slid into the opposite corner. Again Jason hustled after it, but not before putting a hit on another San Diego player, Tommy Park. Again the crowd booed loudly, which only spurred Jason on. *You hear that, Ty? That's the sound of me kicking ass.* The puck came loose, but this time, instead of throwing it behind the net, Jason passed it to Thad Meyers in the slot, who snapped it right through Wingo's five hole. New York was on the board.

Jason skated back to the bench. Ty patted his shoulder, but no words of praise crossed his lips. They weren't necessary: Jason sat only one shift before Ty sent him back out on the ice with another line.

Jason suppressed a cocky smile. *Glad it's finally dawning on you what I can do, old man.* There was a scramble at center ice as the puck was once again dumped deep into San Diego's offensive zone. *Dominate,* Jason thought, flying in after it. Marty Cuff chased it down and looked to skate it out. *Didn't learn your lesson last time, huh, asshole?* Jason checked him against the boards, satisfaction surging through him as he watched Marty crumple to the ice. His delight was short-lived as Marty's teammate Wynton Brawdy smashed Jason into the boards from behind. Jason whipped around, dropping his gloves.

"Fucking cheap shot, Brawdy!" Jason yelled.

Brawdy shook free of his gloves. "Bite me, you fucking yokel."

Grab his sweater, Jason urged himself as the two went at it. *Lock the bastard up. Watch his left.* Adrenaline pounding, Jason swung his right arm, connecting with Brawdy's jaw. Brawdy hit the ice just as the linesmen arrived to break them apart. The sound of the crowd booing was like music to Jason's ears as he skated back to the Blades bench, where his teammates stood banging their sticks against the boards to show their support. Jason was double-shifted for the rest of the game. In the end, New York won, 2–0, both goals assisted by Jason.

"Yo, Mitchie. You rocked out there."

Denny O'Malley's compliment made Jason smile as he emerged from the shower, knotting a towel around his waist as he walked to his locker. Feelings of invincibility were singing through his veins, making him hyperalert. He was sure he could hear every conversation taking place. He had dressed and was just removing his lucky gold cross from around his neck when Ty came up and patted him on the back.

"Good game, Mitchell."

Jason nodded humbly. "Thanks, Coach."

Ty raised an eyebrow. "Trying to prove something?"

"Just to myself, Coach."

"Well, keep up the good work."

Jason watched Ty walk away. "You da man," he whispered to himself. He'd restored himself in his coach's eyes. He couldn't wait to get back to New York. He was going to find every newspaper clipping he could get about his on-ice performance, and he was going to tape them to Eric's apartment door. Then he was going to share his triumph with Delilah over coffee.

"Stanley, down!"

Delilah shook her head in disbelief as she commanded Stanley off her couch for the second time. The first time it happened, it shocked her. Hadn't Jason been working with him on this? The second time it happened, she was in the kitchen putting an empty bowl of popcorn in the sink. When she came back, Stanley was beside Marcus on the sofa, nose sniffing the popcorn-scented air.

"Honey, that dog is allergic to the floor," said Marcus.

Delilah watched as Stanley tried to slink his way into her bedroom, only to be stopped at the bedroom door by Shiloh, who emitted a low growl. Stanley looked puzzled, turned, and headed straight for Delilah.

Delilah knelt in front of him. "I need you to be a good boy, Stan, okay?" Stan's breath on her face was warm and yeasty. His tongue flicked out to lick her cheek, and Delilah wrapped her arms around his neck. "You can't deny Newfs are great for hugging," she said to Marcus.

"Nor can you deny Miss Shirley MacLaine is the greatest actress *ever*." Marcus pointed the remote at Delilah's TV, and the DVD player spat out *The Turning Point*.

"Put on ESPN a minute, will you?" Delilah asked.

Marcus cupped his left ear. "Excuse me, what did you just say? I could have sworn you just asked me to put on ESPN."

Delilah frowned. "Don't get surly with me, Marcus. Just do as I asked. Please."

"Your wish is my command, madam." Marcus pressed a bunch of buttons on the remote, and three men in suits talking loudly appeared on the screen. Delilah had no idea who they were or who they were talking about. She waited patiently for one of the men to say the word "NHL." Then she listened closely.

"The New York Blades beat San Diego tonight in a two–nothing win," said one of the newscasters, a tackily dressed man with a greasy mullet and thick Canadian accent.

"Huzzah!" mocked Marcus. Delilah shot him a look.

"I think the Blades are going to find Jason Mitchell is worth every penny of his three million dollars a year contract," the mullet man continued.

"Three million dollars?!" Marcus rasped. "Honey, if you won't have coffee with him, *I* will!"

"You can turn it off now." Delilah knew it was silly, but hearing that Jason had done well on the ice made her feel proud. It had dawned on her earlier in the evening that if she followed what was going on with the Blades, she'd have something to talk to Jason about when they had coffee. Her elation over his gift had worn off, replaced by a terror of being tongue-tied. To keep fear at bay, she'd started making a list of potential conversation points in her mind. So far she'd come up with Stanley, hockey, and whether he was enjoying New York. She would keep her questions and comments as simple as possible to prevent herself from lapsing into incoherence.

"When's he due back?" Marcus asked.

"Late Sunday night. He said he'd come by for Stan Monday morning."

Marcus raised an eyebrow. "Which means we're going to put on a little makeup that morning, aren't we? Maybe do up our hair nice and purty?"

"God, you're worse than my mother!"

"No one is worse than your mother, Delilah, but that's beside the point. Don't you want to seal the deal?"

"What I want is for you to leave so I can walk these monsters and get to bed. I'm exhausted."

Shiloh trotted into the kitchen to get some water. The minute the coast was clear, Stanley shot into Delilah's bedroom. Sighing, Delilah followed, flipping on the bedroom light. Stanley was up on her bed, his tail wagging happily as he waited for her to join him.

Marcus appeared in the doorway. "What a good boy! He's warming the bed for his master."

Delilah spun Marcus around and pointed him toward her front door. "Leave. Now."

Marcus thrust out his lower lip. "But Marcus wants to watch the little woman try to get the big dog off the lumpy bed."

Delilah scowled. "Out. Now. And my bed isn't lumpy."

"Hmm," said Marcus, planting a kiss on her cheek as he headed out the door, "I'll have to remember to ask Stan about that next week."

• • •

It dawned on Delilah, as she gave her doorman the go ahead to allow Jason upstairs to pick up Stanley, that he'd never been to her apartment before. All their previous meetings had taken place either at his place or in the park. Worried that he might think it a bit too unkempt, she hurriedly gathered up her dogs' toys and stashed them in the wicker basket in the corner, then folded into a neat square the fleece blanket she liked to snuggle under on the couch. There was nothing she could do about the current dog population, though; in addition to Stanley, she was boarding three other dogs, bringing the total to seven. All had been fed, walked, and were now settled down for their midmorning snooze. It was doubtful Stanley would be alone in greeting his master when he arrived; the other boarders were likely to want to check him out, too. Delilah hoped he didn't mind.

"Hey." Jason sounded relaxed as Delilah ushered him inside.

At the sound of his voice, Stanley drowsily lifted his head, then scrambled to his feet and headed straight for the door, followed by Delilah's other three canine guests, who pressed and sniffed and nosed Jason's jeans.

"Hello, guys. Nice to meet you, too. Now where's my buddy?"

Stanley was so excited by the sight of Jason he was going around in circles.

"There's my man." Jason knelt to let Stanley feverishly lick his face in an overwhelming show of affection. Delilah's heart melted as Jason closed his eyes, letting Stanley moisten his cheeks, his forehead, even his eyelids. Was there anything sexier than a man who loved his dog?

Delilah knew that if it were up to Stanley, he'd happily lick away forever, so she wasn't surprised when Jason eventually rose to his feet. The contented smile on his face was proof he was just as happy to see Stanley as Stanley was to see him.

"Was he a good boy?" Jason asked.

"Define good."

"Uh-oh."

"I guess you haven't yet trained Stanley not to climb up on the furniture?"

"Yeah, I kinda meant to talk to you about that." There was a hint of the naughty boy in his apologetic expression that made it hard for Delilah to be cross with him.

"What did you kinda want to say to me about it?" she replied.

"I kinda like having him on the couch with me."

"But that's kinda not good behavior. And I kinda can't have him doing that while he's boarding here, since the other dogs are kinda not allowed to."

"What if he kinda didn't do it when he stayed here, but when it's just him and me at home, he kinda can. I'm kinda used to having him stretched out on the bed with me, you know?"

"But what if one night you—"

Delilah clamped down on her tongue and stared down at Stanley. *Jason has no idea how that sentence was going to end,* she told herself as she avoided Jason's eyes. *No idea at all.* Realizing she couldn't stare at the dog forever, she eventually made herself look up. Jason's expression was flirtatious. So much for her assumption he lacked basic powers of deduction.

"What if one night I what?" Jason murmured.

"Nothing," Delilah said. "It's—nothing. Really nothing."

"It's okay." Jason sounded as if he were trying to coax someone off a ledge.

"I'm not nuts!" Delilah barked.

"I know that."

"I just get nervous."

"I know that, too. But there's no reason to be." His smile was gentle. "Have you given any thought to coffee?"

Delilah clasped her hands in front of her to keep them still. "Coffee would be nice." There. That sounded sane. "That was so sweet of you to get that coffee press and everything."

Jason looked pleased. "I'm glad you liked it."

"No one's ever given me a gift like that before. Coffee, I mean."

"Well, it's not every day I give a girl a New York Blades mug."

"Oh! Speaking of hockey, congrats on winning in San Diego and L.A. and sorry about Anaheim," Delilah said in a rush. Immediately she wondered if she should have waited until they actually had coffee to bring it up; now they'd have one less thing to talk about, and she'd have to think of something else to hold his attention. But judging from how impressed Jason looked, maybe bringing it up now wasn't such a bad idea.

"You've been following the scores?"

"Yes. I mean I heard it on the TV. I mean, okay, yes, out of curiosity, yes."

"Would you like to come to a game sometime?"

"Maybe."

"Great!" Jason's whole face lit up. Delilah couldn't believe that she, Delilah Gould from Roslyn, New York, could be responsible for such a flash of happiness. It boggled her mind.

"So, coffee?" he nudged.

"Yes."

"Here? Or my place?"

Delilah thought a moment. Her place was okay, except the dogs could be demanding. And clients called her cell a lot. And what if her mother called and made some comment about her hockey player boyfriend and Jason heard it and then she had to strangle herself with one of the dogs' leashes because she was so humiliated? "I think your place might be better. Quieter." She gestured at the menagerie behind her.

"That's fine. How about tomorrow night?"

Tomorrow *night*? Delilah had been picturing them sipping coffee at Jason's as morning sunlight filtered through the windows he really needed to get blinds for. When she was really feeling racy, she'd picture them lingering over steaming mugs in the late afternoon. But never night. Night-sipping had a completely different set of connotations.

"I can't tomorrow night," she said, which was true. "I'm having dinner with my dad."

Jason looked interested. "What does he do?"

"He's a businessman on Long Island," she said, deliberately vague. Now wasn't the time to tell him her father was Sy Gould, Long Island's Mattress Maven. "I could do Wednesday night, though," she offered. In her head she heard Gemma's voice telling her to stop being so afraid.

Jason was frowning. "I have a game on Wednesday. Thursday?"

Delilah nodded. "Thursday's good."

"Seven?" Jason asked.

"Seven's fine." Delilah bent over and kissed the top of Stanley's head. "See you Thursday night, big boy."

"Don't I get a kiss, too?"

Was he kidding? Delilah checked his expression. No, he wasn't. He looked like a guy who really wanted to be kissed. At least, she thought he did. Not that she was at all certain what guys looked like when they wanted to be kissed. Though if she *was* certain, she was pretty sure they'd look like Jason. *Oh, for pity's sake, just do it!*

Delilah leaned in, planting a chaste but lingering kiss on his lips. She liked the way he smelled. Maybe they could talk about that over coffee. "I like your cologne," she'd say, sipping demurely. "Oh, thank you," he'd reply huskily. "I put it on just for you." Then—

"Delilah?"

Delilah blinked. "Oh. Sorry. I was just thinking about all the stuff I have to do today."

"You and me both." Jason fastened Stan's leash to his collar and opened the door. "So, I'll see you Thursday around seven."

"Yup," Delilah chirped.

The minute she closed the door behind them, her heart began to pound.

"He likes me!" she announced giddily to the snoring

dogs. Little Belle opened her good eye and looked at her a moment, then yawned before returning to sleep. Pretty boring news for a dog. But to Delilah, it was the most exciting thing in the world.

CHAPTER 08

"There's my pussycat."

Delilah pasted the best smile she could onto her face as she made her way to her father's table at Ming Dynasty, his favorite restaurant. She'd been looking forward to seeing him, though the reason for their dinner date was less appealing: she was there to meet her father's new fiancée, Brandi.

At least it's not Junie, Delilah thought to herself as her father rose to kiss her cheek. After vociferously defending him against her mother's charge of infidelity with his secretary, the last thing she wanted was to be wrong. Her mother would never let her live it down.

"Look at you." No sooner had her father kissed her than his face contorted with consternation. "You're thin as a rail! Let's sit down and get some egg drop soup into you."

Delilah complied, sitting to her father's left. In her mother's eyes, she always weighed too much. In her father's, too little. She wondered if she really was thin, or if her father was just saying so out of force of habit. Even when she was younger, she'd never been entirely sure if he meant it, or if it was just a way to oppose and aggravate her mother.

"Where's Brandi?" she asked.

"Powdering her nose. She's so excited to meet you, you don't know."

Delilah manufactured another smile. "Powdering her nose" . . . what an antiquated expression. Then again, some people would say her father was antiquated, despite being robust for his sixty-seven years. Always concerned about him, Delilah discreetly looked him over. He appeared happy and healthy, his glowing complexion enhanced by the perpetual tan he maintained courtesy of TanFastic, a tanning salon he was half owner of. Delilah had been warning him for years about the dangers of skin cancer, but her father refused to listen. Eventually, Delilah gave up. There was no convincing Sy Gould he was mortal.

Delilah's father eyed his Rolex. "What the hell's taking her so long?" he grumbled.

"There's no hurry, Dad," Delilah assured him, glancing around the restaurant. The decor hadn't changed in decades: same black lacquer tables, same sad paper lanterns. When Delilah was small, she loved coming here with her parents, eagerly anticipating cracking open her fortune cookie after dinner. By the time she was in her early teens, she dreaded it: her mother would always send something back, claiming it was too hot, too cold, too spicy, or not spicy enough. Her father would get annoyed, and the bickering would begin.

"Here she comes," Delilah's father announced.

Delilah turned in the direction of the ladies' room, unprepared for the sight of the *very* young, *very* buxom, and *very* blonde woman wiggling her way toward the table. She was twenty if she was a day, with blinding white teeth and a tan as natural as her father's.

"Leelee," he said to Delilah proudly, "I want you to meet my soul mate, Brandi."

"Hello." Delilah extended her hand, shocked when Brandi enfolded her in an embrace.

"Leelee!" Her voice reminded Delilah of Minnie Mouse.

The temptation to tell her that only her parents were allowed
to call her by her childhood nickname was strong, but
Delilah resisted, not wanting to sound peevish. "I'm so glad
to finally meet you. Your daddy talks about you all the
time!"

*Does he talk about the fact I'm probably almost ten years
older than you?* Delilah wondered.

"Sit, sit," her father enjoined. They all sat. Her father's
face remained animated as he clasped each of the women's
hands. "My two best gals," he gushed. "Can I tell you how
happy this makes me?"

Brandi smiled at Delilah. Delilah smiled back, wondering if it would look suspicious if she excused herself so she
could call Marcus to tell him her father was engaged to a
Bratz doll.

A waiter appeared at the table to take drink orders.
Delilah, who rarely drank, ordered a gin and tonic. Her father and Brandi both ordered extra-dry martinis. Brandi was
looking at her expectantly. Delilah took that to mean *she*
was supposed to get the ball rolling.

"How did you meet my dad?"

"Well, I went into Mattress Maven because I needed a
new mattress—"

"The Syosset store, not the one in Levittown," her father
added as if it made a difference.

"And your dad was there. We got to talking, and both of
us could tell there was chemistry there, you know?"

"Especially after I sold her the Sealy Posturepedic
Dream, extra firm," her father chuckled.

"Then," Brandi continued in her high-pitched voice, "I
invited him to come for a free facial at the spalon where I
work."

"Spalon?"

"Oh, it's a combo salon and spa," Brandi explained helpfully.

"Gotcha."

"Anyway, Sy went in the sauna, and I gave him his facial,
and the rest, as they say, is history." She beamed adoringly

at Delilah's father before reaching across to grasp Delilah's hand, the giant engagement ring on her finger nearly blinding Delilah as it caught the light. "I love your daddy so, so much."

I bet you love his bank account even more, Delilah thought angrily. Her heart was racing. She loved her father and hated to see him being taken advantage of by this gold digger with a voice that could drive dogs insane.

Delilah took a sip of her drink, striving for calm. *Don't judge yet,* she admonished. *Maybe Brandi really does love him, despite his tacky TV commercials and old-man boobs and pinky ring. After all, you love him. Yes, but he's my father!* An image forced its way into her mind of a naked Brandi bouncing happily atop her father in bed. Delilah shuddered. It was no big mystery why her father would love Brandi: she allowed him the illusion of eternal youth and virility. She didn't want to think about how much he had to be spending on Viagra.

"Your dad says you own a pet store," said Brandi with wide-eyed interest.

Delilah shot her father a look that could stop the world on its axis. "I think you might have misunderstood; I own my own dog walking/training business in the city."

Brandi looked wistful. "I had a dog once: Butchie. He got some kind of disease, and his tail fell off, and he died."

"My poor baby," Delilah's father murmured, making kissing noises at Brandi. Delilah crammed a handful of fried noodles in her mouth to keep herself from gagging.

"Leelee's always loved animals, haven't you, honey?" her father asked.

"Always," Delilah mumbled through the noodles.

"We got her her first puppy when she was five. Of course, I would have preferred we had another child, but her mother—"

"Dad." Delilah flashed him a warning look. "Let's not talk about Mom, okay?"

"Dat's wight, Sy," Brandi baby-talked with a pout.

"Bwandi doesn't want to hear abwout the big bad bitch tonight."

"Excuse me?" Delilah glared.

Brandi looked uneasy. "I didn't mean that *I* thought your mother was a bitch." Her eyes pleaded for backup from Delilah's father. "It's just that Sy—he—your father—"

"I get the picture," Delilah snapped.

"Can you excuse me a minute?" Brandi whispered. Eyes filling with tears, she picked up her purse and wiggled her way back to the ladies' room.

"Did you have to upset her that way?" Delilah's father asked.

"Upset *her*? She called my mother a bitch!"

"Your mother is a bitch!"

"That doesn't give *her* the right to say so! She doesn't even know Mom!"

"Let's just drop it," her father muttered.

"Gladly," Delilah muttered back. Maybe Brandi would sob her way into a headache and want to leave. Delilah could only hope.

Her father took a long, slow sip of his martini. "How *is* your mother?"

Delilah turned to him with anger. "Do you really care?"

"No."

"Then why are you asking?"

Her father shrugged. "Curiosity."

"Funny, that's the same thing she said when she was trying to pump me about you."

Her father pricked up his ears. "She asked about me? What did she say?"

"I'm not telling you. Call her yourself if you're so hot to know! Honestly, I don't know why the two of you split up! If you ask me, you both seem waaayy too concerned with what the other is doing."

"Oh, I know what she's doing, all right," her father snorted. "Correction: I know *who* she's doing. That *schmegegge*, Bruce Whatsisface, from the temple."

Delilah was close to exploding. "Dad, we are not having this conversation, okay? It's completely inappropriate."

Delilah's father sighed. "You're right." He patted Delilah's hand. "Sorry, doll."

"It's okay."

"What do you think of Brandi, eh? Is she an angel or what?"

"She seems very . . . buoyant."

"Apologize for upsetting her when she gets back, okay?"

"Dad!"

"Fine, fine, fine," her father groused with a frown. "I'll repair the damage later, I guess. Here she comes."

Delilah tried not to tense as Brandi resumed her place at the table.

"I was afraid you fell in," her father said to Brandi.

"Delilah," Brandi began humbly, "I'm really sorry for what I said about your mother. That was wrong."

This was the last thing Delilah expected to hear. "It's okay. We're all a little nervous tonight. Sometimes when people are nervous they say things they don't mean."

"That's right." Brandi seemed relieved. "I was wondering," she continued. "Are you open to going on a blind date?"

"Why?" Delilah asked.

"My brother, Randi? He's looking for someone nice to date. He's very handsome."

"An actor," Delilah's father put in, wiggling his eyebrows with significance.

"Have I seen him in anything?" Delilah asked.

"He just did a movie called *Bareback Mountain*."

Delilah choked on her drink. *Bareback Mountain* was a gay porn film. She knew because Marcus had just seen it. She looked at Brandi; she was in deadly earnest. That's when it dawned on Delilah: Brandi wasn't an evil gold digger. She was just dumb.

"Thanks for thinking of me, Brandi, but I'm not really interested right now."

Her father frowned. "A beautiful girl like you shouldn't

be home every night. What, you think Mr. Right is going to jump out of your TV set?"

"Actually, I'm seeing someone," Delilah lied.

"What were you waiting for, a formal invitation?" her father chided. "Tell us!"

Delilah nervously pushed her hair behind her ears. What was it about her parents that made it so easy for her to lie? She hated people who lied! Yet here she was, talking once again about her imaginary boyfriend.

"He's a professional athlete. A hockey player."

"I hope he has a good dentist," her father joked, Brandi giggling as if Delilah's father was the soul of wit. Delilah refrained from checking the time. She had no desire to know just how long she'd been in hell.

"Who does he play for?" her father asked.

"The Blades."

"Does he have a name?"

"Jason Mitchell. And don't even ask the next question."

"When do I get to meet him?" her father asked. "Why didn't you bring him with you tonight? Then we both could have celebrated being in love!"

Delilah's head was beginning to ache. *Keep it simple,* she reminded herself as her anxiety level began to climb. "He's on the road. An away game. Hockey isn't just played on home ice. They play away."

"Well, I think I need to meet this boy—"

"Man," Brandi corrected with a big stage wink to Delilah.

"—as soon as possible." Her father touched Delilah's cheek. "Does he make you happy?"

"Very happy," Delilah murmured, amazed at how quickly a lie could *feel* real. Actually, it wasn't really a lie. Right now, thinking about Jason did make her happy, when she wasn't worried about saying something so stupid she made Brandi look like the president of Mensa.

"If he makes you happy, that's all that matters." Her father cracked open his menu. "Now let's order. I'm starving."

•   •   •

Later that night, Delilah learned the hard way that lies can have consequences: she arrived home from Ming Dynasty to find a message waiting for her.

"This is your mother, inviting you and your hockey player for brunch this Sunday at eleven a.m. I already switched my schedule around, so I won't take no for answer. Remember: a little lipstick can go a long way."

Delilah erased the message and sank down on the couch with her head in hands.

Now what?

"This coffee's great."

Jason smiled appreciatively at Delilah's compliment. If she knew what he'd gone through to make a decent cup of coffee, she'd think he was crazy. He'd spent a large part of the afternoon experimenting with varying amounts of water and coffee, trying to get it just right. But caffeine perfection eluded him; either it turned out like coffee scented water or sludge. He called his mother, but she was no help; she'd been using the same electric percolator since before he was born. Finally, in desperation, he called the local coffee bistro around the corner and explained his plight. The haughty barista on the other end of the line took pity on him and explained exactly how much coffee to use per cup of water. The result? Coffee worth complimenting, at least in Delilah's opinion.

She'd been awkward with him at first, as he thought she might be. Awkward and preoccupied. But gradually, she seemed to relax. Stanley helped; just having him there for her to fuss over seemed to calm her. Jason imagined taking Delilah out to dinner, Stanley in tow. There had to be dog-friendly restaurants in New York, right? God knows the city catered to everything else.

Delilah had been telling him about growing up on Long Island, and about her dinner with her father and Brandi. Jason didn't have the heart to tell her he knew who her dad was: whenever the tacky Mattress Maven commercials came on in the weight room, the guys would laugh their heads off, making fun of her father's bad toupee.

"I don't know anything about Long Island, apart from it being the Islanders' home base," Jason confessed.

"That's more than I know about—Flasher?"

Jason nodded, a slow smile spreading across his face. He had only mentioned his hometown to her once, and that had been weeks ago. That she retained the info spoke volumes.

"What's it like?" she continued.

"It's small. Farms, mostly. One supermarket, one bar, one movie theater, one hockey rink."

"Your parents are farmers?"

"Yup."

"What kind?"

"Dairy."

"Wow." Delilah seemed enchanted. "I've always wanted to visit a farm."

Jason was mystified; why would anyone get misty-eyed over a farm? Then it dawned on him: animals. Thank God his parents weren't in the business of raising cattle for slaughter. Delilah would probably never speak to him again.

"Do you ever miss it?"

"Sometimes I miss my folks," Jason confessed. "And occasionally, I miss the quiet. But in general? No." He cocked his head questioningly. "Do you ever miss living on Long Island?"

Delilah burst out laughing. "God, no! Though my mom does have a huge backyard that the dogs love, especially Shiloh. Not that she allows her grandchildren to visit very often."

Jason chuckled. "You talk about them like they're your kids."

"They are my kids."

Jason sipped his coffee. "Ever thought about getting married and having real kids?"

The room became very still. Jason assumed he had blundered. But much to his surprise, Delilah answered.

"I have thought about it. But not very seriously. Not yet. I mean I just haven't met the right person. I guess." She looked down.

Kiss her now, Jason thought. Stealthy yet subtle, he put down his mug and slid to her end of the couch, putting his arm around her. He was just gearing up to kiss her when Delilah burst out with, "Jason I need to ask you a big favor and if you don't want to do it it's okay but I really need your help!"

Jason slowly withdrew his arm. "What's up?"

"It's my mother. She's been on my case forever about not having a boyfriend, and I finally couldn't take it anymore. I lied and told her I had one. Now she wants 'us' to come for brunch on Sunday."

"Well, can't you tell her you're busy? Or that your boyfriend is in a coma or something?"

"You don't know my mother. She'd bring takeout to the ICU if it meant meeting someone I was dating. She won't take no for an answer."

"So, where do I come in?" Jason wanted to know. He was teasing, though judging by the pained look on Delilah's face, it didn't register.

"I need you to pretend to be my boyfriend."

Jason slipped an arm around her shoulder. "Why does it have to be pretend?"

"I guess you're right. I mean—"

"Delilah?"

"Mmm?"

"Let's make a deal. I'll pretend to be your boyfriend if you'll pretend to kiss me right here, right now. How does that sound?"

"Good." Delilah nodded vigorously. "Really really good. I mean—"

Jason crushed his lips to hers as much to quiet her as to quench his desire. Her kisses were sweet—like sugar, like honey. Tempting and innocent at the same time, making them all the more delectable. When Delilah's lips parted slightly, Jason took it as a signal for deeper intimacy; he gently parted her teeth with his lips, kissing her full on the mouth as he drew her tighter to him. Delilah didn't resist; in fact, a little "Mmmmm" of pleasure rose from the back of her throat. Jason kissed her more passionately, delighted when Delilah returned his ardor. Kissing her was like entering a magic world: breathtaking, shimmering, completely enchanting.

And then the pounding began.

"Open up, you pussy!" Eric's voice was strident on the other side of the front door. "You think you're funny, taping those press clippings to my door? Let me tell you, bro, that's pathetic!"

Jason wanted to kill him, especially when Stanley, who wasn't renowned for his abilities as a watchdog, began barking his head off.

"Maybe if we pretend we're not here, he'll go away," Jason whispered.

"But what about Stanley?"

Stanley's deep-chested woof grew more ferocious the longer Eric kept hammering on the door. Caught between a rock and a Newfie, Jason had no choice.

He flashed Delilah a look of disbelief before storming to the door. "Settle down, Stan!" Jason slid back the locks and opened the door. The minute the two brothers made eye contact, Eric threw his mouth back into overdrive.

"Big deal, so John Dellapina thinks you're hot shit! Let me tell you something—" He stopped short when he caught sight of Delilah. "Uh . . ."

"You were saying?" said Jason.

Eric looked mortified. "Did I interrupt something here?"

"Take a guess," Jason replied. Delilah had a nervous smile plastered to her face, like she didn't know what else to do. Jason closed the front door and grabbed Eric by the collar of his rugby shirt.

"Can you excuse us a moment?" Jason asked Delilah, dragging his brother toward his bedroom. "This will only take a minute."

Delilah just nodded.

Jason shoved Eric over the threshold to the bedroom, kicking the door closed behind them.

"What, did you plant some kind of tracking device on her?" Jason exclaimed, releasing Eric from his grasp.

Eric blinked uncomprehendingly. "Huh?"

"Every time I'm close to getting something started with Delilah, you manage to appear and kill the moment! How did you get up here, anyway?"

"Duh, the doorman knows I'm your brother."

"I'm going to have to talk to him about that." Jason glowered. "Guess what you're doing now?"

"Leaving?"

"That's right. Leaving. You're going to walk back out into the living room, you're going to tell Delilah it was nice to see her, and then you're going to disappear. Got it?"

"I hear you." Eric dug his hands into the front pockets of his jeans. "Look, I'm sorry about this. Seriously. If I'd known you were trying to catch a ride on the Poontang Express, I would have left you alone." Eric playfully punched his arm. "So, how far did you get? Second base?"

"You're such a dick, you know that?" said Jason, shaking his head in disgust.

"Yeah, but you love me anyway."

"Only because I have to. Now get *out* of here."

When Jason and Eric returned to the living room, Delilah was no longer there. She was in the kitchen with Stanley, washing the coffee mugs and press. *Great.* Jason thought glumly. *Guess this party is over.*

"Hey, Delilah," Eric called meekly from the kitchen doorway. "Nice seeing you."

Delilah turned from where she stood at the sink and smiled. "You, too, Eric."

Eric ducked out of the doorway, and Jason led him to the front door.

"For what's it worth," Eric concluded as Jason practically shoved him out into the hall, "you still suck on the ice."

"Blah, blah, blah," Jason replied in a bored voice. He

closed the door behind Eric and locked it. One problem solved, one more to go. He went to join Delilah in the kitchen.

"I'm really sorry." Jason put his hands on Delilah's shoulders as he stood behind her. "Eric has this knack for turning up when he's least wanted."

"It's okay," she assured him as she carefully placed the coffee press on the drying rack. "I should be going anyway."

Goddamn Eric.

"Delilah, please don't let my brother run you off." He leaned down to plant the lightest of kisses on her shoulder. "We were having such a great time."

"I know," Delilah agreed as she turned to face him. "But I really do need to go. I have dogs to walk."

"Right." Jason's heart sank. *Dogs, dogs, always the dogs.*

In a move unexpected—and therefore thrilling—to Jason, Delilah reached up to caress his cheek. "I had a really nice time tonight."

"Me, too. Can we do it again?"

"I would like that," Delilah murmured demurely.

Going with the moment, Jason drew her into an embrace. The next thing he knew, Stanley was trying to nose his way between them.

Jason groaned. "Today is not my day."

"He doesn't want to be left out, that's all," said Delilah. She crouched so she was eye level with Stanley. "You'll be my dream date tomorrow night, right, pal?" She looked up at Jason for confirmation. "You've got a game tomorrow, right?"

"Yeah. I need you to take Mr. Suave here out for his final nighttime jaunt."

"Thought so." She rose. "And Sunday?"

"Sunday?" Jason was puzzled. "Oh, right, Sunday! I'll go to your mom's with you, no problem. Is there anything I should bring?"

"Flowers. And a thick skin."

"Hey, I'm a hockey player. My skin's as thick as it gets."

CHAPTER

09

"Don't freak out. I can explain."

Delilah stood openmouthed in her doorway, staring at Eric. She'd been feeling unusually optimistic, even excited, about what the day might bring. After giving a command performance at her mother's, maybe she and Jason would come back to the city, have dinner, kiss and cuddle. For the first time in a long time, Delilah was feeling connected to a human rather than a canine. Until this.

Eric looked uncomfortable. "Can I come in?"

Delilah nodded, ushering him inside. Shock was slowing turning into worry.

"Was Jason hurt on the ice?"

"No, nothing like that." Eric ran a hand through his wet hair. He looked as though he'd just come from the shower. "Jace woke up this morning sick as a dog. He called and asked me to go with you to your mom's—something about needing me to pose as your boyfriend, and your mom not taking no for an answer if you tried to bail. So here I am."

"Oh." Delilah was worried about Jason being sick. But that did nothing to quell the anxiety hiccuping its way into existence as she thought about spending half the day with Eric, whom she barely knew. "Um. I guess this is okay. I mean I guess."

Eric peered at her questioningly. "Are you all right?"

"Fine." Delilah drummed her fingers against her side. "Totally, I mean really. Can you hang on one minute?"

"Sure."

Delilah picked up the phone and calmly dialed her mother's number. She got the answering machine. Delilah knew Mitzi: she was there and simply choosing not to pick up. She also knew that if she left a message saying she couldn't make it for brunch, she'd get the "I almost died giving birth to you and you can't even come to my house for a nosh" speech. Delilah hung up the phone.

"We should go," she said as she walked back to Eric. "Are you as smart as Jason?" she asked abruptly. "Because if you're not we might need to rethink this whole thing because it's just not going to work and my mother—"

Eric held up a hand. "Whoa, hang on there. First of all, I'm probably ten times smarter than my younger brother. Second, chill out."

"I'm sorry," Delilah said, forcing herself to meet his eye. "Sometimes when I get anxious I get a little"—*What was the word Jason used?*—"twittery. I'll calm down. I promise."

"If you say so." Eric jangled the keys in his pocket. "Were we planning on driving?" he asked, sticking his nose into the store-bought daisies he held in his hand.

"Yes. Is that a problem?"

"What kind of car have you got?"

"A mini. Why?"

"Let's take my Mercedes instead." He nudged Delilah. "That'll impress Mommy Dearest, eh?"

Delilah put on her jacket and grabbed her purse. "Are you sure you're up for this?"

"Hey, Jason's paying me five hundred bucks."

"That answers that." She kissed each of her dogs, telling them to be good until she got back. She opened the front door. "I guess we can use the drive there to cook up some fake history for ourselves."

Eric looked taken by the idea. "Cool. This is going to be fun."

Eric didn't know Mitzi Gould.

Delilah tried seeing her mother's house through a stranger's eyes as Eric's Mercedes rolled to a stop behind her mother's white BMW. The house, a large colonial, sat far back from the road on an acre lot. A winding stone path led up to the front door; the house itself was flanked by two large maple trees.

"Pretty swanky."

Delilah supposed he was right. They were just emerging from the car when the front door swung open, and Delilah's mother stepped outside to greet them. Delilah tried not to be embarrassed by the shuffling baby steps her mother took toward them so she didn't fall in her too-high heels. Mitzi was fully made up, her hair so stiff with hair spray it looked like platinum meringue. Her eye shadow matched her canary-yellow cashmere sweater. Her mother was not going gentle into that good night. If Mitzi wasn't careful, she was going to wind up looking like an anorexic drag queen.

"Helloooo." Her mother waved as frantically as a drowning victim. "You must be Jason!" she squealed as she drew Eric into a crushing embrace.

"Uh . . ."

"So handsome." She pinched Eric's cheek before glancing at Delilah, pleased. "What a looker. You did good this time."

"I try." Delilah's eye caught Eric's as her mother released him from their hug. He looked shell-shocked, and the "fun" hadn't even begun.

"C'mere, let me look at you." Delilah tensed as her mother perused her right there in front of Eric. "Gorgeous," her mother pronounced unexpectedly. She turned to Eric for confirmation. "Isn't my baby gorgeous?"

"Gorgeous," Eric agreed.

"You must be starving after your trip out from the city."

Delilah felt compelled to point out that the trip was only forty minutes by car, if that.

"Men have appetites," Mitzi replied with a knowing wink at Eric. She playfully wagged a finger at him. "I hope you brought yours."

"Of course." Eric offered Mitzi his arm. "Shall we?"

Mitzi looked impressed. "Good looking *and* a gentleman. We like."

Delilah's mother took Eric's arm, and together the three of them headed for the house. *So far, so good,* Delilah thought, especially when her mother turned around to give her a quick thumbs-up.

"Let me take your coats," Delilah's mother said as soon as they were inside. Delilah watched Eric take in the living room. There was no mistaking the confusion in his eyes as it dawned on him that everything in the room was the color of sun on snow: blinding white carpet, walls, and furniture. The only splash of color were the daisies he held in his hand, which he now thrust awkwardly at Delilah's mother.

"For you."

"Beautiful. I'm just going to find a vase for these. You two take off your shoes, and I'll meet you in the dining room." Slipping off her own heels, Delilah's mother padded off in the direction of the kitchen.

"Doesn't your mother believe in color?" Eric asked as soon as she was gone.

"Only when it comes to her eyelids, lips, and fingernails."

A few years ago, Mitzi had gotten the idea that white was chic. Her father claimed it was like "living in a goddamn asylum." That only seemed to spur her mother on.

Eric couldn't stop staring. "I feel like we're in a museum. Like we should be quiet."

"We *are* in a museum. Come, let us tour the eggshell-colored dining room, not to be confused with the ecru kitchen."

Eric chuckled. He must have thought Delilah was joking until they entered the dining room, which indeed was all beige, save for an enormous glass-topped table upon which sat enough food to feed the entire population of Roslyn.

"Please, make yourself at home," Delilah's mother urged as she swept into the room holding the daisies in a white vase, which she placed at the center of the table. Eric pulled out one of the upholstered dining room chairs and gestured for Delilah to sit. *Oh, he's good,* Delilah thought as she took her place. *He's got the whole chivalry thing down pat. This is going to be a breeze.*

Eric sat, and Delilah's mother poured coffee for everyone. Delilah was starving; she hadn't eaten a thing since the night before, and the sight of the bagels, muffins, and fresh fruit were making her stomach rumble. She reached for a chocolate chip muffin, only to have her mother gently slap her hand away.

"We want to keep nice and trim for Jason, don't we?"

"Jason thinks I look fine just the way I am," Delilah replied sharply. "Don't you, Jace?"

"Yes, I do, my little—polecat," Eric improvised, putting an arm around her.

"They're your hips," Delilah's mother murmured at her beneath her breath.

"You're damn right," Delilah murmured back, putting the muffin on her plate with a flourish.

"So, Jason." Delilah's mother's voice was loud and overly bright—not a good sign. "Where are you from?"

"Flasher, North Dakota."

"Really." Mitzi pursed her lips thoughtfully. "Do you mind if I ask you a question? Are there a lot of J—"

"Mom! I already *told* you."

Eric looked confused. "Are there a lot of what?"

"Jews," Delilah said flatly. "My mother wants to know if you're Jewish." She glared at her mother. "Why don't you just pull down his pants and find out?"

Eric looked panic-stricken. *"What?"*

"Pay no attention," Delilah's mother replied. "My daugh-

ter can be very crude sometimes, especially when she's trying to hurt me."

Delilah rolled her eyes. "That's right, I forgot: it's all
about you." She glanced at Eric; he still looked somewhat
terrified. "I'm sorry. We usually wait until dessert before we
step into the ring."

Eric responded with a nervous smile.

"So if you're not Jewish"—Delilah's mother glared back
at her—"what religion are you? If you don't mind me asking."

"Methodist," Eric replied.

"That's some kind of birth control method you people
use, right?"

Delilah groaned. "You're thinking of the *rhythm method*,
Mom. And it has nothing to do with being a Methodist.
Let's just get off the subject of religion, okay?"

"Fine." Her mother gave an annoyed shrug. "Whatever
you want." She piled her plate high with grapes and melon
slices before pausing to hollow out a bagel. "Am I allowed
to ask how you two met? Or is that off-limits, too?"

"We live in the same neighborhood," Eric replied,
launching into the romantic history he and Delilah had concocted in the car, which wasn't far from reality. "She was
out walking dogs, and we got to talking." His eyes sought
Delilah's. *How'm I doing?* Delilah patted his knee reassuringly beneath the table.

"Very romantic." Delilah's mother popped a grape in her
mouth, chewing carefully. "What do you think about
Delilah's dog-walking business, Jason?"

"I think it's great," Eric enthused, chugging down coffee.

"Really?" Delilah's mother did nothing to hide her surprise. "The hair doesn't bother you? The smell? The *drool*?"

"Not at all, Mrs. Gould." He sounded so supportive of
Delilah she wanted to throw her arms around his neck and
kiss him. "I think it's great Delilah has followed her heart.
She has a real way with dogs. Everyone in the neighborhood
is in awe of her."

Hear that, Mom? Awe. Me. Awe and me in the same sentence. Ha!

"I suppose it's all right for now," her mother sniffed. "Once she gets married and has a family, it'll be a different story. I hope."

"Delilah tells me you're an interior designer," said Eric, helping himself to a bagel.

"I like to think of myself as more of a habitat intuitive," Delilah's mother corrected. "I'm able to go into people's living spaces and read the energies there. Then I use that info to make design choices. For example," she continued, turning to Delilah, "remember Coco Kaplan?"

"No."

Mitzi clucked her tongue. "Oh, please, Delilah! She was at your Bat Mitzvah."

"You invited three hundred people to my Bat Mitzvah, Mom! I didn't know most of the people there!"

"She exaggerates," her mother said to Eric. "Anyway, Coco hired me because she wanted to redo her living room. So I went over there, and immediately I was overcome with a strong, intuitive sensation of primal heat. I thought: jungle."

"Not 'hot flash'?" Delilah asked.

Her mother ignored her. "We went with zebra stripes with leopard spot accents. Do you know that to this day, everyone who comes to Coco's says it's the most amazing room they've ever been in?"

"I'll bet," said Delilah.

"So tell me: do hockey players make a good living, Jason?" Delilah's mother asked casually.

"The good ones do. I'm a good one."

Her mother nodded approvingly. "A boy with confidence. I like that."

For the next hour and a half, Delilah's mother proceeded to grill Eric. Mitzi would claim she was "just making conversation," but to Delilah's ears, it sounded like an interview. Were his parents still married? Did he have any siblings? Where did he see himself in five years? Was he putting away money for when his hockey career was over? Delilah half expected her mother to conclude the brunch by pulling out a calendar and picking a wedding date. At least Mitzi had been so wrapped up in appraising Eric, she'd forgotten to pump Delilah about her father.

Brunch over at last, Delilah's mother insisted on walking them back to the car. Taking Eric's Mercedes had been a wise choice. Mitzi oohed and aahed over it.

Delilah and Eric climbed into the car and waved good-bye to her mother, their relief palpable as Eric threw the car into reverse. They weren't even out of the driveway before Eric turned to her and said, "Delilah, I may not know you that well, but after today, I know one thing: You are *so* not like your mother."

Delilah settled back in the passenger seat with relief. "That might be the best thing anyone's ever said to me."

Conversation on the ride back to New York was not nearly as awkward as it had been on the ride out to Roslyn. For one thing, they hadn't had to cook up a fake history for themselves in case Mitzi succumbed to her addiction to minutia. Delilah attempted to explain the Jewish mother phenom to Eric, but since he had no real point of reference, he couldn't quite grasp it. Offering reciprocity, he told her about his and Jason's childhood growing up in North Dakota, lacing it with long anecdotes about their time spent on the ice. Delilah wondered how Jason might feel knowing Eric revealed the way he'd cried the first time he saw a calf being born, or how when they were fourteen, two hoods from a neighboring town wrecked the snowman their little cousin had carefully built. Accidentally catching sight of them commit the crime from his window, Jason ran out of the house in his long johns to catch them, dragging them back to rebuild the snowman while the whole family watched. Delilah loved hearing these stories. They gave her a clearer sense of who Jason was. A picture was beginning to emerge of an impulsive but driven man with a tender heart.

Eric pulled up in front of her building and kept the engine idling. "Well, thanks for an interesting morning."

"I can't thank you enough."

"True, you can't." The door lock released with a dull click. "Look, I probably shouldn't say anything, but my brother really likes you."

Delilah already knew that, but she didn't want to sound egotistical. "Then why are you?"

"Because any woman who can deal with that slobbering mop of a dog is the right woman for Jace."

After lavishing some TLC on her dogs, Delilah decided the least she could do was check on Jason to see how he was feeling. She knew how depressing it was to be sick when you lived alone. She'd bring him some chicken soup, walk Stan for him, and see if he needed her to fetch anything for him from the grocery store.

Approaching his apartment, she heard the sound of the TV and men talking. Eric. He must have gone straight to Jace to give him the lowdown. She knocked twice. Jason opened the door. Sitting on the couch was a hulking man she didn't recognize. A football game was on.

"Delilah." Jason looked startled. "What are you doing here?"

Delilah held up the bag containing the chicken soup. "I brought you some chicken soup. It'll make you feel better. Plus I thought I'd walk Stan for you." Stan trotted over and sat down beside her. "How are you feeling?"

"Uh, better."

The man on the couch slapped his thigh. "Yo, dog, I wish someone would come by *my* place with some soup when I was hungover!"

Delilah stared at Jason in confusion. "He—you—you're not sick?"

The man on the couch chuckled. "He was sick this morning, all right. On your knees praying to the great porcelain god, weren't you, Mitchell?"

"Shut the hell up, Thad, okay?!" Jason snapped over his shoulder. His expression was desperate as he turned back to Delilah. "Let me explain."

"No need. You were hungover. You blew me off. You sent Eric. You told him to lie to me and say you were sick. I understand." She held the chicken soup out to him with a trembling hand. "Take this. If I eat it, I'll vomit."

"Delilah, you have to let me explain."

"No, I don't." She kissed Stan's head. "Good-bye."

CHAPTER

10

"How about the hair of the dog walker who bit you, bro?" Eric asked, offering Jason a beer.

Jason shook his head no and went back to cradling his head in his hands. He'd been at a loss for what to do when Delilah left his apartment. Plead? Chase after her? She didn't seem in the mood to listen to anything he had to say, and who could blame her? He booted Thad out, brooding alone for a while before showing up at Eric's.

"Do you think I should go over there?"

"Give her time to cool off," Eric advised. "You should have just told her the truth, you know."

Jason's head snapped up. "What? That the Blades kicked ass out on the ice and our postgame celebrations got a little carried away?"

"Yeah. How could it have hurt? You could have apologized, said you were sending me, and that would have been the end of it." Eric shook his head. "I knew this was going to bite you in the ass."

"If you knew, why did you let me do it?" Jason snarled.

"I was helping you out, you asshole. You should have heard yourself on the phone! You sounded pitiful."

"Yeah, well, you'd sound pitiful, too, if you did so many tequila shots you were seeing triple." Jason returned to cradling his head, which felt like a thirty-pound pumpkin. "I let her down."

"Not completely: you sent me. And by the way, I'd like that five hundred dollars in small bills, please."

Jason wasn't listening. "What if she won't talk to me?"

"She'll lighten up. You've got to impress her with a big gesture. Chicks love the big gesture."

"You know, for someone who loves dispensing advice about women, I never actually see you with any. When's the last time you had a girlfriend?"

Eric stretched out his legs and folded his arms across his chest. "I'm a rollin' stone, my man. Valedictorian of the School of Love 'Em and Leave 'Em. These boots were made for—"

"Please shut up." Jason closed his eyes. The headache he thought he'd vanquished earlier in the day seemed to be punching its way back with a vengeance. "You were saying?" he eventually asked, rubbing his temples. "About the big gesture?"

"You've got to do something that will really blow her away. She loves dogs, right?" Jason nodded. "Get her a puppy!"

"I'm not going to get her a puppy!" Jason scoffed. "She's already got three dogs!"

"What about jewelry? Jewelry always goes over big."

"She's not my girlfriend. I can't buy her jewelry."

"Flowers?"

"Maybe flowers."

"Flowers say you care," Eric agreed facetiously.

Jason cracked open an eye; Eric was smirking.

"The thought that you and I share the same genetic material scares the shit out of me," said Jason.

"Hey!" Eric unfolded his arms and lurched forward. "I saved your sorry ass today!"

Jason deflated. "You're right." He continued rubbing his temples. It wasn't helping. "How'd that go, by the way?"

"Let's just say I earned every penny of what you owe me."

Delilah was miserable as she made her way to pick up Stan for his walk. Though Jason was at practice, there was something about returning to the scene of her humiliation of two days previous that had her choking back tears. She should have known better than to just show up at his apartment.

Things could have been worse: he could have forgotten about brunch entirely. Still, if he knew he had to be somewhere Sunday morning, why hadn't he taken care not to overindulge the night before? Was she that forgettable?

"See, this is why I like you better," she explained to Chucky, a shepherd, and Cinderella, a Great Dane, whom she picked up before Stanley. "You don't lie. You don't let people down."

Entering Jason's building, Delilah guided her charges into the elevator, pressing the button for Jason's floor. What if she'd read Jason's schedule incorrectly, and he was there? She squared her shoulders. So what? She'd come for Stanley, not him.

Delilah opened the door to Jason's apartment. As always, Stanley was sitting right there waiting for her, his wagging tail sweeping the floor. Delilah did a double take: there was a small gift-wrapped box dangling from his collar along with his tags. Stanley lumbered to his feet and while the three dogs merrily sniffed each other's butts, Delilah removed the box, pondering it as she held it in her hand. If she opened it, she was forgiving Jason. If she left it on the kitchen table, she wasn't. Torn, she kept staring. Then she remembered: she needed to play an active role in her own destiny. Did she really want to end things before they'd even begun? She looked at Stan, whose tail resumed wagging the minute their eyes met. "Your master is a jerk, you know that?" Delilah told him.

Nervous, Delilah's fingers gently tore open the package. Inside were two reserved seats for the Manchester Kennel Club Dog Show at Met Gar. But that wasn't all: there were also two coveted backstage passes as well. Delilah gasped loudly. Immediately the gaze of all three dogs shot to her.

"No need to worry, guys," she assured them. "I'm just a little overwhelmed, is all." She tucked the tickets into one of the compartments in her fanny pack and picked up her charges' leashes. "It's a beautiful day outside. Let's go for a walk."

"*I guess this* means you've forgiven me?"

Jason found himself shouting in Delilah's ear as they strolled—or tried to—around the dog show. Hockey fans had nothing on these dog people. If one more person accidentally elbowed him, rudely pushed past him, or stepped on his foot, he was going to lose it. The only thing saving him from going ballistic was the beatific expression on Delilah's face as they jostled their way along. Delilah seemed determined to check out every stall lining the walls, selling everything from waterproof booties to diamond-studded collars.

Jason kept his skepticism to himself as Delilah chatted with a rotund woman in a booth selling something called Seameal. The woman wore a black sweatshirt covered in tiny images of dachshunds. Silver dachshund earrings dangled from her ears. The chair from which she'd just risen boasted an embroidered cushion with the image of a dachshund on it. Jason imagined sitting on a cushion bearing Wayne Gretzky's face and suppressed a snort.

Delilah carefully perused the plastic bottle the woman handed to her. "Thank you," she said politely, returning the supplement to the woman before tugging on Jason's hand, indicating they should move on.

Jason kept his fingers woven through hers and held

tightly, fearful of her getting swept away in the momentum of the crowd. "You still haven't answered my question," he pointed out.

"About forgiveness?"

Jason nodded.

She squeezed his hand. "Of course I forgive you. Just promise it won't happen again."

"I promise," said Jason. She'd said "again." That meant the dog show wasn't a one-shot deal.

"Can we go backstage now?"

Jason hesitated. What he really wanted was to duck outside for some fresh air and follow it up with a nice, greasy hot dog from a street vendor. But the eager expression on Delilah's face made it impossible for him to refuse. "Sure," he said. "Let's go."

The backstage area was less crowded, but that didn't mean it was any quieter: Jason could barely hear himself think above the whir of the hair dryers. There were dogs the size of pigeons sitting atop ironing boards, being lovingly groomed; dogs with their hair in curlers; dogs getting their teeth brushed. Jason locked eyes with a large brown poodle whose owner was baby-talking while teasing its hair into a pompadour the size of a tsunami. "Who's daddy's coco baba boy, hmmm? Who's daddy's piggly wiggly devil dog?" *Just kill me now,* the dog's expression seemed to say. Poor bastard. Jason couldn't believe the humiliation these poor creatures were being subjected to.

He scanned the room. "Where's the Newf?"

Delilah's eyes lit up. "C'mon, we'll find it."

They wandered the backstage area until they finally came to a large banner hanging on the concrete wall that said "Working Dogs."

The Newf, named Abel, sat regally behind a bench, being adored by a passel of adults and children. He was chocolate brown, not black like Stan. But his expression was just as friendly and lovable.

"Would you like to shake paws?" his owner asked Jason as he and Delilah drew nearer.

"No, thank you," said Jason. Shake paws? Did this *yutz* think they were five years old? Abel's coat was trimmed and gleaming, his nails immaculately clipped and shaped. He smelled vaguely of strawberry. *Poor bastard,* Jason thought again.

"You know, Stan could look like that if you brushed him out more often," Delilah pointed out.

"Stan's not a pansy."

Delilah shushed Jason as she led him away. "I can't believe you said that."

"I can't believe what some of these people are doing to these dogs!"

"I know," Delilah admitted in a low voice. "The owners are just trying to give the crowd a little something extra." She glanced around anxiously. "We should probably get to our seats." She seemed almost flirtatious as she stood on tiptoes and placed a tiny peck on his mouth. "This is the best present anyone has ever given me. Seriously."

He drew Delilah to him. "You call that a kiss?"

Delilah glanced around, embarrassed. "Jason . . ."

"No sweat," he assured her as released her from their embrace. "We'll wait till after the dog show to make out."

Delilah blushed, but he knew he had her.

"Su-ki! Su-ki! Su-ki!"

Jason shook his head in disbelief as the Manchester crowd chanted the name of a Chinese crested circling the ring with its handler. Most of the crowd—some formally attired—appeared seriously invested in the outcome. Even Delilah was sitting on the edge of her seat.

"That dog looks like a powder puff with toothpicks for legs. In fact—"

"Sshh. I'm trying to watch."

"Sorry."

Jason forced his tired eyes back to the show ring. He couldn't believe he'd be sitting through two nights of hearing things like, "The dappled Tunisian rat catcher first came to these shores in 1814 . . ." Still, one look at Delilah's face, and he knew it was worth it. Getting the tickets and back-stage passes from the Met Gar staff had been easy. Waiting and wondering if she'd accept them had not. When he returned home to find the gift gone and a note on the table that said "Call me," he'd pumped his fists and whooped so loudly he frightened Stanley. The "big gesture" had worked.

He'd been an unthinking idiot. He felt horrible about blindsiding Delilah the morning of the brunch. The look of betrayal on her face had been devastating. But Delilah—beautiful, shy, softhearted Delilah—had forgiven him. He vowed never again to let her down that way.

"The Maltese is a fearless animal, loyal beyond compare . . ."

Jason blinked at the sound of the announcer's voice and dragged his gaze back down to the "action" in the ring. A dust mop with two button eyes was anxiously waiting to strut its stuff. Drowsy, Jason let his eyes drift shut. He'd open them when they announced the Newf.

CHAPTER

11

"*I can't believe* you fell asleep!"

Delilah affectionately punched Jason's shoulder as they entered his apartment. She'd been so absorbed in the dog show she failed to register Jason's trip to dreamland until he startled himself awake with a window-rattling snore. He stayed awake for the rest of the competition, but Delilah could tell it was a struggle.

"I can bring Marcus with me tomorrow night instead if you want," she offered, handing him her coat to hang up.

Jason looked wounded. "No way. I don't want to miss the Newf. I loved being at the dog show. I just need to, you know, make sure to have some coffee with me or something."

Delilah was skeptical. "If you say so."

She calmly petted Stanley's head, waiting for a cue from Jason what to do next. When he'd asked her back to his place, she'd hesitated, but then said yes. It was time she started paying attention to instinct.

"Why don't we sit down?" Jason asked. Together they started in the direction of the couch, Stanley right on their heels. "Stan, down," Jason commanded. Delilah was impressed when Stan actually obeyed.

"Do you want any wine? Coffee?" Jason offered.

Delilah shook her head. "No, thanks." One would make her hyper, the other knock her out. She wanted to stay on an even keel.

They sat together on the couch. Delilah glanced around; the lighting in Jason's apartment was unusually subdued. Perhaps he'd been intending to invite her back here all along. There was no sound save for that of Stanley's panting, which seemed to grow louder each second that Jason didn't touch her. Delilah began to get nervous. When was he going to kiss her? When—

His mouth clamped down on hers softly. Delilah closed her eyes as the room slowly tumbled. It felt like there were feathers in her blood. She returned his ardor, careful not to appear overeager. Still, there was no ignoring how dizzyingly wonderful this was. How was it that time and time again, their lips fit so perfectly? How was it that he always tasted as delicious as she remembered? Time unspooled lazily as Jason drew her into a strong embrace. This, she thought dreamily, was exactly what she'd been waiting for. This sensation. This man.

Her breath hitched as his mouth moved down to feast on her neck. Anticipation juddered through her. Whatever he wanted to do, she would let him. Wherever he wanted to go, she would follow. When he pushed her shirt up and closed his mouth over the thin white fabric of her bra, she thought she'd die of shock and pleasure. He was taking his time, teasing. By the time his mouth latched onto her bare breast to suckle, Delilah could barely think straight. All that mattered was enjoying each delicious moment here on the precipice before taking the plunge.

And then Stanley woofed for attention, and she remembered.

"Shoot!" Delilah fumbled out of his embrace, pulling her bra back down over her chest and fixing her shirt. "The dogs."

Jason blinked in confusion. "What?"

"My dogs," Delilah replied frantically. "It's way past the time I usually take them out! I have to go."

Jason looked astonished. "You're kidding me, right?"

"Please don't be pissed, Jason," Delilah pleaded. "We got out of the dog show much later than I expected."

"I'm not pissed. I'm stunned."

The sweet languor that moments before had cradled her disappeared. In its place came the old familiar anxiety.

"I'm sorry but I have a responsibility to my animals and if you can't deal with that well—"

"Delilah, shut up a minute!" Jason's voice was so loud and so abrupt even Stanley looked shocked. He took a deep breath, slowly massaging his forehead. Delilah held in her breath. Whatever he was going to say, she was sure it would be bad. She steeled herself.

"I need to tell you something, okay?" Jason asked in a measured tone.

"Okay," Delilah replied timidly.

He put his arm around her. "I really like you, Delilah. I think you're sweet, and caring, and gorgeous." He tilted up her chin so their eyes met. "I want to take you to bed and show you how I feel about you. And I'm going to."

"You are?" Delilah squeaked.

"Uh-huh. Tomorrow night. After the dog show. I don't care what you have to do or who you have to pay to take care of your dogs, but you're spending the night with me. Got it?"

Delilah nodded dazedly. "Yes."

"Good. Now Stanley and I will walk you home."

"Oh dear God, child." Marcus shook his head in dismay as he held up a pair of Delilah's underwear for examination. "Who's been picking out your panties for you? Your grandma?"

"Give me that." Delilah snatched back the plain white bikini brief and shoved it back into the drawer. "I knew it was a mistake telling you why I needed you to stay over tonight."

"You don't think I would have figured it out? It's about time you and Jason did the deed. If I were you, I would have jumped his bones long ago."

"I'm not a bone jumper." Delilah began biting her nails. "I don't know if I can do this, Marcus."

He patted her shoulder consolingly. "It's like riding a bicycle. Once you learn how, you never forget."

"Not the actual act! What it signifies."

Marcus addressed the ceiling. "Saints in heaven, help me." His expression was stern as he looked back at Delilah. "Do you want this guy or not?"

"Yes." Delilah closed her dresser drawer. "It's just—what if we start going out, and we fall in love, and we get married, but then things fall apart, and we have a horrible acrimonious divorce, and I wind up bitter and alone like my mother?"

"Honey?" Marcus looked worried. "You haven't even slept with Jason yet. Don't you think appearing on *Divorce Court* is a little premature?"

"I know." Delilah sank down on the edge of her bed. "I'm afraid of the actual act, too," she admitted. "It's been so long. He's probably slept with hundreds of women sexier than me."

"That's why we're going to get you some sassy undergarments."

"I don't do sassy undergarments."

Marcus lifted an eyebrow. "You do if you expect me to spend the whole night here with your dogs."

"That's blackmail!"

"Damn straight it is. Now put on your happy face and get your ass in gear. We're going panty shopping."

"How about this?"

Delilah could feel the heat surging to her face and neck as Marcus held high a red silk thong for her and everyone

else in Portia's Boudoir to see. Marcus told her if she looked
sexy, then she'd feel and act sexy, and Jason would respond
in kind.

Delilah had never felt sexy in her life.

"Put that away," Delilah hissed, forcing his arm down. "I
would never wear that in a million years."

Marcus slipped the thong back on the rack. "Don't you
want to look special for him?"

Of course she did. But she was afraid of making a fool of
herself.

"How about this?" Marcus was holding up a skimpy purple bikini bottom encrusted with faux rhinestones.

Delilah stared at him. "You have got to be kidding."

"I am, actually." He put the offending garment back on
the rack and grabbed Delilah's hand. "Come with me."
Delilah barely had time to think before she found herself
standing before a smiling young saleswoman wearing the
tightest skirt Delilah had ever seen in her life.

"Good day," Marcus said to the woman. "My friend here
is having sex with her boyfriend for the first time tonight—"

"Marcus!"

"—and she's completely clueless when it comes to alluring panties and the like. Could you help us find something
sexy yet simple that won't cause her to have a breakdown?
A matching bra to enhance her totties would be great, too."

"Of course." The woman regarded Delilah kindly. Or
maybe it was with pity. "Please follow me."

Delilah shot Marcus a murderous look as the two of them
followed the saleswoman to the back of the store. "Lots of
women have a hard time buying sexy things for themselves," the saleswoman assured Delilah. Delilah did not
feel comforted.

After trying on dozens of thongs, V-strings, tangas, and
push-up bras in every color and fabric imaginable, Delilah
chose a pair of black lace boy shorts with matching bra.

"Black is always sexy," the saleswoman said approvingly
as she rang up Delilah's purchase. Delilah went to take out
her credit card but Marcus stopped her.

"This one is on me, sweet pea. Have fun tonight."

"I can't believe the Newf didn't win."

Delilah made herself smile as Jason led her into his apartment. Her anxiety had completely ruined her enjoyment of that evening's dog show. All she could think about was the lingerie she was wearing under her clothing. She found it itchy. And strange. She was worried about how Jason would react to it. What if he didn't find it sexy at all? Marcus assured her that any man with a pulse would find her deliciously hot, but you never knew. Human behavior was unpredictable. That's why dogs were preferable.

"Hey, boy." Jason crouched down to hug and kiss Stanley, who'd been snoozing faithfully by the door. "Were you good?"

"He's always good," Delilah chimed in, rubbing Stanley in his favorite spot behind his ears.

"Do want to come with me to take him on his final walk?" Jason asked, reaching for Stan's leash.

"No, I'll stay here."

"Okay. Well, there's wine in the fridge." He fastened the leash to Stan's collar. "We'll just be a minute."

"Have fun," Delilah said, regretting it immediately. *Have fun?* What a stupid thing to say.

Jason and Stan departed, leaving Delilah alone. It was funny; she was in and out of here almost daily, yet she never really bothered to take the place in. It was still sparsely furnished, but at least Jason had gotten around to putting shades on the windows. Her interest was drawn toward the many photos crowding the mantelpiece. Many were of Jason out on the ice throughout his life, but some were of his family. There was a picture of him and Eric in matching hockey uniforms standing side by side on a pond; they looked to be about four years old. In another frame, a news clipping proclaimed, "Mitchell Twins Drive Flasher to Victory!" For someone who claimed to find his brother "a huge pain in the ass," Jason certainly had a lot of pictures of them together. Jason would claim the link between them was simply inescapable, but Delilah knew better. The brothers loved each other.

"Checking out the peanut gallery, I see."

Delilah turned to see Jason and Stanley coming through the door. Feeling guilty, she put the photo in her hand back on the mantel. She hoped it didn't look like she'd been snooping around.

Jason unsnapped Stanley's leash, and Stanley immediately bounded up onto the couch. "I know, I know, I know," Jason said before Delilah had a chance to speak. "It's bad behavior. But just for tonight, let's let it go."

The meaning behind his words had Delilah blushing. This was it, the moment of truth. Beneath the itchy lace of the miracle bra giving her cleavage for the first time in her life, Delilah could feel her heart beginning to pound. She wondered if Jason was anxious, too. He certainly didn't look it.

"C'mere," he whispered.

Stiff as a robot, Delilah walked toward him. *You can do this,* she thought to herself as panic began to rise. *You can be as sexy and alluring as the next woman.*

Jason wrapped his arms around her. "You okay?"

Delilah nodded woodenly.

His expression was tender as he swept back some hair from her face. "Look, I realize I came on pretty strong last night. If you don't want to, you know, that's fine with me. We can just kiss and cuddle and stuff."

"But we have to have sex!" Delilah blurted. "I bought special underwear!"

God, I'm an idiot. Delilah cast her head down, wishing she were in a Godzilla film. That way, the monster could appear out of nowhere *right now* and crush her flat. She couldn't stare at the floor forever; that much she knew. With what little dignity she had left, she made herself look Jason in the eye. He wasn't looking at her like he she was an idiot. He was looking at her like she was hot.

"Special underwear," he murmured, sounding intrigued. "Like the Mormons wear?"

Delilah's fingers squeezed his arm. "Don't joke. I'm a nervous wreck." As if he didn't already know. Still, she felt better confessing it, despite the fact it could ruin the moment completely.

Jason looked puzzled. "I don't understand why you're nervous. It's just me."

"I'm nervous *because* it's you. I want everything to be perfect."

"It will be. You just need to shut up and relax."

They stared at each other a moment, then burst out laughing.

"I'm usually a bit more smooth than that," Jason assured her.

"I hope so."

"So," he began as he caressed her cheek, "can I see the special underwear?"

Delilah nodded, trembling involuntarily at his soft touch.

"C'mon," he whispered, taking her hand as they tiptoed past the slumbering, snoring Stanley.

Jason's bedroom was cool and dark. Delilah paused just inside the door, waiting as he went to turn on the bedside lamp. She wished he wouldn't. It would so much easier to remain in the dark, to hide all she felt for him in shadows. Light meant truth. She'd be revealed to him. Delilah wasn't sure she was ready.

The light came on, bathing the room in gray twilight. Jason stood by the bed smiling in invitation, his hand held out to her. Delilah joined him, trying to hide her trembling. His mouth touched hers, gentle, reassuring. "It's just me," he murmured, kissing her neck. "Only me."

"I know," Delilah whispered back. Her own voice sounded shaky in her ears.

"It's going to be fine," he assured her as he drew her into a loving embrace. "Here, wrap your arms around my neck."

Delilah did so, completely enchanted when he lifted her up and placed her down gently on the bed, lying down beside her. "You have to trust me," he whispered, his fingers playing down her cheek. Delilah looked into his eyes; there was such tenderness there, such concern. But there was also hunger.

Delilah nodded, her eyes lazing shut. His mouth dipped to hers, the pressure barely tangible. Delilah allowed herself to sink into the sweetness of the moment. His mouth on hers . . . his body against hers . . . how could something so simple feel so perfect? Timidity waned as her hands began exploring his back. It felt hard beneath her fingers; hard and muscled. Jason responded to her touch with a moan. An unexpected surge of power awakened in Delilah, and she shifted her hands lower, skimming his hips. He was already hard. Already wanting.

His mouth was roaming now, teasing first her lips, then her neck. Delilah felt herself melting beneath him. "You're so soft," he marveled, unbuttoning her blouse.

"Ah," he continued, his fingers tracing the swell of her breasts above her lacy bra. "This must be the special underwear."

Delilah smiled, then shuddered as his fingers continued exploring. One moment his hand was cupping her; the next he had slid the bra up and had started to suckle. Sensation after sensation rippled through her body, accompanied by amazement. She was teetering on the edge of ultimate desire, and they hadn't even gotten close to the actual act yet.

"Relax," Jason urged, reaching around to unfasten her bra. Delilah complied, helpless to resist when he gently tugged off her top and bra, leaving her naked to the waist.

"Look at you," he marveled, lowering his mouth to taste her. "As perfect as I imagined."

Delilah groaned, stirring beneath him. She was arching up into him. Arching and pressing, making her need known. Jason took a ragged breath and reared up, tearing his shirt off over his head. Then he returned to pleasuring her, his mouth taking its time feasting, sparks shooting from their skin each time flesh touched flesh.

Delilah held her breath as Jason's mouth journeyed lower

over the heated terrain of her skin. He kissed her ribs, kissed her torso. And with each kiss, Delilah wanted more.

Jason lifted his head, looking into her eyes. "I want to see all of you."

Delilah swallowed, heat circling her body like the vortex of a storm. "I want to see you, too."

Jason nodded, rose from the bed. Delilah had the distinct feeling that he knew baring himself to her first might ease her nerves. He stripped—slowly, unselfconsciously. Clambered back down beside her to take her in his arms and let her fingers touch him, learn him. His skin was hot. Her hands played over his rippling muscles. He was so solid, so *male*. Her touching him seemed to inflame him. He was breathing harder now, moans of desire coming from deep within his throat. Delilah skimmed a finger up his thigh, and he shuddered.

"Don't do that," he said hoarsely. "Don't do that unless . . ."

Delilah silenced him with a kiss. Jason grabbed her face between his hands and kissed her hard. Delilah felt her will drain away. Whatever he wanted, she would do.

Jason's hand crept down to Delilah's jeans, a question in his eyes. Delilah nodded her compliance, lifting her hips so he could remove her pants. She watched to see how he would react to the lace briefs, whether Marcus was indeed correct that he'd find the sight of her in them enticing. Her heart leapt to see he did, a guttural groan crossing his lips as he moved to cup her. Delilah let her head drop back, moving against his hand. How she wanted. Ached. Did he know? Could he see?

One moment her panties were on. The next they were sliding down her body, silk trailing against her legs as Jason freed her.

"I want you," he declared, eyes shining as he drank in every inch of her body. Earlier, Delilah had feared feeling exposed. But the way he was looking at her made her realize she was beautiful, at least to him. That was all that mattered. The two of them here, now, together.

Delilah clasped him tightly to her, her body giving assent. Jason rose up slightly, put on protection, then eased himself into her. Pleasure burned through her as he began moving atop of her. Delilah drew herself in around him, saw the shocked pleasure in his eyes as she cleaved to him. They were indivisible; one heart, one mind, one soul. Joy rocketed through her until Delilah felt as though she were flying into the face of the sun, the heat nearly unbearable. Then she came sailing back down to earth, moving with Jason as he, too, reached the heights. Delilah smiled to herself. Special underwear indeed.

CHAPTER

12

"Stanley!"

Jason looked mortified as the bedroom door swung open and Stanley jumped up onto the bed, pushing right between him and Delilah.

Delilah scrambled to cover herself with the sheet. There was still the faintest sheen of sweat on her body; the last thing she wanted was to find herself coated with Stan's hair as if she'd been tarred and feathered. She'd had a feeling all along Stanley was going to make an appearance. Newfs hated to be alone. Plus the noise from the bedroom must have alarmed him.

Jason rolled off the bed, glaring. "Stan! Down!"

Delilah took one look at her naked lover trying to cajole his dog into leaving the comforts of bed and laughed. "I wish I had a camera."

"And I wish I had a cattle prod." Jason gently took hold of Stan's collar. *"Down!"*

Stanley threw him a baleful look, but he did what he was told. Jason slid back into bed, taking Delilah in his arms. Delilah had no sooner snuggled close to him than Stanley, conveniently forgetful, hopped right back up on the bed, though this time he had the good sense to curl up at their feet.

"Jesus Christ," Jason muttered.

"I told you you should train him not to come up on the bed."

"You're right. You did." Jason frowned apologetically. "Sorry about this."

"It's okay."

The truth was, Delilah liked that the three of them were together. Before she began boarding dogs, her dogs always slept with her. Why snuggle with a stuffed animal when you could hold on to the real thing? Her dogs were her family. But once she started her business, she had to stop: the boarder dogs would get jealous, and fights would erupt. Though it saddened her, she trained her beloved pooches to sleep on the floor like the rest.

Jason seemed to have accepted Stan's presence. "That was great," he murmured as he sweetly stroked Delilah's hair. "I really enjoyed that."

"Me, too." She was still feeling blissful.

Stanley shifted position, and Delilah found herself with a head resting on her calf. "You're a pip, Stan," she called down to him. She sighed. "I wonder how my three are doing."

"You left them in capable hands, right?"

Delilah nodded. "Marcus." He was one of the few people she trusted with her animals, or anyone else's, for that matter.

"Maybe he could watch them for a weekend, and we could go away somewhere."

Delilah just smiled. Now was not the time to tell Jason she would never leave her dogs for an entire weekend. Lots of other people did—it was how she made much of her money, after all—but Delilah herself had never felt comfortable doing so. They'd given her so much. She repaid them by always being there for them.

Jason kissed her neck. "Any chance of you coming to a game this week?"

"It depends," Delilah replied honestly. "I think I have some boarders. I have to check."

"I don't see what difference it makes," Jason replied, sounding confused.

"I can't just *leave* other people's animals left in my care. They'd bark their heads off. Or rip each other to shreds."

"But if you never leave them, how do you have a social life?"

"I have one when it's just me and my dogs."

Jason looked worried. "How often is that?"

Delilah felt the first stirrings of anxiety. "Is there a problem?"

"No. I'm just trying to figure out how we'll go out and do things when you're boarding dogs."

Delilah shrugged. "I don't need to go out all the time. I'm perfectly happy to hang out at home with my dogs. In fact, I prefer it."

She could see from the expression flashing quickly across Jason's face—a cross between a grimace and a cringe—that it wasn't the answer he'd hoped for. Delilah's anxiety spiked. "Is everything all right? Because—"

"Everything's fine," Jason hastily assured her. He drew her close, kissing her forehead. "We should probably think about getting some sleep. Maybe in the morning, you can show me that special underwear again."

"My pleasure," Delilah murmured. She reached down, patting Stanley's head for her own reassurance as much as his. She should have felt contented. Instead, she felt uneasy. Delilah closed her eyes, and talked herself into sleep.

God. Damn. Eric.

Jason jammed his pillow over his head to block out the sound of the ringing phone. It was six thirty in the morning. *Six fucking thirty.* What was Eric doing calling him at this hour? He must have known Delilah was there and he was out to bust Jason's balls. Jackass.

Jason toyed with letting the answering machine pick up, then thought better of it. He knew Eric; the jerk would deliberately run out the tape. Groaning in resignation, Jason snaked his arm out from under the comforter and grabbed the phone.

"Yeah?" Jason tried to turn over onto his back, but found he couldn't: sometime during the night Stanley had crept between him and Delilah. Worse, Stan was snoring. "Shit."

"Excuse me?" asked the imperious male voice on the other end of the phone. There was a tense pause. "Jason, this is Marcus."

Marcus. Delilah's dogs. Double shit.

"What's up?" Jason murmured, trying to keep his voice as quiet as possible. The phone hadn't disturbed Delilah at all; she was sleeping soundly, the comforter bunched up around her neck, making her look like a disembodied head in the bed. An adorable disembodied head, Jason thought tenderly.

"I need to talk to Delilah," said Marcus. "It's urgent. Something's up with her mother."

"Hang on." Jason reached across Stanley to gently shake Delilah's shoulder, trying to rouse her. Eventually Delilah's eyes fluttered open.

"Hi," she whispered with a sleepy smile Jason doubted she knew was sexy. His heart sank. He hated having to kill the moment, but he had no choice.

"Marcus needs to talk to you," he said, handing her the phone.

The alarm instantly transforming her face was so severe that Jason had to look away. He found himself stroking Stanley, if only to give himself something to do.

"What happened?" Delilah asked breathlessly as she sat up in bed. "When? . . . Well, what did she say? . . . *Shit* . . . Thank you, Marcus. Love you, too."

Delilah handed the phone back to Jason. "I have to go."

"What's going on?"

Delilah's expression was tense. "It's my mother. She called Marcus—I mean, me—a few minutes ago in hysterics, saying there was a family emergency, and I needed to come out to the house right away. When Marcus pressed her, she wouldn't say what was wrong." Delilah clamped her eyes shut. "God, I hope my father's okay," she whispered.

Jason rubbed her shoulder. "If it was something that serious, wouldn't she have said so?"

"No." Delilah's eyes sprang open. "My mother doesn't believe in giving bad news over the phone."

"No offense, but that's nuts."

"Yeah, no kidding." She looked as though she were going to cry. "I have to go," she repeated flatly.

Jason got out of bed along with her. "Do you want me to come with you?"

Delilah looked touched. "No. But thanks for asking."

Jason hung back, unsure of what to do. He watched as she gathered her clothing together. Her movements seemed abrupt, distracted. Twittery Delilah was back.

"Delilah." He came up and hugged her tightly from behind. He could still smell her perfume from the night before. "We're here if you need us," he whispered.

"We?"

"Me and Stan," said Jason.

"I know that," Delilah sniffled.

"Do you?"

Delilah nodded.

"Good."

Reluctantly, he let her go.

Delilah took it as a positive sign as she pulled into her mother's driveway that the house wasn't blocked off with police tape, nor was it a smoking pile of rubble. She had tried repeatedly to call her mother on the ride out to Roslyn, but got no answer. Her mind had run through dozens of disaster scenarios. Whatever it was, it couldn't be good.

Delilah threw her car into park and raced to the front door, slipping inside.

The house was eerily quiet, its bleached walls making her feel as though she were cocooned within an egg. She paused, listening. Her mother was upstairs weeping. Delilah padded up the white carpet of the stairs, praying she could handle whatever bombshell Mitzi was about to drop.

"Mom?"

Delilah stood in the bedroom doorway. She'd always been wary of her parents' room, since that was where much of their fighting took place. To her it was a dark place, a place of turmoil, not marital harmony. Even now she found herself hesitating.

Her mother was sitting up in the massive king-sized bed purchased years ago from one of her father's stores, mascara running in black rivulets down her powdered cheeks. Delilah couldn't believe she was already made up for the day. Hearing Delilah's voice, Mitzi wanly extended a hand.

"You came," she whispered, sounding like she was on her deathbed.

Delilah was alarmed. "Of course I came! You said it was an emergency!"

Mitzi's face crumpled as she resumed sobbing. "Oh, Leelee."

Delilah swallowed hard as she approached the bed. She hadn't seen her mother this upset since Grandma Ida died. Steeled, she took her mother's hand.

"What is it, Mommy? Is it Daddy?" Delilah's mother nodded frantically. "Oh, God." Delilah felt as though her chest would crack open from pain. "When did it happen?"

Mitzi swiped at her nose. "I'm not exactly sure."

She seemed dazed. Delilah wasn't surprised she didn't have a grasp on the hard facts. Grief did that to people. It scrambled their brains.

"Can you tell me where?"

Her mother squeezed her eyes shut. "No."

This was worse than Delilah thought. "Who told you?" she gently pressed. "Can you remember that?"

"I found out this morning when I opened the newspaper!" Mitzi wailed.

"Oh, Mommy." Pain mingled with anger. For her mother to find out from *Newsday* . . . it was awful, just awful.

"It was the last thing I ever expected to see," her mother continued in a disembodied voice. "There was no warning, no nothing."

As delicately as she could, Delilah reached across the bed for the newspaper lying facedown on the pearl comforter. She herself was finding it hard to think straight. Did Brandi know that her father was supposed to be buried within twenty-four hours of his death?

Queasiness creeping up her throat, Delilah made herself look down at the paper. There was a headline that read: " 'Mattress Maven' Sy Gould To Say 'I Do' to Model Brandi Rose." Delilah stared at the boldface type for a long time. She stared until the letters ran together in one black, rushing torrent of fury. Then she began to yell.

"This is the emergency you made me *schlep* out to Long Island for?! This?!"

"Leelee—"

"I thought Dad was dead! I thought something awful had happened to you!"

"Something awful did happen to me!" her mother insisted, picking up the paper and rattling it in Delilah's face. "The rat bastard is going to marry that stupid *shiksa*! You don't think that's an emergency?!"

Delilah clutched her head in despair. "You divorced him, remember?! You have no right to be upset!"

"You're wrong. This"—she poked repeatedly at the engagement announcement with her finger—"is against the rules. He wants to *shtupp* some bimbo? Fine. But remarry? Jeopardize my baby girl's inheritance? No. That is not fine."

"Oh, so this is about me?" Delilah chortled. "You're upset on *my* behalf?"

Mitzi nodded.

"That's the biggest bunch of bull I've ever heard!"

"Don't you care that she could rob you of your mattress millions?!"

"No! What I care about is that my own mother doesn't think twice about interrupting my life for no good reason and manipulating me into coming out here!"

"You don't understand."

"No, I don't. If you still love Dad, then cut out the melodrama and just tell him."

Mitzi stuck her nose up in the air. "I can't live with that man."

"Then don't! Maintain separate residences and get together when you want to screw! Do whatever! Just keep me out of it!"

Mitzi pressed her back against the white wicker headboard. "You're angry."

"You missed your calling, Mom. You should have been a brain surgeon."

Mitzi narrowed her eyes. "Who answered the phone when I called this morning?"

"Marcus." Delilah suddenly felt claustrophobic. "Look, I have to go."

"One minute." She grabbed hold of Delilah's hand before she could rise from the bed. "How's that adorable blond boyfriend of yours?"

"What?" Delilah squinted at her mother in confusion. She thought, *Jason's not blond.* Then she remembered: *Eric.* "He's fine," Delilah answered distractedly.

"You look tired."

"I was up all night having sex."

"Don't be rude, Delilah."

"Oh, it's all right for you to tell me about Lance or Bruce or whoever it is you're seeing just for kicks—"

"It's Bruce, thank you very much, and for your information he left me for Myra Talman—"

"—but when I say it in the context of an actual relationship, it's rude."

Mitzi wagged a finger under Delilah's nose. "Men don't

buy the cow when they can get the milk for free. Remember that, Leelee."

"Quotes from Chairman Mitzi. How could I forget?" She stood up.

"You're not really going, are you?" Mitzi asked in alarm.

"Yes, I really am."

She clutched at Delilah's arm. "I don't think I can be alone right now. Please."

"Sorry, Mom." Delilah shook her off. "But you don't really have a choice. And if you ever pull another stunt like this, I will never speak to you again."

"Check it out: major tail at ten o'clock."

Jason turned discreetly to see what his former teammate, Guillaume, was murmuring about. Though road trips were a pain in the ass, Jason had been looking forward to returning to Minneapolis as a Blade. Not only did the Blades kick the Mosquitoes' asses out on the ice in a 4–2 victory, but it also gave Jason a chance to hang with his old friend.

They were sitting at a table at Harvey's, the Mosquitoes' usual hangout. The place was crawling with puck bunnies. Once upon a time Jason might have considered inviting the two women Guillaume was slobbering over to the table. But not now.

Jason turned back to his friend, whom he'd known since they were both in the minors. "They're okay."

"Okay?" Guillaume's eyes doubled in size. "They're grade A prime beef, my man."

Jason shrugged. "I'm not interested."

"Is your dick broken?"

"No." Jason sipped his beer. "I'm kinda seeing someone," he confessed.

Guillaume looked horrified. "What are you, nuts? You just got there! Why are you tying yourself down?"

It was a good question, one that Jason had been trying to avoid thinking about. He'd been so pumped after making love with Delilah. Everything was coming together: his ca-

reer, his personal life—he felt invincible. But then came
Delilah's comment about holing up at home with her dogs,
and suddenly things seemed a little less exhilarating. She
couldn't be serious, could she? She'd gone to the dog show
with him. Clearly she could get away when she really
wanted to.

He was about to admit his doubts to Guillaume when the
image of Delilah waking up popped into his mind, and he
experienced a warm fuzzy feeling bordering on the mawk-
ish. They'd work things out. They would.

Jason finished his Stella Artois and ordered another.
"She's special," he told Guillaume.

"What does she do?"

"Trains dogs."

Guillaume looked impressed. "Has she managed to tame
Stan the Man?"

"Oh yeah." He found himself wondering what the two of
them were doing right now. Stan was probably sleeping. Or
trying repeatedly to hop up on the couch. As for Delilah,
he'd left her a couple of messages trying to find out what the
story was with her mom, but she'd yet to get back to him. It
worried him. He hated the idea of her having to go through
a crisis alone.

"What does she look like?" Guillaume asked.

Like an angel, Jason thought, thankful he hadn't said so
aloud. "She's pretty. Petite."

"Got a picture?" Guillaume asked, his gaze still tracking
the women he'd tried to get Jason interested in.

Jason shook his head. "Not yet." He'd make it a priority
as soon as he got back to New York. He'd just bought himself the most expensive digital camera he could find to play
with.

"Good body?" Guillaume continued.

"Really great." Jason wasn't sure why, but for the first
time ever it felt intrusive discussing a girlfriend like this.
Maybe it was because he knew Delilah would be upset if
she knew she was being talked about this way. Or maybe it
was because she was the first woman he'd ever started dat-

ing that he felt so strongly about. Whatever it was, he didn't care to parse Delilah's physical attributes like she was some heifer being assessed for purchase.

Guillaume nodded thoughtfully. "I'd like to meet her sometime."

"You will, the next time the Mosquitoes come to New York to get their asses kicked." He checked his watch. "Shit, I better take off if I want to make curfew."

Jason turned to see three more of his old teammates heading for the table. He checked his watch again. Screw it. He could probably squeeze in one more brew and still make it back to the hotel in time if he hustled. Who knew when he'd next get to hang with his pals again? He waved them over and ordered another beer.

"You're late."

Jason's heart jolted to an abrupt stop as Ty's voice rang out across the hotel lobby. It was twenty-five minutes past midnight. Jason couldn't believe the hard-ass was going to give him a hard time about a piddling half an hour.

Busted, Jason stopped, waiting for the dressing down he knew was to follow. One look at his coach's face told him he was in deep shit. Ty was in full glare mode, his brown eyes gleaming like a feral animal's. When Ty looked like that, it was scary.

"Where ya been, Mitchell?"

Jason scratched nervously behind his ear. "I was, uh, meeting some old friends for a beer."

"I see. Do these old friends play for the greatest hockey team in the NHL?"

"No, Coach."

"But you do, don't you?"

"Yes."

Ty stepped so close to Jason he could smell his breath: peppermint. "What time is curfew, Mitchell?"

"Midnight."

"Take a look at that pretty little Rolex you're wearing and tell me what time it is now."

Jason looked down at his watch. "Twenty-seven minutes past midnight."

"You can tell time; I'm impressed." Ty rubbed his chin. "Let's see if you can guess what I'm thinking right now."

Jason fought a flinch of humiliation. "You're thinking that I'm stupid. Or impulsive. Or both."

Ty nodded. "Not bad. Maybe you can make your living as a mind reader after you get kicked off the team." He folded his arms across his chest, shaking his head. "What the fuck am I going to do with you, Mitchell?"

"With all due respect, Coach, it was only twenty-five minutes."

It was the wrong thing to say. Whatever crumb of mercy Ty might have offered he had just snatched back as a result of Jason's stupidity. Jason tried not to stare at the vein pulsing wildly on Ty's forehead.

"How about I bench you for twenty-five games?" Ty proposed. "Would you like that?"

Jason's gaze darted away. "No."

"Why not? It's only twenty-five games."

"I see your point, Coach."

"I'm not sure you do." Ty was so close now his nose was practically touching Jason's. "Rules are created for a reason. Contrary to what you're thinking, I don't just pull them out of my ass to make your life difficult. When I make a rule, it's to ensure maximum performance from my players. And when my players follow my rules, it tells me two things: one is that they understand who's in charge. The second is that they're willing to do what it takes to win. I'm not sure you give a shit on either count."

"I—"

"Don't interrupt me when I'm talking, Mitchell."

Jason slumped. "Sorry."

"Since I'm such a great guy, I'm only going to fine you a thousand bucks. Creep in past curfew again, and it'll be double. Fuck up a third time, and you're gonna be benched through Christmas. Are we clear?"

Jason's voice was strained. "Totally, Coach."

"Good." Ty stepped back. "Now get your ass upstairs."

CHAPTER

13

"*Hey! How're my* two favorite—beings?"

Delilah smiled as Jason stepped over the threshold of her apartment to give her a long, lingering kiss before crouching to pet Stanley.

"Is he okay?" Jason asked uneasily as he stared deeply into Stanley's eyes. "He seems kind of out of it."

"He's been a little under the weather. Sit down a minute, and we'll talk."

Jason headed for the couch while Delilah hung up his coat and pushed his luggage away from the door. "No more emergency calls from your mother, I hope."

"I'm really sorry about that," Delilah said as she sat down next to him.

Jason looked concerned. "Is everything okay?"

Delilah sighed. "Everything's fine. My mother's a total drama queen. She saw my father's engagement announcement in the paper and had a complete meltdown. Apparently, she couldn't convey this to Marcus over the phone. I had to *schlep* out there so I could see the full performance."

Jason smiled in sympathy at how crazy parents could be. "Okay, so what's up with Stan?"

"Have you been feeding him a different kind of dog food?"

"No."

"New treats?"

Jason stared at her blankly. "Don't think so."

"Hmm." Delilah hated asking the next question, because she knew the answer would be upsetting, but she had no choice. "Have you been letting him eat table scraps?"

The quickness with which Jason averted his gaze gave her the answer. "Sometimes."

"Jason! You shouldn't do that! What did you give him?"

Jason glanced guiltily at Stan. "I don't know. Some Cheetos, I think. The last piece of pizza in the fridge."

"The Cheetos would explain the bright orange vomit. He also had very loose stools. Did you feed him table scraps when you two were living in Minnesota?"

"Sometimes," Jason muttered.

"And would he get sick?"

"Sometimes."

Delilah was incredulous. "Why didn't you tell me this before?"

"Because I didn't think it mattered."

"It matters a lot. Stan's not the only dog living here when you're away. I didn't know what was going on at first; I was afraid he might have had some kind of virus he could pass on to the others."

"Well, he doesn't."

"That's not the point," Delilah said sharply. His cavalier attitude was annoying, not to mention baffling. One minute he was on the edge with concern over Stan. Now he seemed defensive. It was crystal clear he didn't like being reprimanded.

"Can we start over?" Jason asked. "I hate that I just got back and we're starting off on the wrong foot."

"You're right," Delilah conceded.

Jason took her hand in his, brushing his lips softly across her knuckles. "Did you really miss me?"

"I really did."

"I missed you, too." He nuzzled his nose in her hair. "Your hair smells great."

"It's Mane 'n Tail Shampoo."

Jason pulled back. "Isn't that for horses?"

"People can use it, too," Delilah explained enthusiastically. "It makes your hair very shiny."

"I see." Jason was staring at her head. "Please don't tell me you moisturize with Bag Balm, or I might have to rethink this whole relationship."

"I'm shocked you even know what Bag Balm is!"

"I grew up on a farm, remember? I smell Bag Balm in my dreams." He stole another look at Stan, who was sleeping peacefully. "He's okay now, right?"

"He's okay *this time*." Delilah reached forward, pulling a piece of paper off the ugly but trendy kidney-shaped coffee table Marcus had bought for her at a yard sale. "I came up with this diet for Stanley. I think you should follow it."

Jason studied the paper. "Vitamin supplements . . . kelp . . . alfalfa . . . raw meat . . . cooked yams . . . this seems a little complicated, Delilah."

"It is at first, but once you get into the routine, it's pretty easy."

Jason appeared unconvinced. "Is this what you feed your dogs?"

Delilah nodded.

"With three of them, it must cost you a small fortune."

"They're worth it."

"So's Stan, but I don't see why I can't keep feeding him his regular dog food and just cut out the table scraps."

Delilah hesitated. "He doesn't like that kibble you feed him. It tastes disgusting."

Jason looked distressed. "Please don't tell me you eat dog food."

"Of course I don't!" Delilah hesitated. "He told Marcus."

Jason looked confused. "Who told Marcus what?"

"Stanley told Marcus he hates the kibble you feed him."

"I'm sorry, could you repeat that, please?"

"I know, it sounds nuts. But Marcus can read animals' thoughts. They talk to him. And Stan told Marcus he hated that kibble. He hates those liver treats, too. But he likes the little doggie bagels you get him."

"Okay, um, Delilah?" Jason rubbed his forehead as if warding off a headache. "I'm not really sure I'm up to having a conversation like this right now. Could we just unwind?"

"Sure. But promise me you'll at least try the diet."

"I promise. Now you come here." Jason drew Delilah to him. "Two things."

"Mmm?" said Delilah, leaning against him. He looked tired; there were faint circles beneath his eyes and the first hints of stubble on his chin.

"Thing number one," said Jason, kissing the top of her head. "Can I stay the night?"

Delilah flushed with pleasure. "Of course." She hadn't made any assumptions on that front. She was afraid if she did and he wanted to go back to his own place with Stan, she would feel slighted. His wanting to stay spoke volumes.

"Thing two: what are you doing Wednesday night?"

"Nothing that I know of," Delilah answered slowly.

"Great. I want you to come to my game, and afterward we'll grab a drink with some of my friends."

"Oh." Delilah's pulse began fluttering. "That sounds . . . fun."

"It'll be fine. I promise."

"I know, it's just I'm not really good with people, you know? I mean groups of people. I—"

Jason silenced her with a kiss. He smiled at her playfully as he pulled away. "I'll ask all of them to wear dog collars. How about that?"

"That's not funny."

"There's nothing to be scared of, Delilah. It's just one drink."

"Okay." Delilah knew his expectation wasn't unreasonable. This is what couples did. They met the people in each other's lives. So what if the only people in her life at present were two bat shit crazy parents and a frustrated dancer slash dog psychic? That didn't mean *his* friends were screwballs. In fact, they were probably refreshingly normal; so normal they'd think *she* was a screwball. She'd give anything not to have do this, but she knew it wasn't right. There was a possible out, though. "I don't know anything about hockey."

"You'll be fine."

Was he getting tired of saying that? Of having to hold her hand and reassure her before she splintered into a million irrational pieces? Delilah checked his face; he didn't seem particularly bothered.

"Just tell me when and where, then," Delilah heard herself say in a voice shockingly convincing. Her arms were beginning to itch. She was worried she was about to break out in hives. But she wanted to make Jason happy, and so she agreed to attend the game.

Walking down the street with Brandi, who kept referring to herself as Delilah's "stepmom," Delilah tried to think of creative ways she could exact her pound of flesh from her father. He'd been haunting her for *weeks* to go shopping with Brandi, hammering home the point that it was important that "you girls get to know each other better."

So here she was, helping Brandi carry her many packages after an exhausting morning of traipsing from store to store. They'd shopped the East Side. They'd shopped the West Side. They had even ventured into the crowded hell that was midtown. Brandi bought lingerie, a number of tight sweaters with plunging necklines, five pairs of shoes, and a pair of fur-lined handcuffs that Delilah preferred not to think about. Delilah bought a new leash for Shiloh.

"Oh, this has been so much fun!" Brandi squeaked.

Delilah imagined dogs for miles around covering their

ears and howling. Delilah herself longed to howl. From boredom.

"This is a darling little neighborhood," Brandi continued. "But aren't you nervous living in the city?"

"Why would I be?"

"It's so dangerous. You could be mugged or raped or murdered or run over or kidnapped or pushed under a subway train or—"

"Gotcha." The shoe-laden bag on Delilah's shoulder began slipping, and she paused to hoist it back up. "Those things can happen on Long Island, too, you know."

"But it's more likely to happen here," Brandi insisted. "I haven't seen one spalon," she noted with disdain.

"Nope. We don't have dinerants, either. Yet somehow we survive."

They had just rounded the corner of Delilah's street when they ran into Eric.

"Hello, Delilah," he said smoothly. Delilah noticed right away the way Eric sized Brandi up, his eyes lingering on her impressive chest and tiny tush. "Aren't you going to introduce me to your friend?" He flashed a smile that could charm the spots off a leopard.

"Eric, I want you to meet my *father's fiancée,* Brandi. Brandi, this is my friend Eric."

Eric gave a small bow. "Enchanted, I'm sure."

"So gallant." Brandi turned to Delilah, impressed. "Isn't he gallant?"

"Very gallant," Delilah agreed flatly, glaring at Eric. Her shoulder was beginning to throb. She dropped the bag of shoes to the sidewalk.

"I bet you're a model," Eric said to Brandi.

"I am!" Brandi grew excited. "Maybe you've seen me? On the Mattress Maven commercials? I'm the girl who rolls around on the bed in an angel costume and says, 'Oooohh, this bed is heaven.'"

Eric's gaze again traveled her body. "I think I've seen that, yes."

"We have to get going," Delilah said coldly.

"What's the big rush?" Eric asked, winking at Brandi as if the two shared a secret. Brandi covered her mouth with her hand, giggling girlishly. "Can you guess what I do for a living?" he asked Brandi.

Brandi fluttered her eyelashes. "You're a model, too?"

"I'm sure I could have been," Eric boasted. "But no, I'm a professional hockey player."

Brandi was awed. "You are?"

"For New Jersey." He seemed to remember Delilah was there. "I'm playing Jason tonight."

"I know. I'm going to the game."

"Really." Eric seemed intrigued. "Well, you'll have to let me know what you think."

Brandi sighed. "I would love to go to a hockey game sometime." She clutched Delilah's hand. "Maybe I could go with you? Tonight?"

"You're having dinner with my father tonight, remember?" Delilah pointed out frostily.

Brandi dropped her hand. "Oh. Right."

"There's still lots of games left in the season," Eric assured her. "I can get you free tickets any time. Just say the word."

"I would looove that," Brandi purred.

Eric smiled slyly. "I thought you might. Do you have a pen and paper? We can exchange numbers, and maybe I can arrange for you to come to a game sometime."

While Brandi fumbled in her new Fendi bag, Delilah couldn't decide whether to kiss Eric or kill him.

Brandi found a scrap of paper and scribbled on it, handing it to Eric.

"That's my home number *and* at the spalon."

Eric's nose crinkled in confusion. "The—"

"Don't ask," said Delilah.

"Thank you," Eric said to Brandi, slipping the info into a back pocket of his jeans.

"Don't you have to be somewhere?" Delilah asked him pointedly. "Resting for tonight's game, maybe?"

"As a matter of fact, I do." He leaned over to kiss

Delilah's cheek. "Good to see you, Delilah." His gaze fastened onto Brandi. "A very, *very* great pleasure to meet you, Brandi."

"You, too," Brandi said breathlessly, watching him as he walked away. Once he was out of sight, she turned back to Delilah. "Wow."

"Wow what?"

"He's so, like, hot."

"And you're so, like, engaged to marry my father."

"I know," Brandi sniffed. "But a girl can still *look*."

"Looking's fine," Delilah agreed. "But don't touch. Because if you hurt my father—"

"I would never hurt my Sy Guy," Brandi insisted. She actually looked insulted, which Delilah took as a good sign. "Never, ever, ever."

Delilah hoisted the bag of shoes back onto her shoulder. "Glad to hear it."

"Goddamn, Eric's on fire tonight."

Jason grunted in response to Thad Meyers's comment, watching as Eric broke up another cross-ice pass, thwarting a Blades rush. The first period was nearly over, and Eric was playing like a man possessed. The two hadn't yet met on the ice, but given how Ty liked to switch lines to generate sparks, Jason had no doubt they would.

He had seen Delilah briefly in the Green Room before the game. She seemed overwhelmed. She smiled and nodded politely to everyone he introduced her to, but she looked petrified. He saw to it she was seated with Barry Fontaine's wife, Kelly, and hoped it would work out.

"Mitchell, get out there for Webster!" Ty barked.

Tully Webster came sailing back to sit on the bench as Jason jumped over the boards and headed up the Blades' left wing. Eric was on the ice. The Blades dumped the puck into the Jersey corner. Jason went to dig it out. He and Eric got there at the same time. "I hear Delilah's here," Eric panted, scrambling furiously for the puck that Jason was trying to keep away from him by kicking it along the boards. "Wait until she sees what a pussy you really are."

"Bite me," Jason replied, snapping the puck into the slot where center Duncan Connors deflected it just wide. The crowd groaned.

In the middle of the second, it was still deadlocked 0–0. Jason nailed Eric in the corner with a hard check. "Who's a pussy now?" Jason breathed in his ear. "At least I've *got* a girlfriend."

They froze the puck, and New York won the subsequent face-off. A slap shot by Duncan Connors from the point caromed off the goal post, sending it to Jason near the half boards. As he went to one-time it, he was knocked off balance by a spear in his side. It was Eric.

"You're stupid as shit," Eric taunted as he picked up the puck and sent it sailing to center ice. Furious, Jason smashed his brother's helmeted head into the boards. The whistle blew.

"Number Fifteen, New York, two minutes for roughing!" the ref called.

Jason's mouth fell open. "What are you, shitting me?" he yelled. "He speared me!"

The ref glared at him. Jason took the hint and skated to the penalty box. He wondered what Delilah was making of all this, if she was even cognizant that he and Eric were battling.

After the Blades killed off his penalty, Jason skated to the bench, where his team captain stood glaring at him. "Ignore your fucking brother," Michael commanded. "He's trying to get in your head."

Back on the ice, he and Eric met up along the boards near New York's blue line. "Delilah offered to blow me on the way back from her mom's," Eric jeered, tipping the back of Jason's helmet up so that the front was covering his eyes. *Ignore it,* Jason told himself as he headed back to the bench. But his fury grew.

The Blades scored on a power play at the end of the second and took a 1–0 lead into the dressing room. Jersey, led by Eric, came out for the third on fire. But despite carrying the play, they couldn't score on David Hewson. Midway through the period, the Blades scored on a counterattack to make it 2–0 with about twelve minutes left.

When there were eight minutes to go, Ty barked for Jason's line to get back out on the ice for a face-off at center ice. The Blades got control and dumped the puck deep. Jason raced in after it. His stick had barely made contact when Eric cross-checked him from behind into the boards.

"Delilah says you suck in bed," said Eric as the ref blew his whistle.

"Fuck you!" Jason howled, hooking his brother between the legs with his stick so he couldn't skate away. Before the linesmen could get between them, the two brothers started circling one another, dropping their gloves. "You upset I can get it up and you can't? Delilah says—"

Bam! Bam! Jason punched Eric with two quick right jabs before Eric could finish his taunt. Panting, he went to hit Eric again, shocked by how exhausted he suddenly felt. Eric grabbed his jersey and connected with a short left to the chin. They both grabbed at each other's shoulder pads, each determined to thwart another blow from the other. Jason glanced down; there was blood on the ice. *Good,* Jason thought. *I nailed him.* The crowd was roaring. Jason felt like a gladiator in the ring.

"I can't wait to find out how sweet she tastes," Eric murmured in Jason's ear.

Jason roared and, rearing up, threw Eric to the ice and jumped on top of him. At that moment, the two linesmen jumped in and pulled them apart. Jason could hear the sound of hockey sticks being banged against the boards as both teams' players "voiced" their support.

"Good go, boys. Now both of you get the fuck off the ice," one of the refs scolded. The crowd cheered as Jason pushed the linesman off him and stormed off the ice to the locker room. It wasn't until he was inside that he realized some of the blood was his.

CHAPTER 14

"You're sitting next game."

Jason lowered the ice pack he'd been holding to his stitches and stared at Ty, who had just invited him to step into his office. Since all his teammates had been patting him on the back for not taking any shit from Eric, Jason assumed Ty was about to do the same.

"Sit down, Jason."

He did as Ty asked, working hard not to look dumb-founded. He'd played his guts out, and when push came to shove, proved no one could get away with cheap-shotting him, not even his brother. So why was he being punished?

"You played pretty well tonight," Ty started, throwing a Nerf basketball into the small hoop set up in the corner.

"Thank you."

"But I could have used you the rest of the third period."

Jason didn't know what to say. They'd won, hadn't they? What difference did it make?

"What you did tonight was dangerous," Ty continued.

"I don't understand."

"You made it personal. This is a team, remember? But you let your brother play you like a cheap violin."

Jason slumped, defeated. Ty was right: Eric had intentionally gotten up his nose in the hopes he'd lose his cool, and he'd succeeded. It was so obvious that Jason was mortified.

"I don't care if your brother killed your pet pony or is fucking your girlfriend. When you're on the ice, only one thing matters: doing what we have to to win. What you did actually set us back. It fractured people's concentration."

Jason squirmed with frustration. "I was taught not to take any crap."

"And that's admirable. But unless you get the okay from me, keep your gloves *on*."

"I see your point," Jason grumbled, "but I don't get why you're benching me next game."

"Because I'm a prick," Ty answered glibly, shooting another hoop and scoring. "You buy that?"

"No."

"Then you tell me why."

Jason frowned. He was getting tired of answering Ty's rhetorical questions.

"You want to teach me a lesson," he recited, bored.

"Bingo." Jason tensed as Ty bounced the Nerf ball off his head. "I want you to sit on the bench, and watch your teammates play, and see how they all put the team first."

Jason couldn't hold his tongue any longer. "He speared me, Coach!"

"And if he wasn't your brother, then maybe—*maybe*— you could have made a case for going after him. But he knows you, Jason." Ty spun the Nerf ball on his index finger. "He knows what buttons to push, and you played right into it. You think that's good?"

"No," Jason muttered.

"I've told you before: you're a good hockey player, Mitchell. You might even be a winner. But until you curb your impulsiveness, neither of us is ever going to know for sure, are we?"

• • •

"*C'mon, let's get* the hell out of here."

Jason's gruffness surprised Delilah. She'd done as he'd instructed, waiting patiently for him in the Green Room after the game. She was still trying to process the game itself; having never seen one before, she'd been amazed at how fast the action was. She could barely keep up, but she felt stupid asking Kelly Fontaine, or any of the other hockey wives/girlfriends, what was going on. They all seemed to know, cheering certain calls in unison and booing others. It felt like they were speaking a foreign language.

They'd been cordial to her before the game. She was pretty sure she hadn't sounded like a complete idiot when they asked her what she did for a living. People immediately wanted advice about their own pets, and Delilah was always glad to help, because it saved her having to talk about herself.

Her eyes had been glued to Jason every time he was on the ice. She couldn't believe the speed at which he was able to skate. It must feel like flying.

Delilah also couldn't believe how tough he was. Every time he hit someone or was hit by someone else, her heart would stop. Rationally, she knew it was part of the game, but emotionally, it was hard to watch.

The way he and Eric had gone after each other was particularly upsetting, the more so because the surrounding crowd seemed to enjoy the fact they were beating the hell out of each other! Delilah didn't get it. When neither appeared for the final half of the third period, she worried. She was relieved when Jason finally appeared in the Green Room, though the stitches in his chin did give her a little jolt.

"Are you all right?" she asked. She moved to touch his face, but Jason jerked his head away.

"I'm fine."

"The game was fun to watch," she offered lamely.

Jason snorted. "I bet."

"Kelly Fontaine seemed nice," Delilah continued. Jason shrugged like he didn't care.

Bewildered, Delilah grabbed her coat. "Where are we going?" she asked in what she hoped was a cheerful voice.

"Home."

"But I thought—"

"I changed my mind. I'm tired, and you'd probably just sit there and not say a word anyway, so what's the point? Let's just go home."

The air fell still. Delilah reached for her purse, deliberately avoiding Jason's eyes. She'd seen this movie before, starring her parents. It had a very long title. It was called, "I'm angry about something that's happened to me, so I'll lash out at you. I'll make you feel bad to make myself feel better." Delilah hated that movie. Were she her mother, she'd snarl back and storm off the set. But she wasn't, and so she just kept her head bowed, intent on getting home without incurring further wrath.

At the dog park the next day, Delilah laid out the previous night's scene for Marcus. Leaving Met Gar, she and Jason had cabbed back to their neighborhood in silence. When Delilah screwed up the courage to tell him she thought he should stay at his own place that night, Jason didn't protest. He had kissed her before leaving her, true, but it felt perfunctory. Now she was worried.

"So, what exactly are you asking me?" Marcus asked, keeping an eye on Quigley, who'd lately taken to scrapping with a Great Dane four times his size.

"Do you think he hates me?" Delilah asked pathetically.

"No. I think he had a bad night, and he took it out on you. Call him on it. He should apologize. And if he doesn't, well, then you have something to worry about. But right now? Don't make a mountain out of a molehill."

"I just hate the way it made me feel. It was like bad déjà vu. I shut down."

"For the nine hundredth time, the two of you are not Sy

and Mitzi. Thank God." Marcus rose abruptly. "Excuse me," he called out to a young woman on a cell phone whose Doberman was attempting to mount Daisy, an aging cocker spaniel whom Marcus walked, "but we don't *do* humping at this dog park, especially not before ten a.m." The woman made a face, but she did pull her dog off Daisy. "Stupid little girl," Marcus muttered under his breath as he sat back down. He broke off a piece of his corn muffin and passed it to Delilah. "You've been holding out on me."

"What?"

"The *sex*," Marcus practically shouted in her face. "How's Jason in the sack?"

Delilah blushed. "Great."

"Really great, or 'anything's better than my last boyfriend who thrust five times and was done' great?"

Delilah choked. "Really great."

"*Mazel tov.* You deserve it." Marcus licked corn muffin crumbs off his fingers. "I have some good news of my own."

Delilah perked up. "Yes?"

Marcus looked like he was about to burst. "Remember I told you I was auditioning for that new musical based on the life of Dr. Phil called, *My Mustache, My Self*?"

Delilah clasped her hands together excitedly. "Yes?!"

"Well, I got it!"

Delilah threw her arms around Marcus's neck. "That's wonderful!" Her voice was unnaturally high and loud, so much so that Sherman, Shiloh, and Belle all came racing to her side, worried. "It's okay, guys," she assured them as she petted them. "Mommy's just excited." She squeezed Marcus's arm. "I'm so proud of you. Really."

"You might not be when you hear what I have to say next." Marcus smiled uneasily. "Rehearsals begin this week, Lilah, and they're intensive, because they want to get this show up before Christmas. I'm not going to be able to help you out anymore."

Delilah had always known this moment would come. But now that it was here, she was unprepared for how sad she felt.

"I'm sorry to be leaving you in the lurch like this—"

Delilah stilled Marcus's apology with a wag of her index finger. "I don't want to hear it. You've been waiting years for this. I'll be fine."

In her mind she was already reconfiguring her day, trying to work out how she'd do double duty. It would be hard, but not impossible. The hard part would be coming up with a suitable replacement. Unlike *some* dog walking services, Delilah wasn't about to hire just anybody. Whoever worked for her had to really care about the animals. It had taken her months and countless interviews to find Marcus. She had no doubt the same would be true when it came to finding his successor.

Marcus's eyes were misty as he gazed into the middle distance. "This could be it, Lilah. My big break."

"It could," Delilah agreed breathlessly. She was so proud of him! He'd worked so hard and had never given up hope. He was finally being rewarded!

"This show is going to be a big hit," Marcus continued, trancelike. "You know how I know?" Delilah braced for her friend's latest canine communiqué. "Little Cha-Cha appeared to me in a dream—you know, Ginny's Cha-Cha who died in August?"

"I *know* who Cha-Cha is, Marcus."

"Anyway, he had this big silver sombrero on, and there was a blue light around him. He jumped up onto my lap and said, 'Prepare for all your dreams to come true, compadre.' So I *know*."

"I wish Cha-Cha would appear to me," Delilah murmured, half joking.

"You don't need Cha-Cha," Marcus admonished. "What you need is an exorcism to get rid of those childhood ghosts. *And* you need to tell that boyfriend of yours what for."

"I know. It just makes me nervous."

"Then forever hold your peace, lady. Because I for one am sick to death of your wishy-washy ass."

• • •

"*I need to* talk to you."

Delilah was shaking so hard as she approached Jason she had to shove her balled fists in the pocket of her coat. She'd spent an entire day and night mulling over Marcus's words, and came to the conclusion that he was right: she had to call Jason on his rudeness to her after the hockey game. He needed to know right from the get-go that he couldn't treat her like that. She'd called and asked him to meet her at Starbucks.

She kept her coat on as she slid into the chair opposite him. Without her even noticing, fall was rapidly giving way to winter, and there were rumors in the air of a first snow before Thanksgiving. All morning Delilah had felt unable to keep warm.

Jason looked uncertain as he pushed a cup of coffee across to her. Delilah lifted the coffee to her lips. The brew was delicious, and the aroma calmed her as she prepared to say the words she'd been rehearsing all morning.

"Look, I want to apologize to you," Jason said. "I was pissed about something that happened after the game, and I took it out on you. That wasn't right."

Delilah's mouth fell open.

Jason leaned across the table, concerned. "Are you okay?"

"I'm fine," Delilah replied, trying to blink away the dazed and happy feeling of having been beaten to the punch.

"Is that what you wanted to talk about?"

Delilah nodded.

"I thought so," said Jason, sounding regretful. "As soon as the cab dropped you off at your apartment, I thought, *You moron, what did you do that for?* It won't happen again, I promise."

Too warm now, Delilah shed her coat. His apology made her feel confident.

"What happened after the game?" she ventured.

Jason absently fingered his stitches. "My coach is benching me next game. Said I have to learn discipline."

Delilah bristled. "I think your brother's the one who needs to learn discipline."

"I'll tell my coach you said that."

"Are you and Eric speaking?"

Jason looked perplexed. "Why wouldn't we be?"

"You made each other *bleed*, Jason!"

"It's part of the game, Delilah," Jason replied matter-of-factly, taking a gulp of coffee. "It's nothing personal."

Delilah tried to imagine beating the hell out of Marcus in the dog park and then the two of them rolling along as if nothing had happened, but couldn't.

"So, I was thinking." Jason sat up straighter, and his eyes seemed to brighten. Delilah loved when he was enthusiastic about something; his entire being became animated. "Since we bailed on drinks with my friends the other night, what if we all go out to dinner Friday night?"

Delilah pulled out her PalmPilot and studied it. "I can't. I'm boarding three dogs this weekend."

"What about the following weekend?"

Delilah shook her head. "Four dogs, two of them puppies."

Delilah watched Jason's grip tighten around his coffee mug. "Can't Marcus spot you one night?"

"Marcus resigned. He got a part in a show!"

"That's great. I guess." Jason fiddled with the teaspoon on the table before him. "I mean, it's great. For him."

"Jason, you need to understand: I run my own business, and I'm not in a financial position to turn down work. And until I find someone to replace Marcus, I'm basically tied to my business morning, noon, and night."

Jason nodded like he understood, but his rigid posture said otherwise. "How long will it be before you replace Marcus?"

"I don't know. I can't hire just anyone."

Jason laughed curtly. "No offense, but how hard can it be to find someone to walk dogs?"

CHAPTER

15

"Piece of cake," Jason murmured to himself as he walked down West Seventy-eighth Street to fetch his first dog of the day. Granted, the list of instructions Delilah gave him seemed more complicated than the plans for the D-day invasion, but he was pretty sure he could handle it.

He came to the first address on the list, a neo-Gothic building complete with grinning Friars' heads and the odd gargoyle. There were three dogs waiting for him here.

"Can I help you, sir?"

Jason was surprised to be stopped by the doorman, a behemoth of a man with jowls Hitchcock would envy. For a moment, Jason felt stupid; he assumed he'd be able to just breeze into the building and pick up the dogs.

"Hi, I'm Jason Mitchell. I'm here to pick up"—he glanced down at his instruction sheet—"Quigley, Miranda, and Luscious."

The doorman eyed him suspiciously. "Where's Marcus?"

"He landed a part in a show."

"May I see some ID, please, sir?"

Annoyed, Jason fumbled for his wallet, producing his

driver's license as well as one of Delilah's business cards. The doorman looked at the license, then Jason. The license, then Jason. His gaze was suspicious as he handed the license back to Jason.

"Any particular reason you're walking around with a Minnesota driver's license?"

It's all part of my big dog scam. I'm going to kidnap them and sell them to Garrison Keillor. "I just moved here from Minnesota," Jason explained patiently. "I play for the New York Blades?"

The doorman sniffed. "I'm afraid I don't follow sports, sir."

Jason rolled his eyes. Even the doormen in New York had attitude.

"I'm a hockey player."

"And you walk dogs because—?"

Who did this guy think he was? Columbo? "I'm helping my *girlfriend*." Jason punched a finger at Delilah's card. "Delilah Gould? Owner of the Bed and Biscuit?"

"I'm familiar with Miss Gould, sir." Appeased, he motioned for Jason to proceed.

"Thank you."

Taking the elevator up to the nineteenth floor, Jason double-checked his instructions: "Quigley's apartment is the one on the left. Don't forget: you have to pet him five times and say 'Quigley, you da man' before giving him a biscuit and putting him on the leash." Jason frowned as he fumbled in his coat pocket for the key to the apartment.

He opened the door to find the little pug sitting there, eagerly waiting. "Hey, guy." Jason went to put the leash on him and Quigley backed up, beginning to growl. Loudly. Jason sighed. "You're really going to make me do this, aren't you?" Glancing around to make sure no one was there to see, he quickly petted Quigley five times then whispered, "You da man," producing a biscuit from his pocket. Quigley happily devoured the treat while Jason attached his leash to his collar.

"One down, two to go." Keeping Quigley on his left as

Delilah instructed, Jason proceeded down to eleven to collect "Miranda, a high-strung Irish setter. She'll be in a crate to your left as you open the door. Give her one pink pill from the mantlepiece before you leave the apartment." Jason shoved the instructions back in his pocket.

Whistling confidently, Jason opened the door to Miranda's apartment. Upon seeing him, Miranda began barking loudly, throwing herself against the side of the crate.

"Um . . ." Jason looked down at Quigley. "You stay here."

He dropped Quigley's leash, grabbed a pill off the mantelpiece, and crept toward the crate as if stalking wild game. The closer he got, the louder Miranda barked. "It's okay, girl," Jason soothed. He opened the crate, and Miranda shot out, sliding across her owner's teak floor with a yelp. Scrambling to regain her balance, she legged it away from Jason as fast as she could. Jason followed, cornering her in the kitchen. Despite her desperate, nonstop barking, he somehow managed to grab her head and slide the pill as far down her throat as he could, holding her muzzle the way he did with Stan so she wouldn't spit it up.

Jason patted her head. "See, that wasn't so hard." Attaching Miranda's leash to her collar, he led his reluctant charge back out to the living room. Quigley had vanished.

"Shit." Jason looked down at Miranda. "I—you stay here."

He dropped her leash and slipped out into the hall, closing the door behind him. Miranda resumed barking madly. Jason stood in the vestibule, completely perplexed. No Quigley. He reentered the apartment, where Miranda was now wildly chasing her tail. High strung? The dog was crazy.

"It's okay, girl," Jason assured her absently on his way back to the kitchen. No Quigley. He checked all four bedrooms. No Quigley. Finally he ventured into the bathroom. Quigley stood in the tub, quivering.

"What the—?"

It was clear Quigley had no idea how he'd managed to wind up in the tub, and he had no intention of hopping back out. Annoyed, Jason lifted him up and led him back out into the living room, where Miranda had vomited up her pill before resuming her tail chasing.

"Goddammit!"

Overwhelmed, Jason tore Delilah's now crumpled instructions from the pocket of his coat. There it was, clear as day but blithely ignored: "Make sure you give Miranda some water after her pill."

"Sorry," Jason muttered to Miranda, stomping into the kitchen a third time for some paper towels with which to clean up the dog puke. Less than ten minutes into the job, and already he'd screwed things up. Good thing Quigley and Miranda couldn't rat him out to Delilah.

He had no problems with Luscious, an Australian shepherd, but there were still three more dogs to fetch from two other buildings. Jason had seen Delilah walk up to twelve dogs at the same time, so he had no doubt six would be a stroll in the park. He was wrong.

One dog wanted to go one way, one another. One would stop to pee, and the others would pull. Delilah claimed they knew the basic commands, but all appeared deaf when Jason used them. Maybe he wasn't using a forceful enough voice, but he felt kind of guilty, yelling at other people's dogs. More than once he had to stop to disentangle them from each other, as well as prevent them from wrapping themselves around his legs. He never knew one half hour could last so goddamn *long*. He was nearing the end of his first "shift" when Eric came strolling around the corner, a copy of the *Post* under his right arm and a steaming cup of coffee in his left. Naturally he stopped to savor the sight of Jason and his unruly charges.

"You know, all you need is a chariot and you could reenact *Ben Hur*."

Jason shot him a withering look. Why was it that Eric always managed to materialize at the most inopportune times? Did he have a twin's sixth sense for these things? Or were these random meetings simply one of the drawbacks of living in the same neighborhood as a jerk?

"Having fun?" Eric continued as he fell into step with Jason.

"It's harder than it looks." Jason glanced at his brother out of the corner of his eye. Three days on, patches of his face remained black and blue after their fight on the ice. "You look like shit."

"Nice stitches," Eric shot back.

Jason tugged gently on Luscious's leash, trying to get the dog to stop straining. It worked. "I'm being benched next game thanks to you, you asshole."

Eric was unapologetic. "Hey, don't blame me for your lack of control."

"That crap you said about Delilah—"

"Was meant to rile you, and it worked." Eric's mouth twisted with scorn. "You're such an easy mark."

"Only when it comes to my girlfriend."

"Speaking of whom"—Eric gestured at the dogs taking up the sidewalk—"is she sick?"

"No, her assistant quit. I figure if I pick up some of the slack, she can find his replacement faster." Jason frowned. "She won't go anywhere when she's boarding dogs, which is the case most weekends, apparently."

Eric shrugged lightly. "I'll spot her for a couple of hours if she'll let me."

"Yeah?"

"Sure, what the hell? How hard could it be to dog sit?"

"Famous last words." Jason regarded Eric suspiciously. "Why are you being so nice all of a sudden?"

"I'm nice to you all the time, prick bag."

Jason snorted.

"I am!" Eric looked indignant. "Hey, who saved your ass with Delilah's mother?"

"You're right. I stand corrected." Jason nodded curtly at the imperious doorman as he delivered Quigley, Miranda, and Luscious back to their homes. "I'm heading over to

Delilah's after this," he told his brother. "Come with me, and we can present our case."

Delilah knew it was wicked, but she actually enjoyed picturing Jason being overrun by the dogs. She had no intention of sending him out again in Marcus's place. She just wanted him to see that proper dog walking wasn't something any idiot with a leash and a bag of biscuits could do.

She'd placed an ad in the paper for Marcus's replacement and had put out the word among her acquaintances at the dog park. The truth was, she didn't mind carrying the business on her own shoulders for a while. It was more important she find the right person than rush into hiring someone.

Jason materialized at her apartment half an hour late, with Eric in tow. Seeing the frazzled look on her lover's face, it took all Delilah's restraint not to burst out laughing.

"So, how was it?" she chirped.

Jason wearily raised his palms in surrender. "I apologize. It's not an easy job. You were right."

"Thank you."

"He did have me helping him at the end," Eric pointed out.

"Yeah, you were a big help," Jason jeered. He looked hopefully at Delilah. "Any bites?"

"Jason, I just put the word out today. It might take a while, you know."

"Great."

Delilah chose to ignore the note of displeasure in his voice.

"Well," he continued with a cautious expression, "I might have a temporary solution. For one night, anyway."

"What's that?"

Jason pointed at Eric.

"I don't understand," said Delilah.

"Him." Jason continued pointing at his brother. "He can watch the dogs one night."

Delilah felt the color drain from her face. "You've got to be kidding me."

"Hear me out." Jason came to sit beside her. "All I want is for us to go out to dinner one night with my teammates. It'll be three hours, max. You're telling me Eric can't sit here watching TV for three hours? Especially if the dogs have all been walked before he arrives?"

"But what if there's an emergency?"

"You've got a cell."

That was true. She did have a cell, and it would only be a few hours. She looked at her three dogs. They'd behave for Eric, no problem. But there was no telling how her boarders would react. "I'll do it on one condition," she said.

The brothers exchanged glances. "What's that?"

"Eric has to come and hang out beforehand with the animals so they know him."

"Done," Jason answered. He shot his brother a piercing look. "I'll hang out, too," he added.

It took only a few seconds for the first tentacles of anxiety to begin winding themselves around Delilah. "You swear it will only be a few hours?" she asked Jason.

"Deep breath time," Jason murmured to her under his breath as he wrapped an arm around her shoulder. "You can do this. They're nice people. We're just going to eat and talk. The end."

"I'm not good at talking to people."

Jason rubbed her shoulder. "You talk to people all the time."

"I mean in groups," Delilah clarified, growing more nervous. "I suck at talking to people in groups."

"Pretend they're dogs," Eric suggested. Was he making fun of her? Apparently not, if his helpful expression was any indication.

"It'll be three hours, max, Delilah," Jason repeated. "Anything's doable for three hours."

Delilah's eye caught Eric's. *Do it,* he mouthed, nodding with encouragement. Delilah turned to look at Jason. How could she deny him something so simple? So intrinsic to a relationship?

"All right. Eric can watch the dogs, and we'll go to dinner with your friends."

"Yess!!" Jason squeezed her tight. "They're gonna love you, Delilah. I just know it."

Delilah was intrigued when Jason announced they'd be dining at an Italian restaurant in Bensonhurst, co-owned by his team captain, that had somewhat of a cult status among the Blades. Jason spoke of it with the religious intensity of one about to embark on a pilgrimage, fanning the flames of Delilah's anxiety even more. Was she worthy of a visit to the shrine?

Pathetically, she'd allowed Marcus to dress her. The results were simple but tasteful. Marcus had tried to push funky on her, but Delilah was adamant: if ever there was a woman who couldn't pull off funky, it was she. She did allow him to prevail on the issue of makeup, however, putting on one coat of mascara, a little blush and some clear gloss on her lips. It was hard to admit, but all these years her mother had been right: a little makeup did seem to brighten up her pallor, though she still could see no reason to wear any in her day-to-day life with the dogs.

Her hand was soldered to Jason's as they entered Dante's. The place was packed, which she took as a good sign. "Psst." Jason nudged her, discreetly pointing to a handsome couple with two small children tucked away in a corner. "That's my team captain."

Delilah followed his gaze. The man was good-looking, and the woman, hugely pregnant, was one of the most beautiful women Delilah had ever seen.

"Maybe we should say hi," said Jason, beginning to pull her in their direction.

Delilah stilled him with a touch to the arm. "Let them eat their dinner in peace, Jason. You can always stop over when they're finishing up."

"You're right."

They were led to their table by a wizened waiter named Aldo. Delilah was thrilled to see they were the first to arrive. One of her fears had been that everyone else would be there before she and Jason, and she'd approach the table feeling like she were about to face a firing squad. At least this way, she could compose herself enough to appear relaxed when the others arrived.

They were seated and had just started to enjoy the Pellegrino they'd been served when a man in chef's whites emerged from the kitchen, his arm around a female cop's waist. Jason nudged her again. "That's the captain's brother, Anthony. He's the head chef here."

Delilah studied Anthony. He was broadly built and handsome, and clearly smitten with the policewoman, whom he was escorting to the front of the restaurant. He actually looked forlorn as he kissed the woman good-bye and released her into the night, returning to the kitchen by way of his brother's table. The two shared a strong resemblance.

Just when Delilah thought she might indeed have a few minutes to calm herself down, Jason announced, "They're here." She'd been disappointed when Jason told her Barry and Kelly Fontaine wouldn't be there; at least she vaguely knew Kelly Fontaine. The two couples approaching the table were total strangers. She reminded herself that she, too, was a stranger to them. She put down her glass and rose with Jason to greet them.

"Hey, guys." Jason slid out from behind the table to warmly clasp hands with his teammates. He put an arm around Delilah, for which she was grateful, since the case of nerves she'd been hoping to quell was beginning to dominate. "I want you to meet Delilah." He turned to her. "Delilah, I want you to meet David and Tierney"—an extremely good-looking couple smiled in Delilah's direction—"and Denny and"—Jason hesitated—"Suzie, is it?"

"Suze," the small, freckled woman corrected.

"Rhymes with ooze," Denny offered cheerfully. Suze didn't appear to appreciate the remark.

Everyone sat, and two bottles of wine were ordered for the table. The info Jason had given Delilah on the two other couples was starting to come back. David was the Blades new goalie, and his girlfriend had just moved to New York from Chicago to be with him. Denny was the backup goalie; Jason hadn't said anything about his girlfriend beyond her name. Delilah found herself flanked by Denny on the left. He seemed affable, and comfortable enough with the company at hand to devour half the bread basket before they'd even received their menus.

Delilah held up her menu in front of her like a shield, fretting over what to order. Should she get an appetizer? That would leave no room for dessert. She craved pasta, but if the other two women ate like sparrows, she'd look like a hog if she sucked up a plate of spaghetti. It didn't help that everything on the menu sounded wonderful.

Just when she thought her indecision couldn't get any worse, Anthony Dante appeared, pleasure lighting up his face as he recognized Jason and his teammates.

"Can't get enough of my brother, huh?" His voice was a deep, pleasant ripple. Coupled with his physique, which seemed as solid as any of the athletes seated at the table, Delilah imagined he could be incredibly intimidating. Her eyes brushed the simple gold wedding band on his left ring finger. The cop must have been his wife.

"Let me tell you about tonight's specials," Anthony continued. Delilah had never been to a restaurant where the chef himself came out to relay the additions to the menu, but she could see from the proud look in his eyes that cooking was more than just a job for Anthony; it was his calling. "As an appetizer, we've got acquacotta, a hearty peasant soup made with cabbage and beans."

"Nothing with beans for me," Denny O'Malley chortled. "Not unless you want to clear the restaurant."

Anthony politely ignored him, along with everyone else. "Additional entrées tonight are veal stew with sage, white wine, and cream; and eggplant patties lovingly made with garlic, fresh Parmesan, and parsley. We have some dessert specials as well, but I won't overwhelm you with them now." He bowed deeply. "Aldo will be back shortly to take your orders." He disappeared into the kitchen.

Five minutes later, Aldo appeared, their orders were taken, and the evening officially commenced. Delilah had been hoping she'd be able to fade into the background, nodding and smiling her way through the evening. Instead she found herself immediately in the spotlight.

"So, Jason says you walk dogs for a living," said Denny, swiping another piece of bread from the basket.

"Yes," said Delilah. "I run my own business, the Bed and Biscuit. I board them as well."

Suze wrinkled her nose, moving the bread basket out of her boyfriend's reach. "Doesn't that get kind of stinky? Having dogs in your house?"

"No," said Delilah.

"I'm not a big dog fan," Suze continued. Delilah fought a knee-jerk reaction to instantly dislike her.

"I'm dying for a dog," Tierney confessed with a sigh. "But someone doesn't want one right now." She stared hard at David.

"Hey, don't make me out to be the bad guy here," said David. "You yourself said you didn't know if you had the patience to train a puppy."

"Delilah trains dogs, too," said Jason. He turned to her. "Why don't you give them one of your cards, babe?"

Delilah shook her head frantically. "No—I don't think—"

"C'mon," Jason urged. He turned to the table at large. "She trained my dog, Stanley, like that," he confided, snapping his fingers. Delilah froze as he reached down beneath the table for her purse, extracting her business cards and passing them around the table. Delilah was mortified; she hated the idea of these people thinking Jason was shilling for her, trying to drum up business.

"Delilah Gould," said Denny coolly. "Interesting name."

"I'm definitely going to hang on to this," said Tierney, tucking the card into her own purse. Her smile was friendly as she regarded Delilah across the table. "Are you enjoying going out with a hockey player?"

"Yes. I mean I never dated an athlete before so that's been new especially adjusting to his schedule and such and I don't like seeing him get hit on the ice but so far so good."

Tierney nodded slowly as if she were not quite sure how to respond. *Shit*, Delilah thought with mounting panic. Babbling Brook was coming out of hiding. Delilah reached for her wineglass, practically chugging down the contents. *Speak slowly,* she told herself. *Small sentences. Slow.*

She sat back and listened while Jason, Denny, and David talked hockey. She supposed when there was a break in the conversation she should ask something of Suze. Or Tierney. That was how it worked. People asked about you, and you asked back.

"So what do you do?" she blurted.

Momentary silence blanketed the table.

"Who, me?" Suze asked, looking confused.

Delilah nodded.

"She's a full-time pain in the ass," Denny offered.

Suze's expression was deadpan. "Denny missed his calling as a comedian." She turned back to Delilah. "I'm a nursery school teacher."

"That must be fun. And you?" she said to Tierney.

"I was a concierge at a Chicago hotel. I'm looking for work right now."

Delilah nodded woodenly, unsure of her next move. Had she messed this up? She probably should have asked Suze a follow-up question rather than turn to Tierney right away. Now Suze would think she didn't really care, and Tierney didn't seen eager to elaborate on her job search. Delilah reached for her wine and took another gulp.

"Slow down with wine, okay?" Jason said under his breath. Delilah didn't respond. As discreetly as she could, she wiped her increasingly clammy palms on the cloth napkin in her lap. She couldn't wait for the food to arrive. She would chew and chew and not have to talk and chew.

Denny glanced at Jason's chin. "When do your stitches come out, my man?"

"I'll probably pull them out myself in a day or two," Jason replied dismissively.

David shook his head. "Your brother's a monster on the ice."

Delilah piped up. "He's nice in real life, though." Jason shot her a sideways glance, but it was so fast she didn't know whether it meant *Be quiet,* or *Good, say something, so they know you have a brain.*

Delilah continued, "Eric came to brunch with me at my mom's house once when Jason was too hungover. I didn't know Jason was hungover at the time he actually lied to me and said he was sick but anyway he sent Eric in his place because I'd told my mother I had a boyfriend and she'd been nagging me to meet him and so, well, Jason wasn't really my boyfriend yet, but anyway Eric came in his place and it went really well."

There was stunned silence. Delilah twisted her napkin in her hands. "I'll shut up now," she announced to no one in particular as she shrank back in her seat.

"That might not be a bad idea," Jason said in a very low voice, looking pained.

A sudden rush of tears came to Delilah's eyes, and she blinked them back. Jason was ashamed of her, which was unfair. She'd warned him she didn't do well in groups, but he'd pushed her anyway. He was as much to blame for her ineptitude this evening as she was.

By the end of the night, Delilah was of the opinion that Denny O'Malley was a coarse moron and that Suze, despite her dislike of dogs, was too good for him. David and Tierney were incredibly nice, especially Tierney, who kept trying throughout the evening to engage Delilah. Delilah got the sense she actually cared whether or not Delilah was having a good time.

She couldn't say the same for Jason.

CHAPTER
16

"Well, that was a disaster."

Jason had promised himself he'd be gentle with Delilah on the ride back to the city. But the minute he pulled out of Dante's parking lot, all the frustration he'd held in check over the course of the evening began bubbling over, and he couldn't hold his tongue.

Delilah said nothing, which only increased Jason's frustration. He wanted her to vehemently defend herself. He wanted to *fight.* He was glad when she finally gave him something to work with by murmuring, "It wasn't that bad."

"From whose perspective? You babbled. You blurted."

He got what he wanted: Delilah's eyes flashed with anger. "I told you I didn't do well with groups of people!"

"You have to learn to, Delilah! Otherwise, you're doomed."

"You mean *we're* doomed."

"Yeah. Maybe. I don't know."

Jason put on the AC, despite it being late November. High emotion had him perspiring. He waited for Delilah to protest, but she didn't. Maybe she was afraid to.

They drove in interminable silence. Jason turned on the radio, surfed, turned the radio off. Every song annoyed him, as did the manufactured, convivial patter of every DJ. Silence was better, even if it was the stony kind.

Eventually Delilah blurted, "If you want to break up with me, do it now!"

That was his cue. Jason pulled the car over. "I don't want to break up with you."

"Then what?" said Delilah, flicking off the AC. Glaring, Jason leaned forward to turn it back on, then stopped: Delilah's hands were shoved deep in the pockets of her coat, her scarf wound tightly around her neck. She was freezing her ass off. Jason compromised by opening his window just a crack, grateful for the thin gust of cold air tickling the back of the head.

"I want you to get help," he said.

Delilah cocked her head as if she hadn't heard him quite right. Ironically, she reminded him of the RCA dog. "Excuse me?"

"Lots of people suffer from social anxiety, Delilah. And they get help. They go see a therapist or take drugs."

"What kind of drugs?"

"The kind that make you less anxious," he offered face-tiously.

Delilah's eyes burned like two coals in the dark of the car. "I'm not taking drugs."

"Fine." Jason was annoyed she rejected this option out of hand without even considering it. "Then talk to someone. There has to be some kind of support group: I'm Afraid of Humans Anonymous or something."

"Now you're just being mean."

"You don't think you have a problem?"

Delilah stared down at her lap. "I do, but I don't think it's as bad as you make it out to be."

"It's bad enough to make you want to avoid groups of people."

"You know, not everyone likes to socialize in large groups."

"No, but I do."

"Well, I don't. I'm shy."

"You're more than shy. You're—"

"What?" Delilah challenged.

Jason paused, taking time to choose his words carefully. He cared about Delilah. He did not want to wound her with any further criticism, especially since he got the feeling that was the root cause of her problem in the first place. On the other hand, he didn't see how they could move forward as a couple unless they faced this difference between them head-on. Maybe he was selfish, but all he could think was: how was he supposed to relax in company if he knew she was miserable, or if he worried about what might come out of her mouth?

"Well?" Delilah prompted.

"You're more than shy. You've got some kind of phobia."

"I talk to you. I talk to Marcus. I talk to salespeople and clients and other dog walkers."

"Congratulations: you're not a complete social cripple." Delilah flinched. "I didn't mean that," he said, reaching out to touch her. Delilah pushed his hand away.

"This is why dogs are better. They don't criticize. They don't *say* hateful things."

"They also don't hug you, kiss you, make passionate love to you, tell you you're beautiful, make you laugh, take you to the dog show, or defend you against refrigerator-sized assholes in the park."

"That's true," Delilah said quietly.

Jason reached again for her hand; this time she let him take it. "I'm not asking you to completely change your personality," he said, brushing his lips against her knuckle. "I'd just like us to enjoy going out with people without it being a major source of stress for you."

Delilah seemed impatient. "I know, but can I point something out?"

"Sure."

"You were bored senseless at the dog show."

"That's not true."

"Jason, you fell asleep! Not only that, but if your schedule allowed it, you'd be out every night of the week." Delilah peered at him accusingly. "Am I right?"

"I just moved to Manhattan! Do you have any idea how amazing this city is to me? How much stuff I want to do?"

"You're right to want to explore everything the city has to offer. But our 'problem,' if you want to call it that, isn't just my shyness. It's that we like different things." She dropped his hand. "Tell me your idea of a perfect evening."

Jason squirmed. "I can't answer that."

"Try."

Jason forced himself to be honest. "A perfect evening would be the Blades completely destroying another team out on the ice—preferably my brother's—followed by you and me partying afterward with a group of my friends. It would conclude with you and me having mind-blowing sex."

"Want to hear my version of a perfect evening?"

No, thought Jason, but he nodded anyway.

"My perfect evening is: you come over to my place, we order in pizza, we watch *Animal Planet* or a movie we've rented, and then we go to bed and make love."

"That sounds okay."

Delilah looked surprised. "Does it?"

"Occasionally."

"How often is 'occasionally'?"

"Once a week?"

"How about half the week? To be fair?"

"I'm usually playing hockey at least three nights a week. Sometimes four."

"Fine." Delilah sounded huffy. "Let's say you've got four games one week, which leaves us with three evenings free. How are we spending them?"

Jason felt the first stirrings of tension at the base of his neck. "This is one of those trick questions, isn't it?"

"Just answer."

"I'd say we spent two evenings out—not necessarily with

friends, maybe just going to the movies or out to dinner"—
he said in a rush—"and one evening in."

Delilah shook her head. "Two evenings in, one out."

"No way."

"No way to what *you* want!" Delilah retorted.
"Especially if I'm boarding dogs."

Jason ran his hands back and forth over the top of the
steering wheel. "Maybe you could gradually phase out that
part of your business."

Delilah looked indignant. "You're not serious."

"Yeah, I am."

"I need the money, Jason. I'm self-employed."

Jason shrugged easily. "I'll give you the money to make
up for that part of your business."

"No!"

"You don't want to give it up because it gives you an excuse to be a hermit," Jason accused.

"I don't want to give it up because it helps me pay my
rent, and I enjoy doing it! You enjoy hockey, don't you?"

"Hockey isn't interfering with our relationship!"

"Says who?"

Jason scrubbed his hands over his face. "We're going
around in circles here."

"No kidding." Delilah sounded tearful.

Jason's hand groped for hers. "I care about you, Delilah.
I want this to work."

"Me, too."

"Then we're going to have to figure out some compro-
mises."

Her hand squeezed his. "Like what?"

Jason looked at her sadly. "I don't know."

"What's the matter, dolly? You seem distracted."

Delilah shook herself out of her daydream to see her father peering at her with concern. He and Brandi had come
in to the city to "treat" Delilah to Sunday brunch, a gesture
she could hardly turn down. Ever since she'd consented to

shop with Brandi, her future "stepmother" considered them
fast friends, and Delilah was too much of a wuss to disabuse
her of that notion. Plus, it seemed a small price to pay to
make her father happy.

"It's nothing," Delilah fibbed. The last thing she wanted
to do was confide her romantic woes to her father. The man
had sparred his way through nearly thirty years of marriage
and was now engaged to a living, breathing Barbie doll. She
was better off turning to Marcus for relationship advice.

Her father crinkled his eyes. "Don't lie to me, Leelee.
And while we're at it, finish those eggs. You're way too
thin."

Delilah ate a mouthful of runny eggs to please him.
"Better?"

"I'd be happier if you cleaned your plate. Now what's
wrong?"

"Just—stuff." Delilah pushed aside the sausage her father had insisted she order to the side of her plate.
"Boyfriend stuff."

Her father's hackles immediately went up. "He's treating
you well, right?"

"He's treating me fine, Dad." Delilah reached for a piece
of toast. "We just have a few differences we need to iron
out. That's all."

"If you say so." He looked unconvinced. "Why didn't
you bring him with you today?"

"He left for a road trip this morning." This time Delilah
wasn't lying.

Delilah couldn't decide if Jason's leaving so soon on the
heels of their disastrous date was a blessing or a curse.
Maybe a few days apart would give them time to mull over
what they'd discussed and what, if anything, could be done
about it. But Jason's departure also left Delilah with a lingering sense of uncertainty; she hated that they'd parted
without any real closure.

"How's his team doing?" her father asked.

Delilah knew her father; he had zero interest in sports
whatsoever. Yet here he was, making an effort in a noncriti-

cal, minimally intrusive way. She wished her mother were here to learn a thing or two.

"They're doing well. They're leading their division right now."

"Very nice," said her father.

"How's that other hockey player doing?" Brandi asked, staring innocently at Delilah over her mimosa. "You know, that friend of yours we ran into after shopping?"

"He's fine," Delilah said tersely. Brandi wasn't supposed to be thinking about Eric. Not while she was sitting next to Delilah's father.

Brandi sipped her drink. "He was nice."

"He's my boyfriend's brother."

"They both play hockey?" Delilah's father seemed surprised. "It must be a very athletic family."

Brandi suppressed a giggle, while the insinuation seemed to fly right over Delilah's father's head.

"They grew up in North Dakota, Dad. There wasn't much else to do."

"As long as he's treating you well," her father reiterated.

"He is."

"I'd like to meet him sometime."

"You will."

"Does he have a good mattress?"

"Dad."

"Don't 'Dad' me, Delilah. A good mattress is crucial to one's health, as you know. You tell him if he needs a good mattress, he should come to me. I'll give him a great deal."

"I'll tell him. I promise," Delilah muttered. Anything to get off the subject of mattresses, which her father could go on about for hours.

Her father grunted into his salami and eggs, then asked offhandedly how her mother was. Delilah couldn't hide her surprise; usually her father waited until Brandi was off "powdering her nose," or at the very least out of earshot, before enquiring after Mitzi.

"She's fine." At least that's what Delilah assumed. They

hadn't spoken since Mitzi had lured Delilah out to Long Island for the "emergency."

"I heard through the grapevine that *schlemiel* she was seeing dumped her." There was a touch of unrepentant glee in her father's voice. "For Myra Talman, of all people. That had to sting."

"Dad, why do you care? I mean, really?" Delilah stole a quick glance at Brandi. She didn't seem to be listening, fascinated instead with twirling the tiny paper umbrella that came with her drink.

"I don't care," her father insisted gruffly. "I just hear things."

Things you sniff around for, thought Delilah. "Can we change the subject, please?"

Her father frowned. "Sure." He took another bite of salami. "How's business?"

"It's going great, except it's a little crazy right now: I lost my assistant, and I haven't found a new one."

"I'll help you!" Brandi volunteered.

Delilah smiled politely. "I thought you were working at the spalon."

Brandi's eyes began filling up. "I got fired."

God, please don't let her weep into her huevos rancheros, Delilah prayed. She supposed she should feign concern. "What happened—if you don't mind me asking."

Brandi cast down her eyes. "I messed up a spray-on tan."

"The woman had orange and white stripes!" Delilah's father hooted. "She looked like a creamsicle with eyes!"

"It's not funny, Sy!"

Delilah's father patted Brandi's hand. "I know, bunny wunny, I know." Delilah didn't like the expectant look in his eyes as he turned to her. "Brandi could be a wonderful asset to you, Leelee."

"I love dogs," Brandi added.

"I appreciate the offer of help," said Delilah, trying to keep in check the feeling of being guilted into something she didn't want to do, "but it doesn't make much sense. You live out on Long Island, Brandi."

"So? I'll commute in."

"No offense, but when we went shopping I got the sense that you weren't a big fan of the city. You seemed obsessed with crime."

"No one's gonna hurt me if I'm protected by doggies," Brandi pointed out brightly.

There was no way Delilah was going to win this one. If she turned Brandi down, her father would begin lobbying by phone day and night, and Brandi would do the same. It was easier to let Brandi try it and then quit.

"Let's give it a try then," said Delilah. "We can work out the details later."

"Oh, goody!" Brandi clasped her hands together. "I can't wait to work with the dogs! And get to know everyone in the neighborhood."

Delilah smiled sweetly. "I'll bet."

"Yo, Mitchie."

Jason hated admitting it, but he'd been avoiding David and Denny since dinner the night before. He'd shown up at Met Gar in the sourest of moods, convinced they were going tease him about Delilah. Now, hearing Denny's voice behind him as he was about to climb onto the team bus, he knew he'd simply been forestalling the inevitable. Jason stepped aside to make room so others could board.

"What's up?" Jason asked, turning up the collar of his coat. He couldn't believe how cold it could get in the open-air tunnel between Met Gar and the adjoining train station, the wind whipping through with a vengeance. It reminded him of standing on the school bus stop in North Dakota as a child. He and Eric would freeze their nuts off. It would get so cold their snot would freeze before it even had a chance to leak from their noses.

"Last night was fun," said Denny.

"Yeah," Jason agreed cautiously.

Denny's mouth tilted into a slight smirk. "Your girl-friend's a little shy."

"She can be."

"I have to confess," Denny continued with a derogatory chuckle, "that I was a little surprised."

"Why? Lots of people are shy."

"No, not that." Denny glanced around. "You know."

"No, I don't know."

"C'mon, dude. Think."

Jason was in no mood to play games. "I have no idea what the fuck you're talking about, Denny."

Denny leaned in and whispered, "I was surprised you're going out with a Jew."

Jason felt as if someone had just kicked his heart up into his throat. "What did you say?"

"C'mon. Delilah *Gould*? Total Hebe name."

Jason grabbed Denny and threw him up against the side of the bus. "I should beat the shit out of you right now."

"Go ahead," Denny sneered. "Kike lover," he added under his breath.

Jason's right fist landed a solid blow to Denny's jaw. Denny looked dazed for a second; then he began swinging wildly. It was no use: Jason had him pinned like a butterfly mounted for exhibit. Jason used it to his advantage, landing two more short jabs to Denny's ribs before releasing him with a shove. Denny crumpled to the asphalt with a groan. Before Jason could get in a much-desired kick, two of his teammates jumped in, holding him back. Struggling against them, Jason watched as two more helped the dazed Denny to his feet.

"Someone want to tell me what the fuck is going on here?" Ty Gallagher's voice echoed ominously through the tunnel as he strode into the center of the melee.

"It's nothing," said Jason. He tried to shake off the teammates restraining him, but they wouldn't let him go.

"Don't give me the 'It's nothing' line of bullshit. It doesn't wash." Ty inspected Denny and his rapidly swelling jaw. "What did you say to him?"

"I didn't say anything!" Denny protested.

"Don't insult my intelligence, O'Malley." Ty pushed

Denny's handlers away, planting himself in front of him. "I'll ask it another way: Why did he hit you?"

Denny hesitated. "I dissed his girlfriend."

"Good one." Ty's glare was cringe-inducing. "I'm trying to build a team here, and you two are fighting like pussies on the playground."

Jason hung his head. "I'm sorry, Coach."

"You should know by now that sorry doesn't cut it." Ty turned to Denny. "You. Get your ass on the bus. *Now.*"

Denny nodded, holding his face as he dragged himself onto the bus.

"Get one of the trainers to give you some ice!" Ty barked after him. He wheeled around to Jason, his expression of disgust holding steady.

"You gentlemen can get on the bus, too," he told Jason's teammates. Jason hadn't realized how hard they were holding him until they released him: His arms were throbbing as he waited for Ty to tear him a new one.

Ty took his time, staring at Jason as if he were an exotic yet somewhat repulsive specimen in the zoo he'd never seen before. The longer he stared, the more Jason longed to yell in sheer frustration. Finally Ty just shook his head sadly and sighed. "What the hell am I going to do with you?"

"With all respect, Coach—"

"Did I say you could talk?" Ty snapped.

"No."

"Nice to see you're not deaf." Ty tilted back his head, staring up at the concrete ceiling. "I'm trying to think of a nice way to say this."

Jason awaited his coach's next pronouncement. The longer they stood there with everyone else on the idling bus, the more time Denny had with their teammates to spin his version of what happened. Jason didn't want this ugly incident hanging over the rest of the season. He was relieved when Ty finally deigned to speak to him.

"I don't care if O'Malley said your girlfriend is a dead ringer for Jabba the Hutt. I care about one thing: the team. Fighting fucks that up. It wrecks morale, and I won't have it. If you want a future with this *team*, Jason, you better start thinking seriously about impulse control both on *and* off the ice. Am I making myself clear?"

"Totally."

"Good. Now get on the bus."

Jason nodded humbly and climbed up on to the bus, which fell silent. Not quite looking at anyone, he scoured both sides of the aisle for a seat. There was one open next to Michael Dante. That was out, since that's where Ty usually sat. The other available seat was next to Denny O'Malley. Jason would never understand God's perverse sense of humor as he made his way down the aisle to sit beside the man who judged his girlfriend on her religion, not her personality or values. Neither said a word the entire way to the airport.

CHAPTER

17

"I've never seen a dog that big in my life!"

The childlike wonder in Brandi's voice almost made Delilah like her. Delilah had just brought Stanley downstairs from her apartment, and together she and Brandi were taking him to the park. Jason paid extra to have him walked privately, and Delilah enjoyed spending time alone with Stanley. It was fun to see people's reactions to him. Plus, silly though it might be, it was a way for her to feel close to Jason.

Stanley wasn't built for speed. Even so, Brandi was struggling to keep up with them. "You might want to wear sneakers rather than high heels if you're serious about wanting to help," Delilah pointed out.

Brandi glanced down at her Candies. "I guess you're right." She eyed Stan nervously. "Does he bite?"

"Does he look like he bites?"

Brandi bit her lip. "No. He looks like a big mush."

"He *is* a big mush." Delilah patted his back affectionately. "Aren't you, Stan?"

A woman and small girl approached. As they drew

closer, the little girl's eyes doubled in size. "Mommy, look! Beethoven!"

"I saw that movie!" Brandi chimed in.

The mother flashed an indulgent smile and quickly moved the child along.

Brandi watched them go. "Wasn't Beethoven actually a Saint Bernard?" she asked after a considerable pause.

"Yup." Delilah was impressed; not everyone knew the difference between a Newf and a Saint Bernard. Maybe Brandi wasn't a total ding-dong after all.

Delilah took a deep breath, enjoying the rush of cold air to her lungs. There was a metallic tang to the air; it felt like it might snow. Delilah hoped it didn't. Walking dogs in the snow could be a huge pain in the butt, and it distressed her when people paved the snowy sidewalks with rock salt, not knowing or caring how irritating it could be to dogs' paws.

"So, um, could I ask you a question?"

Brandi's high, squeaky voice never failed to catch Delilah by surprise. How could her father stand it, day in, day out? Perhaps he'd lost both his mind *and* his hearing.

"Sure," said Delilah.

"Why did your parents break up?"

Delilah wasn't sure how to respond. "I'm sure my father's told you all about it," she said.

"Yes, but he's, you know, biased."

"So am I." Delilah couldn't help herself. "What did he say?"

Brandi sighed with the relief of someone who's been holding in something forever, and had finally been given the green light to speak. "Well, he said she could be a drama queen and a bitch and that she accused him of having an affair with his secretary but he wasn't but she wouldn't listen and he thinks she just wanted him out so he wouldn't dirty up her white house."

Terror struck Delilah's heart. Was that what *she* sounded like when she babbled? If so, Jason was right: she was doomed and needed help.

"It had nothing to do with the house," said Delilah. She opened the gate to the dog park, ushering Stanley inside.

"Then what?" asked Brandi, kicking up a small spray of gravel with each shuffling step.

"They fought all the time." Delilah unclipped Stanley's leash, and he immediately trotted off to play with Tango, his shepherd friend at the dog park. And to think that just a few months ago Stanley couldn't even relate to another dog! Delilah filled with pride. She'd done her job well.

"If they fought all the time, then why does he still want to know about her?" Brandi sat down on the nearest bench and took off her right shoe, massaging her cramped toes. "I hear him on the phone sometimes with his friends. He's always asking about her, wanting to know what this one's heard or what that one knows. It bothers me."

Much to her surprise, Delilah actually felt sympathetic. "They still have a lot of mutual friends, Brandi. And they were married for close to thirty years. You can't just erase that overnight."

Brandi pressed her lips together. "I guess."

Delilah longed to ask *her* a question or two, like, *Do you really love my father, or do you just want his money?* She suspected it was a bit of both. She had no doubt Brandi was fond of her father. But it was Sy's net worth that enabled Brandi to look past the liver spots, of that Delilah was sure.

"Ladies!"

Delilah turned. *Eric.* She couldn't believe it. Jason wasn't kidding when he said Eric had an innate GPS. He was jogging toward the dog park with a big smile on his face. Delilah shot a quick look at Brandi. Her poutiness was rapidly transforming itself into the mindless vivacity Delilah knew all too well. She made a decision right there: if Brandi flirted wildly with Eric, Delilah was going to go running to her daddy and tell.

Eric entered the park and flopped down on the bench beside Brandi, breathless and sweating. "God, I hate exercising."

Brandi looked surprised. "But you're an athlete."

"All the more reason I hate having to do it in my spare time." He mopped his brow, gaze scouring the dog park. "Ah! There's my nephew."

"Nephew?" Brandi looked totally confused.

Eric pointed at Stanley. "That black beast over there is my brother's dog."

"He's a mush."

"I think you mean wuss."

"Hey!" Delilah protested. "No one's allowed to say anything mean about Stanley. Got it?"

"Wouldn't dream of it." Eric tilted his head back and shot a stream of Gatorade down his throat. "So, Brandi." His voice was caressing.

Delilah tensed.

"I've been meaning to call you about those hockey tickets, but things have been kind of crazy."

"Oh, don't worry about it," Brandi assured him. "I've been busy, too."

"Yeah, doing what?" His gaze slowly crept down to Brandi's cleavage. "Acting?"

"Planning my wedding."

Eric deflated. "Oh."

Delilah suppressed a smirk.

"But I'd still love to go to a game," Brandi enthused.

Shit.

Eric smiled flirtatiously. "Should I call the number at the spa-thingie?"

"You mean, the spalon?" Brandi whispered in a pained voice.

Eric nodded.

"I was fired."

Eric looked indignant. "How could anyone *ever* fire you?"

He was laying it on so thick Delilah wished she had a trowel she could hand him.

"It's okay, though," Brandi continued. "I'm going to be helping out Delilah."

"Really."

"Temporarily," Delilah clarified.

"Well, Jason will be glad," Eric said to Delilah. He regarded Brandi. "Jason is my brother, by the way. He's also Delilah's boyfriend."

"Yes, Leelee mentioned that at brunch the other day," said Brandi.

"Leelee?" Eric snorted.

Delilah gave Eric the death stare. "It's a childhood nickname." She rose. "We should be getting back. The dogs need to be fed." She handed Brandi Stanley's leash. "Why don't you go see if you can get this on Stanley and bring him over here?"

"Oh. Okay." Brandi looked displeased with her assignment, but she did what she was told. As soon as she crossed the park, Delilah poked Eric in the shoulder.

"You better quit this right now."

"Quit what?"

"You know what! She's engaged to my father! If you wreck his life, I will break your knees with a baseball bat. I will tie you down and have Stanley stand over you and drool. I will shove your hockey stick up your—nose."

Eric's eyes flashed with surprise. "Delilah! I never knew you were so feisty."

"I'm not kidding, Eric."

"I can see that," Eric replied, sounding impressed. His eyes were glued to Brandi. "How old's your father?"

"Sixty-seven."

"You think she really loves him?"

"She better."

Eric squirted more Gatorade down his throat. "You think he really loves her?"

Now there was a question worth pondering. Did her father really love Brandi? He certainly seemed smitten. And having someone so young and beautiful on his arm had to be a huge boost to his male ego. But love? That thing her parents seemed to share when they weren't fighting? No way.

"I don't know," Delilah answered, noticing that Brandi

was having trouble getting Stanley to budge. "But it's no concern of yours."

She threw Eric a final look of warning before calling out "Stanley, *up*!" in exasperation. Hearing Delilah's command, Stanley reluctantly rose to his feet and ambled toward them, Brandi smiling proudly as if she'd been the one to get him moving. *God help me,* thought Delilah.

Eric stood. "It was nice seeing you again, Brandi."

Brandi blushed deeply. "You, too, Eric."

"Good-bye, Eric," Delilah said loudly.

Eric winked at her over his shoulder as he jogged off. "See you 'round the campus, Leelee."

"*Are you gonna* tell me what the hell happened?"

Jason stopped brooding into his beer long enough to lift his head and consider David Hewson's question. The two were sharing a drink following the Blades' 4–2 victory over Indiana, the second goal courtesy of Jason. Returning to the hotel after the game, Jason had proceeded directly to his room with every intention of holing up and calling it a night. But David wouldn't let him. "One drink," David cajoled, "just to take the edge off." Since Jason's edge had been dangerously sharp since boarding the bus back in New York, he agreed.

Though all the Blades knew there had been a fight, Jason was certain no one but he and Denny knew the details: their teammates treated both of them the same as always, though he did detect an undercurrent of wariness, as if Ty's displeasure might somehow rub off on them. Jason understood completely.

Denny's words had haunted him all the way to Indianapolis. Jason couldn't believe the ease with which such poison had slid off his teammate's tongue. He couldn't believe he had the balls to say something so sickening aloud. Obviously, Denny knew what he was saying was offensive; why else would he have he spoken to Jason in hushed tones? The whole confrontation left Jason feeling bewildered and betrayed. How could one friend say to another what Denny said to him and think it was okay? He thought he knew Denny. Apparently he was wrong.

Jason sipped his beer, wondering how best to answer David's question. "We had words," was all he'd offer. "That's all."

David raised his eyebrows. "They must have been some pretty powerful words for you to deck him."

Jason grunted in response. He was surprised David was pressing this. It was rare, but not unheard of, for two players on the same team to fight. When they did, they usually kept the reason to themselves, especially if there was no one else there to witness the dispute. Even then, a code of silence tended to prevail. As Ty had so forcefully pointed out, when all was said and done, it was an issue of morale. The more people who knew, the higher the odds of distraction—for everyone.

Perhaps sensing Jason had no intention of divulging any more details, David changed the subject. "I had a good time the other night. Your girlfriend seemed really nice."

Jason's eyes hooded. Was David mocking him? "She can be a little shy," Jason replied.

He waited for David to chime in with some comment about Delilah's bumbling and fumbling, but he didn't. "That's okay. It just takes some people a while to warm up."

"She's not big on socializing in groups," Jason continued.

David seemed unfazed. "Some people aren't."

Who are you, friggin' Gandhi? Jason thought with irritation. It dawned on him that he'd been hoping David would confirm his own belief that Delilah's extreme shyness was unusual, even unacceptable. That he didn't gave Jason pause; maybe he was overreacting to Delilah's ineptitude.

The bar door swung open, and Denny entered, along with Thad Meyers and Tully Webster. It was inevitable the trio would make their way over to where Jason and David were sitting; they were teammates, after all. Thad reached the table first, slapping Jason on the back.

"Good game."

"You, too," said Jason. He could feel Denny staring at him and returned the favor, saddened by the contempt in his eyes.

Jew lover, Denny mouthed silently.

Jason crushed his right hand into a fist beneath the table. Why the fuck was Denny trying to provoke him? He heard Ty's voice in his head telling him to exercise control. He wondered how controlled Ty would be if someone insulted his wife. Answer: not very.

Thad pointed to the three empty chairs at the table. "Mind if we join you?"

It was a simple question with no hint of challenge or sub-text. Whatever hostility existed was purely between himself and Denny.

"That would be great," said David, flashing Jason a quick look of confirmation. Jason nodded curtly, even though the last thing he wanted was to bend an elbow with Denny. In fact, what he really wanted to do was crush Denny's melon-sized head like a grape. But since that would be considered unacceptable social behavior, even between boneheaded jocks, he refrained.

As Jason knew he would, Denny sat down right next to him. Jason drained the final dregs of his beer, noticing David was already done. "Next round's on me," he announced.

"Get the fuck out of here," David scoffed. "You paid last round."

"Hey, let him pay," said Denny with a smirk. "You've got access to a lot of money now, right, Jace?"

Tully looked at Jason with envy. "You SOB! You land an endorsement deal?"

"Something like that," Jason muttered as he pushed his chair back from the table and headed to the bar, as much to place orders as get the hell out of Denny's orbit. There was no fucking way he was going to spend the rest of the night—or the rest of the season, for that matter—dealing with this bullshit. No way.

He returned to the table with five Guinness drafts, thanked by everyone but Denny. If anyone else noticed, they didn't say. Together, they conducted a post mortem on the evening's game, each one with his own opinion on what went wrong and what went right. It seemed Denny had decided to give the hate mongering a rest. Then Jason leaned over to grab a tortilla from the plastic basket at the center of the table, and the gold crucifix from his mother fell free from his shirt. Back in New York, he only wore it during games. But on the road he wore it all the time, a safeguard against losing it.

"Nice necklace," Denny observed quietly. "Though I would have thought a Star of David—"

Jason grabbed Denny by the throat, lifting him spluttering out of his chair. He didn't give a flying fuck if Ty suspended him for life, or even sent him back down to the minors. This crap was going to stop here and now.

"Shut your mouth now, or I'll shut it for you."

Tully, Thad, and David jumped to their feet in alarm.

"Jesus Christ, Jason." David looked disturbed as he pried Jason's fingers from around Denny's throat. "What the hell is going on?"

"Asshole," Denny rasped. He looked embarrassed at having been physically bested, shaking himself off before storming off in the direction of the exit. "The fuck you lookin' at?" he snarled at no one in particular as all eyes in the bar watched him go.

Tully stared at Jason with pity. "I so would not want to be you when the coach finds out about this, dude."

"Yeah, yeah, yeah," Jason muttered. He tucked his cross back into his shirt and departed before the bartender had a chance to throw him out.

Jason was neither surprised nor alarmed when Michael Dante called a team meeting the next day. Jason knew word would get back to Ty and Michael about him and Denny mixing it up again; he also knew there was no way either of them was going to cough up the reason why, unless they were totally, balls to the wall pressed.

The mood was somber as the team filed into one of the hotel's conference rooms. Michael was already there. Ty was not. Jason could imagine the discussion that must have taken place between the two, Ty reminding Michael that as Blades captain, it was his responsibility to squash team disputes before they mushroomed into something more serious. Despite the ring of empty chairs circling the sleek, oblong table at the center of the room, Michael had chosen to stand against the far wall, arms crossed against his chest. The team followed suit, everyone standing rather than sitting. Jason had no idea whether it was conscious or not, but most of the players stood at a distance from Michael, a fact their captain noticed immediately.

"I'm not gonna bite, you *cafones*. Come closer so I don't have to yell to be heard. That would put me in a really bad mood. And you do not want to see me in a bad mood, *capisce*?"

The team shuffled closer to Michael. Jason had visions of the door swinging shut behind them, trapping them inside forever. He felt as if he was being sealed up in a vault; there were no windows, no air moving. Michael enjoined the team to form a semicircle around him before employing Ty's time-honored technique of making eye contact with each player. Jason waited his turn; when it came to him, Michael's gaze lingered. Jason looked back unflinchingly. He'd had a whole night to think about his actions, and the conclusion he'd come to was this: he may not have dealt with Denny in the most effective or intelligent way, but he knew what he'd done was *right*.

"Okay." Michael looked grim. "Just in case some of you boys have been in a coma and don't know why I've called this meeting, I'll lay it out: Mitchell's attacked O'Malley twice, and no one seems to know why." Michael's gaze lit on Jason. "Care to share?"

Jason shook his head, fixing his gaze on a spot on the

wall right above Michael's head. He heard Michael sigh in frustration. "What about you, O'Malley?"

"No idea at all," Denny said.

You lying sack of shit, Jason thought, his pulse ratcheting up. If he could get away with clocking the asshole again, he would.

Jason looked at Michael, who was rubbing a weary hand over his face. *"Madonn',"* he marveled to himself, "I'm captain of a team of idiots." Someone snorted and Michael's world-weary expression turned into a glare. "Something funny?" There was a nervous cough and the room returned to silence.

"One more time." Michael came and planted himself right in front of Jason. The two men locked eyes. "What happened?"

"Nothing."

"Son of a goddamn bitch," Michael muttered. He approached Denny. "What happened?"

"Nothing," Denny echoed.

"So, Mitchell hit you for no reason." Michael shook his head, frustration in his eyes. "What am I going to do with you two? Murder's against the law, so that's out."

"Fine Mitchell," Denny murmured under his breath.

Michael thrust his head forward. "What did you say?"

"I said, 'Fine Mitchell.' "

"Why should I do that?"

"It'll hit him where it hurts," Denny explained. He shot Jason a sidelong glance. "Mitchell's become very cheap all of a sudden." Denny chuckled at what he obviously believed to be his own cleverness.

"Explain," Michael demanded sharply.

"What?" Denny asked, all innocence.

"What do you mean, 'Mitchell's become very cheap all of a sudden'?"

Denny shrugged. "It's just, you know, he's hanging out with people who don't like to part with their money."

Michael looked completely exasperated. "What the hell are you talking about, O'Malley?"

"You know." Denny started to hum "If I Were A Rich Man" from *Fiddler on the Roof.*

Jason thought: *You've just dug your own grave, you idiot.* He could see Michael piecing two and two together, disbelief pinching his face as the source of the conflict became clear to him.

"Let me make sure I'm getting this straight," Michael said slowly. "You've got a problem because you think Mitchell is Jewish?"

"He's not Jewish," said Denny. "His girlfriend is."

"And you were giving him a hard time about that?"

"I wouldn't say I was giving him a hard time," Denny claimed. "It was more expressing my surprise, you know?"

Michael raised an eyebrow. "At—?"

"You know. That he was going out with—"

"A Jew?" Michael supplied.

"Well, yeah," Denny sniggered as if it were self-explanatory.

"You know what, O'Malley?" Michael sounded contemptuous. "If I were Mitchell, I would have beaten you to a fucking pulp."

Denny's face fell. "What?"

"You heard me." Michael rounded on him. "Tell me: What do you think of me as? A guinea? A wop? A greasy dago?"

"Of course not!"

"How 'bout you?" Michael continued. "Maybe I should start calling you the stupid Mick. Or Paddy. Want me to start calling you Paddy?"

"No." Denny's face was turning red.

"Let me clue you in to something, O'Malley. You play in New York. Know what that means? It means that lots of people who pay good money to see you play are Jewish. It means that lots of the top brass at Met Gar who sign your paycheck are Jewish. It means that if you're ever fucking stupid enough to say anything anti-Semitic again, you could wind up with more than Mitchell's fist in your face; you could find yourself without a job—not only because your views are disgusting, but because they're dangerous to the whole franchise.

"So the next time you feel the urge to show one of your teammates what an ignorant jackass you are, try to restrain yourself, okay?"

Denny was silent.

"Okay?"

Denny jerked his face away. "Okay!"

"That goes for the rest of you," Michael concluded with a scowl. "If I catch wind that any of you clowns are talking that type of trash, it's over. And PS, what went on in this room stays in this room. Am I making myself clear?"

Heads nodded, and voices murmured assent. Jason, who'd been expecting a personal reprimand from Michael as well, was surprised when it didn't come. He looked down at his hands; without even realizing it, he'd balled them into two fists. Vindicated, Jason slowly unfurled his fingers and filed out of the conference room with his teammates.

CHAPTER

18

"I think you know who is coming down the hallway, Stanley."

Delilah paused, waiting for the sound of Jason's key turning in the lock. It was a bold move for her, but she'd decided to surprise him, letting herself into his apartment and preparing him a nice meal that would be waiting when he got home. Delilah saw it as propitious offering to Cupid, designed to banish the lingering uncertainty that had prevailed since their "disaster" of a date with his friends.

That Jason called it that wounded her incredibly. She knew she'd been shy and stuttery, but she hadn't thought things had gone *that* badly. Jason's immediate departure with the Blades gave full rein to her overactive imagination: She was convinced he was going to return to New York and dump her for some female *bon vivant*. When he called from the road, Delilah nearly wept with relief, though he did sound somewhat preoccupied. Sensing he might need cheering and reassurance as much as she did, she convinced Marcus to dog sit for her on his one night off from rehearsal.

"You're going to be too exhausted to do anything else

anyway," Delilah pointed out. Marcus agreed to spend the night at her place on one condition: if *My Mustache, My Self* tanked, he could immediately have his job back, with a small raise included. There'd been no question of that anyway, but Delilah readily agreed.

Jason opened the door, and Delilah felt her pulse suspend mid-beat. She'd been worried he might view her being there as an intrusion or an overstepping of bounds, but his expression of pleasant surprise said otherwise.

"Well, what have we got here?" Jason crouched down so he was eye level with Stanley and let him giddily lick his face. The sight of it never failed to move Delilah.

Eventually Jason pulled back from Stanley's loving ministrations, spluttering, "Okay, pal, that's enough. There's someone else here that *I* want to kiss." Rising to his feet, he wiped his face on his shirtsleeve as he approached Delilah. "You okay with being kissed by a guy covered in dog schmoo?"

Delilah laughed as she slid into his arms. "Schmoo-covered men are my favorites."

Jason smiled and crushed her to him. She was surprised by the urgency in his kiss. Perhaps her intuition had been right; perhaps he'd been just as unsettled as she by their post-date discussion. Delilah relaxed into him, reaching up to cup his cheek. "I missed you."

"I missed you, too." Jason lifted his nose, sniffing the air like a dog. "Something smells good."

"I made lasagna. Is that okay?"

"It's great. I didn't know you could cook."

"I can cook some things."

Which was true: Delilah could cook some very simple, basic dishes. But cooking wasn't something that had ever been valued or encouraged when she was growing up—unless it was a holiday. Holidays were the only times Mitzi broke out the pots and pans, and even then, Delilah's father usually wound up taking over, since the slightest spillage or errant puff of flour could send Mitzi into fits. Delilah half suspected it was an act, her mother's way of getting out of doing the actual hard labor while still being able to maintain she'd done something "special" for her family.

Jason glanced in the direction of the kitchen, then back at Delilah. "How much time do we have before the lasagna's done?" he murmured seductively.

"About twenty minutes. Why?" The question was purely rhetorical. Delilah knew why, and so did her body, which was beginning to hum to life.

Jason nipped at her neck. "I think I can make you happy in under twenty minutes." He maneuvered her to the couch, laying her back gently. Delilah was already beginning to tingle, anticipation of what was to come feeding an uncharacteristic impatience. Jason slid his body on top of hers, heat touching heat as he kissed her deeply.

Then Stanley came trotting over, torpedoing Jason in the ribs with his nose.

Jason jerked up his head. "Stan! Settle down!"

Stanley sat, but he didn't move. Delilah took a deep breath, trying to find her way back into the moment. Jason's mouth reclaimed hers. But Delilah couldn't enjoy it with Stanley's moist dog breath blowing on her face as he panted away.

Jason lifted his mouth from hers, sighing with resignation. Delilah opened her eyes to find him coolly regarding Stanley. So much for being moved by the bond between them.

"This isn't going to work, is it?" he asked Delilah.

Delilah stretched out a hand to pet Stanley. "Well, I guess it depends on what you mean by 'work.' "

"You. Me. Couch. Quickie."

"I don't think so." Delilah trailed her free hand up and down Jason's back. "We could try the bedroom. Close the door."

"Let's go for it."

They tumbled off the couch and began tiptoeing toward the bedroom.

"Why are we tiptoeing?" Delilah whispered. Why was she whispering, for that matter?

"Don't know," Jason whispered back, looking amused.

Stanley followed, reaching the threshold just as Jason was closing the door.

Guilt swamped Delilah. "I feel badly closing the door in his face."

"I don't," said Jason, feverishly pulling off his shirt.

His ardor revived Delilah's. As quickly as she could, she stripped off her own shirt and bra. Jason came and held her tight, the feeling of his hot skin against hers the only aphrodisiac she'd ever need. When he dipped down, running his tongue along the smooth plane of her collarbone, Delilah thought she'd shoot out of her skin. That's when Stanley began to howl, scratching at the bedroom door.

Jason hung his head in mock defeat. "I don't believe this."

"I do. You've been away, Jason. He wants to spend quality time with you."

Jason raised his eyes to Delilah's. They burst out laughing.

"I guess we'll just have to wait until we've put junior to bed," said Jason. His finger traced a lazy circle around the nipple of her left breast. "You *are* staying the night, aren't you?"

Delilah nodded, feeling dizzy. "I persuaded Marcus to stay with my guys."

"I thought he was in intensive play rehearsals," said Jason as he opened the door to let Stanley in.

"He has a night off," explained Delilah, quickly gathering up her top and bra before Stanley happily trampled them. "Speaking of which, the play opens in two weeks, and we're invited to the opening."

"Oh."

Delilah fell silent, thrown off balance by his distinct lack of reaction. She thought he'd be thrilled that they were going out and *doing* something. "I think it will be fun," she said, sounding a bit more strident than she intended.

"Did you check the date against my playing schedule?

Are you sure there's not a conflict?" There was a prick of hopefulness in his voice that annoyed her.

"No conflict. You're free that night."

Jason smiled weakly. "Then I guess it's a date."

I should never have agreed to this, Jason thought as he sat beside Delilah, suffering through *My Mustache, My Life.* When the balding actor playing Dr. Phil had belted out, "Oprah / She's no dope-rah / She sees something fine in meeee," it had taken every ounce of Jason's strength not to bust a gut. He checked his watch discreetly. The play was limping toward intermission, and Dr. Phil hadn't even been given his own show yet. Shit.

Still, he had to give credit where it was due: Marcus was an outstanding dancer. Every time he appeared onstage, Delilah's face lit up like a Christmas tree. Jason knew it was selfish, but part of him hoped the show flopped so that Marcus would go back to working for Delilah. Her father's fiancée hadn't worked out; the minute she realized there was dog poop involved, she bailed. Delilah had been working solo the past two weeks, so she barely had any time for Jason.

The curtain went down, and the audience applauded, pulling Jason out of his own head.

"Well?" Delilah asked him eagerly as the house lights went up.

Jason glanced around furtively. "It sucks," he whispered. "Don't you think?"

Delilah looked offended. "No!"

"It's awful, Delilah. Admit it. It'll close in three days."

She wouldn't. "Marcus is good," she pointed out defensively.

"I agree. But everything else . . ." He stood up. "Want to split?"

"What?"

"If we leave now, we could probably catch a movie somewhere."

Delilah looked incredulous. "You're not serious."

He peered at her, interrogation style. "Do you really want to sit through an hour and a half more of this?"

Delilah flicked back her hair. "Yes, I do. And even if I didn't, I would do it anyway. For Marcus." Her expression was bewildered. "I thought you'd be happy that we're out *doing* something."

"Not when we're doing something boring."

"You're the arbiter of what's worth doing and what isn't?"

"No." Jason could feel the walls closing in.

"Then this counts as a legitimate night out for us."

Jason hesitated. "Yeah. I guess." He didn't dare tell her *he* counted it as a night of making Delilah happy, not a night consisting of an agreed-upon leisure activity mutually enjoyable for both of them. In other words, *fun.* Speaking of which . . .

"There's going to be a surprise birthday party next Friday night for David—you know, one of the guys we went to dinner with?" *The one who isn't an anti-Semite,* Jason added in his head. "You up for it?"

"If I don't have any boarders." Delilah looked tense. "Weekends are hard, Jason. I told you that."

"They might not be if you looked a little harder for a replacement for Marcus."

Delilah drew back and just stared at him. Oh, fuck. Had he really just said that? It was the type of thing she herself might say in one of her more blurty moments.

"Would you mind explaining what you mean by that?" Delilah asked quietly.

I mean that running your business alone gives you an excuse to be a hermit. Jason couldn't say that, but deep down it was what he thought.

"Jason?"

He blinked, realizing he'd yet to answer her question. "I didn't mean that the way it sounded. I meant"—*Think fast, bucko*—"I miss you. I don't get to see you as much now that you don't have an assistant."

"I can't hire just anyone," Delilah protested.

"Right." Jason took her hand, wishing the whole conversation away. "Look, forget I said anything. It's not important."

Delilah didn't look too convinced. "If you say so."

Delilah might be twittery, but she wasn't a twit. Jason knew damn well she wasn't buying the line he'd just handed her. He feigned interest in his Playbill to avoid her eye. Somehow, in the course of five minutes, everything had changed: He couldn't wait for the play to resume.

"The play sucked. I sucked."

Delilah's heart went out to Marcus as she handed him a cup of jasmine tea. As Jason so cruelly predicted, *My Mustache, My Self* didn't last a week. The critics were ruthless, one newspaper describing it as a "car wreck." Cha-Cha's prediction of success from beyond the grave had proven completely wrong. Poor Marcus! He so deserved a break, and Delilah was beginning to fear he might never get one. She pictured him a bitter old man, hovering outside the American Ballet School, trying to trip young dancers on their way inside. It could happen.

"You didn't suck," Delilah assured him as she joined him on her couch.

"Whatever." There was pain in his eyes as he gazed down at Delilah's sleeping dogs curled up at their feet. "Can I have my old job back, boss?"

"There was never any question of that. And don't call me 'boss.' You know I don't think of myself that way."

"Any new clients?" Marcus asked, mindlessly scratching Belle beneath the chin.

"A female poodle named Puddles on West Eighty-second."

Marcus stopped scratching. "Please tell me the name isn't in any way related to canine incontinence."

"It's not. Apparently, the dog likes to walk in puddles."

"Not on my time, she's not." Marcus scowled.

Delilah patted his arm. "Don't worry. She's on my route, not yours."

Marcus sighed, resting his head on her shoulder. "Tell me you missed me. Tell me no one could ever replace me. I need for my life to have *some* meaning."

"I did miss you, and no one could ever replace you. I told you: my dad's fiancée helped out for two days. The minute she found out she had to scoop poop, she was out of here. Jason even helped out one day, though that was more to teach him a lesson and show him the job wasn't as easy as he thought."

Marcus lifted his head. "How are things going? You've been tight-lipped about him, sweet pea."

"Things are fine," Delilah murmured.

"Just *fine*?" Marcus prodded. "Not fantastic, magnificent, crazy ass in love with one another?"

Was that how love was supposed to be? Delilah knew she was falling in love with Jason, and she was pretty sure he felt the same way about her, though neither of them had spoken the actual words yet. Yet Marcus's description made her uneasy. What if the quiet romance unfolding between her and Jason was fundamentally flawed? What if she was "doing" love the wrong way?

"What's wrong with plain old *fine*?" Delilah made herself ask.

"Nothing. I just thought, since you wanted this guy so bad and were even willing to buy special panties to delight him, that you might be more enthused about being his girlfriend."

Delilah found herself frowning and reached for her tea. "We've got some things to work out."

"Like—?"

"We're opposites." She hated admitting it to herself, never mind someone else.

"Not completely," Marcus replied. "Didn't you tell me he can be impulsive? That he bought himself a bike before he even stocked his fridge?" Delilah nodded. "Well, there's something you share. You're verbally impulsive, and he's physically impulsive."

Delilah wasn't buying it. "We're opposites, Marcus," she repeated.

"So?" Marcus was nonplussed. "Everyone knows opposites attract."

"Yes, but once they've acted on that attraction, can they make things work?" Delilah asked plaintively.

"That depends on the two people involved. I'm no *Dr. Phil*"—Marcus spat the words like a curse—"but it seems to me that a little compromise on both sides is all you need."

"We're trying. But it's hard." She hesitated. "He doesn't get that hanging out in a group makes me nervous."

Marcus was painfully frank. "You've got to get over that. Seriously. You cannot expect this guy to hang out here all the time with you and the dogs."

"I know that," Delilah countered heatedly. "But he needs to understand that I run my own business, and that takes precedence over—"

"Making the relationship work?" Marcus cut in, lifting an eyebrow. "Look, now that I'm back, you've got way more flexibility. And God knows Mr. Right ain't anywhere on my radar screen. Anytime you need me to do nighttime pooch patrol, I'm your man."

"Are you sure? Because I don't want you to feel I'm taking advantage of you."

"I would never feel that way."

"Hmmm." Delilah took a sip of her tea. "One of his teammates is having a birthday party Friday night. I told him I probably couldn't go."

"Well, now you can."

But I don't want to! Delilah thought. Just imagining herself at a party made her feel nauseous.

"I have an idea," Marcus continued, his old enthusiasm returning. "Why don't you surprise him? Think of the look on his face when you walk in and he realizes you made the effort just for him?"

Delilah felt her eyes bug out of her head. "You want me to walk into a party alone?!"

"I'll give you a Xanax. You'll be fine."

"You might have to give me one now."

Surprise Jason; it was a thought. He'd liked it when he came home to find her in his apartment. And it would show that she'd made a special effort to spend time. Still . . . *a party* . . .

"I don't know where it's being held," Delilah pointed out.

Marcus's gaze was withering. "Nice try. You'll be seeing him before that, right?"

"Probably."

"Then casually ask him about it. Or find out from the brother. Aren't they thick as thieves?"

"I would describe it as more of a love/hate relationship."

"Well, appeal to the love side of him and get the details." Marcus turned up his palms, mimicking the two sides of a scale. "Think about it, Delilah: Relationship with Jason"— he lifted his left hand—"or winding up the crazy old dog woman of the Upper West Side." He raised his right hand. "You decide."

CHAPTER 19

"*When am I* gonna get to meet your girlfriend?"

Jason looked up from his plate of spaghetti to see Michael Dante standing beside him. Like all Blades affairs, the surprise party for David Hewson was being held at Dante's. Michael, who had organized the party as part of an ongoing effort to build team camaraderie, had been making the rounds since the festivities began, making sure everyone had enough to eat and drink. It was obvious he was very proud of the restaurant, even though his brother Anthony looked like he wanted to kill him every time he emerged from the kitchen with new dishes for the banquet table.

Jason blotted his mouth with a napkin. "She's working."

He started to rise, but Michael patted his shoulder, urging him to remain in his seat. "Sit, eat." Michael grabbed an empty chair from another table and sat down. "What does she do?"

"She has her own business. She's a dog trainer. She walks them and boards them, too."

"Yeah? Can she train little kids? I'll pay her beaucoup

bucks to whip little Anthony into shape. Four years old, and already he's busting my horns."

Jason smiled. "I'll find out." He figured since Michael asked something personal about him, maybe he should do the same. "Your wife should be giving birth any day now, right?"

"Any *minute* now," Michael amended with a chuckle. "That's why she's not here. She's bone tired."

Jason nodded sympathetically as if he understood the way it was with pregnant women, though he hadn't a clue.

Michael grabbed a piece of foccacia from the basket on the table and popped it into his mouth. "Everything okay between you and O'Malley?"

"Fine." Jason pushed his plate away. "Look, I meant to thank you—"

Michael made a zipping motion across his lips. "Over. Finished. No need."

Jason flushed. "Okay."

"Good." Michael rose, patting him again on the back. "Give me a shout when you're ready to leave. I'll have Anthony fix up a plate to bring home to your girlfriend."

"Thanks," said Jason, impressed by Michael's generosity.

Michael took his leave, leaving Jason to finish his appetizer. Some people were eating, others standing in small groups, talking. Jason had arrived at the party ravenous, having forgotten once again to grocery shop. He could hear Delilah's voice in his head, teasing him about impulsively buying a second digital camera when he didn't even have any food in the house. She was right, of course.

Jason turned to talk to Barry Fontaine, sitting on his right, then refrained: Barry was having what sounded like an argument with his wife over her excessive spending. It embarrassed Jason to be able to hear them. Still, at least Barry had someone to argue *with*.

"Hey, look who I found."

Jason turned. Birthday boy David Hewson stood behind Jason's chair, beaming. Beside him was Delilah.

In the split second it took her to register Jason's delighted smile, Delilah knew the anxious buildup to this moment had all been worth it: worth her hands trembling on the steering wheel as she drove to Bensonhurst; worth the nausea that almost kept her pinned to the driver's seat as she turned a little too sharply into Dante's parking lot; worth it all.

"Hey, you." Jason jumped up to give her a kiss. "This is the best surprise I've had in a long time! I'm really glad you came."

"Me, too," David chimed in, giving Delilah a quick peck on the cheek. "Unfortunately, our esteemed captain is motioning for me to join him. I'll catch you guys later."

"Bye," said Delilah.

"This is really, really great," Jason marveled in amazement. That she was the one responsible for his happiness made Delilah feel terrific. She still felt a little anxious, but if Jason kept looking at her the way he was now, as if she were the most beautiful woman in the world, then she was sure it was only a matter of time before her nervousness disappeared altogether.

Delilah smiled up at him. "I'm glad you're happy." Jason looked fantastic; he was a man born to wear tight, faded jeans. His rolled-up shirtsleeves revealed strong, muscled forearms, and there was something about the way the soft light of the restaurant bathed his face that made him look especially striking. Delilah let her gaze linger appreciatively on her boyfriend's body, then remembered she was in public.

"Are you hungry?" Jason asked solicitously.

"Not really." Delilah pointed to the half-eaten plate of pasta before him. "Finish your food."

"In a minute."

Jason put his arms around her, drawing her close. Instantly there was heat, along with a pleasant jolt of shock: Delilah had never had a boyfriend embrace her so lovingly in public. Perhaps her mother had been right when she'd characterized all Delilah's previous boyfriends as "losers."

"I'm sorry about the other night," Jason murmured, looking contrite. "It was wrong of me to try to get you to leave your friend's play early."

"It's okay. The play sucked."

Jason winced but looked mildly vindicated. "It really did, didn't it?"

"Yes."

"Is Marcus okay?"

"He's upset, but he's a trooper," said Delilah, touched by Jason's concern.

"Is he staying with your dogs tonight?" Jason asked tentatively.

Delilah could tell he was nervous of sending the conversation in a direction he didn't want it to go. She nodded.

"I'll have to thank him."

"He would like that, I think."

"Consider it done." Jason's lips pressed against her forehead. "You okay? With being here?"

"I'm fine," Delilah assured him. She'd come up with a little mantra to help her cope: *Think before you speak.* She'd chanted it to herself in the car all the way over to the restaurant, and was, in fact, repeating it even now in the back of her mind. She would not embarrass herself or Jason.

Jason's lips brushed the tip of her ear. "It means a lot to me that you're here."

Think before you speak. "It means a lot to me that you want me here."

Jason broke their embrace to take her hand. "C'mon, let's get you something to drink."

Hand in his, Delilah followed where Jason led. Maybe her insecurity was insisting on reasserting itself, but it seemed to Delilah as if Jason's teammates were turning to look at them. At her. She supposed it made sense; most of them didn't know her, so of course they'd be curious. Normally, her impulse would be to try to shrink somehow or pray to blend in with scenery, but she held her head high and even smiled. Before she knew it, they had reached the bar.

"What can I get you?" Jason asked.

"A Diet Coke would be fine." Delilah didn't want to drink. Drink loosened her tongue.

"Hello, Delilah!" The voice of David's Hewson's girlfriend Tierney felt like a ray of sunshine beaming down directly on Delilah. It was friendly and warm. Delilah smiled in greeting.

"Hi, Tierney. How are you?"

"Great! It's so nice to see you here. Jason said you were working."

"I was. I mean I should be. Someone else is. I mean—" *Think before you speak!* "My coworker managed to fill in for me tonight," Delilah managed to finish smoothly.

"Well, I'm still working on David about getting a puppy. If we do, I promise we'll give you a call to talk about training him. Or her."

"My pleasure," said Delilah.

Tierney rolled her eyes heavenward as she gave the wrapped present in her hand a small shake. "More treasures for the birthday boy. Can you guys excuse me a minute? This thing, whatever it is, weighs a ton."

"Go ahead," said Jason.

"She's really nice," Delilah observed as Tierney headed toward a table piled high with gifts.

"She is," Jason agreed, handing her a Coke.

"Did you get David anything?" Delilah asked delicately.

Jason looked insulted. "What do you think I am?"

"Someone who ran out to buy a Bowflex before he even had a bed?" Delilah teased.

"Hey, I'm getting better." He stole a sip of Delilah's drink. "I got him a couple of DVDs he wanted." He opened his mouth to say something else, but a sudden frown overtook him instead. *"Fuck."*

"What?" Delilah responded with alarm.

Jason handed her drink back to her, pointing to a large blond man with a piercing gaze gesturing Jason join him. "My coach wants to see me. I wonder what I've done wrong now."

"Relax," said Delilah. "It might be nothing."

"You're right." Jason gave her shoulder a quick squeeze. "I'll just be a minute."

Delilah watched him go, taking a big chunk of her self-confidence with him. Here she was, standing alone at the bar in a hot, noisy room full of strangers. She had two choices: she could keep standing here while her jitters returned with a vengeance, or she could venture into new territory and force herself to make human contact. Terrifying though it was, she determined to do the latter. Jason would be proud of her, and she would have proved to herself that she wasn't a completely inept loser when it came to certain social situations.

Delilah scouted the room. Denny O'Malley stood at a nearby buffet table, heaping a small mountain of food onto his plate. Perfect. At least she vaguely knew him, which was better than going up and introducing herself to a total stranger. Delilah took a deep breath and walked over to the table.

"Hi, Denny," she said brightly.

Denny glanced up and seemed to register she was there, but said nothing. Delilah blinked, confused. Maybe he hadn't heard her?

"It's Delilah, Jason's girlfriend," she continued in a slightly louder voice. "How are you?"

Denny remained silent as he continued loading his plate. Delilah felt herself slowly sliding into panic. Was it possible he didn't remember her? She swallowed hard, determined to give it one more try.

"Maybe you don't remember me? I—"

"I remember you." Denny's gaze was hostile. "Excuse me."

He walked away, leaving Delilah burning with humiliation and confusion. She looked around wildly. Jason was in deep conversation with his coach. It seemed unlikely he'd be "back in a minute." Delilah's pulse pounded her ears, a bitter taste filling her mouth. Why had she even bothered to try? She *was* inept. She *was* a loser. Tears already beginning to blur her vision, Delilah deposited her drink back at the bar and fled the party.

What the hell happened? Jason's mind hadn't stopped racing from the time he discovered Delilah left the party right up until now, as the cab deposited him in front of her building. One minute, Ty was talking to him about mixing up the lines to beef up the offense; the next, Delilah had disappeared. Alarmed, Jason asked Tierney and David if she'd said anything to either of them or if they'd seen her go, but neither had. Something must have happened to her mother. Or her father. Or worse still, one of her dogs. Knowing Delilah, she didn't want to interrupt him while he was talking to Ty. His worry increased the longer he tried to come up with reasons for her abrupt disappearance. Jason left the party, cabbing from Bensonhurst back to Manhattan. If she needed him, he wanted to be there for her as soon as he could.

He was granted a small reprieve from the mad, unchecked thoughts in his head when he presented himself to the night doorman, and Delilah buzzed him up right away. Too impatient to wait for the elevator, he flew up the stairs two at a time. He knew from past experience that she would have unlocked the door for him, so he plunged right inside. Delilah sat on the couch, wrapped tightly in the oversized fleece blanket she liked to snuggle beneath when watching TV. Her eyes were red-rimmed, the lids puffy from crying.

"Delilah." Jason rushed to her side. "What happened?" He did a quick scan of the room; all three of her dogs were safe and sound, sleeping on the floor. That took care of that possibility. Perhaps Marcus had had an emergency?

"I'm sorry," Delilah apologized quietly. "I should have let you know I was going. But I couldn't think."

"Honey, what happened?" Jason searched her eyes; all he saw was pain. "Are you sick? Is everything all right?"

"No, I'm not sick. But I don't know if everything's all

right." Delilah looked distraught. "If I ask you a question, do you promise you'll answer me honestly?"

"Of course." Jason was completely mystified.

"The night of our date—when we went to dinner with your friends?" Her eyes began filling up. "Did I say or do anything offensive?"

"No. Why would you even think that?"

"Because tonight"—Delilah seemed on the verge of completely breaking down—"when you went off to talk to your coach, I thought I'd make myself be sociable. I went to say hello to Denny, and he wouldn't even talk to me. In fact, he looked like he hated me. So I thought I must have done something—"

"You didn't," Jason interrupted fiercely. "Believe me."

Delilah blinked in bewilderment. "But—"

"Listen to me, Delilah. It's him, not you."

"I don't understand."

Agonized, Jason glanced away. "I don't know how to say this."

Delilah's eyes clamped shut. "I know I'm a loser. I know I suck when I'm in big groups of people and I bleat and blurt and—"

"*Stop.* I told you: it's not you." He hated seeing her rip herself to shreds like this because of that asshole, Denny.

"Then what?" she asked plaintively. "Do I smell? Have bad breath?"

"Nothing like that," Jason scoffed.

"Then what?"

Jason grimaced. "Denny's anti-Semitic."

Delilah looked stunned as she drew the blanket around her shoulders tighter. "He is?"

Jason frowned. "Yeah."

"How do you know?"

"He said some things," Jason replied evasively, leaning over to pet Shiloh, who had just settled at his feet. He wondered how Stan was doing.

"What things?" Delilah asked.

How much should he tell? All of it? Some of it? Didn't she have a right to know?

"He made a crack that he was surprised I would go out with someone with the last name Gould. That's how it started. We got into it on the road."

Delilah looked like she was sinking in a quicksand of confusion. "What do you mean, 'Got into it on the road'?"

Jason rubbed a weary hand across the back of his neck. "He started saying some really offensive things, and I basically beat the crap out of him."

Delilah looked away. "Oh, God."

Jason put his arm around her shoulder and squeezed tight.

"I'm so sorry, babe."

"I'm sorry, too. I hate the thought of being a source of trouble between you and your teammates."

"You're not. It's one teammate, and he's an asshole."

"Are you sure he's the only one who feels that way?" She shed the blanket, revealing hands clasped so tightly her fingertips were turning red. "What if the others feel that way?"

"They don't."

Comprehension flickered in Delilah's eyes. "Is that why you were so aloof when you called from the road? Because all this was going on?"

"Yeah," said Jason, hating to admit it.

"God," Delilah repeated, disgusted. "Some people are so ignorant." She laughed bitterly. "Guess I won't be inviting *him* to my mother's for Hanukkah."

Jason's interest was piqued. "Your mom's having a Hanukkah party?"

"Less a party than dinner for a few people." Delilah brightened a bit. "I can't wait for her to meet you."

"She already did, remember?"

"Shoot." She'd spaced on her adventure with Eric. "I'll explain it all to her when we get there."

"I'm sure it will be fine."

Delilah sighed, resting her head on his shoulder. Jason liked it; it made him feel as though he were her protector, the person she relied on to buffer her from the storms of self-doubt that seemed to besiege her. She was so vulnerable. If only he could figure some way to bring out the self-confidence she displayed when it came to dogs. She'd be unstoppable!

He kissed the top of her head. "I was so proud of you tonight. I know how hard it must have been for you to come to that party, especially all alone."

Delilah's gaze was soulful as she lifted her head to look at him. "I wanted to do it. For you."

"That means a lot to me." He couldn't take his eyes from hers. "I love you, Delilah."

Jason couldn't decide which of them was more shocked: Delilah, who clearly hadn't expected to hear it, or himself, who hadn't expected to say it. He couldn't believe how easily the words had glided off his tongue. He'd always thought that when he finally told a woman he loved her, it would be a monumental moment, the emotional equivalent of the ocean surf crashing in his ears. Instead, the moment had crept up on him quietly, like the moon slowly rising over the crest of the hill.

"I love you, too, Jason," Delilah said quietly, so quietly he almost didn't catch it. He kissed her then, her body pliant in his arms. Gentle as the moment was, he felt something surge within him, greedy and demanding. He wanted to stake claim to her, the terrain of her body a map he wanted to memorize. He paused, pressing his burning forehead against hers, and then, like the explorer he'd deemed himself to be, he carried her off to the bedroom, kicking shut the door behind him. It was clear right away how poorly Stanley was trained in comparison to Delilah's dogs; not one of them howled or scratched at the door.

He laid her back gently on the bed, debating whether or not to turn on a light. Darkness could be its own mystery, a tool for lovers to wrap themselves in or hide in if they so chose. But light was better. Explorers needed light, especially when it came to being guided toward their treasure. He turned on just one of Delilah's bedside lamps, throwing her small but tidy bedroom into subdued relief. Her eyes were wide but excited as she looked up at him. Jason knew that whatever journey he was about to take Delilah on, she was a more-than-willing participant.

He lay down beside her, kissing her fully on the mouth. The urgency he tasted there matched his own, but he didn't want to hurry. Rather, he wanted to tarry. He gathered her up in his arms, his lips moving gently over her face, pausing to kiss sweetly her closed lids. She was so beautiful; why couldn't she see that? As if reading his thoughts, Delilah's eyes fluttered open, and she looked at him with complete surrender and trust. Moved, he pressed his mouth to the soft terrain of her throat, as his hands slid down her back to cup her small, firm bottom. A quiet but unmistakable purr of delight stole past Delilah's lips. For a moment she looked embarrassed, almost abashed. Jason decided to banish the look with a swift nip to her right earlobe. It had the effect he wanted: Delilah seemed to surrender to her own desire, a moan escaping her lips as Jason dipped his head to reacquaint himself with the soft, ivory skin of her neck and throat. His mouth teased and tickled; it skimmed and played. He knew Delilah could feel how badly he wanted her, just as he could tell how bad her own need was for him, as each touch of his mouth to her skin had her pressing her body harder against his.

"Jason," she whispered. He lifted his head to look at her. Her eyes glimmered with need. "I'm going to go crazy if you don't—"

He crushed his mouth to hers, her small gasp inciting him. Sweetness was turning to juddering lust; he needed to slow down and take his time, even though the ache pounding through him could easily drive him over the edge. Slowly, deliberately, he took his mouth from hers, eyes catching hers as his fingers took their time unbuttoning her blouse. He pushed her shirttails back, revealing the beautiful lace bra she'd worn the first time they made love. It dawned on Jason she'd worn it on purpose in anticipation of just such a moment as this, wanting to please him. The realization sent a fresh surge of desire through his body. Head reeling, he undid the clasp at the back of her bra and freed her, cupping her breasts in his hands. Delilah tensed, her breathing unsteady as he took his time caressing her. By the time he took her into his mouth to suckle, she was trembling in his arms, rocking against him in a way he thought would drive him mad.

And then it all stopped.

Wild-eyed, Delilah sat up, trying to tug off his shirt. Jason complied, his breaths becoming shallow as he waited to see what she was going to do. "Close your eyes," Delilah commanded. Jason obeyed just as the burning skin of her palms made contact with his chest, caressing him slowly. Control was beginning to fade. If he didn't take this woman now, he would burst.

Determined to drive both of them into oblivion, he grabbed Delilah and pulled her back down onto the bed. He could not stop kissing her, his lips landing wildly on her body, one moment on her mouth, the next clamping down on her shoulder. Delilah's breath was hitching now, her head thrown back in a posture of total and willing submission. Frenzied, Jason ran his fingers over every available inch of bare flesh, groaning in frustration at the inconvenience of their having to shed the rest of their clothing. He rose up, fumbling for his wallet and protection before hastily undoing his jeans and kicking himself free of his pants and his briefs. Beside him, Delilah was doing the same as she shimmied out of her pants and panties, the sultry smell of her body like incense, like heaven. Delilah lay back, the naked desire in her eyes making it hard for him to keep any thought but her in his head. One minute they were both panting with desperation. The next he had slid inside her, Delilah moaning with unabashed pleasure as she wrapped her legs tightly around him and they began moving together.

Jason twined his fingers through hers, hungering to get as much contact with her as he could. He would start slowly, taking his cues from her when it came to tempo. But Delilah didn't want that; there was fire in her eyes, a plea for holy immolation made all the more enticing as she strained against him, wanting more, wanting all he could possibly give. Jason complied; she came in a dazzling flash, the passionate cries cascading from her lips driving him insane.

Satisfied she was sated, Jason took his turn, throwing himself into the moment with joyful abandon, Delilah's body both his shelter and his treasure. When he came, it was accompanied by that roaring tide he'd so long ago imagined would herald love. Jason let it carry him away.

CHAPTER

20

Jason was still feeling on top of the world as he returned home from practice the next day. Practice had gone well, and there was something about the icy December air he found invigorating. With Christmas less than a month away, the city was alive with good cheer and anticipation.

Eric was sitting on the couch watching TV, his feet stretched out on the coffee table. A crumpled bag of potato chips lay against his side, which he reached into with hypnotized regularity.

"What the hell are you doing here?" Jason asked, tossing his keys onto a nearby table. He'd been looking forward to relaxing, maybe taking Stan for a stroll and catching up on back issues of *Sports Illustrated* before heading back out for tonight's game. Instead, he'd be playing reluctant host to Eddie Haskell.

Eric dipped into the chip bag. "Nice to see you, too."

"I'm serious: what are you doing here?"

"My TV died."

"Ever think of picking up a book or going to a movie?" Jason asked as he hung up his coat. Stanley, who'd been fast

asleep snoring when he entered, trotted over to greet him.
Jason bent down to rub his nose against Stan's; that's when
he noticed tiny crumbs flecking Stan's muzzle.

"Have you been feeding Stanley potato chips?" Jason
asked angrily.

"Yo, check this out." Eric shook the bag of chips, and
Stanley turned tail and raced back to the couch, jaws drip-
ping. "Stan the Man's learned a new trick." Eric reached in
the bag, holding a potato chip high above the dog's head.
"Stanley, speak!" Stanley barked, and Eric fed him the chip.
He turned to Jason, grinning. "Pretty cool, huh?"

"You're an idiot." Jason stormed over to the couch,
plucking the chip bag from his brother's fingers with a
glare. "Don't ever feed him anything again without my permission! Got it?"

"What's the big deal?"

"I've spent months training him and feeding him the
right foods, and then you come along and feed him this
crap. *That's* the big deal."

"He liked it."

"Dogs like to eat horseshit, Eric." Jason scoured the list
of ingredients on the bag—not that he had any idea which
might be bad for Stanley. "If he gets sick, I'm blaming you."

"Relax, he's not gonna get sick." Eric hit the Pause button on the remote, freezing the image of a woman dancing
in a see-through sari.

"What are you watching?" Jason asked.

"Some movie. *Debbie Does New Delhi*, I think."

"Let me guess: you rented it on pay-per-view, which
means I'll be footing the bill."

"I'll pay you back," Eric insisted lackadaisically.

"With interest." Jason glanced down at his beloved dog,
salivating heavily as he stared at the bag of chips still in
Jason's hand. "Moron," Jason cursed at his brother beneath
his breath as he threw the chips out in the kitchen garbage.
When he returned to the living room, he swore Stanley gave
him a dirty look.

"What just happened?" Eric asked, sounding almost resentful. "You looked like you were in a pretty good mood when you walked in."

"I was, until I saw you."

Eric gave him the finger. Without even thinking, Jason gave it back. They'd been flipping each other off for as long as he could remember; it was more ritual than self-expression. Eric was right: he was in a good mood when he walked in. He shouldn't have let his brother's stupid pet trick spoil it.

"So, what's going on?" Eric asked as Jason parked himself beside him on the couch.

"Nothing." Jason smiled enigmatically as he, too, stretched out his legs on the coffee table, lacing his fingers behind his head.

"Don't give me 'Nothing.' " Eric leered. "You score big time last night or what?"

"Why do you always have to reduce everything to these stupid, macho clichés?"

"Because I'm stupid and macho?" Eric offered without the slightest hint of self-deprecation.

"That must be it."

"You gonna spill or what?" Eric asked, his attention drifting back to the frozen image on the TV screen. Annoyed, Jason lunged for the remote and turned off the TV. "Hey! I was watching that!" Eric protested.

"You can watch it on your own TV when it's fixed."

"Whatever." Eric grabbed a nearby pillow and positioned it behind his head. "There's only two reasons why you'd have that goofy smile pasted to your face: either Ty Gallagher's lost his mind and put you on the first line, or something mondo is up between you and Delilah."

"The second," Jason admitted, surprisingly happy at being able to share his good news with his brother. But Eric didn't react the way he expected.

"Oh, man. It's not serious, is it?"

"Define serious."

"You didn't say the three magic words that guarantee you'll never see your balls again, did you?"

"Where do you come up with this shit?" Jason asked incredulously.

"Did you?"

"What if I did?"

"Oh, man," Eric repeated in a voice dripping with pity. "Bad move."

"Tell me why—as if you were going to hold back."

"Because it's going to fuck with your game. Have you ever seen me in a serious relationship during the season? Answer: No."

Jason snorted. "I've never seen you in a serious relationship during the off season, either!"

"That's because I keep my friends close and my women closer," said Eric. "Dude, you do not want to be entangled during the season. Especially *this* season, when you need to prove yourself to your new team. Dating? Fine. Screwing? Nice added bonus. I love you? Recipe for total destruction. Take it from Dr. Love: the prescription for good game is to stay footloose and fancy free."

"If what you're saying is true—and by the way, don't ever call yourself Dr. Love in my presence again—then I'd think you'd be happy, because it would mean you could best me on the ice."

"I always best you on the ice," Eric replied immodestly, "but that's another story. Look, I like Delilah a lot. You know that. But you haven't even been in New York six months."

Jason gaped at him. "Excuse me, but aren't you the one who advised me to 'go for the big gesture' with Delilah?"

"There's a difference between buying a chick flowers and giving her license to start picking out china patterns. You don't know what you're getting into, my man, tying yourself down this way."

"I'm not tying myself down," Jason said tersely. The warm glow he'd been carrying within him was beginning to flicker out, replaced by a whisper of uncertainty.

"You will when you want to hang out with some of your friends and she tells you you can't, because you promised to go to her cousin's for dinner. Or when she starts simpering, 'What are you wearing *that* for?' Or when some gorgeous piece of ass in a Blades Jersey offers you a pussy pass good for one night only and you have to turn her down. Or—"

"I get the picture!" Jason snapped as Eric sank back, chastised, against the couch cushions. "But you're wrong. Delilah isn't like that."

Eric smirked. "They're all like that."

"Yeah, like you'd know."

"I *do* know," Eric retorted. "Why the fuck do you think I don't have a steady girlfriend? Remember Barb Harmon?"

Jason squinted in confusion. "You mean Barb Hard-on?"

Eric frowned. "Yeah, her."

"What about her?" Jason hadn't given a thought to poor Barb with the unfortunate last name since high school. The only thing he could remember about her was that her brother couldn't skate to save his life.

"Well, when I was playing in Binghamton, guess who was living there at the time and looked me up? Barb. We got serious, and within a couple of months I went from cock of the walk to balls in a box. It was a friggin' nightmare, Jace. I vowed right then I would never get seriously involved with anyone until my NHL career was over."

Jason eyed his brother curiously. "How come you never told anyone you were seeing Barb?"

"Think about it: If Mom and Dad knew, all of Flasher would know. I didn't want to come home for Christmas and read my own engagement announcement in the paper."

"You could have told me," Jason pointed out, mildly wounded.

"Forget about who knew and who didn't, okay? My point is, you tell a chick 'I love you,' and that's it, your life isn't your own anymore."

Jason smirked with disbelief, but the uneasiness within him was gaining. Hadn't Ty basically said the same thing to him the night he and Michael took him out to dinner? He resented the insights of both his brother and his coach, not only because they were so bloodlessly pragmatic, but because he couldn't help but feel the comments were directed specifically at him, as if *he* as a player would be distracted, or *he* as a player couldn't manage a good season on the ice simultaneous with being romantically involved. Did they think he was a fucking simpleton or what?

"I'm sure I can make it all work," Jason maintained stubbornly.

"Whatever you say." But the skepticism in his brother's eyes told Jason he believed otherwise.

"*What the hell* is wrong with you tonight?"

Panting, Jason reached up from the bench to accept the water bottle proffered to him by one of the trainers, rinsing out his mouth and spitting. The Blades were five minutes into the second period against Boston, and already Jason had missed one cross-ice pass and coughed up the puck, leading to one of Boston's goals.

"There's nothing wrong with me," Jason replied defensively, though it wasn't true. Ever since hanging out with his brother earlier in the day, he'd been unable to get rid of the nagging feeling that Eric was right. That he'd already fucked up twice on the ice seemed to prove his brother's point. He should have been concentrating on his game; instead he was thinking about Delilah. Then again, every player experienced an off night now and again. Maybe tonight it was his turn—not that that was any excuse.

Ty said nothing, but his displeasure was obvious. Once again Eric's words came back to Jason. He knew he especially needed to concentrate this season, his first as a Blade. He knew he'd gotten off to a rocky start, but things had been going pretty well. But Ty's silence was damning.

"Get out there." Ty tapped him on the shoulder, and Jason climbed over the boards and out onto the ice with the rest of his line. David was down with a killer stomach bug, so Denny was in goal tonight. Their eyes met briefly as Jason positioned himself on the wing for the face-off. New York cleared the puck to center ice. Out of the corner of his eye, he saw goonish Boston defenseman, Sam MacGinty, making a beeline toward the puck. Jason was confident he could outrace Macs—he always had in the past—but a millisecond later, Macs was on it. The crowd booed, and Jason cycled back to the blue line, furious with self-loathing. He should have been able to outskate Macs. That he didn't was solid proof he was truly off his game. Split-second, erroneous judgments in timing continued to dog him for the remainder of the second period and well into the third. He was losing all his battles in the corners and was having a tough time getting to loose pucks.

The Blades lost 2–0.

"What did I tell you? You put pussy first and your play goes out the window."

Jason couldn't believe it: Eric was in his apartment again. With his feet up on the coffee table again. Eating chips again.

"Are you living here now, or what?" Jason snapped as Stanley rushed to give his customary greeting. At least Stan still thought he was great. He checked Stan's mouth; there were no potato chip crumbs that he could see.

"My TV's still broke."

"You couldn't go watch the game at a bar? Or get Met Gar to comp you?"

"I like the comforts of home."

"Yeah, *my* home." Jason went into the kitchen and pulled two beers out of the fridge, tossing one to Eric. "Did you at least take Stanley out?"

"Delilah swung by about an hour and a half ago to take him out."

Jason frowned uneasily. "You didn't say anything, did you?"

"Like what?" asked Eric, opening his beer.

"Gee, I don't know, maybe something like, 'I think having you in his life is messing up my brother's concentration'—you know, something like that."

"I would never do that," said Eric, tipping his head back to drink. "Even though it's true."

"My concentration would have been fine if you hadn't planted seeds of doubt in my head." Jesus, he'd never learn, would he? Eric's chief pleasure in life was pushing his buttons, and time and time again, Jason fell for it.

Eric chuckled meanly. "Oh, so now it's my fault you sucked?"

"I did not suck," Jason snapped. "I was off my game. It happens occasionally—to everyone but you, I suppose."

Eric's gaze was disdainful. "You call that a defense?"

"It is what it is." Jason sank down wearily on the couch. "I'm done talking to you about this stuff. One minute you're offering to watch Delilah's dogs so I can take her out to dinner, the next you're telling me she's the worst thing that could happen to my career, short of breaking my leg."

"I never said she was the worst thing that could happen to you. I simply advised you to date her."

"That's what I'm doing now."

"People who are just dating don't say 'I love you.'"

"I can't talk about this anymore, okay?" Jason said irritably, taking a sip of beer. He hated that he'd let what Eric said make him second-guess himself. *Why do I even listen to him?* Jason asked himself. What he and Delilah had started was good. Yeah, there were a few kinks to work out, but nothing that seemed insurmountable—until Eric put in his two cents.

"You're just jealous," Jason muttered.

"In your dreams."

Each instinctively retreated to the opposite ends of the couch, nursing their beers in silence as they watched the news. When the sports segment came on, Jason tensed. He imagined the sportscaster booming, "The Blades lost to Boston tonight, thanks to a pathetic showing by winger Jason Mitchell. Boy, I bet Blades management are sorry they traded Krakov and Ballinger for him!" Thankfully, the only one on the team who got an on-air nod was Denny, whose netminding had kept the game close.

"I've been meaning to ask you." Eric's voice was studiedly casual as he regarded Jason. "What happened with you and Malls on the road?"

Jason shook his head in disbelief. Honest to God, the NHL was worse than a bunch of old biddies gossiping over the back fence. Word of altercations spread fast, though the salient details were usually missing due to team loyalty. He wasn't surprised his brother knew.

"What did you hear?" Jason asked.

"Just that you two tied up. Something Malls said to you. Was it about Delilah?"

"Yeah."

Eric looked intrigued. "What did he say?"

"You know the rule: what goes on in the locker room stays in the locker room."

"I'm your *brother*, man. Give me a break."

"Yeah, and I was your brother when you were seeing Barbara Hard-on! I can't believe you didn't tell me."

"I'm sorry, okay? Now tell me."

Jason hesitated. "You promise you won't say anything?"

"Who the fuck am I going to tell?"

"Your whole team?"

"Blood's thicker than a three-year contract," Eric declared. "Just fucking tell me."

"Denny's an anti-Semite."

Eric looked surprised. "Really?"

"Really."

"Damn. Well, I always knew Malls was dumb. You were right to kick the shit out of him."

"Fuckin' A," said Jason, taking a sip of beer.

"You know," said Eric, "I was supposed to go out with him and a couple of the guys on my team next Saturday, and I was gonna ask you if you wanted to come. But I guess it's a moot point. And now I'm not so sure *I* want to hang out with him, either."

"I couldn't have come anyway. I'm going to Delilah's mom's house for Hanukkah."

"Balls in a box," Eric sang with warning. "See?"

"Just shut up, Eric, okay?" Jason was hit with a wave of exhaustion so strong he could have fallen asleep right there on the couch. "I want to go. It's important to Delilah."

"Can I come?"

"Sure, why not?" Delilah wouldn't mind. Besides, Eric had already met her mother. Having him in tow might make Jason less nervous.

"Cool." Eric looked pleased. "This is going to be fun."

CHAPTER
21

Delilah was dumbfounded when she went to pick up Jason to bring him out to her mother's, and both he and Eric appeared beside the car.

"What is this, a field trip to see the Jewish exhibit?" Delilah asked.

Jason looked at her, surprised. "I'm sorry. I didn't think you'd mind."

"Besides," added Eric, "I thought you'd want me here since your mother and I are like *that*." He crossed his fingers.

Delilah sighed. "Get in." She turned to Jason as he slid into the passenger seat. "I wish you'd checked with me first, Mr. Impulsive," she murmured under her breath. "I don't mind Eric coming, but I don't know how my mother's going to react to an unexpected guest. Plus, having both of you there is going to confuse her."

"Sorry," Jason repeated, heartfelt.

"I'm sure it will be fine," Delilah said, as much for his peace of mind as her own. The truth was, she was a nervous wreck about bringing Jason home to meet her mother. She

wasn't delusional enough to think he'd earn the Mitzi Seal
of Approval right off the bat, but she hoped her mother
would at least let him talk about himself a bit before
quizzing him about his bank balance and his goals for the
next thirty years. Her anxiety was heightened by the fact she
hadn't actually seen her mother since the "Plunge a dagger
in my heart; your father's engaged!" debacle. Just remembering it made Delilah feel itchy with nerves, like she was
breaking out in a rash. Detente had been reached over the
phone, but still, you never knew what melodrama Mitzi
might cook up for this special occasion. If she pulled a
Sarah Bernhardt in front of Jason, Delilah would just have
to kill herself.

"So, Hanukkah's like the Jewish Christmas, right?" Eric
piped up from the backseat. Delilah's eyes met his in the
rearview mirror. The naïveté she saw was genuine.

"No."

Eric looked befuddled. "But don't you get presents?"

"Yes, but it's really not a big holiday."

Eric nodded, seemingly mollified. Delilah was glad: She
didn't have the energy to explain about Maccabees, dreidels, oil, and menorahs.

Jason seemed unusually quiet as he gazed out the window. Delilah touched his leg.

"Nervous?"

"Nah," he scoffed.

"No need to be," Eric assured him. "Old Mitz is a pussycat. As long as you can keep a straight face when she starts
spouting the bull about being a 'design intuitive,' you'll be
fine."

"Excuse me," said Delilah. "It's one thing for me to find
my mother occasionally ridiculous, but you have no right."

"Sorry." Delilah could hear the sulk in Eric's voice. "I
was just trying to be helpful."

"Apology accepted."

For a few seconds, strained silence reigned the car. Jason
reached over and began kneading the back of Delilah's
neck. "Just relax. You're wound tighter than a—"

"Cheap watch," Eric interjected.

Jason's fingers stopped moving as he turned around to regard his brother. "Here's an idea: Why don't you count how many blue cars you see before we get to Roslyn?" He turned back to Delilah. "Relax," he repeated. "Everything will be fine."

"I know," Delilah said tersely.

Jason's fingers resumed kneading, deep and hard. "Not to bring up a sore subject, but is there anything I should or shouldn't say when I meet your mom?"

"Don't mention my father, do tell her you love the house, don't tell her you love dogs, do tell her she looks too young to have a daughter my age, don't eat or drink too much, do reassure her that you're not going to go bankrupt in the next five years."

"Is that all?" Jason teased, his touch transforming into a caress. "I bought you a Hanukkah present, you know. Eight, in fact."

"You did?" Somehow the fact that she'd get gifts for Hanukkah had slipped Delilah's mind.

"Of course I did. I'll give you the first one when we get back later tonight," said Jason suggestively.

"Excuse me while I puke," said Eric.

We won't be back too late, Delilah thought to herself. She had no intention of spending hours under scrutiny at Chateau Mitzi. Her plan was to introduce, eat, and leave. If push came to shove, she'd invoke the "We have to get home to the dogs" clause.

The ride out to Roslyn seemed shorter than usual, aided perhaps by the joking, easy banter between Jason and his brother. Sometimes Delilah wished she had a sibling, someone with whom she shared childhood memories. Maybe if she'd had a sister or a brother, her mother wouldn't have been so focused on her. Who knows?

She turned left onto her old block, driving slowly, the better to enjoy the menorahs blazing in the front window of some of the neighbors' homes. Though it was only the first night of the holiday, the contrast of the single, flickering candle against the plum-colored darkness of the winter sky seemed to herald hope. Perhaps tonight wouldn't be so bad after all.

Delilah pulled into her mother's driveway, eyes misty as she caught sight of the elaborate brass menorah in the window that her great grandmother had brought with her from Russia at the turn of the century. Mesmerized, Delilah watched the flame of the slim white candle flicker and dance. It wasn't until she switched off the ignition that her eyes glanced on the license plate of the car parked in front of hers: MATTRESS.

Her father was here.

If ever Delilah's penchant for blurting out the first thing that came to mind was tested, it was now, as her mother floated to the front door in a cloud of Shalimar.

"Happy Hanukkah," Delilah's mother greeted her, her lips lightly skimming Delilah's cheek before moving to crush Eric in a viselike hug. "There he is! How are you, darling?"

"Great, Mrs. G," chirped Eric. Without missing a beat, he divested Jason of the bouquet of flowers in his hand and presented them to Mitzi. "These are for you."

"Always so thoughtful," Mitzi sighed, gazing up at Eric like a lovelorn teenager.

Delilah shot a look at Jason, who stood gaping at his brother's impudence.

Mitzi stuck her nose in the fragrant bouquet, which was now competing with her perfume for dominance. Raising her head, she seemed to become aware for the first time of Jason's presence. She resumed her role as pint-sized diva, lifting a severely plucked eyebrow to ask, "And you are—?"

"Jason Mitchell, ma'am. It's nice to meet you." Jason thrust his right hand forward to shake hands, his left clutching the bottle of wine for dear life. Delilah knew just what he was thinking: No way was Eric going to steal that sucker.

Mitzi squinted as she shook Jason's hand, trying to place him. "You're the boyfriend's brother," she said slowly.

"Actually, I'm the boyfriend," said Jason.

Mitzi's face petrified into a mask of incomprehension. "I don't understand." She turned to Eric for help. "I thought you were the boyfriend."

"I was," Eric replied cheerfully before Delilah could answer, "but now I'm not."

Now it was Delilah's turn to gape. What the hell was he doing? She knew having both Jason and Eric here would cause her mother confusion, but she'd had the whole car ride to LI to figure out how to handle it. In the end, she decided she would come clean, telling her mother that she'd brought Eric for brunch because Mitzi had hounded her so much about having a boyfriend, Delilah didn't dare disappoint. This man, Jason, was her real boyfriend. Eric had never been. Instead, Eric had impulsively thrown a monkey wrench in the works.

Mitzi was peering at Jason apprehensively. "You're all right with this? Going out with someone who was with your brother?"

"Oh for God's sake!" Delilah exclaimed in irritation, her back beginning to itch madly. A rash was definitely coming on. "I'll explain it to you later, Mom, okay?"

Her mother covered her ears. "Better I shouldn't know."

Delilah turned with imploring eyes to Jason. "Why don't you and Eric head toward the dining room and we'll catch up?"

"Sounds great," Jason replied with a frozen smile.

"I'll show you how to get there," added Eric, rubbing his hands together eagerly. "I don't know what you're cooking in there, Mrs. G, but it smells great!"

Mitzi pursed her lips demurely. "Thank you."

Jason and Eric disappeared down the long white hallway. At least Eric hadn't been totally sucking up to Mitzi when he said the food smelled great; it did. Delilah stood savoring the aroma of potatoes and onions fried in oil, complemented perfectly by the sweet-spicy scent of the pot roast.

She wondered if Mitzi had had dinner catered, or if she'd actually cooked it herself. She'd ask, just as soon as she found out what scene she was about to walk into.

"What's Daddy doing here?"

Mitzi shrugged as if it were self-explanatory. "I invited him."

"No kidding. *Why?*"

"For you, Leelee." She put a hand on Delilah's arm. "I know how upsetting it's been for you to be from a broken home. I thought maybe, just for tonight, we could all be together again. A family."

Delilah stared at her before spluttering with disbelieving laughter. "You really believe it when you're saying it, don't you?"

Mitzi lifted her nose in the air. "I don't know what you're talking about."

"Oh, please. You didn't invite Daddy here for me! You invited him to check out Brandi!"

"Don't be ridiculous!" her mother spat. Her vehemence was all the proof Delilah needed that she'd hit the nail on the head.

"I wish you'd warned me," said Delilah. This was the second time tonight she'd had to say that to someone. It didn't bode well.

Mitzi's eyes flashed. "I wish you'd warned *me* that you've been playing musical beds!"

"I didn't. I don't. I—"

"Better I shouldn't know. What goes on between a man and a woman, or a woman and two men"—Mitzi's nostrils flared with disapproval—"is their business." She jerked her head in the direction of the hall. "Come on. I'm sure Daddy and that pair of talking boobs he calls a fiancée are dying to see you."

Two minutes at Mitzi's house, and I'm already feeling shell-shocked, Jason thought to himself as he followed his brother down the long white hallway. It reminded him of TV shows in which someone has a near-death experience, their soul leaves their body, and they talk about walking down a long tunnel toward the light—except in this case, the light was a dining room on Long Island.

He glanced at his brother, so smugly confident. "I can't believe you gave Mitzi the flowers *I* bought!"

"Move fast or die," was Eric's glib reply.

As they drew closer to the dining room, the smell of the food grew stronger, as did the sound of people talking. Jason listened attentively; it sounded like a man was talking to a small child, the latter's voice high-pitched and tinkly. The thought there might be a child here relaxed him a bit; he did well with kids. If things got really tense or weird, he could always hang out with little Bobby or Susie and avoid adult conversation altogether.

Jason was already sure of one thing: except for their petite stature, Delilah was nothing like her mother. He knew from Delilah—and from Eric, too, unfortunately—that Mitzi could be trying. He knew she'd be sizing him up. What he wasn't prepared for was her bluntness, or the sense he got that everything about him was being scrutinized, from the length of his hair to the measure of his character. Of course, Eric hadn't helped in that arena. Delilah's mother probably thought the three of them belonged to some weird sex cult.

They rounded the corner into the dining room, and conversation stopped. Sitting at the food-laden table was a balding older man with sagging skin and a warm smile. Beside him was a bright-eyed young blonde whose breasts were potentially lethal weapons. Delilah's father and his fiancée. Had to be.

"Hello, hello," the man said happily, coming out from behind the table to shake their hands. "Which of you is the hockey player?"

"I am," Jason and Eric answered at the same time.

The old man looked confused. "I thought—"

"They both play hockey, remember?" Brandi squeaked. "But that one's the boyfriend." She pointed at Jason. "The

other one"—her gaze was flirtatious as she looked at Eric—
"is his brother."

Delilah's father regarded the blonde suspiciously. "How
do you know?"

"Leelee and I ran into him when I was helping her walk
dogs. Right?" she said to Eric.

"That's right," Eric said smoothly. Jason shot his brother
a sideways glance; there was something vaguely wolfish in
the way he was looking at the blonde. Even more disconcerting, the blonde was returning the look.

"Huh," Delilah's father grunted. He seemed satisfied
with her answer. "Well, as I'm sure you've guessed by now,
I'm Sy, Delilah's father, and this lovely young lady at the
table is my bride-to-be, Brandi."

"Jason Mitchell." He flashed a quick smile to cover his
shock. The woman was young enough to be the man's
daughter; maybe even his granddaughter. No wonder
Delilah was so freaked out over the whole thing. And no
wonder Brandi didn't work out as Delilah's assistant. No
way could Jason picture this girl scooping poop.

"Eric Mitchell, sir." Eric stuck out his hand again to
Delilah's father. "It's a great honor to meet you."

Jason looked away. Jesus, his brother was sickening. And
obnoxious. And making him look bad—though his effusive-
ness did seem to somewhat baffle Delilah's father. *Good,*
thought Jason.

"Sit, sit," Delilah's father urged.

Eric made a beeline for the empty chair on Brandi's left.
Jason put down the bottle of wine on the table, then sat opposite, tossing his brother a quizzical look, which Eric was
either ignoring or pretending not to see.

"Do you boys have good mattresses?" Delilah's father
asked.

Jason exchanged glances with Eric. "Uh . . ."

"A good mattress is crucial to well-being."

"Crucial," Brandi echoed in her cartoon-character voice,
her gaze caressing Eric.

"You've probably seen me on TV," Delilah's father continued boastfully. "The Mattress Maven?"

"I thought I knew you from somewhere!" said Jason, though of course he knew who Sy was.

Delilah's father smiled, pleased with the recognition. "Well, if either of you need a good mattress, I'm your man. I'll give you a nice discount."

Jason cleared his throat to rid it of the immature laughter there just waiting to erupt. "I appreciate that, sir."

"Why hockey?" Delilah's father asked abruptly.

"What do you mean?" Jason replied.

"Why did you boys pick hockey? Why not a teacher or doctor or entrepreneur?"

"I've always loved the sport," Jason answered simply.

"Me, too," said Eric. "You and Brandi should come to a game sometime, sir."

Brandi giggled. "Wouldn't that be fun, Sy?"

"We'll see," Delilah's father grumbled. Jason was trying to figure out how he could be oblivious to the sexual tension crackling back and forth between Brandi and Eric. Maybe he wasn't, which was why he suddenly looked so cranky.

Just when Jason feared all ensuing talk would revolve around hockey and mattresses, Delilah's mother swept into the room bearing herself like a queen. Delilah followed a few seconds later, looking extremely anxious until her eyes lit on Jason, and she smiled. He pulled out the chair beside him, and Delilah sat down, squeezing his knee hard beneath the table.

"How's it going so far?" Delilah said under her breath.

"You know, I'm not sure I can even put it into words," Jason murmured back, prompting Delilah to snort loudly.

"Sorry," she said to no one in particular.

"Everyone, listen up." Mitzi's voice was commanding as she took her spot at the head of the table. "We've got pot roast, potato pancakes, carrots—"

"None of which you cooked, I'm sure," Delilah's father cracked.

"I cooked all of it, as a matter of fact," Mitzi retorted.

"You mean Ben's Deli cooked all of it. If you'd cooked it, dinner wouldn't be on the table until midnight."

Delilah's mother smiled sweetly at Brandi. "Have you grown bored of his nastiness yet? Or are you still in the 'He's so witty' stage?"

Delilah groaned. "Mom. Don't."

"You *wish* I was still being nasty to you," Delilah's father continued, unheeded. "Admit it."

"You know what I wish?" Mitzi hissed. "I wish you should get hit by a truck!"

"Why did you invite me, then?" Sy challenged.

"For Leelee! I wanted to make a nice Hanukkah for *our daughter*!"

Jason glanced at Delilah. She sat extremely still, head bowed as she stared down at the table. Jason got the impression she was somewhere else in her head, or else she was trying to make herself as unobtrusive as possible to keep out of the line of fire. It seemed to work; as her parents continued hurling insults at each other like poison darts, they seemed to forget Delilah was even there.

Jason caught Eric's eye. He looked uncomfortable yet fascinated, which was exactly the way Jason was feeling. This was so different from the way their family interacted that it was like being on another planet. The intensity of the emotion between Delilah's parents was unnerving. Jason had once heard there was a thin line between love and hate. Mitzi and Sy lived on the line. The gleam in both their eyes wasn't purely malice; there was also excitement there. *This is a kind of foreplay for them,* Jason realized.

As quickly as the nastiness had flared, it was over. Sy grumbled something, Mitzi muttered something, and then they were acting like nothing had ever happened as Sy asked Mitzi to pass him the pot roast, and she did so with a smile. Delilah slowly lifted her head, as if it were safe to come out now.

"Baby, what can I get you to eat?" her mother said to her.

"I'll have some potato pancakes, please."

Her mother's mouth twisted with displeasure as she put

some potato pancakes on Delilah's plate. Mitzi put pancakes on Jason's plate, too, nearly three times more than
she'd given Delilah. If Delilah noticed, she didn't say anything.

Jason had never had a potato pancake before, so he
watched to see what everyone else was doing. Delilah's father was slathering his in sour cream. Jason did the same,
passing the sour cream to Delilah when he was done.

"She doesn't need that!" Mitzi called out sharply.

Jason blinked in confusion. "What?"

"You don't want the sour cream, do you, honey?" Mitzi
asked Delilah. "So fattening. Why don't you have the apple-
sauce instead?"

"Why don't you leave her the hell alone, Mitzi?" Sy
growled. "She's skin and bones!"

"She takes after your side of the family, Sy. Too much
sour cream, and she's gonna wind up looking like your
cousin Temma—that blimp!"

"Temma was not a blimp," Sy said indignantly. "She had
a gland problem."

"You mean she had a cake problem! I don't want
Leelee—"

"Hello," Delilah interrupted loudly, "please stop talking
about me like I'm not here!"

Sy looked apologetic. "You're right, pussycat. I'm sorry.
I still think you should eat what you want."

"Thank you, I will," said Delilah, glaring at her mother.
There was relish in her movements as she plopped a huge
dollop of sour cream on her plate.

"I have a headache," Brandi announced. She turned to
Delilah's father. "I want to go home."

Sy looked embarrassed. "We just got here."

Brandi looked annoyed. "I can't control when I do or
don't get a headache, Sy."

"Sweetheart, if you could take an aspirin and just hang in
there—"

"I can run her home if you want," Eric offered. Everyone
at the table turned to look at him. "Really, it's no problem.

I can take Delilah's car, run her home, and then come back. That way you can stay here and enjoy your dinner, Mr. G."

"Well . . ." Delilah's father seemed uncertain.

Jason looked at Delilah, who was busy glaring at Eric, who refused to glance at the side of the table where Delilah and Jason were sitting. *What the hell?* Jason thought.

"It's a perfect solution, Sy," said Brandi, patting his hand. "This way I won't ruin your night."

Delilah's father looked at Eric uncertainly. "Are you sure about this?"

"Absolutely," Eric declared. "As long as Mitzi promises to save me some of that delicious pot roast."

Jason pushed his plate away. Eric was making him nauseous.

"All right, then." Delilah's father glanced across the table. "Can he take your car, Leelee?"

"Of course. I can see poor Brandi is just dying to get to bed," Delilah said pointedly.

Eric rose. "I promise I'll get her there in one piece, Mr. G."

"This is very nice of you, young man. Delilah, will you give Jason your keys?"

"You mean Eric, Dad. Jason's right here." Delilah leaned her head for a moment on Jason's shoulder.

"Jason, Eric, you hockey players all look the same to me," Delilah's father joked feebly.

Delilah handed over the keys.

"Don't even ask," were the first words out of Delilah's mouth as soon as she and Jason were in the kitchen. Ostensibly, they were there to help clean up after dinner. The real reason, though, was that Delilah feared she'd lose her mind—and her temper—if she had to spend one minute more with her parents.

"What do you mean, don't even ask?" Jason replied. "What the hell is going on with Eric and Brandi?"

"I guess we'll find out, won't we?" Delilah replied bitterly.

"Maybe he really is just driving her home," Jason offered. Delilah's impulse was to blurt something horrific about Eric, but she held back. She could see Jason was clutching at straws, not wanting to believe his brother really was as devious as he appeared. It was touching in its own sad way.

Jason cringed as Delilah's mother's voice grew louder. "Your folks really—"

"Don't go there, either. Please."

Mortification didn't even begin to cover what she was feeling. The minute she saw her father's car parked in the drive, the evening was already a goner in her mind. She couldn't believe her parents didn't even *try* to be on their best behavior when meeting Jason. She told herself she should be used to it by now; that when her parents were together, everything became about them. But this was different. This night was supposed to be about introducing Jason to her mother. Her parents' behavior embarrassed and infuriated her.

At least her mother hadn't done her impression of Torquemada. Instead, she hadn't asked Jason anything about himself *at all*. Which was worse?

All the tension she'd been holding back all evening came rushing to the fore. Delilah stood at the sink, blinking back tears. Jason came up behind her, wrapping his arms around her waist. "It's okay," he said, pressing his cheek against hers.

"I'm so embarrassed," Delilah choked out.

"Don't be. Everyone's parents are insane."

Delilah gave a hiccuping little laugh. "Really?"

"Well . . ."

Delilah turned in his arms. "It might not be true, but hearing it makes me feel better."

"Good." Jason's expression was tender as he looked down at her. "Tonight has helped me 'get' you."

"What do you mean?"

"Your parents. I can see why you wound up being so nervous and shy. Anytime they open their mouths, it's big-time drama."

"No kidding. It's like *Who's Afraid of Virginia Woolf?* without the booze."

"I saw you trying to make yourself disappear at the table," Jason said softly.

Delilah's eyes burned. "You did?"

"Of course. Your folks suck all the oxygen out of the room; there isn't space for anyone else."

As Jason held her close, Delilah slowly became aware that the shouting in the dining room had ceased. She paused, listening. There wasn't a sound: no talking, no sound of china clinking against a plate, nothing. Terror struck her heart.

"Can you excuse me a minute?" she asked Jason.

"Sure."

Back stiff as a poker, she walked back into the dining room. Her parents were kissing. In fact, her mother was sitting on her father's lap.

"What the hell is wrong with the two of you?!" Delilah shrieked.

Her parents broke apart guiltily. "It was just a kiss for old time's sake," her father offered lamely.

"Oh, that's nice! I wonder what Brandi would think if she found out you were kissing Mom!" She couldn't believe it; she'd actually been put in a position of feeling sorry for Brandi. If that wasn't proof of how screwed-up the situation was, what was?

She heard movement behind her and turned. Jason was standing in the dining room doorway, looking completely disconcerted.

"Please go back in the kitchen," Delilah begged.

"We're all adults here," said her mother, rising from her father's lap.

"I'm not so sure about that," Delilah snapped. An image flashed in her mind of herself as a little girl, sitting between her parents on the *Dr. Phil* show. "You need to get with the program!" Dr. Phil scolded them. "Or you're really gonna mess this child up!" *Too late,* thought Delilah.

Her father's face was flushed. "Leelee, you need to understand."

"No, *you* need to understand! Get back together, or leave each other alone!" Delilah continued angrily. "This is ridiculous! My nerves can't take it anymore! And while we're at it, it would have been nice if one of you tried to engage my boyfriend in conversation at some point! But no—you were too caught up in the 'passion' of your own stupid melodrama!"

"I'm sorry," Delilah's father said to Jason.

"Me, too," said Delilah's mother, though she didn't really look it. Delilah hated the way she was smoothing her blouse, as though she were fresh from a roll in the hay.

"I'm back," Eric announced, strolling into the dining room with a great, big smile, which slowly faded as he picked up on the tension in the room. He peered at everyone in turn. When his eyes got to Delilah's, she jerked her gaze away, unable to stand the sight of him. "Did I miss something?" he asked.

"Armageddon." Delilah held out her hand. "Keys, please. We're leaving."

CHAPTER 22

"Delilah hates me, doesn't she?"

Jason wasn't even sure he wanted to dignify Eric's question with a response, since the answer seemed pretty obvious. The ride back to the city following the Hanukkah debacle was spent in abject silence, Delilah doing her impersonation of a powder keg about to explode behind the wheel. Both Jason and Eric were smart enough not to strike up conversation. When they got back home and Delilah said she was tired, Jason decided it would be wise to take a rain check on giving her her Hanukkah gift. He was tired, too, which made Eric's insistence on coming with him on Stanley's final walk of the night all the more annoying.

"Jace?"

"What do you want me to say, Eric?" Jason gently tugged Stanley away from a small stack of moldy newspapers sitting by the curb. "You invite yourself to dinner at her mother's, then you take off and fuck her father's fiancée. How do you think Delilah feels?"

"I didn't fuck her!" Eric's voice rose in protest. "She just needed to talk."

"Yeah, right."

"I'm serious."

"And she just decided to pick you to bare her heart to, huh?"

Eric glanced away. "We know each other vaguely."

"I saw the eyes you were making at each other. I was tempted to tell you to go get a room."

"I'm telling you," Eric insisted, "she's confused."

"Boo-fucking-hoo."

Confused? thought Jason. *A double D cup disaster was more like it.* They were all wrecks: Delilah's parents, Brandi, his brother, him, and Delilah.

"Okay, so maybe I shouldn't have been so eager to drive her home," Eric eventually conceded.

"And nothing happened?"

Eric hesitated. "A few kisses."

Jason shook his head disgustedly. "I knew it."

"I swear to you, bro: it was mainly talk. You want to hear something sad? She's not sure Delilah's father loves her."

"Which means what? It's okay for her to fake a headache so she can slink off to suck face with you? Think about this: if she's cheated on Delilah's father, she'd cheat on you, too."

Eric arrogantly tilted his nose up in the air. "I think not. For one thing, I'm about thirty years younger than Sy. Better looking. Possibly richer. *And* I don't have man boobs."

"Yet."

"Fuck you."

"Seriously, Eric: can you blame Delilah for being ticked? She might not be thrilled about her father being with Brandi, but she doesn't want to see the old man hurt, either."

"That old man can take care of himself, believe me. He survived life with Delilah's mother, didn't he?"

Jason just groaned.

"What the hell was going on there when I got back to the house?" Eric continued.

"Nothing." Jason turned up the collar of his coat. He wished Stanley would hurry up and do his business; it was

beginning to get seriously cold outside. "Delilah was just
having a disagreement with her parents." No way in hell
was he going to give Eric ammunition by telling him about
Sy and Mitzi's bizarro canoodling. Plus, he couldn't do that
to Delilah. The look of humiliation on her face when he'd
wandered out into the dining room to see what was going on
had broken his heart. How vulnerable she'd seemed standing there, facing off against her parents. It made Jason want
to scoop her up and shield her in his arms.

That's when it hit him: he would invite Delilah to spend
Christmas with his family. His parents were flying in from
Flasher for the holiday, beside themselves with excitement
at coming to New York for the first time. His mom was planning to cook a big dinner with all the fixings at Eric's. It
would be the perfect opportunity for Delilah to see how a
relatively functional family interacted.

Jason decided to feel out his brother. "How do you think
Mom and Dad would react if I asked Delilah to join us for
Christmas dinner?"

"I think they'd be fine. I also think you're nuts if you do
it. You bring a girl over to meet Mom at *Christmas*, and by
New Year's she'll have knitted three pairs of booties for
your firstborn child."

Jason ignored the wisecrack, though it wasn't far from
the truth. "I just thought it might be nice for Delilah to
spend some time around a normal family, you know?"

"Normal?" Eric chortled.

"More normal than her parents."

"True."

"And you know Mom: she'll make a big fuss over
Delilah, it'll be great."

"If you say so," said Eric, sounding doubtful. "But don't
come crying to me when Mom starts calling you with sug-
gestions for baby names."

"*I can't believe* you're saying you can't. Can't Marcus
watch the dogs?"

Delilah glanced away, unable to take the disappointment in Jason's eyes. He'd been so excited when he'd shown up at her apartment, a little boy bursting to tell a secret. Delilah had been excited, too. Then he asked her to spend Christmas with his family, and she'd had to spoil his fun.

"I told you," Delilah said gently as she turned back to him. "It's not that I don't want to; it's that I can't. The holidays are my busiest time of the year, Jason; they're right up there with summer vacations. Not only am I walking the maximum amount of dogs, but I have the maximum amount of boarders. It's a twenty-four-hour thing."

Jason's lips pressed together in a thin line. It was something he did when he didn't like what he was hearing. "Like I said: can't Marcus spot you?"

"Marcus has a family, too, you know. He goes home to Virginia at Christmas."

Jason took her hand. "Delilah, this is really important to me."

"I know, but . . ." Delilah searched for an alternative. "How long are your parents in town for? Marcus usually comes back the day after Christmas. If your parents are in town for the whole week, maybe I can meet them then."

She smiled encouragingly; even though the thought of meeting Jason's parents brought on the itchy feeling. She couldn't help thinking back to that one failed foray to meet a boyfriend's family, when she'd mistaken a painting of Jesus for a member of the family. Things would probably go worse with Jason's family, since Jason meant more to her than that boyfriend ever did.

"They're in town until the twenty-eighth, but that's not the point. I wanted you to spend *Christmas* with us."

Over the years, various friends had invited Delilah to join them for the holiday, and until she started her own business, she often accepted, though sometimes she did feel a bit like an outsider with her nose pressed up against the window. When she was little, she didn't understand why her family didn't have a tree or sing carols or attend Midnight Mass or believe in Santa Claus. Christmas dominated the culture. It was everywhere: on TV, in the stores, in school.

"I would love to spend Christmas with you and your family," Delilah said softly. "But I can't. If I were only taking care of my dogs, then maybe I could get away for a few hours. But I'm going to be taking care of other people's dogs, too, and that's my first priority. How would you feel if you boarded Stanley with someone, and something bad happened, and you found out the person you'd hired to watch him hadn't been doing their job?"

"I'd be pissed," Jason admitted reluctantly.

"There you go." She ran her thumb back and forth across the top of his hand. "I have to confess something to you. Remember when I let Eric watch my boarders for a few hours while you and I went to dinner with your friends?" Jason nodded uncertainly. "I was wrong to do that. And I'm sure it's part of the reason I was so uptight that night. It was an irresponsible thing to do."

"You're allowed to have a life, Delilah."

"I do have a life."

"Not enough of one to accommodate a serious boyfriend."

Delilah swallowed. "What do you want me to do, Jason?"

"I don't know." He ran a hand through the dark, unruly mop of his hair, the hair Delilah loved trailing her fingers through. "There's got to be some way we can work this out."

"I told you: I'd love to meet your folks later in the week if they're still here."

"We'll see."

It pained Delilah to be the source of his dismay, but she didn't see any way around this. Sometimes she longed to say to him: *Excuse me, you're a professional athlete who makes tons of money! Not all of us do! Some of us have to pay ourselves a salary, pay others a salary, and carry our own health insurance!* But she didn't want to sound shrill, or worse, bitter. Jason had worked hard to get where he was. But so had she. She'd started out by posting a card on a bulletin board in a pet food store. Now she had to turn clients away. It was a dream scenario, except when it came to her and Jason.

Shiloh was pawing her for affection, so Delilah leaned over to scratch her behind the ears. "We haven't talked about the other night," she said tentatively.

Jason's voice was quiet. "I got the impression you didn't want to." Seeing Shiloh get attention, Belle and Sherman headed over to Jason and Delilah. Jason began petting them both, one with each hand.

"I'm sorry about what you were subjected to. I had no idea my father would be there. Or Brandi." Delilah could barely hide her displeasure as she asked, "Did your brother have any comments about that?"

Jason sighed. "He said they just talked."

"Oh, please."

"He said Brandi's not sure if your father loves her."

"As if she loves my father!" Delilah exclaimed.

"That's a whole other issue."

"True." Delilah analyzed the situation. "I think my dad loves the ego stroke of having this young, hot babe on his arm. But I also think he's still in love with my mother. And I think she's still in love with him." She shuddered. "Not that I want to think about it."

"Why did they split up, then?"

Delilah sighed heavily. "My mother thought he was having an affair with his secretary, Junie."

"And was he?"

"God, no. I also think my mother thought they'd be happier apart, so she cooked up this stupid affair accusation. And then she realized she missed him, but she had too much pride to ask him back, and my father had too much pride to ask to come back. Plus, as you can see, they love the thrill of the fight."

"Why didn't they try couples therapy?"

"They did. The therapist offered to pay them to leave."

"I don't understand how they can live at a fever pitch like that all the time."

"No kidding," said Delilah dryly. She stopped scratching Shiloh. "Go lie down now. Good girl." She turned to Jason. "Well, that was a Hanukkah you'll never forget."

"Speaking of which." Jason rose, fetching the gym bag he'd left by the front door. Unzipping it, he pulled out a wrapped present and handed it to Delilah. "For you."

The gift was wrapped in Hanukkah wrapping paper, with white menorahs and dreidels scattered against a royal blue background. Self-conscious at being the only one with a present, Delilah tried to make a joke. "Well, it's too light to be gold bars," she said, shaking the gift.

"Open it." The excitement Jason had shown earlier returned. It was one of the things Delilah adored about him: his unbridled enthusiasm when something was important to him.

As delicately as she could, Delilah began unwrapping the present, carefully running her index finger beneath the gift's taped seams to do the least damage, the way her mother had taught her. That way Jason could reuse—

"Just tear it off!" Jason exclaimed impatiently.

"Okay, okay."

Delilah tore off the wrapping paper with great flourish, revealing a plain box beneath. Trying not to look overeager, she pried off the lid. Inside was a beautiful leather fanny pack, much larger than the beat-up nylon one she currently used.

"Oh, Jason," she whispered, holding the fanny pack up. "This is wonderful! Look how big it is! I can hold tons of biscuits and poop bags and God knows what else!"

"That's the idea."

Delilah stood up and put it on, adjusting it so it properly fit around her waist. "What do you think?"

"Looks great."

A momentary sense of unworthiness fluttered through her. "I hope you didn't spend too much on this."

"That's my business."

Delilah left it at that, though the thought that he'd laid out a lot of money on the present was somewhat unsettling,

especially since there was no way she could afford to recip-
rocate.

She carefully took off the fanny pack, reveling in the
scent of new leather. *It's almost too beautiful to use,* she
thought. A month on the job and the poor bag would be
scored with scratches and seasoned with drool.

She laid the pack back in its box. "I don't know what to
say."

"You don't have to say anything." Jason stood and
wrapped his arms around her. "Happy Hanukkah, Miss
Gould."

"Delilah? Jason's here."

"Send him up."

Pleasantly puzzled, Delilah released the intercom button.
The last thing she expected was a visit from Jason on
Christmas Day. She imagined him in his apartment with
Eric and his parents, all of them sitting around sipping
eggnog while carols played softly in the background.

After so many years of living there, Delilah had noticed
the city had a different feel on Christmas. The sense of anticipation that built steadily throughout the month of
December was gone, replaced by a special hush unique to
the day. Walking the dogs earlier that morning, Delilah actually found herself wishing for a soft snowfall to complete
the picture.

She glanced at her canine house guests, all of whom
were extremely well-behaved. Of course they were: Delilah
had trained each and every one of them. She was surrounded by eight dogs in total, including her three. Not a
few heads had turned when she'd walked them all together;
but for Delilah, it was a piece of cake.

Unfortunately, Jason's surprise visit didn't give her time
to change into something a little less *zhlubby* than sweats
and a ratty old fleece. She decided not to stress about it;
he'd seen her in her hermit wear before. When the doorbell
rang, a few of the dogs barked, but most were content to ex-

citedly scramble to their feet and follow Delilah to the door.
"Sit," Delilah commanded them. All eight dogs took a seat.

Delilah flung the door open wide. "Merry Christmas!"

There stood Jason with Stanley. And Eric. And an older
man and woman who were extremely sensibly dressed. All
were carrying shopping bags.

Delilah wanted to die.

"Since you couldn't come for Christmas, we thought
we'd bring Christmas to you!" Jason exclaimed happily.
Delilah could feel her heart wanting to drop to her feet, but
she managed to halt the plummet and just stare at him. She
wanted to kill him. Truly. She wanted to lure him up to the
rooftop of her building and push him off. How could he am-
bush her this way with his parents in tow?! He knew she was
taking care of lots of dogs. He knew what her winter dog
walking "uniform" was. Yet here he was. Chalk up another
one for Sir Jason the Impulsive.

Stanley, who once hadn't known how to react to other
dogs, was dying to get inside Delilah's apartment. Though
he was sitting like a good boy at Jason's side, he was panting heavily, his eyes glued to the other animals.

"Let him go," Delilah told Jason.

"Up," Jason said to Stanley, and he trotted past Delilah to
join the other dogs. "Down," Delilah commanded all of
them, Stanley included. All sank down to the floor, the way
Delilah wished she could.

"Come in." Delilah ushered her unexpected company inside, willing herself to produce a smile meant to indicate
good cheer. How was she going to fit five people in her
apartment along with nine dogs? A fresh wave of in-
credulity washed over her; what had Jason been *thinking*?
Delilah glanced at him surreptitiously. If Jason had any
sense she was about to lose it, he didn't show it.

Chiding herself for forgetting her manners, she awkwardly stuck out her hand toward Jason's mother. "I'm
Delilah."

"And I'm Jane," the tall, pear-shaped woman said cheerfully. She pointed to the craggy-faced man beside her. "And

this is Dick. I know, Dick and Jane, ha ha ha. But it can't be helped." She began unbuttoning her coat. "We've heard so much about you—more from Eric than Jason, actually. You know what a chatterbox Eric is." She looked at Eric affectionately. "Anyway, I really hope you don't mind us being here. Christmas is a time for people to be together!"

Overwhelmed, Delilah resumed her false smile. She was dressed like a hag. A zit had decided to make a holiday appearance right in the middle of her forehead. Her apartment smelled of dog.

"I'm so sorry," she said to Jason's mother. "I've been working today, and I wasn't expecting you so I didn't clean, and all these dogs—"

"Are wonderful," Jason's mother finished for her. She put down her shopping bags and went to kneel amid the dogs, letting them sniff and lick her face if they wanted to. "Look at them all!" she marveled. "I don't think we've ever seen so many dogs together at one time, do you, Dick?"

"Nope," said Jason's father.

"None of them are as handsome as Stanley, though."

Delilah made a conscious effort not to gape as Jason's mother reveled in the dogs' attention. If this were Mitzi, she would be halfway down the street by now.

"That's enough for now, kids." Jason's mother rose. Her black corduroy pants were covered in dog hair. Delilah cringed as she began brushing herself off.

"I'm so sorry, Mrs. Mitchell. Let me see if I can find a lint remover."

"Don't be silly," said Jason's mother with a dismissive wave of the hand. "Most of the time I'm up to my ankles in mud and cow dung and God knows what else. This is nothing."

Up until now, Delilah's head had been spinning so fast she hadn't paid much attention to Jason. Their eyes met. With Stanley again parked beside him, Jason looked like a man without a care in the world. How could she stay mad at him? What he'd done had come from a good place.

"Now." Jason's mother picked up her shopping bags. "If

you don't mind me taking over your kitchen, my plan was to cook a roast beef with gravy, mashed potatoes, carrots, and peas. For dessert we've got an apple pie I baked last night."

"Mom's a baking fool," Eric offered helpfully. He'd been careful to avoid Delilah's eye since arriving.

Mrs. Mitchell rolled her eyes. "There would have been two pies, but a certain set of twins I know decided to be little piggies last night." She regarded Delilah apprehensively. "Are you sure this isn't too much of an imposition?"

"Too late now," Eric murmured under his breath.

Delilah looked at him sharply. "It's no problem at all," she told Jason's mother, trying to believe her own words. So what if her table could seat only two, and she wasn't sure if she had enough plates and cutlery to go around? They'd figure something out.

"Can I help you in the kitchen?" Delilah asked shyly.

Jason's mother cupped Delilah's cheek. "I would love that."

Delilah looked down at her sweats. "Just let me get changed first. I'm feeling a little underdressed."

Excusing herself, Delilah hustled off to her bedroom to change into a pair of jeans and a simple turtleneck. Her feelings of wanting to murder Jason were beginning to wane in light of how relaxed Jason's mother appeared to be. Delilah couldn't believe Mrs. Mitchell didn't care about the state of her apartment and the small fleet of dogs that would be underfoot. If Jason's mother could be so laid back in the midst of an impromptu situation, maybe she could, too. She quickly ran a brush through her hair, putting on some lip gloss for extra measure. She could do this—*and* she could enjoy it. Heart feeling lighter, she went to rejoin Jason's family.

"*It won't be* much longer."

Delilah stepped aside gracefully as Jason's mother once

more basted the roast in its own juices before returning it to the oven.

"Smells good," noted Jason's father, appearing in the doorway. "We almost ready?"

"I was just saying to Delilah it won't be much longer. We won't start without you, I promise."

Mr. Mitchell chuckled and returned to the living room, where Jason and Eric were watching a football game on TV. Their excited cries incited some of Delilah's charges to bark, prompting Delilah to ask them to please keep it down. From the kitchen Delilah could hear their heated murmurings, a cabal of two now joined by their father.

Delilah never would have believed it a few hours ago, but there was actually something heartwarming about the whole scene: the home-cooked meal, the men watching football, the dogs snoozing peacefully on the living room floor. It was as if she'd gone to sleep and awakened to find herself in a Norman Rockwell painting. At first, she was suspicious. Then she realized: Yes, Virginia, there really *are* some families who don't yell and criticize. It was a major revelation.

She edged up shyly on Jason's mom, who had insisted on washing the pots and pans. How different she was from Mitzi, not just in terms of temperament, but in the face she presented to the world. Where Mitzi wouldn't even leave her bedroom in the morning without first putting makeup on, Jane Mitchell wore no makeup at all. She sported glasses rather than contact lenses, and moved with the ease of someone entirely comfortable in their own skin, even if that skin was discernibly slack in places. The same seemed true of Jason's father: Dick Mitchell was quiet but confident, with an easygoing way about him. Watching Jason's parents interact brought a lump to Delilah's throat. They were kind in the way they spoke to another, their teasing playful rather than nasty. The aura surrounding them was one of simple, plain love that some might even characterize as boring. If so, then Delilah yearned for the dullest life on earth.

Initially worried she might embarrass herself, Delilah

had kept her answers to all of Jane's questions simple. But the longer they worked together in the kitchen, the more relaxed Delilah became, which is why she didn't blush and blubber when Jason's mother turned to her and asked, "Are you still mad at him?"

Delilah looked at her uncertainly. "I don't understand."

Jane put an affectionate hand on Delilah's shoulder. "I saw your face when you opened the front door. You looked like you wanted to burrow beneath the floorboards or else give Jason a mountain-sized chunk of your mind."

"It was a bit of a shock," Delilah confessed.

"I knew it would be. When Jason suggested it, I said, 'Are you sure you want to do this?' But he was adamant. You know Jason: he can be very impulsive, but his heart is in the right place."

Delilah nodded in agreement, glad that his mother shared her assessment of Jason. "Has he always been that way?"

"God, yes," chuckled Jason's mother. "Jason's always been a little impetuous, while Eric is always cool as a cucumber. Funny, isn't it, that they're twins and yet so different?"

"It is."

Mrs. Mitchell sighed. "I wish Eric would meet someone nice like you."

Maybe he could if he stopped trying to bang other people's fiancées, thought Delilah. She wondered if Mrs. Mitchell was aware of what a horndog her handsome, blue-eyed son was. Probably not.

"Do you know anyone you could introduce him to?" Mrs. Mitchell continued hopefully.

"Let me think about it."

"Thank you." Jason's mother put the final pot in the drying rack and toweled off her hands. "So, Jason tells me you're Jewish."

Delilah tensed. "Yes." All the self-confidence slowly gaining velocity over the course of the afternoon was in danger of screeching to a halt.

Jason's mother looked embarrassed. "I hope you won't

think me too ignorant, but I know nothing about it. Maybe you could recommend a book for me? Or I can ask you some questions later—?"

"That would be fine," said Delilah, touched by her interest. She realized she'd been tensing in anticipation of an anti-Semitic remark that never came. Damn Denny O'Malley. He'd shaken Delilah up more than she'd realized.

"Geez, Mom, where's the chow?"

Eric stood in the kitchen doorway, rubbing his belly like a hungry little boy. He still seemed uncertain of his status with Delilah. *Good,* thought Delilah.

"I'll tell you the same thing I told your father," Mrs. Mitchell said to Eric. "We won't start without you." She turned to Delilah. "Men!"

"That's all you're eating?"

Delilah looked up from her plate in surprise to see Jason's mother peering at her with concern. They were eating dinner in the living room with their plates on their laps, no easy feat, considering the menagerie sprawled on the floor all around them. The dogs might be well-trained, but dogs were dogs, and all were eyeing the food like vultures. Delilah felt bad, eating this feast in front of them. It seemed deliberately cruel somehow.

She double-checked her plate; she'd taken a single slice of meat and a small dollop of each side dish. She'd deliberately opted for small portions, not wanting Jason's parents to think she was a glutton. Apparently, she needn't have worried.

"I'm okay," Delilah insisted.

"Please, take more. There's plenty here. If you ask me, you could use a little more meat on your bones."

Delilah fought the temptation to put aside her plate so she could get down on her knees and kiss Mrs. Mitchell's feet. Despite her father's insistence otherwise, a lifetime of food supervision by Mitzi had convinced Delilah she ate too much. To have unbiased, outside confirmation that this wasn't so boosted Delilah's confidence immensely.

"Everything's great, Mom," Jason raved. There was a question in his eyes as he glanced at Delilah: *Are you okay?* Delilah gave him a quick smile. Not only wasn't she nervous, but she was actually having a good time.

"What do you plan to do while you're in the city, Mr. and Mrs. Mitchell?" Delilah asked.

"Shop," Mrs. Mitchell replied without hesitation. "And see some Broadway shows." She turned a hopeful glance toward her sons. "Has that play about Dr. Phil opened yet?" She leaned toward Delilah as if imparting a secret. "I love Dr. Phil. He's so handsome."

Delilah and Jason looked at each other. Jason's lips were twitching; he wanted to laugh. "Actually, Mom, that play closed," said Jason.

Mrs. Mitchell looked crestfallen. "It did?"

Delilah nodded. "A friend of mine was in it. He was devastated."

"As am I." She popped a piece of meat in her mouth. "I guess we'll just have to settle for *The Phantom of the Opera*, eh, Dick?"

Jason's father just nodded.

"It's too bad you guys aren't going to be here for New Year's Eve," Eric said to his parents. "You could watch the ball drop in Times Square."

Jason frowned. "Why would you want to subject them to that? There are a gazillion people there crowded into this tiny space. That's not fun."

"I agree with Jason," said Mrs. Mitchell. She took a sip of water. "What are you kids doing for New Year's Eve?"

"Going to Times Square with some of my friends," said Eric, making a face at Jason.

"Delilah and I are going to a party," said Jason.

Delilah put down her fork. "We are?"

"Yeah, I've been meaning to tell you." Jason dabbed his mouth with his napkin. "Tully Webster and his wife are having a party at their house in Westchester. I thought we'd check it out."

"O-okay."

Jason must have sensed her unease. "You're up for it, right?"

"Sure," Delilah told him, and for the most part, she was telling the truth. Still, they did need to talk about it.

Flashing a surprisingly self-confident smile, Delilah resumed eating.

CHAPTER 23

"*I didn't mean* to just drop it on you like that. I'm sorry."

Christmas dinner over, Jason's family had left him and Stanley behind at Delilah's so they could spend some time alone. Jason thought the day went great. His parents seemed to like Delilah, especially his mother. Best of all, Delilah really seemed to be relaxed and enjoying herself. But he could tell she'd been caught off guard when he made his announcement about New Year's Eve. He was wrong to present it as a done deal.

"I should kick your butt," Delilah teased. "You realize that, don't you?"

"You love my butt."

"I do," Delilah agreed. "But in the future, *please*, please check with me first before making plans for both of us. Promise?"

"I promise. What did you think of my folks?" Jason continued, beginning to massage her shoulders. Delilah loved being massaged, and Jason loved accommodating her. Of course, the ego boost of being told he had "wonderful, strong fingers" didn't hurt, either.

"They're amazing," Delilah sighed. "So sane."

"I thought you'd like them." Jason kissed the nape of her neck. "And there was no way I wanted to celebrate Christmas without you." His thumbs made small circles at the base of her skull. "Eric seemed a little skittish, though."

"He's lucky I haven't skinned him alive." Delilah dropped her head forward in full surrender.

"You're under my power now," Jason intoned as if he were a magician mesmerizing her.

"So, about New Year's," Delilah said casually.

"Mmm?"

"I'm not really a New Year's Eve person," Delilah said carefully. "I was kind of hoping we could have a nice quiet New Year's Eve here, or at your place."

"Doing what?" Jason asked.

"Maybe bring in some takeout, rent a few movies."

"In other words, the usual."

"Yes." Delilah lifted her head and turned to look at him. "What's wrong with that?"

"It's New Year's *Eve*, Delilah. We're supposed to be out having fun!"

"Why can't we stay in and have fun?"

"We could," Jason agreed cautiously. "But I'd really like to go to this party. I think it could be fun."

He felt Delilah's shoulders beginning to tense beneath his hands. "Maybe you're right. I don't know."

"How about this?" Jason suggested. "We toss a coin. Heads we go, tails we don't."

"Okay." The prospect seemed to cheer her a bit.

Jason pulled a quarter out of his pocket. "Ready?" Delilah nodded. He threw the quarter up in the air, caught it, then slapped it onto his wrist. "Heads."

"Two out of three," Delilah called.

Jason frowned. "Fine." He repeated the coin trick. Again it came up heads.

"Shit," said Delilah.

"Fair's fair," Jason reminded her, putting the coin back in his pocket.

"I know," Delilah agreed. She swallowed. "Will Denny be there?"

"I don't know. But we can't let him dictate what we do and don't do socially. We play on the same team, honey. Being at the same social events is kind of unavoidable."

Delilah said nothing, but Jason could sense the wheels in her head turning.

"What about the dogs?" she asked quietly. "I have two boarders that night."

"Maybe we could ask Marcus to hang here."

Delilah laughed. "You expect *Marcus* to hang out here on New Year's Eve?"

"Tell him I'll pay whatever he asks."

"Jason!"

"I really want to go to this party, and I really want you to go with me," Jason insisted passionately. "Since Marcus is the only human being in Manhattan you trust with your dogs, it seems logical we ask him, and pay him accordingly."

Delilah bit her lip. "Let me think about it."

"We don't have to get dressed up," Jason added as an additional enticement. "It's casual."

"Well, that's good." Delilah reached for his hand. "Promise me one thing."

"What's that?"

"That we don't stay too long, and that even if some of your teammates are getting drunk, you don't."

"That's two things."

"Those are my terms."

"You really think I'd get drunk on New Year's Eve? Please. I'll leave that to Eric."

"Are we agreed?"

Jason hesitated. "Define 'We don't stay too long.'"

"We leave as soon as the clock strikes midnight."

"Afraid your car might turn into a pumpkin?"

"I don't like the idea of being on the road with all those drunks, Jason. I really don't. I'd like to get home sooner rather than later."

"Agreed," he said.

Delilah's eyes searched his face uneasily. "What if Marcus can't or won't do it?"

"Tell him money is no object."

"Okay. But I still don't think he'll bite."

"*One night of* New Year's Eve's dog sitting sold to the pretty lady with the fancy, leather fanny pack for five hundred dollars!" Marcus whooped. "Yeah!"

Delilah smiled bleakly as heads turned to see who was bellowing in the middle of the dog park. Though winter was here, and with it an increased desire on Delilah's part to hibernate, she had vowed when she started her business that barring a full-out blizzard, "her" dogs would spend part of each day in the dog park. So here she and Marcus sat, their gloved hands clutching large, steaming coffees, Marcus shuddering with cold in his flimsy leather jacket.

"Why don't you wear a warmer coat?" Delilah asked.

"What, and risk being mistaken for Nanook of the North like you? No way. I have an image to uphold."

"Yeah, that of a gay man freezing his butt off on a park bench. You could bring a friend to hang with you if you want," said Delilah, suddenly saddened by the image of Marcus all alone on New Year's Eve.

"You're very sweet, Lilah, but I think I'll pass. New Year's Eve is a trial best faced alone."

"I agree with you there."

The last time Delilah had been to a New Year's Eve party, the host forced everyone to listen to him play "House of the Rising Sun" on his guitar, and by the time the clock struck midnight, the hostess had locked herself in the bathroom, weeping, following a fight with her best friend. Delilah dreaded finding herself in a situation like that ever again.

As if reading her mind, Marcus bumped his shoulder against hers. "Stop fretting. Everything is going to be fine."

•   •   •

Outrageously crowded. Those were the first words that
came to Delilah's mind as she and Jason walked into Tully
Webster's living room. The room was packed with people,
some of them well on their way to inebriation, and it was
only nine thirty. Jason had wanted to hitch a ride from the
city with Barry and Kelly Fontaine, but Delilah resisted. She
didn't want to depend on anyone else for transportation.
Driving themselves insured someone sober would be behind
the wheel on the ride home. It also meant they weren't at the
mercy of the Fontaines who, for all Delilah knew, might like
to watch the sun come up on New Year's Day.

"Hey, guys, come in." Tully's face was flushed, whether
from sheer excitement or alcohol, Delilah couldn't tell.

"Tully, this is my girlfriend, Delilah," said Jason.

Tully's smile was genuine as he held out a big hand for
Delilah to shake. "Nice to meet you." He grinned at Jason.
"You hear about Dante?"

"What about him?"

"The wife dropped the third bambino this morning.
Another girl. Named her Angelina or something like that.
Kid weighed in at nine pounds."

Jason chuckled. "What a bruiser. She might have a future
in hockey."

"You got that right." Tully gestured at the room full of
people behind him. "You know everyone here. Food's on
the table in the dining room, booze on the sideboard behind
it. Go forth and paar-tay."

Tully disappeared back into the crowd as Jason led Delilah
farther inside. She quickly scanned the room for familiar
faces. No David and Tierney. But Denny was there. He was
holding court by a pair of sliding glass doors beyond which a
built-in pool, covered for the winter but still lit by floodlights,
was visible. Delilah felt her face warm with remembered humiliation and tried to put it behind her. He was Jason's teammate. She *would* have to deal with him on some level from
now on, even if it was just breathing the same air he did.

They were in the dining room now. The temperature

seemed to have dropped several degrees, a direct result of less bodies crowding the space. Above the din of voices, Delilah tried to detect what music was playing. She couldn't. All she knew was that it was loud enough to make the bottles and empty glasses on the sideboard tremble.

Jason introduced her to everyone in the dining room, their faces all blurring into one as Delilah did her best to smile and return their salutations. She worried about what would happen once she and Jason filled their plates and glasses. Would he expect her to mingle on her own? Or would he permit her to remain soldered to his side, a nodding appendage too nervous to speak?

"Jason Mitchell. Just the man I was hoping to see."

Delilah watched as a paunchy, middle-aged man in a navy blue blazer approached them. She glanced at Jason. He was smiling broadly. This was someone he liked.

"Hey, Larry. I want you to meet my girlfriend, Delilah. Delilah, this is Larry Levin. He's one of the longtime sportscasters at Met Gar Media. We all love this guy."

"Pleased to meet you," said Larry warmly, shaking her hand.

"You, too," said Delilah. Jason and Larry began speaking, but Delilah wasn't really listening. She had her own monologue going on in her head: *Larry Levin. That means I'm not the only Jew here. Denny O'Malley won't make a scene.* Delilah felt her lungs expand. It was as if she could somehow breathe again. She glanced around at the laughing, chattering couples, at the clusters of young men, all of whom were clearly athletes, their bodies muscled and hard. Maybe the evening wouldn't be so bad after all.

"Larry is great," said Jason, pouring himself and Delilah each a glass of champagne after Larry left to mingle. "Did you hear? He wants to interview me next week on *Blades Banter*."

"That's great," Delilah agreed, accepting the champagne flute from him. She took a small sip. It was good.

Tightly holding Jason's hand, they waded out into the sea of bodies in the living room. Delilah felt Denny's cold gaze zero in on her but refused to let it rattle her. For the next half hour, she was fine. She was holding her own. And then Tully had to go and wreck everything.

"Listen up, all ye lads and lasses." Tully turned down the sound on the stereo, his face one shade redder than before. "It's time for some fun! Y'all up for a game of charades?"

The room echoed with cheers and whistles.

"Good! Then let's start splitting up into teams."

Delilah could feel herself beginning to sweat. She dropped Jason's hand, looking up at him with pleading eyes. "Please don't make me do this."

Jason looked torn. "Delilah . . ."

"Please," she begged again. "I came to the party. I've mingled with you. *Please*."

Jason looked troubled. "What would you do instead?"

"I'll watch you play. Or we can tell Tully I'm not feeling well. Maybe he has a den where I can hang out."

"Okay," Jason said uncertainly. "Just hang here a minute?"

Delilah nodded. No way was Tully going to believe she wasn't feeling well. The timing was too suspect. Delilah just prayed he didn't return with Jason, trying cajoling her into playing, with, "Don't be shy! You're among friends!" or "Lighten up! It'll be fun!" Charades was not Delilah's idea of fun. She'd already done enough acting tonight, pretending to be a moderately social being who enjoyed accompanying her gregarious boyfriend to parties. One more false persona, and she would crack.

It felt like forever before Jason reappeared at her side. "Tully says feel free to hang out in the den. It's down the hall to the left. You sure you don't mind me playing?"

"Of course I don't mind. I want you to have fun."

"Yeah, but I hate the idea of you—"

"I'll be fine," Delilah assured him, giving his hand a reassuring squeeze. "Thank you for letting me be me."

"Me, too." Jason gave her a quick peck on the cheek. "I'll see you in a bit."

• • • •

To Delilah's mind, the word *den* conjured up images of a paneled room dominated by a sectional sofa and a giant TV. At least, that's the way the den of her childhood had looked, until her mother contracted alabaster fever and turned the entire house the color of Minute Rice. But Tully's den was a lot more tasteful. The couch was deep plush leather, the TV hidden away in a tall pine armoire. Shelves of books and trophies lined the room, which was bigger than Delilah's living room and bedroom combined. In fact, the whole house was huge, one of the largest Delilah had ever been in. Hockey had obviously been very good to Tully.

In no hurry to turn on the TV, she circled the room, looking at Tully's trophies, interspersed with family photos. She realized there were no pictures in her apartment of her with either of her parents, or all three of them together. The thought saddened her, especially when she recalled Jason's collection of photos of himself and his brother.

"Thank *God* I'm not the only one who thinks playing charades is *hell*."

Delilah turned to see a rail-thin, fashionably dressed woman her own age coming toward her, champagne flute in hand.

"I'm Wendy Dalton." She covered her mouth as she gave a small burp. "My husband, Burke, plays defense on the first line?"

She was looking at Delilah as if this explanation of who her husband was should ring a bell.

"Of course," Delilah murmured. She had no idea who Burke Dalton was. "I'm Delilah Gould. I'm—Jason Mitchell's girlfriend."

"The new boy in town," Wendy purred. "*Très* hot."

Delilah felt her cheeks flame, unsure of how to respond. Was she supposed to return the favor and say she thought Burke was hot? What was this woman doing blatantly commenting on Jason's hotness, anyway?

Wendy sighed, turning on the TV. "Do you mind? I just

need to, like, zone out. All that noise is giving me a headache."

"I don't mind."

Delilah joined her on the sectional sofa, stunned at the speed with which Wendy channel surfed. The sound of the party floated down the hallway, mingling with the rapid-fire bursts of TV patter. Behind the wall of sound, Delilah could have sworn she heard a dog barking. She listened hard.

"Do you hear that?" she asked Wendy.

Wendy had stopped a moment to peruse an old episode of *The Dukes of Hazzard*. "Hear what?"

"A dog."

Wendy listened. "No."

Delilah frowned with impatience, listening harder. No doubt about it: she heard a dog. Without thinking twice, she got up and unlocked the sliding glass doors of the den, stepping outside into the chill night air. She held her breath, listening again. There it was: a dog howling as if its heart would break. A dog barking in a desperate bid for attention. As if pulled by an invisible force, Delilah moved in the direction of the sound, her feet nearly going out from under her twice as she tiptoed in her not-so-high heels in the frozen grass. She followed the sound to a basement window, crouching to peer inside. A golden retriever puppy was tied with a leash to a pole.

Delilah stumbled back, breathing hard. She had ceased to feel the cold. She felt only fury, a deep, clenching anger that saw her heading back into the house, searching for the entrance to the basement. She didn't care who saw her. She climbed down the basement steps, tears pricking her eyes as the puppy spotted her and began to go crazy.

"It's okay," Delilah whispered, coming closer. There was no water bowl in sight. The dog had pooped on the concrete floor. Delilah untied the leash, scooping the puppy up into her arms. The dog yelped happily, licking Delilah's face. Delilah checked her dog tag. Her name was Marnie. "That's a good girl," Delilah whispered, kissing the top of her small, silky head. "C'mon. Let's take you outside."

Delilah carried the puppy upstairs and back into den. Wendy Dalton's eyes went wide with surprise.

"What a cutie!" she exclaimed as Delilah hustled toward the sliding glass doors. "How long have you had her?"

"She's not mine," Delilah said over her shoulder curtly. "Though she should be."

Outside, the puppy relieved itself in the grass, then tried trotting off, straining at the leash, seeking adventure. Delilah let her explore a bit to work off some of her energy, but it quickly became too cold for Delilah to remain outside without a coat. Delilah scooped the puppy back up and reentered the den. Tully and his wife were standing there, along with Jason.

Jason cleared his throat nervously. "Wendy Dalton said, um, you commandeered a puppy?"

"Commandeered? Saved, is more like it." Delilah tried to keep her voice from shaking as she approached Tully. "I found your dog in the basement. Tied up. With no water. She was crying her head off. But I guess you couldn't hear it because you were so busy with your paar-tay."

"Delilah." Jason started toward her cautiously, as if she were some rabid animal he was fearful might attack. Delilah turned to him angrily.

"I'll be done in just one minute." She took a step closer to Tully. "How would you like it if someone tied you up with no water? How would you like it if you had to poop on the floor?"

"Delilah," Jason hissed.

Delilah ignored him. "Marnie isn't a *toy.* She's a living, breathing creature with feelings and needs and *rights.* If it's too much of a hassle for you to care for her properly, I'll gladly take her off your hands."

"No!" Tully's wife cried. "We love her!" She turned to her husband accusingly. "I thought you gave her water." Tully's wife held out her arms, sniffling with tears.

Delilah reluctantly handed over the puppy. Tully's wife disappeared with her down the hall. Delilah blinked, waiting for her anger to abate. It didn't. In fact, if she had to

spend one more minute in the house of someone who mis-
treated their animal, she was going lose her mind.

"I'd like to leave now," she said to Jason quietly.

Jason looked down at the carpet. "Go ahead. I'll catch a
ride back to the city with someone else."

"Fine, then." Delilah swallowed, holding out a quivering
hand. "I need my keys, please."

Jason pulled the keys out of his front pocket and handed
them over to her without a word.

Delilah's fingers closed around them tightly. Here was
her escape. Just a few more seconds, and she'd be free. She
made herself look at Tully.

"Thank you for inviting us to your party," she said stiffly.

"Yeah, it's been a blast," Tully muttered as he turned
away.

Delilah nodded mutely, blindly moving through the living room and heading for the front door. It wasn't until she
was halfway down the Websters' front walk that she realized
she'd been expecting Jason to run after her, apologize, be-
seech her to stay, anything. He didn't.

CHAPTER
24

Jason spent New Year's Day nursing a slight hangover, halfheartedly watching a football game on TV and wondering what to do about Delilah.

He couldn't believe she'd morphed into the Canine Crusader at a New Year's Eve party being held by one of his *teammates,* for chrissakes. She'd embarrassed Tully, embarrassed him, and embarrassed herself. Jason couldn't wait for the clock to hit midnight so he could get the hell out of there. Unfortunately, he was at the mercy of the Fontaines, who'd offered to drive him back to the city. They didn't leave the party until three a.m. By that time, Jason's eyes were falling out of his head.

A disturbing thought lodged itself in his brain: he loved Delilah, but right now she felt like a liability. Bad enough he'd whaled on Denny and caused a hairline fracture in team morale, even though Denny had it coming. But this incident could turn Tully against him, and that he didn't need.

•　•　•

Walking into the locker room for the first time since Christmas break, Jason felt a sense of excitement growing within him. The Blades were going into the second half of the season sitting first in their division. If they maintained their level of play, they'd make it into the playoffs without breaking a sweat, and would have home ice advantage for most of the playoffs. Jason pictured himself joyously skating the Cup around the ice at Met Gar.

Standing in front of his locker, he stripped off his clothes and was beginning to suit up, when Burke Dalton passed behind him.

"Woof, woof, woof," Burke barked loudly. A couple of the guys in the locker room sniggered.

"Bowwow," someone else growled from the shower area.

"You in the doghouse or what, bro?" Thad Meyers asked, suppressing a smirk.

Jason ignored them and continued dressing. Fucking Tully. He obviously told them everything. Jason knew they were just ribbing him. But that didn't mean it didn't piss him off.

"What'd you do yesterday, Jace?" asked Ulf Torkelson, pulling his sweater over his head. "Watch *101 Dalmations* with your girlfriend?"

Barry Fontaine snorted. "I bet you like to do it doggy style, huh, buddy?"

"Fuck you, you assholes," Jason muttered, donning his cross.

"Oooowwwwooooohhhh," howled Denny O'Malley. The rest of the team joined in, baying like a pack of wolves.

Jaw clenched, Jason said nothing as he sat down to lace up his skates. He could feel his blood rising, but was determined not to lash out. Instead, he'd take his desire to pummel them and use it on the ice.

And then he'd go talk to Delilah.

"I don't think we should see each other anymore."

There, it was done. Delilah had been rehearsing that one simple sentence for two days, practicing different facial expressions and intonations. Sometimes, depending on her mood, the sentence came out angry; other times she'd start getting teary. In the end, she knew the only way she'd get through it was to say it simply. But Delilah being Delilah, it came out as a blurt.

Jason, who'd had the courtesy this time to call ahead rather than just show up at her apartment, stared at her incredulously. "*You're* breaking up with *me*?"

Delilah nodded.

"That's ironic. Because I'm here to break up with *you*."

"I guess I beat you to the punch."

Delilah watched him slowly sink down on her couch in disbelief. Despite maintaining her regular routine with Stanley, she hadn't seen Jason since New Year's Eve. She'd wept all the way back to Manhattan, not only for that poor little puppy, but for herself. She wasn't the right girlfriend for Jason. He needed someone outgoing like he was, someone who liked playing charades and going around in a pack. Delilah's definition of "pack" was limited strictly to dogs.

Harder still to admit was that Jason might not be the right guy for *her*. She loved his adoration of Stanley, and his sense of humor, and his unabashed enthusiasm for what he did. But Delilah needed someone who'd let her just *be*.

"Why are you breaking up with me?" Jason asked quietly.

"I could ask you the same thing."

"I asked you first."

Delilah toyed nervously with her left earring, avoiding his eye. "Because I don't think I can make you happy." She folded her hands in her lap. "Why were you going to break up with me?"

Jason looked pained. "Same reason." He paused. "You really embarrassed me at the New Year's Eve party. Tearing into Tully like that? It was wrong."

"He tied his dog up in the basement!"

"So, you should have come to find me, and then I could

have dealt with Tully diplomatically. You should think before you speak, Delilah."

"And you should think before you act, Jason. You just assumed it was okay to show up here at Christmas, or RSVP a New Year's party without checking with me first."

"I guess we're both guilty, then," Jason murmured unhappily.

"Yes." Delilah's eyes began filling. "We just don't work, do we?"

"No." Jason looked miserable. "I wish we did."

"So do I," Delilah choked. She didn't want to cry, but she couldn't help it. "I tried. I really did."

Jason had turned his face from hers. "I know you did," he agreed hoarsely. "And so did I. But some things . . ."

He turned back to put a comforting hand on Delilah's shoulder as she wept, but she gently rebuffed him. "I know you mean well, but please, don't make it harder than it already is."

Jason nodded, rising from the couch. "I should probably go."

"Okay," Delilah said numbly, swiping at her eyes with the back of her hand.

"What are we going to do about Stanley?"

"What do you mean?" Delilah snuffled. "I'll still walk him and board him as usual—unless you don't want me to."

"Of course I want you to. I just thought, you know, you might not want to."

"Just because we don't work doesn't mean I don't want to take care of your dog." An escaped tear trickled down Delilah's cheek. "I love Stanley. You know that."

"And he loves you."

"It's a nonissue, then."

"Good." Jason's hands looked shaky as he zipped up his jacket. "Delilah."

"What?"

"Thanks for, you know, the good times we did have."

Delilah squeezed her eyes shut. "You, too." *Go*, she

thought. *Please go now before I lose it in front of you completely.*

"Okay, then. Bye."

Delilah held her breath, waiting for the sound of the door closing. When it came, she exhaled hard and forced open her eyes, hoping to release the pain gripping her body. It didn't work. She let herself cry, finding an odd comfort in the knowledge that at least she and Jason had been kind to one another and hadn't gone for the jugular the way her parents would have. Eventually she sought solace in the best way she knew how: sinking down on her knees, she called her three dogs to her, hugging each of them before kissing their furry heads and rubbing their warm, soft bellies. At least she'd never have to let *them* go because their personalities were so different. For that, Delilah was grateful.

"You broke up with Delilah? To quote that great philosopher, Bugs Bunny, 'What a maroon!'"

Jason stared at his brother, debating whether to throttle him within an inch of his life. Leaving Delilah's apartment, Jason expected to be swept away on a tide of relief. Instead, he felt sick and hollow. After walking Stanley, he'd headed directly to Eric's, seeking companionship as well as confirmation that his *intent* to break up with her had been correct. Never in a million years would he tell Eric that Delilah severed ties first. He'd never live it down.

"Excuse me, but aren't you *Dr. Love*, the man who told me for months I was a jackass to tie myself down? The fellow hockey player who claimed my play *sucked* because I was in a relationship?"

"That's before I really got to know the lady in question," Eric replied coolly. "Plus—let's be honest here—you always suck out on the ice."

Jason looked at the ceiling and counted to three. "No matter what I say or do, you're always going to say the opposite, aren't you? Just to break my balls?"

Eric snorted. "You're just figuring this out?"

"For once in your life, could you stop being a dick and maybe act like a real brother?"

Eric actually looked wounded. "I act like a real brother! Who covered your ass when you couldn't make that brunch? Who found you your apartment before you moved to New York?"

"Yeah, yeah, yeah, I know."

"What is it you want me to say that I'm not saying?" Eric asked as he tossed Jason some bottled water from the fridge.

"I don't know." Jason sank down on Eric's La-Z-Boy, his brother's pride and joy. He couldn't believe how freakin' miserable he felt. "Tell me it was the right thing to do. Especially after the New Year's Eve debacle."

"I can't tell you that," Eric said matter-of-factly. "I'm not the one in love with her. You are."

"Help me out here, you *schmuck*."

Eric sighed. "Okay. I like Delilah a lot. I think she's great, and any woman who can deal with that drool machine you call a dog has got to be something special. But you jumped into it too fast, and now you're seeing the error of your ways. And yeah, I do think it was affecting your play, okay? So it's probably better you took the express route to Splitsville."

"Right." Jason wasn't sure he agreed, but it sounded good. Rational.

"Does it suck that you probably devastated her and the next time we see her, she'll turn and walk the other way? Or perhaps kick you in the crown jewels? Yes."

"See, that's the thing. I'm worried it's going to be weird with her still taking care of Stanley. You know—awkward."

"It might be. But what are you going to do? Start looking for another dog minder?"

"I don't really have time." *And I don't really want to,* Jason added in his head. He couldn't imagine anyone taking care of Stanley with the same love and attention as Delilah.

"You'll just have to deal, then. It's over and done now, bro. Just let it go."

"You're right."

"Just don't tell Mom. You'll break her heart."

"Shit." Jason tilted back in the recliner, half expecting a dentist to appear to tell him to rinse. "I totally forgot about Mom."

"She loved Delilah. I mean, *loved* her. You tell Mom you gave her the heave-ho, and she'll probably cut you out of the will."

"You'd like that, wouldn't you?"

"Yeah, like Mom and Dad are rolling in it," said Eric dryly. "When the time comes, you and I are going to be divvying up livestock, not dollars."

"You got that right." Jason glanced around Eric's apartment. For a guy whose taste was clearly in his mouth, he'd done an okay job decorating. Unlike Jason's place, it looked like someone actually lived here. Well, now that he and Delilah were history, he'd have more free time to do things like shop for furnishings, right? Even better, he'd have time to just hang with his buddies—no guilt, no restrictions, no worrying about someone else's schedule or preferences. He was definitely better off flying solo right now. Definitely.

"You got practice tomorrow?" Jason suddenly asked his brother.

"No. Why?"

Jason's feet returned to the floor. "I don't, either. Let's go out tonight and get shitfaced."

CHAPTER 25

Late April

"Mitchell, care to tell me what happened to your New Year's resolution?"

Jason stared at Ty with incomprehension. Back in January, he told his coach that his New Year's resolution was to keep his nose clean: no more hangovers, no more breaking curfew, no more impulsive actions on the ice. He'd kept to it, too. It was a way of keeping his mind off Delilah.

Seeing her all the time, whether out walking in the neighborhood or when they came together over Stanley, always left him feeling melancholy. He still believed they were hopeless as a couple, but that didn't halt his attraction to her. He liked to think she felt the same way, but he had no proof; maybe his male ego just needed to believe it. They were always polite to one another, though Delilah seemed intent on keeping conversation between them minimal.

Without his even noticing it, winter had turned to spring. All the snow had melted, leaving the ground beneath it soggy but full of promise. People had a bounce in their step as they walked down the wide city streets. And the New York Blades had easily clinched a berth in the playoffs, which were one week away.

Ty hadn't asked him to take a seat when he called him to the office, so Jason remained standing somewhat tentatively by the door.

"I don't understand," Jason replied in response to Ty's question.

"I thought you promised to be a good boy," said Ty.

"I have been!"

"Oh yeah? Come here."

Ty motioned for Jason to approach his desk. Coming closer, Jason saw a mound of newspaper clippings. Ty picked one up.

" 'New York Blade Jason Mitchell checked out the Victoria's Secret Spring Fashion Show with brother Eric in tow. Both boys had front-row seats and very big smiles on their faces.' " Ty picked up another clipping. "This is from the *Sentinel*: 'Blades winger Jason Mitchell was spotted dancing with Playboy model Tula at the opening of the Village's hottest new club, Marimba's.' " He picked up another. "Here's a gem from the *Post*: 'Which two hockey-playing twins were seen partying to the wee hours of the morning at socialite Gigi van Lichtenstein's birthday party? Hint: one plays for New York and the other for New Jersey.' " Ty put down the clippings. "I could go on," he said, sweeping his hand above the desk, "but I won't." He folded his arms across his chest. "Well?"

Jason was completely befuddled. "I don't understand," he repeated. "There's nothing there about me getting drunk or misbehaving, because I don't do that. I was just out doing stuff. Nothing controversial." Ty raised an eyebrow, and Jason's hackles went up. "What, I'm not supposed to have a life?"

"You have a life. It's on the ice." Ty picked up the clippings and crumpled them into a ball, throwing them into the garbage. "I don't want this kind of shit dogging us as we go into the playoffs."

"What kind of shit?" Jason protested. "I went to a party. I went to a club. I went to a fashion show. There's nothing unsavory about any of those things! When you played for St. Louis, you stepped out all the time. What's the big deal?"

When it came to Ty Gallagher, silence was anything but golden. The longer Ty stood behind his desk with his laser-like gaze locked on Jason's face, the more Jason wished he'd had the brains to just say "Sorry, Coach" and have done with it—even though in his estimation, he had nothing to apologize for.

"Three things," said Ty in a controlled voice. "Number one: don't believe everything you read. When I played for St. Louis in the early nineties, half of the crap they printed about me in the paper wasn't true. And even if it was, I had three Stanley Cups under my belt to mitigate any damage my supposed partying might have caused. How many Cups do you have, Mitchell?

"Number two: it was a different time. Players weren't put under the microscope with the same intensity they are now, nor were they expected to be role models both on the ice and off. That's not the case anymore.

"And number three: St. Louis was owned by one fat, rich guy named Joe Barza who didn't give a shit what we did off the ice, as long as we delivered—which we did. In case you haven't noticed, the Blades are owned by Kidco Corporation, who pride themselves on providing *family* entertainment, whatever the fuck that means. When Kidco people start coming to me and complaining, then we've got a problem. I have enough on my plate without worrying about corporate breathing down our necks. So, while I appreciate the dedication you've shown on the ice, and the moderate restraint you've shown off it, I have to ask you to avoid events involving models, the word *party*, or anything else these suits might misinterpret. I'm sorry, but that's the way it's got to be." Ty looked empathetic. "Sucks, doesn't it?"

"Big time," Jason muttered.

"If you can't stomach the idea of toeing the line for corporate, then do it for me. I need you to stay one hundred percent focused on the ice. Got it?"

Jason nodded reluctantly.

"Good," said Ty, beginning to sort through items on his desk. "You can go now."

Jason was on his way out the door when he impulsively stopped and turned.

"Coach?"

Ty didn't bother to look up. "Yeah?"

"You really think I've shown dedication on the ice?" he asked, hoping he didn't sound like too much of a dweeb.

Ty glanced up briefly. "You could show more."

Jason shook his head and headed back out the door. He should have known better than to ask Ty for a flat-out compliment. Even if Jason was the greatest player since Paul van Dorn, Ty would never tell him so directly. Instead, he'd give him more ice time, which had definitely been the case the past few months.

No underwear shows, no parties, no questionable activities. He may as well just sit home and watch TV.

It made him miss Delilah all the more.

"Pssst. What's with the little catering tent?"

Delilah rolled her eyes impatiently before answering Marcus's fifth question in as many minutes. Perhaps she should have thought twice before asking him to be her escort to her father's wedding to Brandi.

"It's called a *chuppah*. It's a bridal canopy. The bride and groom stand under it and recite their vows." She peered at him in amazement. "You've really never been to a Jewish wedding before?"

"Never." Marcus tilted the *yarmulke* on his head to a rakish angle. "Does this work for me?"

Delilah pushed the skullcap to the back of his head where it belonged. "No high jinks, Marcus. I mean it. This day is really important to my dad. The last thing he needs is to see me trying not to laugh."

Marcus looked disappointed. "I promise to behave."

"Thank you."

Delilah fanned herself with the wedding program, trying to remember the last time she'd been in temple. It had to be three years ago, when Grandma Ida died. She glanced around; the place was packed with family friends and business associates of her father's, some of whom she recognized, most of whom she didn't. According to her mother, a number of old family friends had refused to come because they thought the wedding to be a farce. She wondered how many were at her mother's house with her right now, helping her through this "difficult day." Delilah herself had made it a point not to stop by Mitzi's today. The last thing she needed was her mother weeping and wailing, or calling her a traitor because she chose to attend.

"Oh my God!" Marcus whispered, pointing discreetly at a male version of Brandi seating himself across the aisle. "I know that guy from somewhere!"

"I think that's Brandi's brother," Delilah murmured. "From what I've been able to deduce, he's a gay porn star."

"*That's* where I've seen him—in *Good Night and Good Lick*! Honey, you better introduce me to him at the reception if you want this friendship to continue."

"I don't even know him!"

"Well, *get* to know him. After all, he's your stepuncle now."

Delilah gave a small shudder. Somehow, in the back of her mind, she never really thought this day would come. Yet here it was, complete with porn stars, packed pews, and a planned reception for over three hundred people at Leonard's of Great Neck. Delilah tried searching for something positive about the day. Well, Marcus was with her, that was one thing. And Brandi hadn't asked her to be her maid of honor.

Delilah closed her eyes, listening to the drone of voices all around her. When she was small, she used to dream about getting married in this temple. For a split second, her mind put her and Jason up there beneath the *chuppah*.

Jason. Every time she thought about him, or saw him, a part of her wanted to suggest reconciliation; she missed him that much. But then she'd remember how incompatible they were, how he wasn't happy unless he was out on the town every night, and she was more comfortable around dogs than people. Every time she opened the paper, there he was with Eric, going to this debutante's party or that club opening. If that's the life he wanted for himself in New York, more power to him. But it wasn't the life *she* wanted to lead.

Jason had been right about one thing, though: the way she'd handled herself at the Websters' party had been wrong. She should have thought twice before reading the Websters the riot act, but she was so nervous about the whole evening she hadn't been thinking straight. Since their phone number was unlisted, she'd tried looking up the Websters' address on the Internet so she could send them a note of apology, but she got nowhere. In the end, she chalked it all up to experience and prayed that if she ever ran into Tully and his wife, she'd have the grace to apologize.

"Excuse me, is this seat taken?"

Delilah opened her eyes and looked up. Standing on the aisle, pointing to an empty space beside her, was Eric.

"What are *you* doing here?"

Eric smiled smugly. "Guest of the bride."

"The bride's guests are over there!" Delilah jabbed a finger across the aisle.

"I'd much rather sit with you," said Eric. "Is that okay?"

"Fine," Delilah hissed. She got up so Eric could move past her and sit down.

"This is getting good," Marcus noted breathlessly.

"Shut up," Delilah commanded. She turned to Eric. "You're unbelievable." Eric just shrugged. "If you do anything to wreck this day, I'll never speak to you again. I *mean* it."

"You barely speak to me now," Eric noted. He looked up her up and down. "You look really nice, Delilah."

Marcus leaned across Delilah toward Eric. "I picked out the dress."

"You have good taste."

"Oh, for pity's sake!" Delilah exclaimed in exasperation. She glanced quickly over her shoulder. As she feared in the wake of her outburst, she was receiving some odd looks. She could just imagine what they were thinking: *That's Sy's daughter. Nutty as a fruitcake, just like the mother.*

If she was feeling edgy before, Eric's presence sent her nerves into overdrive. Had Brandi really invited him? Had they been in touch since Hanukkah? And if so, how closely?

Very quietly, the organist launched into the opening notes of Handel's "Judas Maccabeus," and the temple fell into a hush as everyone rose in preparation for Brandi's entrance. Rabbi Kolton, who once told Delilah in Hebrew school that dogs didn't have souls, waddled his way onto the *bimah*, followed by Delilah's father, dapper in a tux. Seeing him, Delilah's eyes filled with tears. She wanted her father to be happy; God knows he deserved it. But something about this felt all wrong, especially when she flashed back to the image of her mother sitting in her father's lap at Hanukkah, necking in front of a half-eaten plate of potato pancakes.

Her father caught her eye and gave her a quick, reassuring wink. Delilah flashed a quick smile back, determined to put up a good front. If this was what he wanted, she'd follow his lead and accept it.

The guests watched in respectful silence as Delilah's uncle Mort slowly escorted a tall, birdlike woman in a short, poufy lavender dress down the aisle.

"She looks like an Easter egg on stilts," Marcus whispered.

"Shh," said Delilah.

"Almost showtime," Marcus murmured gleefully. Delilah stole a glance at Eric. He seemed relaxed, not at all like someone on the verge of making a scene over his object of lust. People were craning their necks to look at the back of the temple, anticipation running high.

Finally, Brandi appeared on the arm of her father.

Marcus gave a small gasp. "Oh sweet Jesus on a plank of pine."

Not only was Brandi's diamond-studded wedding dress the tightest dress Delilah had ever seen in her life, but her hair was teased into a stiff but lopsided blonde tower, the coiffure equivalent of the leaning Tower of Pisa.

"It's the Bride of Gouldenstein," said Marcus.

"Yum-my," Eric murmured lecherously as Brandi started down the aisle. Delilah shot him a dirty look.

As Brandi and her father approached, Delilah studied the man's face for any telltale signs of stress or disapproval. If he had any objections to his daughter marrying someone older than him, he certainly didn't show it.

The sound of the music faded away. Sy extended his arm to Brandi, the two of them moving to stand beneath the *chuppah* as Brandi's dad took his seat in the front pew. Delilah suddenly, unexpectedly, began to weep. It was as if someone had thrown a switch; one minute she was watching the procession down the aisle, the next she was blubbering. Mortified, she pawed through her purse for a hankie.

Rabbi Kolton stepped forward. "We are gathered here today to celebrate one of life's greatest moments, to give recognition to the worth and beauty of love, and to add our best wishes to the words which shall unite Sy and Brandi in marriage."

Delilah sniffled loudly, drawing a look of consternation from Marcus.

Rabbi Kolton turned to Brandi. "Do you, Brandi, take Sy to be your husband?"

"Uh-huh."

"Say 'I do,' dear," corrected the rabbi with a patronizing smile.

"I do, dear," said Brandi.

"Do you promise to love, cherish, and protect him, in

good times and in adversity, and to seek with him a life hallowed by the faith of Israel?"

"I do."

"Shit," Delilah snuffled quietly as the rabbi turned to her father.

"Do you, Sy, take Brandi to be your wife?"

"I d—"

"Stop!"

There was a split second of silence before the entire congregation turned in unison, gasping as the sound of Mitzi's voice blasted them from the back of the temple.

"Sy!" she sobbed, holding out her twiglike arms to him. "I love you, you stupid old bastard! Don't do this! Come home!"

All eyes swiveled back to the bride and groom. Brandi's mouth was hanging open like a recently caught trout; Rabbi Kolton appeared apoplectic. As for Delilah's father . . .

"If you want me, I'm yours!" he called to Delilah's mother. He looked at Brandi. "Sorry, *bubbele*. When true love comes to bite you in the ass, you have no choice but to offer up both cheeks."

He ran down the aisle toward Mitzi, the two of them disappearing as mayhem erupted in the temple.

Delilah covered her face with her hands. "This isn't happening," she trilled in a singsong voice, the words muffled.

"Daaaaddddyyyy!" Brandi's wail filled the temple as she stood before the now agitated congregation, stamping her foot. Her hair collapsed like a deflated soufflé.

"I better go to her," said Eric, practically climbing over Delilah to get to the bride before her father.

"Who the hell are you?" Delilah heard Brandi's father growl at Eric.

"I'm a close friend of your daughter's, sir."

Delilah took her hands from her face just long enough to see people beginning to focus their scrutiny on *her*, the outlaws' only child.

"Get me out of here," she begged Marcus. "Now."

"This is the most exciting wedding I've ever been to in

my life!" Marcus exclaimed, shielding Delilah in the crook of his arm as the two of them scurried as fast as they could down the aisle.

"Disgraceful, just disgraceful," Delilah heard someone tut-tut.

"Once a jackass, always a jackass," she heard her aunt Lois drawl, never her father's biggest fan.

"That liver-spotted old bastard you call a father is going to pay for this!" she heard Brandi's father call after her.

"He already did!" Delilah yelled over her shoulder.

She and Marcus burst through the doors of the temple just in time to see her parents peel out of the parking lot in Mitzi's blazing white BMW.

"Where do you think they're going?" Marcus wondered aloud.

"Hell," Delilah answered wearily. "Just take me home."

CHAPTER

26

"*I heard about* your folks."

Delilah gave a curt nod of acknowledgment as she ushered Jason and Stanley into her apartment. It had been two days since the wedding debacle, and in typical Sy and Mitzi fashion, Delilah hadn't heard a word from either of them. For all she knew, they'd wound up a twisted wreck on Northern Boulevard after fleeing the temple. Or maybe they were hunkered down at the house for a second honeymoon. Delilah hadn't tried to call, nor did she intend to. If the newly reconciled couple wanted to make contact, they knew her number.

She offered Jason some tea, which he declined. He was about to embark on a road trip with the Blades, so Stanley would be staying with her. Delilah loved having Stanley here, despite his stubborn insistence on trying to hop on the bed or sofa when she wasn't looking. He was the only one of her "students" to test her this way after being trained. Even so, it was hard to get mad at him.

Delilah crouched so she was eye level with Stanley and began scratching his chest, prompting a huge belch.

"You rude boy," Delilah chided as she turned her face away. He'd been burping a lot lately. Delilah had a sneaking suspicion Jason had been feeding him cheap biscuits on the sly, not the organic lamb and rice brand she gave as treats to all her charges. She was tempted to ask him, then thought better of it.

"Think your folks will get remarried?"

The mere mention of her parents made Delilah want to run into her room and pull the covers over her head. "I don't know, and I don't care."

"Of course you care," Jason rebutted softly. "They're your *parents*."

"They're insane."

"Well, yeah. But they're still your parents."

"Is Eric banging Brandi now?" Delilah blurted, unable to help herself. She had to know.

Jason grimaced. "I'm not sure it's gotten to that point yet," he said carefully. "Right now, he's just comforting her."

Delilah snorted. "I'll bet. They deserve each other."

"You won't hear me argue. He's been leaving nasty messages on my cell phone in the hopes I'll mess up on the ice."

"Like what?"

"Oh, you know: 'So and so from such and such paper says you'll probably be traded after this season.' Crap like that."

"Well, don't listen to him."

"I don't. But it still worms its way into your brain, you know?"

Delilah nodded. They hadn't had an actual conversation like this in months. It was nice to be talking to him about something other than Stanley, even if the topic was Eric.

Delilah rose, her hand still resting on Stanley's head. "Where are you off to again?" She knew where he was going, but pretending she didn't made her sound busy, so busy she couldn't keep the simplest facts about him straight in her head.

"Florida," said Jason. "We beat them in the first two, and if we win the next two, we go on to the second round."

"Are you excited?"

"We've got a long way to go yet," Jason said cautiously. "But we could win the Cup. I mean, we have as much of a chance as anybody."

Delilah was touched by the sense she had that he was backing off from being boastful. Maybe he missed talking to her, too.

"Well," she said, "you know I'll take good care of Stan."

"I know that." Their gazes locked, then Jason looked away. He seemed at a loss for words. Delilah felt the same way. She wanted to keep talking to him but wasn't sure there was much beyond hockey, Stan, and Eric. Then she realized.

"How are your parents?"

Jason looked distinctly uncomfortable. "They're fine."

"Good." Was it possible Mr. and Mrs. Mitchell now hated her for breaking up with their son? She supposed she couldn't blame them, though the thought made her sad.

"Please tell them I asked about them. If that's okay. I mean if it's not okay I understand, but if it is okay—"

"I'll tell them," Jason promised.

"Thank you."

Stanley, seemingly bored, gave a big yawn and lay down right atop Delilah's feet.

"Sorry to interfere with your naptime, pal," Jason quipped as he looked down at him affectionately. His expression was almost apologetic as he regarded Delilah. "I better get going. I have a plane to catch."

"Right."

"You have my cell number and everything in case—"

"Yes."

"Okay, then." He leaned over and patted Stanley on the back. "Be good, big guy." He looked at Delilah. "Wish me luck. The Blades, I mean."

"Good luck," said Delilah, trying to read the expression

in his big, brown eyes. Sad? Uneasy? Wistful? She pretended for a moment that he was a dog, and it became clear.

Wistful.

*"**We wanted you** to be the first to know: we're going to get remarried down at the condo in Delray."*

Delilah knew she was supposed to react with excitement to her parents' announcement, but she found it hard to muster sufficient enthusiasm, especially when they'd turned up at her apartment unannounced. Despite the sun and warm late spring temperatures, her mother was wearing an ankle-length raincoat to keep dog hair at bay, while her father appeared dressed for a different season entirely, in tan bermuda shorts and black socks with sandals. She'd give them credit for one thing: they both seemed happy. For now.

"You'll come, right, pussycat?" her father asked hopefully.

"I guess," said Delilah, keeping an eye on Stanley. He'd been acting strangely for the past half hour or so since she'd fed him, pacing restlessly. When she'd command him to lie down, he couldn't seem to find a comfortable position. If it kept up, she was going to call the vet.

"Look what your father gave me." Mitzi proudly wiggled the fingers of her left hand under Delilah's nose, showing off a sapphire ring the size of a gumball.

Delilah nodded distractedly. "Nice."

Mitzi dropped her hand. "I'm not sensing much enthusiasm here."

"Mom, what do you want me to say? I'm happy for the two of you. I just don't believe it'll last."

"It will," her father assured her, looking mildly disgusted when Stanley let out a room-clearing burp. "This time we're doing it right: intensive counseling, anger management, the whole shebang."

"The therapist gave us foam bats to hit each other with when we get angry," Mitzi added. "It's very cutting-edge."

"That's nice, Mom."

Delilah got up and went to Stanley, who was breathing heavily. "It's okay, boy. I just need to check something." As gently as she could, she turned Stanley onto his left side and felt his belly. It was swollen. Delilah sprang to her feet.

"I have to call the vet," she said, hurrying to the phone. As she'd predicted, when she explained Stanley's symptoms over the phone, the veterinary hospital told her to bring him in right away.

Delilah was frantic, searching wildly for her keys. "I have to go."

"Whaaaat?" said her mother.

Delilah pointed at Stanley. "He might have bloat. It's when a dog's stomach twists and cuts off the blood supply. It could be fatal." She grabbed her purse. "What car did you come in?" she asked her parents.

"The caddy," her father answered apprehensively.

"Good. You're going to help me get Stanley into the car and drive me to the animal hospital."

Her mother made a face like she was sucking lemons. "That thing isn't going in the caddy! It has a white leather interior!"

"He might be dying!" Delilah yelled. "Now shut your yap and help me out here!"

Her mother turned to her father. "Do you hear the way she talks to me, her own mother?"

Sy patted Mitzi's arm consolingly. "Later, cupcake. Our little girl needs help."

"I wish I had my bat," Delilah's mother growled under her breath.

Delilah fetched two bath towels, looping one under Stanley's belly behind his hind legs, and the other behind his front legs. "On the count of three," she commanded her father. "One, two, three." Together she and her father heaved Stanley to his feet.

"Go down to the car, start it, and open the back doors," Delilah commanded her mother. "We'll follow."

Too shell-shocked to protest, Mitzi hurried out of the apartment as Delilah and her father painstakingly carried

Stanley downstairs in the makeshift sling. Stanley was limp, his breathing heavy, his eyes dazed.

"You're going to be fine," Delilah promised him over and over again. "You're going to be fine."

She had to believe that or she'd lose her mind.

"Oh my God! Check your messages!" Delilah shouted into her cell phone. This was the fourth time she'd called Jason and left a message. The staff at the vet hospital were waiting for Stanley when Delilah arrived. They immediately put him on a gurney and whisked him off for X-rays, the results of which Delilah was now waiting for.

"Sugar, calm down." Her father put his arm around her. "I'm sure everything will be okay."

"I hope so," Delilah whispered through watery eyes. Her mother had chosen to remain behind at the apartment. Delilah could picture her now, sitting in the middle of Delilah's living room with her raincoat on, stiffening if one of Delilah's three dogs even came near to sniff her. Delilah couldn't worry about that now. Her primary concern was Stanley.

She looked at her father. "How's your back?" By the time they'd carried Stanley downstairs and deposited him in the car, her father was bent over in two.

"How much does that damn dog weigh?" her father groused.

"One fifty, easy."

"If I wind up in a truss, I'll know who to blame."

Delilah said nothing, but she was so tense she feared she might split her skin. What was taking Dr. Shearer so long to take an X-ray?

"You don't have to stay," she told her father, feeling guilty for what she'd put him through.

"How would you get home?"

"Cab."

Her father patted her shoulder. "No. I'll stay."

Delilah swallowed back tears. "Thank you." A minute

later, Dr. Shearer appeared in the waiting room, her expression grim as she approached Delilah.

"It's not good," she said. "His stomach is twisted. He needs surgery immediately."

"But"—Delilah's mind was spinning out of control—"he's not my dog."

"If we wait, he could die."

"Operate," Delilah said without hesitation. "I know it's what his owner would want. Operate."

Dr. Shearer nodded and disappeared. Weeping, Delilah once again pulled out her cell phone and left a message for Jason. "It's Delilah. It's about Stanley. Call me." That's all she could manage before she dissolved into sobs.

"*You gave a* vet I don't even know permission to operate on my dog without asking me?!"

Waiting for Delilah to answer, Jason couldn't believe she had the nerve to be glaring at *him*. The Blades had done great on the road, routing Florida in three to sweep into the second round. He was in a great mood until he came to Delilah's to pick up Stanley, only to discover his best friend in the universe had undergone major surgery.

"Let's try this again." Delilah's eyes were bright with fury. "I left you multiple messages on your cell about Stanley. Multiple! But for some idiotic reason, you never bothered to check your phone! The vet told me Stan needed surgery right away or he might die. What was I supposed to do? *Hope* you'd call me back in time? You've got some nerve taking that attitude with me! I saved Stanley's life!"

Jason pulled his cell phone out of his pocket. Part of the reason he'd been able to focus and perform so well on the ice was precisely *because* he'd taken care to keep his cell turned off to avoid Eric's twisted little messages.

"Go on," Delilah urged heatedly. "Check your messages now."

Jason punched in the code to retrieve his messages and

listened. There were three or four from Eric, all designed to mess with his mind. But there were also multiple messages from Delilah, each increasingly more frantic, the last one ending with, "Stan had the surgery, he came through it great, I'll tell you all about it when you get back to New York." She'd been weeping when she left that message.

Ashamed, Jason turned off his phone and thrust it back into his pocket. "I don't know what to say."

"How about 'I'm sorry,' followed by 'Thank you'?" Delilah snapped.

"I'm sorry," Jason said humbly. His thoughts were coming so fast he couldn't keep up with them. "When did all this happen?"

"Thursday. The day after you left. Stan was fine on Wednesday. Thursday he was listless, burping, and bloated. That's when I knew. I called my vet, and she told me to get him in immediately."

An image of Stan came to Jason's mind, and along with it, a feeling like someone was sitting on Jason's chest, making it hard to breathe. The thought of Stanley ill, in pain, was unendurable. And incomprehensible. He was Stanley. Invincible. Things like this weren't allowed to happen to those Jason loved, goddammit. It was totally unacceptable.

Shaken, Jason sat down on the couch beside Delilah. "And you're sure he's okay?"

"He's doing great," Delilah assured him, compassion returning to her voice. "They did what's called a gastropexy: it's where they sew the stomach to the lining of the abdominal wall to insure it doesn't twist."

"And this . . ." Jason's voice cracked. "He won't die?"

"He won't die. He might get bloated again, but it can't kill him."

"Can I go see him? *Now?*"

Delilah squeezed his hand. "It's not like a human hospital, Jason. They don't have visiting hours. I spoke with them this morning, and they said he was doing well. If his vitals are good overnight, they'll release him tomorrow."

Jason put his head in his hands. "I have practice tomorrow!" he howled in agony.

"It's okay. I'll go get him and bring him back here. It's not a problem."

"How are you going to do *that*?" Jason scoffed.

"One of Marcus's friends is letting me borrow his SUV. Marcus can help me get him in and out of the car."

Jason jerked up his head. "Fuck it! I'm blowing off practice! Screw Ty Gallagher if he wants to bench me or fire me, just fuck it!"

"Listen to me." Delilah's voice was stern as she put her hand on his arm. "I can take care of this. There's no reason for you to jeopardize your career by doing something stupid and *impulsive*, all right? Stanley should probably stay here with me anyway, so I can keep an eye on him while he's recuperating. It's not a big deal."

Jason blinked hard, trying to fight back tears. "I let him down, Delilah. I wasn't there for him when he needed me."

"You're here now. That's what matters."

"That's not good enough."

Emotion rippled through him as he looked into her sweet, beautiful face. It wasn't only Stanley he'd let down. He'd let Delilah down, too, in so many ways. Sending Eric in his stead the first time they were invited for brunch at her mom's . . . getting on her case after taking her to dinner with his friends at Dante's . . . not understanding—not *wanting* to understand—the intricacies and demands of running her own business . . . blindsiding her on Christmas Day. And now this, having the balls to read her the riot act without stopping first to get the details. If it wasn't so fucking pathetic, he'd let himself cry and beg for her forgiveness. Instead, he lifted her to her feet and embraced her.

"Thank you," he whispered, loving the feel of her in his arms again but knowing he had no right to it—was, in fact, nowhere near worthy of it. "Thank you for saving my boy's life."

"You're welcome," said Delilah. Her gaze and voice

were resolute as she looked up at him. "Stanley's going to be fine."

"And what about you?" Jason asked. "Are you fine?"

"I'm always fine," said Delilah with a sad smile as she slipped out of his embrace. "Now go home and get some rest."

CHAPTER

27

"Jesus Christ! We sucked."

No one disputed David Hewson's observation as the Blades filed into the locker room following game two of the Cup playoffs against Detroit. They'd lost the first game by just one goal, but they were sure they'd rebound tonight in the second. They didn't. If anything, they played worse, their equilibrium completely out of whack. They were now facing a major ball-busting fact: if they didn't win the next game, they were probably toast.

Exhausted, Jason pulled his sweater over his head and began untying his shoulder pads. He couldn't figure out what had changed their momentum. Beating Florida in the first round had been a cinch. Ditto winning the semis against Jersey; Jason had taken great pleasure in wiping the ice with Eric game after game, not once letting his brother's usual on-ice antics goad him into some stupid move that could hurt the team. Even battling Boston for the Eastern Conference series looked relatively painless from where he was sitting now, despite going all the way to six games.

He glanced around the locker room; everyone looked

completely demoralized. Ty talked all the time about being driven, being hungry, about wanting the Cup so badly it was all you thought about. Jason thought he had finally reached that place. He thought his teammates were there, too. But judging from tonight's performance, they were all falling short of the mark.

Ty let them know it. Never one for hand-holding or sugar-coating, their beloved but hard-assed coach told them they'd best get their shit together for the next game or else. He told them their play had embarrassed them. That none of them deserved to be playing for New York. Jason knew he was trying to get them mad as a way of firing them up, but judging from the dejected faces around him, it seemed to be having the opposite effect. They looked like a room of sweat-drenched zombies.

David Hewson vigorously toweled his head. "You know, I just realized something: I haven't puked before these last two games."

"That's true," said Tully Webster. "Hewsie *always* pukes before he plays. I wonder if not puking fucked things up for us."

Barry Fontaine nodded knowingly. "It could have."

Doogie Malone shook his head in despair as he pointed at his locker. "My autographed picture of Heidi Klum. I gave it to my cousin three days ago when he was visiting."

"And I shaved last week," Ulf Torkelson confessed quietly, rubbing his smooth chin.

Michael Dante looked exasperated as he began removing his thigh pads. "Guys, forget the woo-woo crap, okay? What we need to be concentrating on is our level of *play*."

"Play, yes," Ulf agreed cautiously, "but also things to bring luck."

David Hewson studied Michael with curiosity. "You saying you don't do anything special to insure good mojo, Cap?"

"Of course I do," said Michael, putting his wedding ring back on and twisting it three times. "But mojo alone isn't going to help us."

"It can't hurt us," Denny O'Malley pointed out.

Tully Webster wore an earnest expression as he jumped up on a bench in the middle of the locker room. "I think everyone needs to remember about *all* the stuff they've done in the past to bring good luck—and then do it." He looked at David. "If that means sticking your finger down your throat before a game, bro, then that's what you've gotta do."

There were nods and murmurs of assent. Jason took the cross from his mother from around his neck and hung it up in his locker, where he always left it between games. He'd only ever forgotten to wear it once, and that night, he'd had his nose broken. That's when he remembered another good luck charm he used to rely on in Minnesota.

"Cap, can I talk to you in private after we shower?" Jason asked Michael.

"I can't believe you talked me into this."

Delilah peered out the limo's tinted windows at muted sunlight as the car glided silently down Seventh Avenue toward Met Gar. When Jason had first come to her saying he'd gotten permission to bring Stanley to his remaining games for good luck, she'd laughed long and hard. He couldn't be serious!

But he was. And since Stanley was his dog, she really didn't have a leg to stand on. The clincher came when he asked her to come with them. Via limo. So she could watch the game with Stanley from a skybox. Her hermit instinct immediately kicked in.

"I have my own dogs to take care of," she'd pointed out.

"There's Marcus," he said. "I'll pay him so much he'll think he died and won the lottery."

"Why can't Eric do it?" Delilah asked.

"Unreliable," Jason had rebutted. "Plus he doesn't like Stan. Plus he might be with Brandi." Delilah pretended not to hear the last sentence.

"What if it freaks Stanley out?" Delilah demanded, starting to feel desperate.

"Have you ever known Stanley to freak out?" Jason retorted. "The only person he loves more than me is you. If you're there, he'll be fine. You know it."

For some insane reason, Delilah had capitulated. Maybe it was the desperation in Jason's eyes. Maybe it was his admission of Stanley's attachment to her. Or maybe it was that the whole thing felt a tiny bit like an adventure, something she didn't embark on very often. Correction: ever.

She looked down at Stanley, snoring happily on the limo's plushly carpeted floor as if there was no place else he'd rather be. He'd been a little listless the first few days home after surgery, and with jagged black stitches lining his shaved belly, he looked a little disconcerting, but overall, he was doing great. He'd even gone back to trying to sneak up on her couch, which Delilah took as a good sign.

"I hope we can get him out of the car when we get to Met Gar," Delilah said. "He looks like he'd be quite happy to stay here."

Jason nodded distractedly. He'd been jiggling his left leg madly ever since they'd climbed into the back of the limo. In fact, it was beginning to drive Delilah a little nuts.

"Are you okay?" she asked.

Jason seemed surprised by the question. "What? Sure. Why?"

She pointed to his leg. "Oh," said Jason. His leg stopped moving. "Sorry about that. I guess I'm a little preoccupied."

"About the game?"

Jason turned to look out the window. "Yeah, pretty much."

Pretty much?

Alarm bells started sounding in Delilah's head. "Jason, you have clearance to bring Stanley inside Met Gar, right?"

Jason's gaze remained fixed on the window. "Kind of."

Delilah could actually *feel* the muscles in her neck beginning to knot. "What do you mean, 'Kind of'?"

Jason reluctantly turned back to her. "I kind of have an unofficial green light. My captain said if I can get him in and out without corporate finding out, then I should feel free. But if I get caught, he'll say he doesn't know a thing about it. So I kind of have one of the security guys and Larry Levin helping me out."

"Oh my God."

Delilah could see it now: Met Gar security breaking into the skybox and putting her in cuffs . . . a story about it on the local eleven o'clock news . . . a picture in the papers the next morning of her and Stanley being led away.

"It'll be fine," Jason assured her, patting her knee.

"If it'll be fine, why are you nervous?"

"I'm not nervous. I'm sure everything will go off without a hitch." He hesitated. "But just in case it doesn't, don't worry. I'll take full responsibility for whatever happens."

Delilah pitched back against the car seat in frustration. "You're insane, you know that?"

"Yeah, but that's why—"

You love me, Delilah silently finished for him. Jason covered the gaffe with a quick clearing of his throat before leaning over to pet Stanley. The sad truth of the matter was, she did love him. But what did it matter? She and Jason had been one of those round peg, square hole couples. No matter how hard you tried to make them fit, they didn't.

"Almost there," Jason murmured, more to himself than Delilah. He hit the button to lower the glass between the front and back seats. "I'm going to direct you to a special entrance," he told the limo driver. "I need you to be waiting there until this young lady comes back outside with the dog later tonight. We're clear on that, right?"

"Yes, sir," said the driver.

Jason turned to Delilah. "Ready?"

"I hate you," Delilah said with a glare.

But both of them knew it was a lie.

Jason would never admit it to Delilah, but he was experiencing some trepidation about the Stan Plan. If anything went wrong, corporate would hang him and his three-year contract out to dry, and Ty would let them.

With the help of Larry Levin and Joey Sacco, a Met Gar security guard whom Jason knew was a dog lover, Jason had concocted a plan. He, Delilah, and Stanley would arrive by limo at one of Met Gar's lesser-known entrances. Larry would be waiting there for them to make sure the coast was clear. If it was, Stan, Delilah, and Jason would take the service elevator down to locker room level, where Joey, the security guard for that floor, would conveniently be "on break." Jason and Delilah would quickly hustle Stanley into the locker room, hanging there until Joey knocked on the door three times. Joey would then conveniently take another break, allowing Delilah and Stan to go up to skybox level once Larry again gave them the heads-up. They'd do the same thing at the end of the game, sans locker room visit. The only other difference would be that Delilah would leave in the middle of the third period to avoid the departing hordes. Was it risky? Yes. Was it worth it? Jason thought so.

Jason directed the limo to the appointed entrance. He was relieved to see Larry Levin hovering at the door as he hopped out of the car.

"Hurry," Larry barked.

As Delilah had feared, Stanley was reluctant to leave the limo, though he obeyed when Jason gave him the command for "Up," albeit with a dirty look. Jason quickly hustled Stanley through the door, Delilah in tow, looking like she was going to throw up.

"This way," Larry commanded, walking briskly toward an elevator at the far end of the hall. Jason could hear voices coming from somewhere; he assumed Joey Sacco was nearby, chatting up people to detain them.

Jason, Delilah, and Larry all seemed to breathe a collective sigh of relief as the elevator doors slid shut, and the elevator began its descent.

"That's not a dog," said Larry Levin, staring at Stanley agog, "that's a friggin' pony. You couldn't own a bichon frise?"

Jason snorted. "No self-respecting jock owns a bichon frise, believe me."

"How you doin', Delilah?" Larry asked, looking concerned.

"I'm okay. Look, Larry, remember when we met at Tully's party and I disappeared for awhile and then left on my own near midnight and—"

"Not now," Jason said sharply. Delilah seemed to shrink against the back of the elevator. "I mean, we just don't have time," he amended gently. This was not the best time for Delilah to turn into Babbling Brook, though he could see how nervous she was.

"It's going to be fine," he told her again.

Delilah just nodded.

The elevator doors squeaked open, and Larry stuck his head out. "The coast is clear." He regarded Jason. "Fifteen minutes, right?"

Jason nodded. "Sacco should knock in fifteen minutes. You be here waiting."

"Go, go, go," Larry urged.

Jason legged it out of the elevator as fast as he could. For once, he wished Stanley was one of those lithe, high-strung dogs; at least they moved quickly. He paused before plunging into the locker room.

"You gonna be okay?" he asked Delilah.

Her eyes flashed with alarm. "Sure, as soon as you tell me what the hell I'm supposed to *do* for fifteen minutes."

"Hadn't thought of that."

"Clearly."

Jason looked both ways down the hallway. "Ladies' room?" He pointed to the left. "It's that way. Or you could just hang out here."

"And if someone comes by, I tell them—what?"

"The truth: that you're my—friend, and you're waiting for me."

Delilah gave him a strange look and leaned against the wall trying, he supposed, to look as inconspicuous as possible. Jesus, he'd nearly done it again, put his foot in his mouth where Delilah was concerned. First in the limo, and now this. He needed to watch himself around her.

"Okay." He patted Stan's back. "Showtime, big guy." He regarded Delilah. "See you in fifteen."

"God willing," she replied dryly.

He started into the locker room, then paused. "Delilah?"

"Mmm?"

"Thank you." A rush of emotion overcame him, rendering him unexpectedly tongue-tied. "For being willing to do this, I mean. It means a lot to me." Shit, he was starting to sound like *her*. "I mean—"

Delilah held up a hand. "I know what you mean. See you in fifteen."

"Ho-ly shit."

Michael Dante's big brown eyes bugged out of his head as Jason ushered Stan into the locker room, locking the door behind them. For a split second, everyone just stared at Stanley in awe. The next thing Jason knew, he and Stan were being surrounded by his teammates, and he was being bombarded with questions.

"What is that, a baby bear?"

"How much does that sucker weigh?"

"Yo, what the hell kind of dog is that?"

"Gentlemen," said Jason proudly, "I want you to meet Stanley."

Appreciative laughter rippled through the locker room. As always, Stanley basked calmly in the attention. He looked damn regal sitting there, his large black head tilted up nobly.

"Is it okay to pet him?" Tully Webster asked nervously.

"Of course," said Jason. "He loves it."

Hands shot out from all directions to pat Stanley's head or stroke his back.

"What kind of dog is this again?" Thad Meyers asked.

"A Newf," Jason answered.

Michael Dante recoiled slightly as Stan panted. "His breath is foul."

"I didn't get a chance to brush his teeth this week," Jason explained apologetically.

"You brush your dog's fucking teeth?" Denny O'Malley jeered.

"Yeah. You might want to try it yourself sometime."

Accompanied by sniggers, Denny stormed back to his locker to continue dressing. David Hewson, meanwhile, had crouched to examine Stanley's belly.

"What's with the stitches?" he asked.

"Minor surgery. Shouldn't you be off throwing up?"

"Oh. Right." David stood and rubbed the top of Stanley's head. "For luck," he explained before trooping off to the bathroom. The entire locker room held its breath, waiting for the sound of David retching. When it came, it was like music to their ears.

"Stanley," each of the Blades intoned solemnly as they took turns petting Stanley's head, Michael Dante included.

"I don't want to know how you got him in here," he said to Jason as the team began dressing. "I just hope to hell you can get him out."

"Piece of cake," Jason assured him. He crouched down, pressing his forehead against Stanley's.

"Bring us luck tonight, boy," he whispered. "Please."

CHAPTER
28

"What are you doing here?"

"What are *you* doing here?"

Delilah closed the door to the team's skybox and waited for Eric to answer. It wasn't stressful enough she'd had to sneak into Met Gar with an animal the size of a pony and pray she didn't get caught. Now she had to deal with her ex-boyfriend's brother, who had her father's ex-fiancée in tow.

"My brother's in the Cup finals," Eric answered. "Of course I'm gonna be here."

"Jason didn't mention anything about you being here."

"That's because he's stupid, and probably distracted." Eric looked down at Stanley. "What is *he* doing here?"

"He's the team mascot." Delilah made a subtle gesture toward Brandi, who'd dramatically turned her back on Delilah the minute she came in. "What's *she* doing here?" she asked quietly.

"She's *my* mascot."

"Spare me."

Eric reached down to give Stanley a cursory pat on the head. "You know you're breaking the law, right?"

"Of course I do." As calmly as she could, since Eric's words made her even more nauseous than she was already feeling, Delilah explained Jason's elaborate, hopefully fool-proof, scheme. Eric's response was a snort.

"Oh, man. You are so going to be an item in the *Sentinel*'s 'Police Blotter.'"

Delilah scowled at him. "That's very helpful, Eric. Thank you."

Eric shook his head. "I can't believe he talked you into this."

"Neither can I." Delilah put a protective arm around Stanley as he sat, leaning against her.

"Why would you help him out on this after he dumped you? If it were me—"

"He told you he dumped *me*?"

Eric looked intrigued. "That's not how it went down?" he asked eagerly.

"I broke up with him first," Delilah declared.

"Then why are you helping the loser out, risking your neck to bring Stan the Man to Met Gar?"

It was a good question, one that Delilah wasn't prepared to answer honestly, at least not out loud. "We're still *friends*."

"Yeah? Let's see how good a friend he is when you get arrested with his dog."

Delilah ignored the comment, escorting Stanley farther into the sanctuary of the skybox. Having never been in one before, she hadn't known what to expect. It was quite plush, with incredibly comfortable seats, its own bar, its own bathroom, and platters of food, one of which Brandi was busily divesting of pepperoni slices. Delilah approached her, uncertain of what to say.

"Your father's a total ween," Brandi declared, not looking up.

Delilah could deal with a lot of things; a gold-digging bimbo calling her father a "ween" wasn't one of them. "You seem to have recovered from your heartbreak pretty fast," Delilah noted dryly.

"Now, girls," Eric chided in a tone so obnoxiously paternal Delilah wanted to smack him, "the only fights I want to see are down on the ice." He grabbed a beer from the fridge before settling down in one of the comfy chairs with a satisfied sigh. "Game three of the quest for the Cup, Blades versus Detroit. This is gonna rock."

"Goddamn, they're kicking major ass tonight."

Delilah smiled nervously at Eric's observation as she peered down from the skybox at the action on the ice below. The score was 3–2 with New York in the lead. Eric explained to her how Jason's teammate Doogie Malone had scored the second goal, taking "a perfect feed in the slot" from Thad Meyers and "wristing" the puck into the net on a "power play." Eric was so excited Delilah didn't have the heart to tell him she had no idea what he was talking about. Her gaze followed the puck on the ice, which she knew wasn't what you were supposed to do; but it was the only thing her eyes could really latch on to, except for Jason. Every time he hit the ice she watched avidly, unable to tear her eyes away from him.

She peered behind her to check on Stanley, who was on his back, snoring, his belly exposed for all the world to see. "Maybe Stan *is* bringing them luck," she mused aloud.

"I think it's more likely the realization that if they don't win tonight, they're fucked," said Eric, eyes still glued to the ice as he tilted his head back to finish off his beer. "Je-sus!" he suddenly spluttered. "Did you see that?!"

"What?" Delilah asked, turning from Stanley as the roar of the crowd filled her ears. What had she missed?

"Jason! The fucker just scored on a low slap shot!"

Delilah looked down on the ice in time to see Jason getting pats on the butt from his teammates as he headed back to the bench. Brandi turned to Eric.

"Why do you pat each other's heinies like that?" she asked him.

Eric looked disturbed. "Hockey players don't have

heinies, honey. We have asses. Don't forget that, okay?" He directed his attention back to the ice. "Jace is playing incredibly well tonight," he murmured.

"You should tell him that."

Eric turned to Delilah with a horrified expression. "Huh?"

"You're his brother," said Delilah. "Can't you tell him he played well?"

Eric looked disgusted. "What is he, a pussy? He knows what I think."

"Maybe he needs to hear it."

"Did he tell you that?" Eric prodded, sounding alarmed.

"No," said Delilah, feeling put on the spot. "I just thought it might be nice."

"I'll tell him if they win the Cup. Any sooner, and he'll get a swelled head." Eric's gaze returned to the action below. Delilah followed suit, watching Jason as he climbed over the boards and back out onto the ice. She didn't know very much about hockey, but even she noticed Jason had been playing a lot. "How are your folks?" she asked abruptly. "You know, I really liked them. They seemed really nice and—"

"Quiet!" Eric snapped. Suddenly he jumped out of his seat. "Yes! *Yes!!* Shot from the left point by the Ulfinator!" He grabbed Delilah and hugged her, hard. "Sorry I told you to be quiet, Delilah. But there are some moments in hockey that require absolute and complete silence."

"I can see that."

"Don't I get a hug?" Brandi pouted.

Eric leaned over and quickly hugged Brandi. "Better?"

Brandi nodded.

"Yes, yes, yes!" Eric chanted, pumping his fist in the air.

His enthusiasm was contagious, as was that of the crowd. The louder they roared, the more Delilah longed to understand what was going on. Though she feared being mocked, she finally plucked up the courage to ask Eric to explain the game to her as it unfolded. Eric, ever the show-off, was glad to be of assistance. When it came time for her to leave midway through the third period, Delilah was actually sad to go; she wanted to see how the game would end. She asked the limo driver to put on WFAN, and listened, rapt. The Blades won.

The mood in the locker room was exuberant after the Blades' 5–2 win against Detroit. They had righted the ship. If they played the next three games the way they'd played tonight, the Cup would be theirs.

Peeling off his uniform, Jason was in an exhausted daze, playing over and over in his mind the goal he'd scored. It had been a long time since he'd been in the zone, a place beyond time and physical boundaries when all the forces of the universe seemed united in your favor, and you just flew. But that was exactly what had happened to him tonight. Each time he was on the ice, everything jelled perfectly; it was almost supernatural. He didn't know how else to explain it, except that it was something he always strived for, but only intermittently achieved. It was great to have been able to get there tonight.

"Yo, Mitchie." Jason turned at the sound of David Hewson's voice. "You were pretty hot tonight."

"Thanks." Jason pressed a towel against his sweaty face with a chuckle. "It must be Stanley's doing."

"Either that or tossing my cookies before the game," David replied.

"Could be."

Compliments flew back and forth across the locker room, along with unprintable barbs about the opposing team. Everyone was feeling pretty damn good, awash in good cheer and high hopes. And then Ty walked in.

"You boys really pulled it out of yourselves tonight. You should be proud. But let's be careful not to get ahead of ourselves," he cautioned. He motioned for the players to draw closer. Jason and his teammates closed ranks around their coach, whose deep, impassioned voice could be as hypnotic as any drug.

"We can win this series. You know it, and I know it. But if we start feeling cocky, we'll start getting sloppy, which is precisely what I want to avoid." Ty's gaze slowly circled the room. Jason knew everyone there was thinking the same thing he was: *God, please don't let me be on the receiving end of a prolonged, ball-shriveling stare.* But tonight, Ty distributed the tension equitably. "Some of you have won the Cup before. Some of you haven't. But all of you have the same hunger inside, and that's what's going to drive us to victory. Not guts. Not determination. But hunger. You keep focused, you stay hungry, and you'll win. It's as simple as that." He headed for the door. "See you tomorrow morning at practice, boys. Oh, and Mitchell?" he called over his shoulder.

Jason froze at being singled out. Shit. What had he done wrong?

"Yes, Coach?"

"Don't forget to bring Stanley to the next game."

CHAPTER
29

"Delilah! It's so wonderful to see you again!"

Slipping Stanley into the skybox for game six, Delilah was dumbstruck at the sight of Jason's mother. Tension was unbearably high: if New York won, the Cup was theirs; if they lost, they'd have to go back to Detroit for game seven. It made perfect sense for Jason's parents to be here, though in typical Mitchell family fashion, their presence had taken her by surprise.

She could forgive Jason for forgetting to mention it; he'd been so tense and preoccupied throughout the playoffs he was barely verbal, handing over complete care of Stanley to her as the Blades jetted back and forth between New York and Michigan to battle Detroit.

There was no escaping the excitement that had turned the city into one big, buzzing hive of hockey fans. Everywhere Delilah turned, someone was talking about the Cup. It was all over the TV, the newspaper, and the radio. Even her father, whose idea of sports was arguing with her mother, mentioned it. "That's the boyfriend's team, right?" he'd asked. "Well, if any of them need mattresses . . ."

Delilah told Stanley to sit. "It's nice to see you, too, Mrs. Mitchell."

Jason's mother nodded with concern in the direction of Jason's father, whose nose was practically pressed up against the Plexiglas of the skybox, even though the game had yet to begin. "He's a wreck," Mrs. Mitchell confided to Delilah. She seemed nervous as she stood there, clasping and unclasping her hands. "Do you know who all these people are?" she whispered to Delilah. The skybox was filled with people, most of them handsome, well-built men with attractive women and a few children in tow. Eric seemed to be holding court.

"I think they must be other hockey players," Delilah offered nervously. All these people she didn't know . . . all these people, period . . . she could feel her anxiety level starting to climb.

"Where's my main man?" Eric called out, his eyes scouring the box. They lit on Stanley, and he ambled over with a good-looking blond man in tow.

"Hey, Delilah. This is Paul van Dorn. Used to play for the Blades. He wanted to meet Stanley."

"Nice to meet you," Paul said to Delilah.

"Nice to meet you, too," Delilah murmured, struck by the man's mesmerizing blue eyes. The urge to blurt out, "My God you're gorgeous!" was strong.

"Hey, Tuck!" Paul called to a dark-haired, lanky boy on the cusp of adolescence. "Come check out this dog!"

The boy shambled over, his mouth falling open. "Holy moly! What kind of dog is that?"

"A Newf," Delilah replied with a smile. She loved it when Stanley caused a sensation.

"Wow! Aunt Katie, look at this dog!"

A reed-thin, blonde woman turned from talking to another woman to join the admiring circle around Stanley. "Wow!" Katie echoed Tuck. "That is one big dog."

"Can I get one?" the boy asked eagerly.

"Sure," said Paul van Dorn.

Katie shot him a look before smiling at Delilah. "As you

can see, my husband has a very active imagination." She playfully tugged on his arm. "Step away from the nice dog now, honey."

Paul chuckled, and together he, Katie, and the little boy went to get some food.

"Chow seems like a good idea," said Eric, following in their wake. Delilah was once again left alone with Jason's mother.

"Jason told me you saved Stanley's life," said Mrs. Mitchell.

Delilah blushed. "Kind of."

Mrs. Mitchell glanced affectionately at Stanley. "You know, when Jason moved to the city, I was worried about how Stanley would adapt. But he's done beautifully, thanks to you."

"I . . ." Delilah didn't know what to say. If the shoe were on the other foot—if, say, Mitzi was dealing with Jason— there would be no pretense at all of cordiality. Jason would be the ex-boyfriend, worthy only of contempt. That Jason's mother was so gracious to her amazed Delilah.

"So, I was talking to Jason," Mrs. Mitchell continued chattily, "and I mentioned that it might be nice if the two of you could come out to the farm for a few weeks this summer. He agreed. It'd be fun, don't you think?"

"It would." Delilah's mind was cycling rapidly. The cordiality, the compliments, the invitation: the woman had no idea she and Jason had broken up. None at all. Delilah nearly blurted out the truth but got hold of herself. What would be the point? It would only cause confusion and discomfort. But why hadn't Jason told his mother they were no longer together?

Jason sat on the players' bench at Met Gar, his gut in knots. After defeating Detroit on home ice in games three and four, they'd gone on to win game five in Detroit in overtime. But now it was balls to the wall time. If the Blades won tonight, he'd be part of history, his name etched on the

Cup along with all those other players down through the years who knew the guts and determination required to win the most difficult championship in sports. Never again would Eric be able to pull rank on him.

His gaze flicked quickly to the scoreboard—which showed the two teams deadlocked 1–1 midway through the third period—before coming to rest a moment on the team's skybox. Everyone he cared about was up there watching: Eric, his parents, friends, Stanley, even Delilah. Former Blades from around the country had come in for the game, including Paul van Dorn and even Kevin Gill, who had been Ty Gallagher's right wing for years. Their presence made Jason feel he was part of something bigger than himself, a brotherhood who knew the value of grit and loyalty.

Jason's heart hammered in his chest as Ty sent the first line back out on the ice for a face-off in the Blades' zone. Detroit won the draw, sending the puck back to Detroit center Larry "Legs" Doherty, whose slap shot seemed targeted for the top left corner. Were it not for David Hewson's lightning-fast glove, Detroit would have put another one on the board. The crowd went crazy over David's save, the air electrified with their shouts and applause. Jason wondered how close David was to puking at this very moment.

"Second line, get out there," Ty commanded as the first line circled back to the bench. Feeding off the energy in the arena, Jason took his place on the left wing, poised in position as he waited for the puck to drop. New York won the face-off, and Ulf chipped the puck out to center ice. Jason hustled after it, a man on fire. The blade of his stick had just made contact when *bam!* Jason felt someone knee him low, and he fell down onto the ice. He could hear the fans screaming their outrage; could hear Ty cursing at the refs to call it. Furious, Jason lifted his head to try to figure out what the hell had just happened. The whistle blew. That's when Jason saw Detroit defenseman Bobby Delacroix smirking down at him.

"You fuck," Jason growled, springing to his feet. The

decibel level at Met Gar rose as the crowd roared its desire for vengeance.

"Whatcha gonna do, faggot?" Bobby taunted as he dropped his gloves.

Panting, Jason almost threw down his stick and gloves, ready to retaliate. Instead, he forced himself to take a deep breath. Quelling his own yen for revenge, and with the impassioned howls of the crowd ringing in his ears, Jason turned and skated away.

"Way to go," Ty said, slapping him on the back as he returned to the bench. Jason paused to listen to the penalty handed out: the refs gave Delacroix a double minor for interfering. Muttering a stream of curses under his breath, the Detroit defenseman skated off to the penalty box, and New York went out on the power play. Three minutes in, Michael Dante scored on a deflection, bringing the score to 2–1, where it remained until the final buzzer sounded.

The Blades had won the Cup.

"*So, what do* you think, dipshit? Is this the greatest moment of your life or what?"

Jason could barely hear his brother over the din in the locker room, which was bursting with family, friends, and the media. Everyone wanted to share in the joy of the Blades once again bringing the Cup to the city. Immediately following the game there had been unbridled rejoicing out on the ice, with players laughing, shouting, and hugging, many with tears running down their faces. Once the hysteria subsided a bit, Michael Dante told each of the players to make one lap around the ice, holding the Cup aloft. When Tully Webster handed off the Cup to Jason for his turn, Jason found himself choking back tears. He'd been dreaming of this moment ever since he was a little boy. Now it was here, and it was every bit as intoxicating as he'd imagined. Making his circuit around the ice, he felt immortal, untouchable. He made sure to pause in front of the skybox, holding the Cup high for those he loved to see.

He turned to Eric, wiping running sweat—or was it champagne?—from his face. "Where are Mom and Dad?" he asked loudly.

"They went back to their hotel. Mom didn't want to deal with this." Eric swept his arm to indicate the chaos surrounding them.

Jason nodded knowingly. "I understand." He smiled happily as he gave an approaching photographer a thumbs-up.

"How about a shot of the two Stanley Cup–winning brothers together?" the photographer asked.

Eric shook his head. "No way. This is his night, not mine. No sibling shots." The photographer shrugged and walked away.

"Thanks," said Jason.

"Hey, anything for my little brother," said Eric, grabbing him in a headlock. "You did good out there."

"I know."

"Egotistical asshole." Eric let him go.

"Where are Delilah and Stanley?"

"They left midway through the third the way they always do."

Disappointment whispered in Jason's ear. "You mean she—they—didn't see us win?"

Eric frowned. "She stuck to your plan, man. What do you want?"

Jason was silent as he took the champagne bottle that had just been handed to him by God knows who.

"You smell rank," Eric observed.

"I'm sure we all do."

"When's the party?"

"Tomorrow night. Dante's."

Eric's eyes bored into his. "I'm invited, right?"

"Of course you are. You, Mom and Dad." He felt a tugging on his arm and turned.

"Team picture," Doogie Malone shouted in his face. *"Now?"*

"For fun, not official," said Doogie. "C'mon."

Jason turned to Eric. "Look—"

"Go," Eric urged. "I'll talk to you in the morning. Enjoy yourself tonight." He patted Jason's shoulder and disappeared into the sea of jostling bodies.

"Where's the dog, Mitchell?" David Hewson asked as the giddy players arranged themselves for an unofficial group shot.

"Yeah, where's Stanley?" Michael Dante asked, holding the Cup front and center.

"He went home."

A collective groan of disapproval went up. "He's our mascot. He should be here, man," said Thad Meyers. "To bask in the glory."

"Fuckin' A," said Ulf Torkelson. "Do *not* forget to bring him to the party tomorrow tonight."

The photographer snapped the picture, and the team began breaking up.

"Whatcha gonna do with the Cup tonight, Cap?" Barry Fontaine asked Michael, since tradition held that the team captain had possession of the Cup for the first night.

"Rebaptize the baby in it," Michael joked. He looked exhausted as he headed off the ice.

"Poor married bastard," murmured Ulf Torkelson.

"Speaking of not being married," Thad Meyers began slyly. "A bunch of us are going to Snatcher's tonight for some R & R. You in?" he asked Jason.

Snatcher's was the most popular strip club in the city. The first year Ty Gallagher played for the Blades, there had been a minor scandal surrounding the fact he and a number of other players had brought the Cup there, as well as some other establishments of questionable repute.

"Who else is going?" Jason wanted to know.

"Anyone without a ball and chain," said Thad. "You comin'?"

"Sure, what the hell." Jason knew Denny would be coming, too, but that wasn't a big deal. Tonight all differences were put aside.

"Great. There's just one hitch."

"What?"

"You gotta bring the dog," said Ulf.

"They're not going to let Stanley in to Snatcher's!"

"That's where you're wrong," said Thad. "Tonight, we own the city. We can do as we please."

Doogie Malone started a chant. "Stan-ley! Stan-ley! Stan-ley!" It grew louder as the other players joined in.

"I get the hint," Jason said loudly, chuckling with amusement. "Just let me shower, then I'll shoot home to pick him up and meet you guys there."

Barry Fontaine pointed at him. "You da man, Jace. See you and Stan at Snatcher's."

CHAPTER

30

Over the years, Jason had imagined countless scenarios of what he would do the night he won the Cup, but dragging Stanley to a titty bar hadn't been one of them. Ah, well. If his teammates wanted to celebrate by going to Snatcher's for few hours, who was he to argue? He just hoped they weren't there all night. He'd much prefer hanging out at the Chapter House.

New York was indeed the Blades' oyster tonight. The city streets were clogged with exuberant fans roaming in large, joyous packs or else hanging out of car windows, yelling and blowing their horns. Flying on adrenaline, Jason hopped into a waiting cab, giving directions to Delilah's. He assumed the lively crowds would dissipate once he got out of the general vicinity of Met Gar. He was wrong; no matter where he looked, the streets were thick with high-spirited pedestrians, many of them in Blades jerseys. The whole city was wide-awake and celebrating.

"Are you one of the hockey players?" the cab driver asked in a thick Caribbean accent.

Jason nodded, loosening his tie before rolling the back

window down halfway. Met Gar PR was adamant players arrive for and depart from games looking like professionals, meaning they wear a suit and tie. Everyone, including Ty Gallagher, hated it. "You a Blades fan?"

The cabdriver laughed. "Not really, sir. But you have made the city very, very happy tonight."

"Thank you."

Restless, Jason settled back in his seat. Holding the Cup out on the ice, he'd been "very, very happy," to quote the driver. But now, even though he was still stoked, it felt like something was missing. Maybe he shouldn't have let Eric leave. It felt strange to be celebrating without his brother in tow, even though he'd be at the party tomorrow night. Maybe it was his folks. He wished they'd braved the post-game insanity in the locker room, though he understood completely their taking a pass: his mother, fond of wide open spaces, would have had a major anxiety attack were she to find herself in a crush of people like that. In that regard she was like Delilah.

He couldn't believe Delilah had missed the Blades' triumph. He knew footage of the final seconds of the game would run endlessly on TV over the next few days, but he wished Delilah had actually *been* there to see him win. It was the proudest moment of his life, and she'd played a part in it by being willing to bring Stanley to Met Gar, not to mention taking care of him over the course of the season. It was hard to admit, but there was also a part of him that wanted her to be impressed by what he'd achieved.

Like so many New York cabbies, this guy seemed intent on breaking the land record for speed. Jason had barely collected his thoughts before the cab glided to an expectedly smooth stop in front of Delilah's building. Jason pulled a wad of cash from his wallet and held it out to the driver.

"No, no." The cabbie waved the money away. "Tonight you're a hero. This is on me."

"At least let me tip you," Jason insisted, peeling off two ten dollar bills and pressing them into the driver's hand.

"You're too generous."

"Tonight I can afford to be," said Jason, sliding out of the cab. He rapped the roof of the cab twice. "Drive safe now."

The cabbie waved and drove off.

Jason paused, looking up at Delilah's window. Her light was on, which was a good thing; he'd been so distracted with celebrating and trying to get out of Met Gar, that he'd forgotten to call to say he was coming to fetch Stan. He pulled out his cell, then put it away. It was idiotic to call when he was standing right in front of the building. Better to just go up and face the accusation of impulsiveness. At least he'd have an excuse.

The night doorman, Vito, broke into a huge grin as Jason entered the lobby. "Way to go, man! You guys rocked!"

Jason grinned. "We did, didn't we?"

"Hell, yeah!"

"Can you buzz Delilah?"

Vito jerked a plump thumb toward the ceiling. "Go on up. She had a feeling you'd come by for Stan. She's waiting."

"Oh." Jason found himself oddly pleased by this piece of information. "Okay."

Energy still ricocheting through him, he decided to take the stairs. There was something comforting in the fact that Delilah knew him so well, she'd anticipated his wanting Stanley with him on this, his night of nights. His teammates had to be at Snatcher's by now, since it was only three blocks from Met Gar. He'd call for a limo, chat with Delilah, and then he and Stan would head back to midtown. The thought didn't excite him the way it should.

He was just getting ready to knock on Delilah's front door when he heard the sound of heavy doggy breathing on the other side. How Stanley knew it was him was a mystery, but he always did. It was one of those weird, psychic pet things defying explanation.

Delilah opened the door, smiling at him brightly. "Congratulations!"

Jason flushed with pride. "Thanks." He bent down to briskly rub the top of Stanley's head. "It's all thanks to you,

big guy, isn't it?" He knew it was nuts, but Jason was dying
to pick up Delilah and spin her around, so giddy did he feel
about winning. He resisted the urge, noticing instead how
excited *she* looked. Her eyes were bright, her cheeks pink.

"I've been watching the end of the game on TV," she told
him. "It was amazing."

"Tell me about it." Her enthusiasm unexpectedly moved
him. Two weeks ago she knew barely anything about
hockey. Now she seemed genuinely fired up. "I wish
you . . . and Stan had actually been there to *see* it, you
know?"

"Me, too," Delilah confessed. "But you told me to leave
in the middle of the third, so that's what I've been doing."

Jason just nodded. What could he say to that?

"Can you stay a minute?" Delilah asked shyly.

"Sure."

"Good."

Jason wondered what was up as she hustled into the
kitchen. A few seconds later, she returned with a bottle of
champagne. "I know you're going out tonight with your
teammates," she began quickly, "but I thought it only right
that Stan and I toast you."

Jason was speechless. This was the last thing he ever expected. He wondered: Would *he* be generous enough to
toast an ex-girlfriend's triumph? Probably not. But his heart
was nowhere as big as Delilah's. Looking at her now, he
couldn't help but catalogue all the wonderful things about
her. Her kindness. Her sweetness. Her willingness to always
go above and beyond for those she cared about. Even her
twitteriness could be endearing, depending on the situation.
To use one of his mother's favorite expressions, they'd broken the mold when they made Delilah. Jason had spent the
better part of the spring thinking that might be a good thing.
Now he wasn't so sure.

"Oh!" Delilah tapped an open palm to her forehead in a
gesture of forgetfulness. "Glasses. Hang on."

She disappeared back into the kitchen. Jason heard the

sound of her rifling through cabinets. When she reappeared, her high color was gone.

"Guess what? I don't have champagne glasses." Her hands twisted together. "This is so embarrassing. I mean I should have checked first. But I was so excited that as soon as the limo dropped me and Stan off I hustled to the liquor store around the corner for champagne and I didn't even stop to think and now—"

Jason instinctively reached out, putting an index finger to her lips. "Relax," he murmured. How warm her lips felt. Warm and plump and soft. Suddenly self-conscious, he pulled his finger away. "It's not a big deal."

Delilah looked disappointed. "But I wanted to toast you."

"You don't need champagne glasses to toast me. We can use something else."

"I have juice glasses," Delilah offered embarrassedly.

"There you go," said Jason.

Delilah returned to the kitchen a third time. It was unseasonably warm for early June, which explained why she was wearing her walking shorts and a T-shirt. Jason's mind flashed back to the first time they'd met; she'd been wearing the same outfit when she'd approached him to take command of the situation with Stanley. God, she'd been a little spitfire. He'd been intrigued. But as he was soon to learn, she only let out that side of her personality when it came to animals. Because he cared, he thought he could help her overcome her shyness. Now he could see he probably hurt more than he helped. Delilah emerged from the kitchen with two tumblers.

"Delilah, I'm sorry I dragged you into social situations that stressed you out," Jason blurted.

"Oh." Delilah looked taken aback as she held out a glass to him. "Where did that come from?"

"I don't know," Jason admitted, feeling like a jerk. Clearly his postgame giddiness was affecting him in unexpected ways.

Delilah's expression was uncertain as she held up her glass. "Shall we toast?"

"After you say you forgive me for telling you that one time that you needed help," said Jason. Suddenly, it felt like the most important thing in the world that she know she was fine just the way she was.

"There's no need to forgive you," Delilah said softly. "I do need help." She swallowed nervously. "I've been doing a lot of thinking, Jason. And you were right: I do have some issues." She looked flustered as she glanced away. "But I'm taking care of the problem. There's this doctor on the Upper West Side who specializes in social anxiety and panic disorders. I'm going to see him next week. I don't want it to hinder my life anymore. Because it has." Her eyes began filling up. "You know what I mean."

Jason put down his glass. "C'mere," he said, opening his arms. Delilah hesitated. "Please," he coaxed, surprising himself.

Delilah put her glass down and moved stiffly into Jason's embrace. *She doesn't trust me,* Jason realized. The thought saddened him tremendously.

"I think it's really great that you're going to talk to someone, Delilah," Jason told her, heartfelt. "That takes a lot of courage. I'm really proud of you."

"I'm sorry I embarrassed you at the New Year's Eve party," Delilah continued tearfully. "That was wrong. I can't believe I did that. When you see Tully tonight, will you tell him how sorry I am?"

"I'm not seeing Tully tonight. Or anyone else."

Delilah looked up at him in confusion. "I thought you were going out with your teammates."

"I thought so, too," said Jason, pulling her closer. "But I'm not. I'm staying here with you. This is where I want to be tonight."

He let himself sink into the realization he'd just given voice to. Never in his wildest dreams had he imagined that this was how he'd celebrate his first night as a Stanley Cup champion. But the heart knew what it wanted, even if it sometimes took the brain a while to catch up. Jason wanted Delilah. *She* was what had been missing.

"Jason." Delilah pulled away, sounding alarmed.

"I know what you're thinking. That I'm being impulsive again. That I'm not thinking straight. But you know what?" Jason felt his heart swell. "I feel like this is the first time I *am* thinking straight. I'm not worried about competing with Eric, or proving myself on the ice, or winning the Cup, or making sure I'm out having a great time because hey, I live in New York, and that's what you're supposed to do when you're a young, single guy. My eyes are wide open."

"But—but—we don't work," Delilah sputtered. "You know that."

"I *don't* know that." He had to make her see. Make her understand what was just now becoming clear to *him*. "Do we have different temperaments? Hell, yeah. But that's not insurmountable." He paused, his words trying to keep pace with his brain. "I think I expected things to be perfect. But it's dawning on me that there's no such thing as perfect." He looked at her sheepishly. "You have to forgive me for that. I'm a guy; I'm a little slow on the uptake when it comes to these things."

"So, what are you saying?" Delilah asked, her expression guarded.

"I think—with a little patience and a willingness to compromise on both our parts—we can make this work." He pulled her to him. "I love you, Delilah. I want to be with you."

Delilah rose up on tiptoes, planting a soft kiss on his mouth. Jason drew her to him, kissing her more deeply. The postgame fever twisting through him had burned away, replaced by a calm sense of certainty he wasn't sure he'd ever experienced. It was all going to work out. He knew it. He *felt* it.

"You and me, Delilah," he whispered. The heat coming off her body made him want her. He moved to kiss the soft, warm flesh of her neck. That's when Stanley pushed himself between them, his tail wagging happily as he stood there, waiting to be petted.

"You, me, and Stan," Delilah amended. Her expression was amused as she caught Jason's eye.

"And Stan," Jason agreed with a contented sigh.

EPILOGUE

"Okay, big guy, it's showtime."

Delilah couldn't resist smiling as she and Jason led Stanley into Dante's. She was determined not to dwell on the last time they'd been here, and she'd been a babbling fool. That was then, she reminded herself, and this was now. Now she wanted to be here—not only for Jason, but for herself.

She glanced over at Jason, so handsome in his jeans and tennis shirt—the same shirt he'd been wearing when they'd met! Part of her was still in shock that they were actually back together. This morning, while Jason slept, Delilah had crept out of the bedroom to call Marcus so he could confirm she wasn't dreaming.

The three of them entered the banquet room and for a moment, all conversation stopped. Then the Blades players began applauding wildly, their chants of "Stan-ley! Stanley! Stan-ley!" growing louder and louder. Delilah glanced down at the hero in question; as always, he seemed completely unfazed as he stood sniffing the air, no doubt attuned to the wonderful, comforting smell of Italian food.

"Promise me you won't give him any table food," Delilah said to Jason above the din.

Jason looked crestfallen. "Not even one meatball? The boy earned it. He helped bring us the Cup."

Delilah shook her head, but her smile was affectionate. "If you must."

"Bring Stanley around to meet everyone!" Barry Fontaine called out.

"Yeah!" echoed others.

Jason turned to Delilah. "Shall we?"

Together they began a circuit of the room. Delilah could see that many of the people there were surprised to see her.

Approaching the first table, Delilah recognized Michael Dante and his wife from her previous visit to Dante's. The wife was no longer pregnant. In fact, it was hard to believe she'd ever given birth at all, so trim was her figure. Sitting next to her was a little girl who was staring at Stanley, terrified. Meanwhile, a little boy who was the spitting image of Michael had scrambled out of his seat, making a beeline for Stanley's tail, which he began pulling.

"Stop it, little Anthony," Michael warned. His face lit up as he spotted Delilah. "Hey! Good to see you!"

"You, too," said Delilah.

Michael commenced introductions. "This is my wife, Theresa, and my daughter, Dominica. The little guy who doesn't have his listening ears on tonight is my son, Anthony." He leaned in to Theresa. "This is Jason Mitchell, the guy I told you about. And this is his girlfriend, Delilah. She's the one who snuck the dog in and out of Met Gar."

Theresa smiled at Delilah in admiration. "You're a brave woman. It's nice to meet you."

"You, too," said Delilah. She decided to be bold, try some conversation. "I think—the last time Jason and I ate here—you were pregnant."

"When was that?" Theresa asked.

"Sometime in the fall."

"Then I was."

"The baby is home with her grandma," Michael explained, scooping up little Anthony. "Enough with the dog's tail."

Dominica, meanwhile, had slid out of her seat and was standing by her mother's chair, chewing on her index finger. "You can pet him, *cara*," Theresa urged. "He won't bite." Dominica took a step toward Stanley, then abruptly changed her mind and rushed back to cling to her mother's leg. Theresa sighed, looking at Delilah as if to say, "Kids! What can you do?"

Michael regarded Delilah warmly. "Your boyfriend here really showed us what he was made of during the playoffs. You should be proud."

Delilah beamed at Jason. "I am." Stanley had started to drool. Without any fuss, Delilah took a small dish towel from her purse and wiped his mouth.

"Eewwwww!" Dominica squealed.

"Eewww to you," Michael said back to her affectionately, tussling her hair. He looked at Delilah and Jason. "Make sure you grab something to eat after your meet and greet with Stanley. There's plenty of food, all of it great."

"You're damn right it is," said Anthony Dante as he approached the table. Delilah recognized him as the restaurant's head chef, the one she'd been amazed had come out to the table himself to tell diners of dinner specials. He did a double take when he saw Stanley.

"What the hell—?" he asked his brother.

"That's Stanley, the team mascot. Remember I told you he was coming?"

Anthony folded his arms across his chest. "You never said a word about bringing a bear in here, Mikey."

"Yes, I did, Ant. But you've been too busy trying to get Angie pregnant to listen."

Delilah glanced away, uncomfortable at hearing something so personal. But Anthony seemed more annoyed than embarrassed.

"Isn't there a pill or something you can give him to make him shut up?" Anthony asked Theresa.

"I can stuff a sock in his mouth," Theresa offered cheerfully.

"Two might be better," said Anthony.

"You want to make sure you get some of the eggplant rollatini. It's to die for," said Gemma Dante as she and a tall, handsome man joined the table. Her eyes lit up when she saw Delilah. "Hel-lo!" she said, giving Delilah a warm hug. "I guess the tarot cards were right, huh?" she whispered in Delilah's ear.

Delilah blushed. "What are you doing here?"

"I'm Michael and Anthony's cousin," Gemma explained. She reached out to shake Jason's hand. "Gemma Dante."

"Jason Mitchell."

Gemma and the handsome man sat down, the man looking somewhat amused. "Don't I get introduced?" he asked his wife in a teasing voice. Delilah suddenly recalled what Marcus said about Gemma's firefighter husband being hot. He wasn't kidding.

"Oops. I'm sorry, honey. Jason, Delilah, this is my husband, Sean Kennealy."

"Nice to meet you," Jason and Delilah said in unison. They looked at each other in amusement.

"Sean's Irish, but we don't hold it against him," ribbed Michael.

"Hey, if your house burns down, don't come crying to me," Sean shot back.

"I think we should get a move on," Jason murmured. Delilah nodded in agreement. "Catch you later, everyone."

They hit two more tables. Delilah always found childrens' reactions to Stanley interesting: they either loved him or cowered in fear because of his size. Stan was reveling in the attention, loving every second of being petted and doted on.

Names and faces blurred in Delilah's mind as they continued their circuit around the huge banquet room. That is, until Delilah noticed that at the next table coming up sat Tully Webster, his wife, and two other couples she vaguely remembered from the New Year's Eve party. The look of displeasure crossing Tully's face when he saw Delilah made her stomach plummet, but she didn't run.

"Stan the Man!" Tully exclaimed, sliding out of his seat to bow before Stanley. "We're not worthy!"

Delilah cleared her throat. "Tully?"

Tully frowned. "Yeah?"

"I want to apologize for the way I behaved at your party. It was wrong, and I'm really sorry."

Tully and his wife looked impressed as they traded looks. "Apology accepted," said Tully.

Delilah swallowed, "Thank you."

"Don't sweat it."

Delilah felt light enough to float away as she and Jason moved on. The incident at the New Year's Eve party had been weighing on her for months; now she was free of it.

"I'm really proud of you, Delilah," said Jason, admiration shining in his eyes. "That must have been really tough for you to do."

"Gotta start somewhere," Delilah replied nervously.

"There's my folks and Eric," said Jason, pointing across the room. "Let's take a detour."

They cut diagonally across the banquet room, Stanley generating comments both positive and negative in their wake. Delilah's heart warmed when she saw the affectionate way Jason's mother was smiling at her.

"God, she really adores you," Jason noted under his breath, sounding pleased.

"Well, well, well," said Eric, rising. "If it's not my baby brother and his—friend?"

"Girlfriend," Jason amended with a proud smile.

"Really." Eric raised an eyebrow as he looked at Delilah. "Get hit in the head with a puck or something, hon?"

"Bite me," said Jason.

"He did," Mrs. Mitchell said quite seriously. "When you were both two."

"That about says it all," said Jason.

Jason's mother rose, crushing him to her. "We're so proud of you, Jason! I can't tell you."

"No, you can tell me," Jason joked. "I can handle the adoration."

"I can't," said Eric.

"We're very proud," intoned Jason's father, poking at his salad suspiciously.

Delilah felt tears pricking her eyes. The love between the members of this family was palpable. She could tell it was the case with the Dantes, too. It was a wonderful thing to see; a wonderful thing to aspire to.

Eric nudged Jason. "You're being summoned."

Delilah followed Jason's gaze to a table near the front of the room. She recognized Paul van Dorn and his wife from the skybox. The other man, the handsome blond with a stern gaze, she knew to be Ty Gallagher.

"That's my coach," Jason said to his parents. He gave his mother a quick kiss. "I'll catch you guys later."

Delilah detected a slight change in Jason's demeanor as they approached the table. He still seemed on top of the world, but there now existed a slight undercurrent of apprehension.

"Why are you nervous?" Delilah whispered to him.

"Because it's like being summoned by God."

God, Delilah noticed, had a very attractive wife. Pert and blonde, she seemed animated as she chatted away with Paul van Dorn's wife, Katie. A small boy at the table jumped up excitedly as soon as Stanley was within petting distance.

"Daddy, look!" he said to Ty. "A baby bear!"

"It's not a bear, Patrick. It's a . . . Newfie?" he finished uncertainly.

"Yup," said Jason.

Paul van Dorn rose to give Jason a hearty slap on the back. "I told Ty to lure you over here so I could pay homage."

"To me or to Stanley?" Jason joshed.

"To you, of course."

"It should be the other way around," Jason said humbly.

"A humble hockey player," Paul marveled with a small snort. "That's a first." He squinted. "Delilah, right?"

Delilah nodded.

"Nice to see you," said Paul.

Delilah always assumed people would forget who she was, or if they didn't, that they'd get her name wrong. That Paul van Dorn remembered impressed her. It also gave her a quick shot of self-esteem. Maybe she wasn't invisible. Maybe she could interact and engage like everyone else.

Delilah noticed Ty's wife looking at her in awe. "I still can't believe you agreed to bring Stanley in and out of Met Gar." She glanced at her husband reproachfully. "If corporate found out—"

"Corporate can kiss my ass," Ty growled.

"Isn't he charming?" Ty's wife asked, regarding her husband with amused affection. "It's his love of humanity that made me fall head over heels in love with him." She extended a hand. "I'm Janna, by the way."

"Delilah."

"That's Patrick," Janna said, nodding toward the little boy to whom Stanley kept giving the paw.

"He wants you to pet him or rub his belly," Delilah told him.

"Mom, can I?" Patrick asked his mother.

"Rub away," said Janna.

"So, Mitchell." Ty's voice was brusque. "I had my doubts about you at the beginning of the season. But you really turned things around. I'm proud of you."

Jason seemed overawed. "Thanks, Coach."

"Now go sit down and enjoy yourself."

"I will, Coach."

Walking away, Delilah was glad of the noise in the room; it masked the sound of her rumbling stomach. "I'm starving," she confessed to Jason.

"Me, too. There's just one more stop we need to make."

He led her toward a table covered in black velvet. Atop it sat a shining silver trophy. The Stanley Cup.

"There it is," said Jason reverently.

It was much bigger than Delilah expected. She took a step closer, inspecting the hundreds of names ringing the

Cup. Soon Jason's name would grace the smooth, shining silver, too.

"I'm so proud of you," Delilah told him as she began to choke up.

"Stan-ley! Stan-ley! Stan-ley!" the room began chanting again.

"I think Stan needs to drink from the Cup," Jason called back.

The room erupted into cheers and whistles.

"I can't tell you how long I've been dreaming of this," Jason said in a voice thick with emotion as he carefully lifted the Cup off the table, placing it on the floor. The whole room was on its feet. Jason grabbed a pitcher of ice water from the nearest table, pouring some into hockey's Holy Grail before tipping it forward. Stanley rose to his feet and plunged his snout into the silver bowl, noisily lapping away. As always, he was oblivious to the water sloshing over the sides. Raucous applause thundered through the banquet room.

Delilah took Jason's hand. "You okay?" she asked. He seemed a bit overwhelmed.

"I'm more than okay," Jason replied, pulling her into his arms. "I've got the Cup, I've got my dog, and I've got my girl. What more could a guy want?"

Be sure to visit the Blades' website at
www.nyblades.com

Enter the rich world of
historical romance
with Berkley Books.

Lynn Kurland

Patricia Potter

Betina Krahn

Jodi Thomas

Anne Gracie

Love is timeless.
penguin.com